This Broken Earth

Roger Colby

Dear reader, I want you to know that I'm about to take you down a road that is full of bumps and pot holes. If you live in Oklahoma, you know all about this. If you don't then you probably have one of those roads nearby if you are willing to travel far enough into the deep woods. This novel is off the beaten path for a reason. Basically I became tired of sharing my ideas about a Bible based post-apocalypse novel with my well meaning Christian friends and finding out that their views on the book of Revelation and Daniel were as varied as the many people with whom I spoke.

This is in no way a bad thing. I think it means that none of us really know what will happen. I write this novel in the fervor and Christmassy atmosphere of the 2012 Mayan prediction that the world will end this December, when I really think the poor fellow carving the calendar became tired and quit. I mean, they had to carve it out of stone, so maybe 2012 was simply too much to carve. My hand would get tired, too. Recent information tells us that we have another year and that the Mayan calendar actually ends in 2013. (Addendum: It's 2014 and we're still here).

I stifle a laugh.

The fact is that even though I'm sure there are a lot of scholars out there who want to predict the end times down to the moment of Jesus' return, no one really knows for sure. Biblical scholars who have spent a lot of time and effort and tuition to ensure that they know everything about it still don't know everything about it. History is filled with prognosticators who spend their lives trying to say that Jesus would come back on such-and-such date or that we are indeed living in the last days.

To some people, we are always living in the last days.

Perhaps we are. Who really knows? As Howard, a character in this book notes: "I'm sure the people during the dark ages thought we were living in the last days, too."

As a writer, I just wanted to tell a pulse pounding story, and it is my hope that this novel will achieve that goal. I am not looking to debunk the pre-tribulation rapture eschatology, or any other "ology". I came to the conclusion that I don't really know what I believe and that suits me just fine. I think I'll just keep it simple and worry about my own salvation and the spread of the gospel and treating others like I want to be treated. God will work out all those other details. I'm sure that when Jesus returns as He said He would, no one will be waiting with a Bible and calendar in hand arguing that he arrived too soon or too late. They'll just be glad to see Him.

This novel is written so that each chapter is a different character speaking from their own point of view, and sometimes the characters may not be that reliable. You be the judge. It hopefully adds to the suspense when the reader is part of the dramatic irony of knowing something that the characters do not.

Above all, if you are offended, I'm sorry. This was not my intention, and hopefully if you read this novel for what it is, you will see that the true message is not end time prophesy at all. But... If you can just realize that none of us really know what will happen anyway, then my hopes are that you will have a lot of fun reading this book, and will laugh, cry, and cringe when you are supposed to.

So find a nice place to read where it's quiet (like a bunker somewhere), curl up with this book and enjoy yourself. This is all I wish for you. If you want to think, go right ahead. I won't judge you.

Roger Colby, 2012

This book is dedicated to all the people who ever had a thought about the end times. I had a lot of help with all the details. I thank Chad Snyder for filling in the military and survivalist information. Rick Young was happy to help line me out on firearms. Michael Dean kept the science straight. Jason Weigand was instrumental in helping me understand Muslim culture and the Middle East. My wife Kristie and my kids all must be thanked for their patience while their Dad spent the better part of 18 months writing this. Dad, if you can read this from heaven, I hope you get a good laugh, because you probably know what *will* happen.

Book I:
The U.S.
of After

Clayton

I's shaken outta my nice dream about a warm bed by something cold pressing against my nose only to realize it was the gun-powdery end of a grimy black shotgun barrel. I's bein' robbed again. I remember bein' in this dream about layin' on my old bed back home, eatin' a nice juicy steak. Robbed again. I just hated this part of the end of the world.

Oh yea, the shotgun barrel. At the end of it there was this shabby young guy, beard all scraggly like ever'body else in the world, two dirt rimmed eyes lookin' square at me.

"Now if you just lay there all nice and quiet, I'll take your bag here and you can just go on your way without any incident," said the shabby, dirty kid standin' over me.

The fella had an air about him as if he did this for a livin', pillagin' and lootin'. I's mostly grateful to God he wasn't right away tryin' to eat me… or perhaps he was and we hadn't got to that part yet. It made me most sore that this bandit was takin' some of my things but at least I might at least live through this if I played the game correctly.

"Look, bud," I managed, my tongue clicking in my dried out mouth. "I don't want no trouble. Just take what you want and I'll find some more food somewheres. Just don't kill me. Ain't no use in doin' that at all, man. I'm just as hungry and thirsty as you are, I figure."

"Hmm," he grunted. "What do you know about what I've been through?"

I figured now was a good time to mind my words, but I forged on and somethin' inside me cringed for the worst.

"You're welcome to take what you want," I said, tryin' my best to smile. "I won't make any trouble. All I ask is that you leave my bag. I really need it in case I want to haul around other goods for people like you to steal."

The grubby fella grinned an ugly possum grin. I could see his dirty finger movin' in and out of the trigger guard while he thought about what I'd just told him. I trusted, and I can't really explain how, that I'd find food again. It was better to be hungry than dead at the moment. As the young hillbilly with the ugly grin and the shotgun turned and fumbled through my bag, I could not help but talk to him. I suppose I figured I had nothing to lose. Maybe it was bein' on my lonesome for so long, but mostly I figure it was the Holy Spirit sittin' up to say hi.

"You ever consider the lilies of the field?" I said, the words spillin' out almost desperate. "They don't work nor make no money nor do they have a job, but they are so pretty to look at. They got the best of clothes."

At this, my fifth encounter with thievery in so many months locked eyes with me, like a snake starin' down a muskrat.

"I don't care 'bout no flowers," he growled, shakin' his gun at me for emphasis. "You'll keep your lip from flappin' if you know what's good for you."

I remember stayin' that way for a while, that bandit grinnin' and me a-layin' there with my hands up above my head in the sit-up position. I was very quiet for a moment and it seemed like forever until the grungy shotgun wieldin' thief told me to get on up. I stood up slowly, my face showin' a wince I guess, and then that bandit began nervously jerkin' the business end of his shotgun to the left and tellin' me to stand "over there" while he took nearly all of my food, me unable to do anything.

I got real sodded out when he found the Spam. I thought I had hidden it better in the little secret pocket I had made in the side of the backpack. A mystery meat eaten mostly by me and my folks before the war, Spam was good eatin' even if one did not cook it over a fire, and now this person was makin' off with it. The thief spent a while goin' through it all, placin' what he stole in a burlap sack, then he turned around and gave me that rodent-like grin again. I watched quietly as the stranger turned to go, made it to the edge of the clearin' before he tripped over a stump, fell to the ground, and accidentally fired his weapon loudly and harmlessly into the bushes. I almost laughed, but lay still. Before I could get to my feet, the stranger was gatherin' up his burlap sack and disappearin' into the darkness.

I felt all powerless…whatever.

This is just how things was in the good old United States of America after everything fell to pieces. People went and had themselves a final and ugly world war like a block party where ever'body gets slammed, bigger than any other one, and then things spun out of control with that Volos virus, the money became worthless and then came several natural disasters. The earth was breathin' its last, but I didn't much care none. All I knew after losin' my food was that now I had to get some more, and that was not an easy task. I didn't cry about it, no sir… nor did I complain. I simply trusted that I would find more. I just went along on faith and figured food would make an appearance at some time or other. As a matter of truth, I had absolutely no idea I was livin' the last few years of my life.

I just sat on the ground for awhile and started to prayin'. I could not remedy my situation by whinin' about it or carryin' on. I went to my bag to see what the thief did not remove from my precious belongings, and man they was precious, all right. I crouched down, opened the grungy grey and blue backpack with the word "Targus" embroidered on the top handle, and with trembling hands found a zip-lock bag of KFC wet wipes, a bent-bristled old tooth brush, my comb (like I'd ever find anybody to impress), and of course the Bible.

At least that fool did not take the Bible, I thought. I didn't know what I'd do without that. I'd found it in an old house, the front porch all fallin' down, a creepy skeletal hand grippin' its leather bound cover. I'd started readin' it out of boredom, mostly, something to do to pass the time between scroungin' for food or water and tryin' not to be seen by people who'd purt near gone off the deep end of their humanity. I'd found somethin' in that little book that sung to me as nothin' had before. My momma used to make me go to church, but I never saw nothin' there but people arguin' over the color of the carpet. I pretty much felt that most church goin' people was living a big fat lie. I's usually shunned by the cliques in that youth group. Didn't fit their cookie cutter mold. Bein' a Christian simply weren't real to me, just a religion used by politicians as a mule to haul corporate greed. This bankrupt earth had stood by and watched all them corporations burn on up. That money was pretty much good for fire kindlin' and stoppin' up holes in yer mud hut.

It took me the better part of a year to read through the entire Bible, 'cuz I'm so slow a reader. But man I found in those pages a hope that I's not able to find anywheres I looked. 'Ventually I read the words of Jesus. My eyes started to dance around when I read about all them miracles and the many teachin's of, yep, a messiah. I 'member sittin' under a pecan tree most of a day and readin' all four gospels. That was the day I got real. After then I's always readin' it when I'd get a spare moment, but now weren't the time. I put it away and got on down the road once it was light.

I sucked in some air, let it out, and gathered up what was left of my stuff to see what lay over the next hill. My shoulders was all slumped down for a while. I tried to stay pos'tive, thinkin' somebody'd prolly have some food somewheres. God'd work it out.

I wandered through the woods for a time and finally emerged at an old road, the sun comin' up over the horizon. I say it was an old road, but really it was just unused. No cars had driven on it in a dog's age, and there was an odd smell in the air like turpentine. I hid behind a bush until I felt safe enough to show m'self. It is good that I did, 'cause a creakin', smoky old diesel flatbed truck came lumberin' along, one wheel a-wobbling like an old donut. I didn't rightly know what they were burnin' but it was really foul. Ragged people were hangin' off it, ever' one of 'em holdin' a gun or a pitchfork or somethin' else just as dangerous. I sat in them bushes at a safe distance and shivered even though it was powerful hot.

The world had shown me lots of really horrible things.

My teeth was chatterin' somethin' fierce. I didn't dare move nothin' else. I had no idea if these wanderers were friendlies or not, but from the looks of 'em this was pretty obvious, their faces full of meanness, all unwashed and grimy. It was good not to show m'self. These were city dwellers out on a raid, from the looks of 'em. Their faces all blotchy and sun-baked with a matted halo of wild hair. As they rolled closer, I saw through the leaves that the driver was an older man with missin' teeth and his cheeks all sunk in, dark as pitch, covered with the grime of this world.

They chunk-kachunked on past. I got a little courage and then crept on out into the road as they were becomin' a fast blurry spider on the next hill, their legs and arms all danglin' down. They seemed to be wanderin' aimlessly like most folks lookin' for food and supplies. I didn't care as long as they left me alone. In the big cities food had become so scarce that they had started in on one another. I thought they were rumors 'till I done seen it myself…and nearly didn't make it out the last time.

Further down the road was an old convenience store, a faded sign out front that read "AST Grocery and Gas". Several of the letters had fallen with time and I chuckled to myself about the price per gallon. That was all gone. The windows, all busted out and sharp edged, caused me to walk a careful line to the front door. I reached in my backpack for my hatchet and then drew my face all up when I realized it wasn't there. I didn't hear a soul, so I moved on quietly. The sound of the wind blowin' through the

shattered windows startled me a little. It was simply somethin'
inside the store hangin' loose, blowing in the wind that rustled off
and on. After seein' the flatbed full of terror roll on by, not to
mention some of the other ugliness I'd been forced to go through
in the year or so I'd been on the road, I was wisely cautious.
Solomon wise.

After about an hour I got a little break: a few cans of beans and
an old zippo. The beans must have rolled under one of them end
caps and whoever looted missed out on a good meal. I threw one
of them cans on the floor, its sides stretched out 'till it almost
looked like a little metal ball. I didn't want to get sick. I opened
one can with my trusty Swiss army knife that had been stashed in
my pocket and sipped on the beans as if I was drinkin' a soda, but
I thought about Dr. Pepper again and most near cried. That thief
had taken my only fork. I thanked God for them beans, 'cause
even though they was all I had, I was still grateful for another day
of life.

I decided to use the store for a shelter that night because it
would be safer than sleepin' outdoors. I lay down on several
bundles of paper sacks and mumbled about New Orleans 'till I fell
out to slumber land.

*   *   *

Not long after my grocery stop I decided that I would have to
find a horse or somethin'. Walkin' was a real chore. I had some
pretty good shoes I found in an overturned truck, some K-Mart
specials, but I just got tired of walkin' all the time. I had eaten all
the food up at the last house I stayed in, gathered up a bunch of
supplies (most of those gone now to thieves) and headed out to
New Orleans. I had heard from some people 'round a campfire a
while back that there was a lot of food and water down there. I
figured I could follow highway nine to a river and then follow
that south. Didn't have a map and didn't know the lay of the
land, so I was just a wingin' it. Everythin' was just so dangerous.

All these people out here livin' like animals. You couldn't trust nobody.

Of course I prayed every day and hoped that Jesus would just protect me from all the dangerous stuff. I knew there weren't no gettin' out of it. Life on this earth was pretty bad. Life has always been pretty bad, but I manage to keep the faith. Dad used to have a lot a faith, even when he passed away in my arms from puffin' on them cancer sticks. I wished Mom hadn't gone off to Iowa to help Krissie with the kids when her husband went to the war. My sister and her kids were prolly fine without her. She just had to make sure. We hadn't had any communication from that part of the country for some time after the big one. I just assumed my family was gone after that explosion over Des Moines. Had to get outta my apartment. I wouldn't dare go back to Norman. Streets there were over-run with gangs. I decided to start fresh.

I'd hear lots of rumors about the state of things. Some sickness called Volos, the war, the quake. You kinda listen in when somebody 'round a campfire somewhere "heard somethin'". Most people were in the dark. I suppose they just went on like most people, tryin' to find some way to get by. My neighbor, Bill, before he lit out for better places said that ever transformer in the country blew. I wasn't sure how. I guess it meant we wouldn't have the power back up forever. It had been what seemed like a few years since the power had been on, so why hope in somethin' that may not happen? I had been livin' like a nomad for a while. I'd decided to light out for better places in the hopes I could find my way down to New Orleans. Maybe Mom had survived and maybe I could find her. I didn't hope in it. I was gettin' pretty desperate.

It was hot. Some old timer whose name I forgot said one time that if you don't like Oklahoma's weather then wait a minute. I had been waitin' for months but it was August and the summer sun beat down on me somethin' fierce. It had been a scorcher of a summer already. Funny thing was that even the winters weren't really cold anymore. I guess that was fine but it made for the strangest weather. I couldn't remember the last time it really snowed.

I had shed my shirt even though there was that little bit of embarrassment left in my mind from the old world about my farmer tan. Who cares, right? It was just so hot and all.

That was the day I met Gabe.

I don't think anyone will believe me about Gabe if I told the story right and true. I don't think he has a last name. Never heard it and prolly couldn't say it right if I did. I had crested the top of a hill on highway nine. There was a deep valley and then yet another hill. Central Oklahoma is like that; just one hill after another. I just remember lookin' at the top of the other hill across the valley and one minute seein' wavy lines of heat comin' up off the blacktop and then in those wavy lines appeared a man. He was sorta bobbin' toward me, his arms swingin' loose, an old ball cap on his head, a full beard coverin' his face. I could barely make out his clothin' really, but it was all brown with dirt and grime. At first I thought I should get off the road and hide, but somethin' told me not to. I quickly put on my shirt again.

The fella started to get closer, and as he did I noticed that he was lookin' dead at me, his face a determined mask. I started to feel uncomfortable, started worryin', and somethin' in the back of my mind started clawin' at the idea that I had made a mistake and I'd get myself robbed again. Well shoot. He could have whatever I had left. A half eaten can of beans wasn't the best meal, and I would pray he got all kinds of stomach cramps from eating it all. I know that isn't the Christian thing to think, but I was plum out of patience with thieves. I said a little prayer for patience just then, and it seemed that just a little talk with Jesus made it right.

He got closer, then he opened his mouth and smiled real big. His teeth was shiny white and he still had all of them. His eyes was kind of shaded by the dirty green ball cap that read "Go Bison". That was powerful strange. He was close enough now to be heard, and said somethin' really weird.

"Hello, Clayton," he said, walkin' forward, puttin' out his hand like he knew me. I kind of got that feelin' you get when a car salesman approaches you on a car lot right before December when they're tryin' to get rid of their inventory. I actually jumped a little and my arms swung backward.

"I'm Gabe," he said. "You don't have to be afraid. I don't mean you any harm, really."

I stood there lookin' at him, nervously foldin' my arms, tryin' my best to stare him down and wonderin' how on earth this dude knew my name. He just stood there smilin', his dirty hand out ready for me to pump it as if this was some kinda normal situation. I didn't know who he thought he was, unless the beard hid his identity from me. Coulda been my old English teacher Mr. Travis for all I knew. There was a time when I hated people, and Mr. Travis was one I hated the most.

"Really, Clayton," he spoke softly now. "I don't have much time. I'm here to give you a message and then be on my way."

He pulled back his hand, looked at the palm briefly, backed up and stood about twelve paces or so away from me. The harsh sun shone down on us but just to spite it I could feel a slight breeze blow across my skin. It felt good. Gabe wasn't sweatin'. It was hot as a coal stoked furnace and he wasn't sweatin'.

"Look, dude," I said, my words sputterin' out of my mouth like an old engine missin' a valve. "I-I don't know how you know my name and all, but if this is some crazy trick to con me out of my food and supplies, then you got a fight on yer hands. I'm right near tired of havin' all my stuff taken by vagrants."

Gabe put up two remarkably dirty hands, palms toward me. I kind of flinched at how strangely quick he moved.

"Honestly, Mr. Delroy," he said with a calm yet firm voice, a voice with a rich quality like James Earl Jones, but not in a bad Darth Vadery way. "I have simply come to give you a message from the Most High and then I will be off to other assignments."

I think I laughed at him at that point. "Most High" to be sure. This dude was buzzin' on some good stuff. If I were one of those spazoids that smoked that garbage I'd be puttin' out my hand, but this was beyond weird, so I just stood there with my arms folded. The guy was sure serious, though.

"The Most High has seen your deeds and knows your faith is strong," said Gabe, using his greasy hands for emphasis. "He has sent me to tell you that the battle will soon be over, but will intensify before it's end. You are to go to Jerusalem and there you will find your purpose."

I laughed again. "You mean to tell me you're some kind of angel?"

"Yes," said Gabe, his warm smile beamin' at me. The guy's face never changed, never flinched. He just stood there with that grin plastered on his face, but somethin' in the eyes told me it was genuine. I could feel some strange electricity in the air like right before a lightnin' strike.

I had one question:

"Where's your wings, dude?"

He laughed out loud with that deep boomin' voice and his face lit up like my Dad's did that time I noodled that fifteen pound catfish.

"That is a common misconception," he said with a smile, then he got all serious. "But I do not have time to talk about that. I have a specific mission. I am to tell you that you are to go to Jerusalem and all will be answered in due time."

"Look, man. I'm not like a super-Christian or anythin'. I barely graduated high school and the best job I ever had was a bag boy at Country Boy grocery. Besides, how am I to know that you aren't just some nut who's got the munchies, if you know what

I'm sayin'."

Gabe stood still for a moment, shoved his hands in his pockets, grinned through his grizzled beard, and started walkin' past me.

"I have not been authorized to do anything else but give you a message," he said as he passed, and his voice was strangely calm. "It is your faith that will do the rest. The Most High is giving you a choice. He has seen your good works and knows that you are a man of righteousness, seen through the filtering curtain of the blood of Jesus. You will do well. Trust in Him. The road will be fraught with peril, and there will be hard things to face, but you will be rewarded in the end."

I stood quietly in the middle of the highway right on the faded, cracked yellow line and watched as this Gabe character walked off over the hill. I waited until I saw that ratty ball cap disappear over the crest and get obscured again by the wavy lines of heat that rose up from the asphalt. I didn't move. I just stared at those wavy lines and then decided I wanted more info, had to know if he was crazy or high or just plain mean. I figured this guy was a nut, but I hadn't talked to anyone who wasn't tryin' to rob me in a while and the conversation was pretty entertainin'. At least he didn't try to eat me. Been through that and that's another story entirely.

I ran about ten feet over the hill after him, but stopped to see the road curvin' 'round toward the Lake Thunderbird dam and not a sign of Gabe at all, only the hot waves of heat ripplin' off of the highway. Did he duck out and hide in the woods? Man, I was too tired to go runnin' after him and I had to make it to a safer place.

That was just nuts... Jerusalem.

Last I heard there wasn't nothin' left of that place or anythin' else in the Middle East after the war 'cept a glowin' hole in the ground. Who knows. Maybe they would rebuild it. I laughed about it a little and kicked a rock down the highway in my original direction and followed it on my somewhat planned route to New Orleans.

Jerusalem. That's a laugh.

I shrugged my shoulders and trudged on, realizin' that the diesel truck that went by with the gaggle of rednecks was a rarity. They's prolly burnin' veggie oil they found in some fast food joint. Some people burned propane and some were also tryin' to make their cars run on other more, well, smelly options. It was a sad state of affairs. Ever once in a while I'd see some people wanderin' on down the road the other direction and I'd slide on off in the bushes to pretend I was a ninja. I's bound and determined not to be robbed again.

"Jerusalem? Why Jerusalem?" I said aloud. Weren't no need to hide my thoughts, so I often talked to myself like a loony.

Wondered what happened to mom after the EMP and the mess in Iowa. I wished I could have got an answer about it. I locked eyes on another crumbling old convenience store on the side of the highway. It might as well be called an in-convenience store at this point, since nearly everythin' had been looted or burned up.

Worse yet, that mean old sun was fallin' below the horizon and I knew that this was the time that all the bandits decided to relieve other people of their goods. Was much better to sleep during' the day and travel at twilight than to wait 'till the thugs came out of the woods. I had to find a place to sleep that was safe from scavengers soon or I'd end up naked this time, or roastin' over a spit like ol'...won't talk about him. I suddenly started thinkin' about aunt Shirley's swimmin' pool and how we used to go over there ever weekend durin' the summers. It was just so hot out even in the later part of the day, even though we hadn't had a really cold winter in a while. People had ruined the sky with their greed, then ruined the rest of the planet with their war.

When I got within arms length of that in-convenience store I found a road that snaked back through the woods. I could just barely see the roof of a house in the distance at the top of a hill. The trees hid most of it from view, but I could see the roofin' material, that black stuff, anglin' up out from between the brown and green leafy branches. If no one lived in it or had lit out of it entirely, then I figured I could prolly stay there for a night and get some rest.

As I moved closer, I noticed that the house sat on a large acreage with an old sheet metal barn just barely visible behind it. I didn't see no livestock or cars or any other sign of life worth mentionin' except for a random squirrel, and they was everywhere. I made a bee-line for the two story house 'cause I could always set some old cans and fishin' line or string along the stairs to warn myself of any intruders while I slept.

I started thinkin' about a big soft bed.

I got a little closer and noticed that this little homestead was very quiet, except for the wind makin' the leaves in the trees hiss and rattle so. I suppose I figured that if there was people livin' in this house, then seein' a dumb redneck like me on their overgrown, weedy lawn would cause them to send out a party to un-welcome me, unless they were otherwise scared and cowerin' like I usually did when I saw strangers.

Man, I decided to take a risk. Sleepin' outside was a much more dangerous thing than findin' a second story house with a soft bed upstairs. The idea of even a little bit of comfort was soundin' better and better, and as I neared the front door of the only two-story house in miles of wooded countryside, I noticed that the front door had a dead bolt. I wondered if it was unlocked.

It wasn't.

I rattled around on the handle a bit, not thinkin' about anybody hearin' me, until I decided I'd have to find a better route inside. Maybe the back door was not locked. I adjusted my backpack on my shoulders and darted on around to the side of the house and into the back yard. No dogs, so that was a good sign. Somebody probably ate them. It was still very quiet, so I still felt a little safe. This, of course, is how all them horror movies take a nasty turn.

I stepped up to the back door, but as I reached on out for the handle that door flew open and there stood some red headed girl wearin' these green joggin' shorts and some dirty white t-shirt with Little Axe Cheer printed across it in blue letters. She gripped tight on this yellow broom, wavin' that handle end right at my face.

I was a little shocked at how pretty she was under all that dirt and how her green eyes sparkled in the dusky light. A faint smile parted my lips, and this is prolly what set her off. Before I could form a thought at all it was knocked savagely out of my head by the broom handle connecting with my right cheek in a yellow blur. I heard a thump and felt the wind go out of me 'cause she had already jabbed the end of it into my stomach, causing me to wheeze in deeply. I felt like I was in an interactive pirate movie. She was lightenin' quick with that broom. Buffy quick. This girl gave me some rapid Zorro punishment, and all I could do was stand there like a chump and groan.

"You get out of here!" she screamed, her eyes two big green globes. My eyes opened up wide to match my gapin' mouth. A string of drool fell past my bottom lip. The grin was long gone.

I put my hands up hoping' she'd back off and she whacked my right wrist , hittin' that little bone that sticks out, and finally I'd had enough so I bowed up and clenched my teeth at her, ready to say somethin' awful unpolite. I tried to grab at the broom, but she magically whipped it around and thwacked me on the kneecap. My legs wobbled under me and I went down on the small concrete stoop, then she started layin' in on me, the sound of it somehow remindin' me of the times my momma used to beat the dust out of a quilt on a clothes line. Each time the broom handle sailed through the air it made the whoopin' call of some insane bird.

I did my best to ball up in a tight bundle and she kept at it, dartin' back inside the door and finally trying to slam it shut, but I think my head was slightly across the threshold. She ended up bangin' the door against my head in an attempt to close it behind her, knockin' the snot out of me once and for all, and that was the last I remember of that fight 'cause everythin' went all black.

Amy

Yeah, so I was just sitting in my house minding my own business when this skinny nerd decided to break in. I suppose I couldn't blame him, what with the world all gone crazy, but a girl's gotta defend herself. I dragged his sorry self into the house and then bound him all up with duct tape. Handy stuff. I pulled him up onto the brown leather couch in the living room because he was kind of light. I decided that when he woke up I'd just have to figure out what to do then.

I wish Dad would have come back. He went off to Europe before the war broke out and that had been like forever ago, three summers. He picked a heck of a time to go on a business trip, but he worked for BP so I guess he had to go. I gave up on him coming back like forever ago. The food had run out, I had gone through all the stores in the safe room and I had been going to that convenience store on the corner for a while. I was tired of being afraid.

Sometimes I heard screams in the night.

That nerd had a backpack with nothing really of concern inside. Just some odds and ends that really didn't help my hunger pangs. I mean... beans? I suppose I could eat them, but eew. Apocalypse weight loss plan. I looked in the mirror and thought that if I really cared about this guy or he was someone I knew I would probably do more to fix myself up. Oh yeah, no water. I hadn't had a shower or a bath in a long time. I never did get used to my own body odor. Ugh! We won't even *talk* about shaving. When scrounging, razors are kind of second in line to water and food. I felt so cave girl. I mean, how come all those girls on *Lost* and *The Walking Dead* had smooth armpits?

Whatever.

Besides, this dude probably was just looking for something to eat when he tried to break in…or not. I ran upstairs, dug through my closet and found the red aluminum baseball bat my Dad used to use when he played in that church league. It had a sort of heavy feel to it. I looked at what I had on, and decided that what I wore to bed would not be a very menacing look, so I sorted through my floordrobe and changed into jeans, then put on an American Eagle hoodie; the blue one, not the white one. I looked in the mirror, tied back my greasy hair all business, put a plain denim ball cap on my head, bore my teeth (Oh, I needed to brush) and then ran downstairs to sit across from the nerd until he woke up.

He moaned a second or two, then he lay there. I think he probably needed sleep. I really smacked his head good in the door. It was kind of an accident. I didn't really mean to do all that. I just got scared and kind of went overboard with the broom. He had caught me in the middle of sweeping the hardwood floor. I had to have *something* to do or I'd go crazy. I was just about losing it already. I'd been cooped up in this house so long I didn't even know what month it was anymore. I knew that it was, like, summertime because it was so hot. I had all the windows upstairs opened up. Man, a house really starts to smell funny when no one lives in it and the power is out for a while. Who knew?

I had come home from OU for the summer, like, summers ago. I lived at the Kappa house and had pledged the year before all the nonsense happened. Dad was always a little worried about his little girl pledging to a non-Christian sorority, but that was what I wanted. At the time I was so concerned with image. A lot of good that did me *now*.

We won't even talk about how I got home. That was a nightmare.

Sometimes I'd feel aftershocks from the big one. It felt like somebody picked up the house and let it fall down suddenly, and usually it happened when you were trying to sleep or when creepy looters were hanging around outside your house. I had to go into the safe room once when that happened, and then when the noise stopped I came out to find the place in a mess. Good thing they couldn't get in to where I was or I'd be done.

Worse, they could have had that Volos virus everybody was talking about on the news before the world went sour. I think it sort of resembled TB but you were contagious for like three weeks and then it didn't respond to any vaccines or antibiotics. I was a pre-med major before school was cancelled forever.

I would have been a really good doctor.

The nerd's head was soaking my fine leather couch with blood. Now was the time to see how good I could be in a pinch. I ran to the kitchen and pulled out the first aid kit from the cabinet and then ran back to the living room to gently lift the guy's head. Yeah, just a superficial wound, but the head bleeds worse than anything. I pulled out some gauze and held it on the cut applying pressure. He moaned again, then he shifted against the duct tape but it held. I held the tape dispenser between my knees and pulled off some coach's tape to fasten the gauze in place, then I took one of my Mom's embroidered pillows and propped up his head. I didn't think she would mind. She didn't mind when she left my Dad for that other guy I can't stand. I was only five but I just remember that he smelled funny. I had not spoken to her since that day I turned sixteen and she called just to "catch up".

Whatever.

Two months ago I sat upstairs and thought I saw her on the road down the hill. It was just some wanderer. The way she was staggering around made me run down to the safe room and hide for three days. I was sick of hiding.

I grabbed the baseball bat and darted over to the recliner to sit across from my dorky hostage and watch him carefully. He'd be waking up soon and I'd have to put on the show so he wouldn't think I was soft. I wasn't soft. I used to be a Little Axe cheerleader, for crying out loud. We were all business.

Clayton

My eyelids eventually parted to let me see that crazy red headed girl sittin' in a brown leather recliner just across from me. Her fiery red hair was all tied up in a pony tail and she had on a plain denim baseball cap pulled down over the smooth, porcelain features of her face. She had some freckles on her nose that made her kinda cute to spite the fact that her soft lips were peeled back to show clenched teeth, but the expression seemed kinda forced as if she was tryin' too hard to be mean. Her thin eyebrows angled down in the middle over green eyes that were squintin' at me all hateful. Even though she was tryin' her best to put on an angry face, I didn't plan on testin' her bluff.

It hurt to laugh, so I didn't.

Of course I was seein' all this in a sort of sideways view because I was layin' down on a couch, my head hurtin' somethin' awful. I couldn't move. She'd tied me up with somethin' I slowly realized was duct tape because the sticky part was pullin' on some of my arm hairs. She'd stuffed somethin' in my mouth and I hoped it was clean. I couldn't get that out either. She picked up a scratched, red aluminum baseball bat and cradled it in her arms like some kinda weird baby and then she started in on me with her words. I was just thankful she didn't use the bat.

"You think you can just break into someone's house and not get the crud kicked out of you?"

"Mhfffmmm," I replied.

She stood up quickly with smooth mechanical motions and I noticed that she had changed into some jeans but was still barefoot. If I was to get away I could prolly outrun her if I got off into the woods, but I pretty much considered that a lost cause. She held the bat in one hand and reached out to pull the duct tape away from my mouth quick but it tore at the patchy stubble I had

21

managed to grow.

"Yaaoowww!" I groaned after spittin' the small wad of cloth out of my mouth. I hoped it wasn't used to clean somethin' even though it tasted a little like Pine-sol smells, kinda bitter and mediciny. An image of a toilet popped into my head and I winced.

She jumped right back into the recliner and pulled her feet up in the seat, her bony knees up near her face. She held the bat out in front of her as if I had the ability to break my bonds and come after her. I tell you if I could get out of that, then makin' any threatenin' moves toward that crazy chick would be the last thought on my mind.

"Ok," she said finally after a short pause. "If, and I mean *if* you can convince me that you are not like some of those other people, I might just drag you outside and cut you free. But you better start talking. If I don't think you are telling the truth, I swear I'll beat you within an inch of your life."

She seemed really calm about tellin' me this, even though her voice was kinda vibratin' funny, but I could sorta tell that she didn't have a clue what to do with me. I figured she hadn't really thought out what she was goin' to do if and when she decided to cut me free. I didn't think she would cut me free anyway. I think she had gotten herself in a bind by bringin' me inside.

"Look," I said, trying to sound as calm as I could but with my voice shakin' kinda like hers. "I don't mean you any harm. I was just lookin' for food like anyone else. You let me go and I promise I'll be on my way, no questions asked."

Right then was when things changed for the weird. Her little mouth kinda opened a bit and then her eyes widened out . She took in a breath of air. She put her feet down on the floor in slow motion and leaned forward.

"Clayton...uh, Clayton..." she gasped.

"Clayton Delroy," I replied. "Am I supposed to know you?"

"Oh my goodness… Clayton..uh.. Delroy?" she grinned pretty big now, and I could see how contagious her smile was and the dirt and grime no longer hid who she was from me.

"Dang," I mumbled, as the memories of her face in the hallway at school came stumblin' back into my mind. "Amy… Lawrence, right?"

She immediately pulled out a knife and I jumped a bit until she started cuttin' the duct tape off of my feet and hands. She didn't slip at all, and made quick work of it until I was sittin' up next to her and she had me in a really uncomfortable but tight warm hug.

"I'm so sorry," she said. "I just didn't recognize you at all, what with the beard… sorry about the tape…and the vicious beating. Things have been rough, you know?"

I sat silent for a while, holdin' the bandage on my head, and I listened to her talk about her Dad goin' off on his forever trip, her food runnin' out, her problems and her life in general. I only really knew Amy from high school at Little Axe and that was at a distance. It had been a few years since graduation on the football field with the sky threatenin' rain. I sat quietly beside her as she chattered away not because of bein' unable to talk to her, but because when we were in high school the only word she ever said to me was "excuse me" as she pushed on past in the crowded hallway. I didn't really run in her social circle, if you get what I'm sayin'. She just sat there by me blatherin' on about her whole experience and then that turned into her boohooin' a bit once in a while until finally she just broke down and put both arms around me and held me close while I sat with my hands firmly planted on my knees. I patted her shoulder once in a while just so she didn't think I was rude. She and her friends said and did some mean stuff to me in high school and even though I was all about helpin' the needy, and the world had definitely ended, she didn't really fit in my grand plan to get back to someplace normal.

Finally, I had to say somethin'.

"Yeah. I'm sorry about all that stuff happenin' to ya," I managed. "Things are kinda ugly and downright awful."

She let me go and brushed the tears away from her eyes. It smeared some of the grime on her face and made her resemble some silly clown, but I didn't say anythin' about it. I mean, I don't want to get into the balance of tellin' a girl she looks funny, 'cause if you tell her then she goes all self conscious on you and then is mad at you. Then if you don't tell her she'll look in a mirror later and is mad at you anyway. Either way, I figured I was done for in that area.

She sighed a little and smiled at me. I could see why them guys at school always fawned over her. She had a pretty smile, kinda like my Mom's.

"I… I'm sorry about all the duct tape and stuff," she said finally, quietly. "Things around here have just been kinda crazy and I'm all out of food, not to mention no water and no way to… Well I'd like to have a shower, y'know?"

"I just don't think about it," I laughed nervously, hoping I wasn't lookin' all troll-face. "I don't even notice the smell anymore. Must be like it was back in the day before deodorant."

"Yeah," she smiled again, wipin' at her wet green eyes. "I guess that's probably how it was. How did they stand it?"

"If everybody stinks, then prolly nobody really does."

She laughed and nodded. She had a really cute laugh, not like one of those snorty ones but one that sounded as if it belonged, somethin' you look forward to hearin'. I just let my natural self come out, tried to dust it off from bein' cooped up inside the hard shell I had built around it. She seemed to take to bein' calm again pretty well, and we talked for a while until it started gettin' to where the both of us were yawnin' more than talkin'. Every time she'd yawn she'd smile at me, and even though she'd taken her cap off, untied her red hair and tried to smooth it down, it was all messed up still. She was still lookin' more and more beautiful to me all the time. I didn't tell her. I said a small prayer for her that she'd find some happiness somehow and that I'd find some, too.

Don't get too attached, Clayton.

Soon we were thinkin' about where to sleep and at the same time not feel all awkward toward each other. She told me I could sleep in her Dad's old room and she would be in her room with the door locked. I figured that was prolly best and what made her feel safe. I went downstairs and made sure all the windows and doors were locked. I only had to re-lock the one door I had tried to open earlier, and when I did I noticed my dried blood on the threshold. Man, my head hurt.

I found her Dad's king size bed to be a welcome relief from sleepin' on the ground. I could get used to this if I didn't have to move on down the road the next mornin'. My stomach told me that I'd have to find some food tomorrow or it would start gnawin' on my backbone, not to mention the dryness of my tongue clickin' on the back of my throat. I think I was gettin' dehydrated. I took these threats seriously, but they would have to wait 'til mornin'. I shed most of my clothin', locked the bedroom door and crawled into the bed (which was still made). Even though the afternoon heat was nearly unbearable, a breeze blew through the open window and the stuffiness of the room had worn off enough so that the sheets felt cool on my legs. I drifted off to sleep and tried to ignore the fact that my head was throbbin' so. I figured I'd deal with that in the mornin', too.

Amy

I just couldn't sleep. Part of it was all the drama that Clayton caused by breaking in, then the duct tape and then me going all blabbity blah blah to him like some thirteen year old girl. I even hugged him, for crying out loud. Ugh, I felt so stupid! Now I had some guy I barely knew sleeping down the hall from me. The feeling of safety was outweighed by the slight creep factor of not knowing him well.

I snuck over and OCD'd the door to see if it was locked for the fifth time.

Laying back in my creaking bed I felt restless. No matter how many times I turned my pillow over and over again, I couldn't get the cool spot to last more than five seconds. The air was a hot, thick lasagna. It wouldn't be so bad if not for all the humidity. I felt so sticky and gross.

I had the window open, and the curtains barely moved. Stupid wind. In Oklahoma the wind always blew when you didn't need it to and didn't blow when you did. I just lay there, rolling back and forth, trying to get comfortable, listening to the bedsprings squeak, trying my hardest to get some shuteye. I finally got sick of it all and bounded out of bed to pull one of my pink Hello Kitty chairs (don't judge) over by the window and just sit for a while. This always helped me sleep even when I was alone.

I was still alone, as far as I could tell. Who knew how long Clayton would stay or whether I'd go with him. Would I go with him? I don't know. Maybe he could find some water to quench our awful thirst. My tongue felt all sticky and dry.

I looked through the window and could see the stars winking. I never used to notice the stars at night until the power went out all over everywhere. We used to have a security lamp that would cast an eerie blue glow in our backyard and another one in our front yard. They were meant to keep people from creeping around, but more for a pre-apocalypse kind of world. Growing up, they never really let me see the night sky. I had to walk a ways from my house off into the woods and then get up on top of a hill to see them back then. I remember it being pretty and romantic and peaceful. One night after all this happened, I tried it again and didn't get to the hill. I had heard someone trolling around in the woods and ran back to the house.

I sat by the window, putting my hands under my legs and just looking out at the night sky, realizing that the stars really do twinkle if you look at them long enough. One of the stars seemed brighter than the others, and I thought it must be the north star, but it wasn't anywhere near north. The moon wasn't out at all so the sky was black as a dead computer screen with little diamond stars, but that one star just got brighter and brighter. It burned up there, getting closer and bigger and bigger until it started to scare me.

I felt like my heart fell into my stomach when I saw that the burning thing was definitely moving toward me, and then there was a sound kind of like a jet taking off but way far away like it was in a dream. That was when I noticed it was spewing out some kind of trail behind it. I first thought it might be a jetliner going down, but it was way bigger than that and there hadn't been a jet in the sky in a few years. It was throwing off little balls of orange light here and there like it was made of molten metal. As it got closer and louder I could see that the little flames were blowing apart and raining down toward the ground.

It got as big as a basketball in my vision before I couldn't look anymore and realized that it was probably headed for somewhere close to the house. I stood up and bolted away from the window but when I looked over my shoulder the thing exploded in mid air just above the house I guess because it made a booming sound that shattered the window glass. This was followed by a high pitched whine that made me fall down on the floor and cover my head with my hands, going total fetal position, trying not to get cut on the little tinkling shards.

I am not ashamed to say I totally lost it.

Through the noise I could faintly hear a banging at the door and I couldn't stand the sound enough to let go of my ears and let whoever it was inside. I then heard the door banging louder and that nerdy Clayton broke into my room, the door jamb splintering everywhere and the door swinging open violently. He didn't cover his ears, but put his arms around me and held me close. I think it was more for comfort than him trying to protect me.

Something hit the ground not far from the house, shaking the floorboards beneath us, and I felt the house sway a bit. That was when we both heard the loudest roaring like somebody in the back yard just turned on a giant flame thrower.

Clayton

All I could hear was a roar at first, then after the explosion outside I grabbed Amy by the arm and we managed to run down the stairs lickety-split. Both of us stopped when we saw that the livin' room had caught fire, and a gapin' hole was in the wall where a chunk of rock had entered, blockin' our exit. The heat was a blast furnace, suckin' the breath out of me. I looked at Amy and she had this kinda wide eyed look that silently told me I'd better do somethin' about it... or that her house was on fire, I couldn't figure which.

The path to the back door was clear, so we made a bee line to it, but it felt as if the thing was wedged shut. I pulled on the brass knob with all I had and then Amy tried to do to it, but we just couldn't get it open. I thought that if it opened outward we could just break it down. We went for the window and that's when I saw the massive fire outside. The wood and sheet metal barn out behind Amy's property was right near destroyed and on fire. It looked like a crew had arrived with a back hoe and dug a giant crater then doused the whole thing in gasoline and set it alight. I turned around and put my hand on Amy's shoulder gently, somehow the Spirit allowin' me to be calm.

"Go get everything you need 'cause we're movin' out in a hurry," I said, my words quiverin' gibberish in between coughin' fits. "We gotta get out of here and you'll need shoes."

She nodded, her eyes glassy with tears, bitin' her bottom lip. She then lit out up the stairs while I looked around for somethin' I could fight the fire with.

No water. Forget that.

Blankets!

I found an old quilt and started to throw it across the fire that was eatin' up the carpet and it seemed to do the trick. She was back down stairs pretty fast, though, breakin' all kinds of stereotypes for me. She gave me that "you're a dork" look and then I thought "yeah she does think I'm a dork anyway. Nothin' new."

"C'mon," she said, and I followed her through the kitchen to another door on the side of the house. We tried to open it and it wouldn't budge either. This was so weird. The house was goin' up in flames and we were tryin' to get out the doors and both of them were wedged shut. We were both chokin' miserably on the smoke. It clogged our nose and everythin' got all blurry 'cause our eyes were waterin'. Snot was stringin' out my nose. We ran back to the window that looked out on the back yard, but the whole yard was up in flames. The dry grasses, not mowed in a long time, were easy kindlin' for the fire as it raced across the ground. I prayed to God for guidance, and silently trusted that He would listen.

"Window!" Amy coughed, and she ran back to the kitchen, dropped the small backpack she carried and opened the only window that did not have flames lickin' at the glass. It was a small openin', about three feet by two just over the sink, and I cupped my hands to help her up onto the counter and out the window but she managed just fine by herself. However, a tree fell just outside that window and it was quickly engulfed in flames. Things was lookin' worse and worse for us, but then the strangest thing happened.

The kitchen door that led outside creaked open ever so gently.

Like a couple of bulls out the shoot, we darted out the door and on down her white gravel driveway where we stood and watched as the house was slowly gobbled up by the billowin', roarin' flames.

"My house," she managed to choke out, her voice cracked and feeble.

I didn't say anythin'. I figured it wouldn't be polite and she didn't really know me that well. Anythin' I said would be like one of them well meanin' strangers who came to my Dad's funeral sayin' "everything would be ok" or "you'll get past this" when they really didn't know what they are talkin' about even if they was well meanin'.

She looked at the house for a while and we watched the fire get bigger and crawl all over the walls and roof, the black smoke and flames rollin' out of the windows as if a flame thrower was mounted inside each one. The roof caved in, then the top story went, and then after a while it kind of fell sideways and internally on the north side. I could feel the heat from it even though we were at least two hundred feet away. We stood on that hard gravel for a bit before movin' to the softer, dried up grass. I guess I kind of lost touch with time, 'cause when I looked over at Amy she was kinda squattin' on the ground and cryin', holdin' her knees and rockin' back and forth.

I took two steps and stood right next to her, thought about crouchin' next to her and puttin' my arm around her slumpin' shoulders, but didn't. I felt kinda awkward. I really didn't know what to say. We didn't have no place to go. Now Amy's house was a mess. I finally just sat on the ground next to her and she eventually leaned over and put her head on my shoulder just because I was the only shoulder to cry on and she'd prolly had enough of all this craziness.

I think we were both prolly thinkin' that this was pretty much the end of the world...again. At least I did. Amy didn't say it but I bet she was thinkin' it. We sat quietly and watched the sun come up over the ruins of Amy's smolderin' house and I wondered where we'd go next.

Strangely, I started thinkin' about Jerusalem. I don't know why. Sometimes your brain does weird stuff when life throws you a bothersome curve. The thought was soon drowned out by thinkin' about what we were goin' to do next, and where we'd find water.

Amy

My clothes were full of the smoke from my house.

When the sun began its oppressive march from its home behind the horizon, we wandered out onto the highway, and I couldn't believe all the smoke rising up across the hills. Many of the trees were on fire and the smoke was thick, covering the sky with a blanket of black smog. We had trouble breathing and had to tie some old shirts around our mouths. Good thing I packed them. The air burned my eyes and I had to stop every now and then to rest, blinking them and wiping at them with my fingers. Clayton was determined to get somewhere safe. I was beginning to wonder if that place existed. There were craters everywhere, and some of them were in the middle of the highway and we had to go around them. Some kind of red stuff was all over the ground making it difficult to walk. It was sticky and smelled terrible. Clayton said it looked like blood but that was impossible. Some kind of residue from the meteor shower would be my guess.

Water.

I wished that we had some water. My mouth felt all sand papery and I had used up all the water I was able to scrounge in the convenience stores near my house. I figured water was the one thing we would be looking for even more than food.

"Just a little further," said Clayton, like, every five miles or so. I didn't think he knew where he was going. I *knew* he didn't know. He kept saying something about New Orleans and that he'd heard that things were better there. My doubt meter was on overload.

We walked along the highway and kept an eye out for anyone who seemed like they would be friendly. Clayton pretty much avoided everyone. He'd duck off the road when he saw somebody at a distance and would say "Those people are probably bad." He did this every time. I started to wonder if being bullied in high school was like survival training for our present day. I guess it's better to be safe than supper. Clayton had told me about what he had seen and the whole horror show.

I could see plumes of smoke all around us, rising up from the wooded areas affected by the meteor shower. Sometimes we had to pass by areas white-hot with burning timber. The smoke filled our lungs and embers from the fires were catching other areas, going up like gas soaked match sticks. It took us a while, but we finally made it to an area that had already burned off, the once large trees smoldering like black fenceposts placed all over what now looked like a barren field. The fires were so quick to fly through areas since we'd had a drought pretty much since forever. Once in a while, a beat up old car or truck would come flying out of the smoke and nearly run us over, and we'd have to jump out of the way if we didn't first hear it coming. Clayton always dodged them or told me to "get out of the way. Those people are probably bad."

Finally, while sitting behind a bush on the side of the road waiting for yet another vehicle to pass I just got tired of it all and went out to flag them down. Clayton tried to grab my arm but I slipped away. It was just one guy in a truck. How much harm could he do? He could at least give us a ride.

The maroon, dinged up Dodge Ram with a missing headlight pulled over and a dark skinned Native guy looked dead at me, the shiny metal circle of the business end of a pistol pointing right at my head. He wasn't smiling.

"What you want?" said the Native, his brown skin shiny with sweat, his close cropped dark hair glistening like black oil. "Either you want to rob me, which you will not be doing, or you just want a ride. Nothing gets handed out for free around here."

"She didn't mean no harm," said Clayton who was suddenly beside me, his arms raised in the air, an inexplicable smile on his face. "We don't want to rob you and we hope you don't want to rob us 'cause we ain't got nothin' to rob."

The guy lowered the gun a little. Behind it was a beautiful face. I could see through the grime that he was probably just a victim of bad luck like the rest of us. He was Native like our neighbor Mr. White Thunder. I have to admit I was a little scared but I found myself smiling at him, sort of a nervous smile, I guess. Funny how your mind goes all to jelly when you see a cute guy, even if he's pointing a gun at your head. Go figure.

"You got any water?" he asked, the gun lowering a little more.

"No," said Clayton. "You?"

"None yet," he said, his face a frozen mask of what could be a smile but was probably more of a wince.

"I'm Amy," I said, my fingers brushing the side view mirror of the truck. It was hot to the touch and I pulled back my hand.

"Ralph Wapekeche," he said, sliding the gun under his

right thigh. Ralph wore dirty faded jeans in this heat. His alert status seemed to be dropping to normal. "I... I guess I could take you a little ways. Got anything to offer?."

I smiled at him and hoped that my hair wasn't too off-putting. Weird thought, I know.

"Oh yeah," I said managing a laugh, a kind of school girl laugh. So embarrassing. "We have some... well, we don't have anything, really."

There was a long awkward moment where we all just stared at each other.

"We can help each other find water," Clayton managed finally. "Plus we will be better together... You know. Strength in numbers."

"Ok," I said, opening the door of the truck as if on a dare and motioning Clayton to get in between me and Ralph. I used my angry face at Clayton for emphasis. Then I shifted to a smile when looking at Ralph. We both got in, Clayton being my safety barrier, and closed the door. "You think you could give us a lift past the next town at least?"

Ralph's face suddenly got all blank and weird like when you see the psycho in the movie shift into his evil voice and start stabbing. I didn't like this look, and started to fumble for the door handle. Clayton was looking at me like I was nuts, and I almost dragged his dorky self out of the truck and bolted for the burned out woods.

"Look," Ralph said softly, his voice taking on a remarkably quiet tone. It was kind of soothing, with a rhythm that was slow and methodical, his "s-es" sounding sort of like he was using the "sh" sound. "I don't have enough gas to get very far. I was just out looking for supplies. I... I mean, I didn't expect to haul nobody around."

"Where do you live?" I asked, genuinely smiling at him, using the moment to get what we wanted. Something in me felt ashamed. I moved closer to the door because I noticed that his right hand rested quietly on the handle of the gun sticking out between the seat and his leg.

We were taking a huge risk.

"I have been kind of roughing it," Ralph said as if reading from a cue card. "My Mom lives in East Texas but I just never made it back after all this happened. Stole this truck and I've been pumping diesel out wherever I can find it. Trying to make my way back there."

"They say there is a lot of food and water in New Orleans," Clayton drawled kind of out of the blue. "Maybe she beat it down there."

Both of us gave Clayton the whatever stare for a minute.

"Well," said Ralph, scratching the back of his head with his right hand and then sheepishly resting it beside him in the seat, just over the gun handle again. "I don't know anything about what has happened back home. I hear rumors, that's all. I guess you guys can go with me a ways and maybe I'll be able to get you a little further to… New Orleans… We can find some water maybe."

"I heard about the reservoir," piped in Clayton, his voice still a little shaky. "I guess we could get a raft or a boat and make it down the river to New Orleans. Those're *my* plans anyway."

Things got a little less tense, especially since Ralph had put the gun away, but he still had it in reach. Without another word, Ralph put the truck in gear (it was a column shifter) and started down the road. It felt good to feel the wind blow a bit on my skin. The smoke was starting to let up, and we could see a ways down the highway. Nobody in sight.

"You two, like, an item or whatever?" said Ralph. There was that cute grin again. His dark eyes made something flip in my stomach. I smiled and then shyly looked away.

Clayton saved me.

"No, no," said Clayton, grinning, squeezing out a nervous little laugh. "I suppose...I suppose we could find a store or somethin' like in a town and maybe stock up on stuff. Not too many people have one of them hand pumps for water like in the movies."

This caused Ralph to laugh and I found even his laugh to be soft and pleasant. I was starting to feel like I should have sat in the middle. I ignored the fact that we all smelled terrible, were dirty, hadn't had a good meal in a while and our lips were all chapped. After a while, Clayton started telling his whole life story to Ralph and he sweetly listened to him like a Dad listens to his son, managing a "yeah" and a "really" every now and again.

I so wanted to know more about Ralph than Clayton. Clayton just kept on and on. I had to interrupt.

"Tell us a little about *you*, Ralph." I said, trying not to look too foolish and needy.

Ralph caught the body language and sort of let out a low chuckle. I was feeling the chemistry, but wasn't sure about him. He was hard to read.

Ralph started talking about growing up in a small town and how his Dad left him when he was three, leaving his mother to raise him. He got a few scholarships from the tribe and then ended up at OU. That gave me an in so I talked to him about that for a while, about campus. Turns out he was working on a horticulture degree. We let the rhythm of the broken road wash away the awkwardness, and after a while it seemed like Ralph wasn't such a stranger, but more like the two of us. Now that the world had been ripped out from under us, it was like we were kind of forced to talk to one another. It was so good to talk to someone who was not Clayton, not that Clayton was all that bad. He was kind of like a little brother to me then.

We listened to Ralph talk about his adventures as we tooled down the road. Clayton seemed to drift in and out of sleep, but I sat intently listening to Ralph, gently pushing Clayton's head off of my shoulder when he'd slump over. I noticed a few times Ralph lost track of watching the highway and gazed into my eyes and then had to correct his driving so he didn't go flying into the ditch. I tried to keep my feelings to myself, not get too involved.

It was really hard to do.

Clayton

I was kinda suspicious of this Ralph guy from the start, but Amy was sure sold on him. I've seen lots of normal lookin' people do strange things after the world fell apart. I just had a bad feeling about the guy, that's all. He was all smiles, but it was similar to when you go to the doctor and he tells you some bad news and you both talk in quiet friendly tones, that is until you leave and you're cryin' in your car.

I figured I'd just keep my mouth shut along the way. At least the guy had given us a lift and it was pretty nice to not have to huff it down the road. Ralph had three fifty gallon drums of diesel in the back of the truck that sorta drew attention everywhere we went, but he would pull out his pistol and shake the business end at anyone who started lookin' our way and then hit the gas when they started towards us. Sometimes they threw rocks or other things or shot at us. Not many people were very good shots, but it was still scary times. We stayed pretty much on highway nine all the way. Every small town we came to, Ralph'd run all the stop signs and barrel on through so's not to attract attention. I was thankful none of them decided to light out in pursuit of us or had set up road blocks. That was what some of the pocket dictators that had control of some of the bigger towns were doin', as I had seen first hand. Now and again he'd stop the truck, and me and Amy would get out to look for supplies with Ralph sayin' he wanted to be the "get-away driver".

The meteor shower we had the night before kind of

shook things up in pretty much every place we passed. Houses were on fire, trees were burnin', and big grass fires could be seen for miles over every hill. Pretty soon we got past Eufaula Lake and then headed south toward McAlester. We'd gas up when we didn't see anyone and made sure we had plenty before goin' through any towns, but we tried to skirt them when we could. Sometimes we didn't have a choice and that was hard to do without feelin' that finger of fear run down my spine. Amy would grip my leg and squeeze. She started sittin' next to Ralph once we figured he wasn't all that bad, and I don't think she minded too much.

I noticed that Amy and Ralph were gettin' more and more chummy by the second and I started feelin' like a third wheel. He started to loosen up after we got down the road a ways and they started lookin' at each other like I wished she'd look at me. I just kinda stood around with my hands in my pockets and kicked rocks when we'd stop for bathroom breaks or I'd work the hardest to find food and water at places that looked abandoned. I was just hopin' that she'd get tired of him when she found out how he really was. But I really didn't know at the time. I was almost as snowed as she was but not really.

When we made it to Lake Eufaula we saw the strangest sight. People was campin' out all around it, a weird village of hippies. We decided to stay away from the tent city. We'd all heard stories. We cut south through some back roads and skirted most of the bigger towns by scootin' down Highway 62. It wasn't until we got in toward McAlester that we saw the big columns of smoke risin' up, like some sort of black markers of evil. We just got closer and closer to it until the bottom fell out of everythin' and Ralph did somethin' that didn't make no sense at all.

Like I said. I was kind of suspicious.

As if to confirm my suspicion, without warnin', Ralph pulled on the wheel of the truck when we caught sight of that big column of black smoke. The truck went over toward the ditch so fast it caught a tire kind of funny and started up on it's side. Before we could blink we were seeing sky-ground-sky-ground. I can't explain it for the life of me, but when that truck stopped its tumble cycle the three of us was totally unharmed if not a little bruised. The truck was trashed, windows spider-webbed, cab all crushed down and pulverized. I was a little dizzy climbin' out but was able to help the two of them onto solid ground where we were checking all of our odds and ends to see if we needed a doctor, like we'd be able to find one.

For a while nobody made a peep. We just stood there on the side of the highway and looked at the large black smoke cloud that used to be McAlester. Weirdest thing was that even though it was purt near obvious that the city was burnin' I didn't hear no sirens or any helicopters or anythin'. For that matter there weren't no people 'round neither. There were plenty of cars stopped in the middle of the highway and abandoned, but I just didn't see any people wanderin' around or hear any voices. It was the eeriest kind of calm.

Amy and Ralph kind of sensed it too 'cause of the drawn up looks on their faces. She was lookin' at me and givin' me that expression like I was supposed to tell her what to do and Ralph was just starin' at the black smoke and the empty cars. It wasn't long before Ralph started walkin' away from us. That dodge was all banged up. The bed was all twisted sideways and it had pretty much spilled all its contents on the highway. The last fuel drum had spilled out the back and there was diesel leakin' all over the road. We had to get away from this area before a spark made it blow up, no matter what them Mythbusters say about it.

"We gotta get out of here," I told Amy. I cautiously took her hand. It was soft and warm.

"Y- Yeah," she replied and pulled gently away from me to fold her arms and stare at the ugly ol' sky. "I wonder where Ralph is going."

We watched Ralph go from car to car and look inside of each one. All the cars had some kind of body damage: windows busted out, dents in the fenders, tail lights and headlights like empty eye sockets. I guess he was lookin' for keys. I figured the best thing for us to do was to skirt McAlester and head southeast. The highway would take us on along toward Texarkana prolly, but then if Texarkana was like McAlester maybe it wasn't such a good idea to find a big city to hole up in. I was beginnin' to lose hope. Where was all the people?

"Hey Ralph," I shouted out. "I don't know if we'll have much luck findin' a vehicle that's not broke down or outta gas. We just need to keep walking or —"

"Here's some keys!" he called back, a nervous giggle stammerin' out of him. "I wonder if it will start?"

He hopped into the seat of a blue Ford Focus with the tail lights busted out and turned the key, but the starter made a funny sound kind of like the breathing of a lung cancer patient.

We ran over there to him and stood outside the driver's side window just starin'. Not much we could do. He tried again, but the thing sat there clickin'. Battery was dead.

"Why'd you do that?" asked Amy, her voice shaky.

"Do what?" snapped Ralph.

"Throw us in the ditch," she said shyly as if speakin' to an angry lion.

Ralph put his hands on the steerin' wheel ten and two and stiffened out his arms straight as baseball bats.

"I don't know," he said calmly, evenly. "It's like the wheel just jumped. Maybe I hit a pothole."

I told him that didn't make no sense and said somethin' 'bout him bein' tired. He lit out of that car like a wet bobcat and knocked me to the ground. I was glad he left that gun in the truck 'cause he was aiming to let me have it and prolly would have shot me if he'd had that pistol. His face was right in mine and I had smacked my head on the pavement. He was on top of me, a wild animal, breathin' in my face and shoutin' curses. I started prayin'.

"You don't now what you're talking about!" he was screaming.

By the time he was on top of me I heard Amy screamin' for him to get off. He was in a crazy rage.

"Get off him!" Amy shouted, and I cocked my eyes to the corner of my vision to see her standin' straight as a board with that shiny pistol cocked and ready, her hands folded over it like a pro. Somethin' ran through my mind, only a flash, that she might have been given lessons.

Ralph jumped up off me and stood there with his hands in the air. I scooted backwards across the pavement and noticed that I had a little open rip in my pants near my left calf just behind the knee. Nothin' important, just a small torn openin', but there was some blood soakin' the fabric. I scooted back, a half-hearted crab walk, and stared at Ralph who looked at us both and then strangely started crying. It was a deep, raspy sound as if he hadn't felt anythin' in so long that he forgot how to let it out.

It looked like he had been bottlin' up that sadness for a very long time and whatever we did or whatever happened with the wheel of the truck or me askin' if he was tired triggered the water works. Ralph's knees suddenly lost their tension and he sank down on the ground and sat not three feet from me, weepin' deeply. I watched Amy slowly lower the gun to her side, tuck it in her waistband, and then she ran over to squat down beside him. Her right arm hesitated as she put a hand on his back.

We sat there on the pavement for a while, the smoke risin' above the hills, the diesel fumes causin' mirages on the road until the only sound was the hitchin' noise that Ralph made when he breathed in. I was thankful the fuel didn't catch fire, but a little sad it was all gone. Perhaps God figured we'd need the exercise.

Ethan

McAlester was a mess. Riots, Volos, disorder… everything went down the drain. I lay on the side of a hill looking across the city at the black smoke rising up and wondered if I my life would ever be the same again. I took this military uniform off a corpse because he sure didn't need it anymore. It helped me get out. Martial law had become madness after that militia attacked the city. I felt kind of sorry about having to leave that lady behind, but the building came down and I panicked. The meteor shower last night put a big one right down in the middle of town. What little order we had crumbled after that, and the militia took advantage.

I wondered if Stacie made it out. I wasn't going to stick around to find out.

I stood up and stretched my legs by walking up and over the hill and through the woods. I figured I'd find a highway and then take my chances. I was so thirsty. Everyone had been taking water from the river and drinking it after boiling it over open fires. Maybe that's the reason the city caught. We haven't had rain in I can't remember when. With no fuel for the fire trucks I suppose the city became a big tinder box. Like they'd be able to pump the water, anyway.

I walked for a few hours before sitting down to rest. I was thankful those guys from Deliverance weren't hunting me anymore. I started looking at the patches on the shirt I wore and started wondering about the man I took it from.

"Farmer".

That was his last name, anyway. I looked on the right

shoulder and saw a Ranger patch and my eyebrows raised. Tough guy. I'm in pretty good shape but not *that* much in shape. I heard those guys ate snakes and squirrels. I don't deserve this uniform, but it got me out of McAlester, at least.

Poor guy, but a huge failure. The army group assigned to our town wasn't a match for those hillbillies.

It felt weird running away. I've lived in McAlester my entire adult life. I sold cars there in town. Used ones. My life before all this consisted of selling cars, P90X, partying on the weekends and being great with the ladies... well, not so great with the ladies. I didn't' have much of a plan at that time other than getting back to Jersey and seeing if my old man was still alive. Surely he'd welcome me back considering the circumstances. You know, now that the world was over.

I pushed that out of my mind as I started back through the trees again headed toward the highway. As I got closer, I heard tires screech and a thumping crash that echoed over the hill. I came through the underbrush and saw a load of cars all parked in funny angles in the middle of the road, probably left there from the EMP, and what used to be a perfectly good pickup all smashed up and in the ditch. I assumed the people who were in it had just wrecked and were recovering, except that one of them, a girl, had a gun pointed at two guys who were on the ground wrestling around. Well, the guy under the dark complected guy was just laying there taking it. I decided to watch for a bit. Didn't want to surprise that girl and get shot.

She was shouting something at the two guys and then the Native guy just sat down on the ground and started sobbing. I figured it was over because the girl put the gun in her waistband and went over to him. I could really use that gun. It would come in handy if I got in a jam, not that I knew how to use one…because I didn't.

It was time to put on my sales face and do what I do best.

Amy

This soldier guy strolled out of the woods, arms up over his head, his face looking something like a salesman or maybe one of my teachers back in school who looked at me with those eyes that had the wrong ideas. First impressions? Shivers.

"Yo kids," the guy called out, his dark eyes flashing back and forth, never really focusing on anyone for too long. He didn't seem too bothered that I had pulled the gun out again and had it carefully aimed at his head. "I just saw the wreck over here and wondered if I could be of assistance."

He had, like, a back eastern accent or something.

Clayton and I stood silent for a bit, and I could tell that he was probably thinking of something to say. Ralph was wiping his eyes with the backs of his hands and slowly rising to his feet. Finally Clayton took the initiative… opened his big mouth.

"I think we're ok," managed Clayton, putting a hand out to touch the shiny metal gun and press downward, causing me to reluctantly lower it. "A little shaken up, I guess. And who're you?"

Clayton took two steps forward and stood with his hands on his hips.

"Sergeant Farmer," said the soldier, his teeth strangely white, his hair a close cropped military style but something was just weird about it all. "Just got separated from my unit back in McAlester. You don't want to go that way. It's a real mess. Whole place has gone ape and the militia are everywhere. We were overrun."

"We were going try to avoid the major cities," I said, my voice strange in the eerie calm. "We guessed that most of the larger ones would be kind of dangerous."

Ralph made a clicking sound with his mouth and folded his arms.

"We don't know *you*," said Ralph cocking his head to the side, wiping at his eyes. "You got some kind of ID or something, soldier man?"

Strangely unflustered, Farmer pulled a wallet out of his pocket and flashed it around quickly. I didn't really get a good look at it, but it looked kind of official.

"Ethan Farmer," he explained, closing up his wallet and putting it away. "First Airborne. Got stuck in the lurch after the war was called off."

"We lost the war, soldier man," growled Ralph. "Or didn't you get the memo on that."

Ethan smiled and put his hands back up.

"Look — uh, what's your name, sir?" asked Ethan.

"No business of yours," Ralph shot back. "I still don't believe you are who you say you are. Where's your unit?"

Ethan dropped his hands a bit and looked at Clayton and I. "Look, that's what I'm trying to tell you. My unit just got wiped out back in McAlester. Riots got out of control, militia took advantage or probably had people working on the inside. We weren't about to shoot innocent civilians, so…the best thing I can do right now is make sure that civilians get clear of this area."

Clayton and I looked at one another while Ralph sat down in the driver's seat of the Ford Focus, the door wide open, mumbling to himself.

"I ain't got no problem with ya, Ethan — er — Sergeant

Farmer," said Clayton as if he were talking to a clerk who gave him too much change. "I figure havin' a soldier along will be good for helpin' us find food and water."

"Well," smiled Ethan. "That is exactly what I will do for you."

I felt like that time when Brayden Schneider said he had run out of gas in his car on our way to the movies…for the second time.

It didn't matter anyway, because our lives were interrupted by the roar of something in the sky, and as we stood in the middle of the highway all of us saw a massive object burning up the atmosphere around it moving from the east to the west. It roared, a sound similar the rockets that used to take off from Cape Canaveral. It rumbled, shook the ground, and I sat down on the pavement and clutched at my chest, feeling like I couldn't breathe. All of us seemed to be frozen in place for a bit, looking skyward and instinctively raising our hands to cover our heads, sure something was going to fall on us and kill us. Ralph and Clayton stared. Ralph's face was stoic yet wide eyed while Clayton's mouth curled on one side to form what could have been a faint smile, his eyes squinting in the sun…some kind of nut. Clayton mouthed something. Was he…was he praying?

The object passed off over the horizon to the west and within a few seconds was gone. We all stood still and quiet as if something inside of us had died. The air around us was silent, not even the birds or insects made a noise. So creepy. We all just looked at each other, one face turning to face another in a random sequence.

"What was that?" asked Clayton.

"Looked like a meteor, " said Ethan quietly. "I wonder if

it hit the ground or if it just passed on out of our atmosphere? That thing was big."

"I don't care, man, let's get in a car or something and get out of here." Ralph said, his sentence seemingly strung together in one long word. "One of these cars has gotta run."

Ralph scurried around, going from vehicle to vehicle, looking at the steering columns, then hunting around the floor boards. The rest of us followed his example all save Ethan who walked calmly to one of the older cars, a Mercedes, and opened the driver's side door to sit behind the wheel. Before turning away from him, I saw him reach under the dashboard beneath the steering column and then his face popped up and looked all strained like he was trying to hot-wire the car.

Heh. Fail.

"I think we are humping it from here." he shouted, sounding like some kind of movie soldier Rambo.

Just as Ralph and I popped our heads up above a mass of many colored car tops, the quake hit. Cars started rocking back and forth on their springs and Ralph lost his footing and fell backward. I looked around for Clayton and that was when I noticed that he was talking to someone, but nobody was there.

Clayton

There stood Gabe in front of me.

He looked a little cleaner this time, and I started to say somethin', but he cut me off.

"Clayton," he said, his voice soft and deep as if it came from underground somewhere. "I thought I told you that your destination should be Jerusalem."

I stood still as a stone statue. My throat was dry from not drinkin' anythin' for a few days. He moved over to me, his boots crunchin' some broken glass on the pavement. His eyes squinted slightly, and he put his warm hand on my shoulder.

"I heard that there's food and water in New Orleans," I told him.

"New Orleans is only a way station for you, Clayton. It is a means to an end. If you will go south to the Red River, you will find your way, but it will be hard. You will find many dangers, but God will guide you. Float the river to the Big Easy."

"I'm so thirsty," I said. I felt as if I'd faint, but he held my arm.

"Look in the trunk of that car," he said, a grin formin' on his mouth. "Ask and you will receive. Now go and do the will of he who sent me."

I thought about the prayer I muttered when the meteor flew overhead. I was so thirsty. Nothin' else really mattered to me. A dyin' man only thinks about what he wants at that moment for comfort. I suppose my greatest wish was water.

I went and opened the door of the car reached under the

dash and popped the trunk. I shuffled my feet to the back of the blue Ford Focus and lifted the lid, my arms feelin' all rubbery. My heart missed a beat at what I saw. I then pushed the trunk lid down to notice that Gabe had disappeared again and in his place stood Amy, her face weary and sweat-smeared.

"Found some water," I said softly.

She brightened, a flower bloomin' in a desert, and walked around the car to stare blankly at the three cases of bottled water sittin' in the trunk. She put a dainty hand on my shoulder and laughed that attractive laugh of hers. I swear I thought I was goin' to get a kiss just then as she focused her beautiful sea-green eyes on mine and got real close, her full mouth openin' slightly. Ralph's voice ruined it all.

"Man!" he shouted, lookin' in the trunk. "Jackpot!"

In a few seconds, Ethan was standin' to my right, hands on the edge of the trunk , feelin' the smooth metal. I had a strange thought that his hands didn't look worn as soldier's hands should. He had fingernails that looked too neat to be the fingernails of a government grunt.

"Good job, Clayton," he laughed. "That will last us a while."

We all commenced to openin' up the thick plastic holdin' the bottles together in neatly packed four by eight rows. We drank two of them immediately, lettin' the warm wetness roll down our parched, cracked throats. We stayed there for a few hours, some of us sittin' on the open trunk and others on the pavement. We had to come up with some kinda game plan, but I knew that I had to follow through with the will of God. I would go to New Orleans via the river and then possibly Jerusalem. Like I had anythin' better to do.

I asked Ethan about the best route, since he was a soldier and all, and he suggested we skirt around McAlester and then move south along the Indian Nation turnpike and that it went straight to the Red River. From there we could head to New Orleans eventually. I hoped he was right.

Ethan

The sky was falling.

I remember as a kid my Dad used to read that story to me about Chicken Little, but now it was real. Whatever smashed into the planet over the western horizon was sending up a plume of black stuff into the atmosphere that was blotting out the sun. Everything was blanketed in a weird darkness. It reminded me of that time I experienced that solar eclipse but was so busy with selling cars and my stupid life that I didn't hear the news for a few days. It was kind of a permanent dusk, but I thought it was just bad weather.

We had been walking for the entire day, but the water was still in good supply. Ralph had found a child's wagon in one of the trucks back in that dead car traffic jam and was dragging it behind us. We hadn't seen anyone at all.

"At least it's a little cooler," said Clayton. "I guess that's a blessin'."

I looked back at them, Ralph and Amy walking side by side, Clayton bringing up the rear. I was leading these kids, but didn't know where. I figured I'd just wing it like always. They were looking to me for help. So trusting. I didn't think I would let on about the truth because the lie was working so well. That was when that Native kid Ralph threw me a curve.

"So what got you in the army, Ethan?" he asked, his voice raspy, methodical.

I paused for a second, my mind whirling. Now would start the dog and pony show. I told him a long story about not having any direction after high school which was partly true until I told him about joining up and going to war, drawing on the war movies my Dad had made me watch as a kid.

I didn't tell him about Dad drinking too much to do anything with me that mattered. I also didn't tell him about Dad disappearing all day to watch the horses. When he was home it was watch what Dad watched on television or get beat for asking to watch something else. Pretty much the extent of my old man's method of parenting.

I tried not to play it too heavy, not to tell too much of a story, just enough to keep them guessing about me. Ralph wouldn't let it go.

"What's it like to kill a man?" he asked, his dark eyes squinting, biting his bottom lip.

I hesitated. Something started to roll inside my head, a hopper full of lotto numbers, except my number wasn't coming up. Think fast, Ethan. This kid has you by the back of the neck.

"You never get over it, kid," I said, using my best Han Solo voice. "It follows you, and you always remember their faces. Let's hope you don't never have to find out."

That seemed to satisfy Ralph and he shut his mouth for a while, but not the smirk he'd always shoot my way. It was easy lying, but keeping it going was tough. Always had to remember what I said to them, or I would just avoid the subject all together.

As it started getting darker, I led them off toward a wooded area where Clayton made quick work of building a fire for us. It cooled off a little more than normal at night now and I figured it was all that debris in the atmosphere from that meteor that went down. Amy and Ralph were talking to each other a lot, flirting mostly, and I thought about what it would have been like to be younger. They started making me feel a little uncomfortable, so I thought up a quick plan to leave them.

"Let me see the gun," I said, calmly. "I'll go out and shoot some squirrels, since there are a lot of them around, and I'll cook us up some food."

Amy winced, but Ralph's eyebrows furrowed. I wasn't really serious about the squirrels. I was really going to just take the gun and dump these kids.

"You aren't taking my gun," Ralph said, standing up. "I'll go do it. You stay here and tend the fire."

He walked off in the woods with my only chance at getting away from these people. I then started thinking about how I could sneak off in the night with some water at least. I could really use that gun, though. I was getting desperate. I didn't care about these kids any more than that lady I had to leave in that building. It was every man for himself, as they say.

"Let me go with you, Ralph," I told him. "I can—"

"Squirrels?!" Amy winced, interrupting. "Really?"

"They're not bad at all if you cook them through," Ralph chuckled. "Just eat it and think about KFC."

Amy looked at Clayton for help, but Clayton only shrugged and smiled shyly.

"You, too?" she said, her eyes wide, mouth open.

"Boy's gotta eat," said Clayton, his bottom lip protruding a bit and his eyes darting around everywhere but at her. He patted his skinny belly for emphasis.

They chatted on about it, which made me forget about

splitting for a while. Ralph wandered off into the dusky forest, ignoring my offer to help, and I didn't follow him. Clayton reached in his backpack and pulled out a worn old Bible. I grinned at him and didn't really say anything. The guy was pretty simple, and saying something about his worn out old dogma would just complicate things so I kept my mouth shut... for once.

It didn't stop Amy.

She sidled up to him and started asking him what he was reading, and he responded by telling her about how much this one passage or whatever made him have hope. I couldn't figure that out. How could a book give anyone hope? Especially a book that was so full of rules and guidelines that not even it's own followers could follow. Dad was Catholic, so I guess that made me Catholic, but that was just more mythology. I got tired of him telling me to live by his code but then watching him turn around and do whatever he pleased. That was what sent me out into the world in the first place. Stupid, unrealistic rules.

About an hour and two distant echoey gunshots later, Ralph returned with two little scrawny squirrels, his dark brown hands stained with their blood. It was the one animal there was plenty of, I suppose. We watched as he produced a knife I didn't know about and proceeded to skin and gut the two forest rats while Amy at first tried to hold down her stomach acid and then walked to the edge of the camp to stare out into the darkness. I had never eaten squirrel or even thought about it.

It didn't taste that bad. Kind of like gamey KFC.

Clayton

We all stood quietly along a rusty, crooked barbed wire fence, starin' at the grazing brown and white horses. They's all lazy, their heads bobbin' along as they ate that golden Johnson grass. A nice breeze had come a-blowin' out of the south and this group of tired travelers had our eyes closed mostly, feelin' the welcome air blow across our skin.

"How I'd love to be able to get one of them horses to ride," I said aloud to no one in particular. "I wonder if they're broken."

"And how do you expect to ride them without bridles and without saddles," Ralph sniffed. "You gonna just talk to the animals like that movie with Eddie Murphy?"

After this comment there was a few chuckles at my expense and then there was dead silence, only the sound of the wind blowin' the leaves on the trees and the cicadas chireein' in the branches.

Just then, out of nowhere, some old man came sneakin' up on us all ninja-like, lay his hickory staff against a fence post a few feet to the left of us, parted the barbed wire and stepped through, walkin' all slow and methodical across the field. I's surprised that none of us jumped, but I guess it's 'cause we was so dog tired…or maybe 'cause he was somehow not a threat…I don't know.

I watched him pull a small metal bucket from his over-the-shoulder brown satchel and pretty soon he was circlin' around, huntin' along the ground for small rocks that he placed inside that bucket, each one fallin' in with a little plunk. Before anybody was able to utter so much as a peep, the gray headed old feller sat down in that tall grass and commenced to rattlin' the bucket of rocks in his left hand while usin' his right hand for support.

"What is that guy doing?" whispered Ethan. "And…did you guys see him before now?"

"Yeah, um, he was sitting over there across the highway," said Amy, shrugging her shoulders. "I think I'll watch and see what happens."

"Why didn't you tell me—."

"Shhhh!" said the three of us to the soldier man.

All of us stood real quiet as the old man rattled his little bucket of rocks. Quietly, like in a movie, each horse stopped grazin' and raised their heads to finally look over toward the old man. After a couple seconds of them standin' around as if they was discussin' the matter, the horses started off toward Jacob, their heads bobbin' gently along. All of us yahoos on the other side of that fence looked at each other with toothy smiles, my face feelin' like it hadn't made the expression in a while. Ethan put his fist up for Ralph to bump it with his own, and after some weird expressions, Ralph didn't "leave him hangin'" as they say. Amy's cheeks had streaks of tears cuttin' through the dirt and grime, but she was still so pretty.

The horses came closer to the old man, curious I guess, thinkin' prolly that the bucket was filled with oats or sorghum mash or somethin' like that. The old guy reached in his satchel slowly and with a tremblin' hand pulled out three white paper packets which he tore open all at once and poured into his hand. He didn't stand, but raised his cupped hand containin' the sweet stuff toward the waitin' and eager lips of the brown and white painted stallion. Its chocolate mane billowin' in the wind, it sniffed the old man's hand and then a pink tongue shot out and started to lickin' at the sweet and wonderful sugar.

The old man rose to one knee and then creaked to his full height as he stood, his knees protestin', to stroke the neck of what had looked to us like a wild horse.

I chuckled to myself, thinkin' I'd prolly have to learn to ride one of them.

Jacob blinked once.

"Indeed," the old man said calmly, his voice floating over to us. "But he always provides a way."

I watched the joy drain out of the old guy's face but his eyes narrowed and his mouth got real small.

We didn't even hear the four militia guys who walked up behind us with guns drawn. The only way I knew that somethin' was up was when Amy turned and gasped and then all the blood ran out of her face. I'd heard stories about these types, mostly told by mothers to scare their children into not goin' out at night, but here they was as big as life, starin' at us through ugly hawkish eyes. They each had little half grins on their grizzled faces. Out of reflex I put up my hands in surrender. That's when I heard the old man's voice, echoin' behind us like he was usin' a megaphone.

"You boys don't need to start any trouble," he said, soundin' remarkably like my former high school principal. "All of you along the fence should now lay down on the ground so you don't get hit."

I could imagine, even though I did not turn to see, that the old guy had a gun or somethin' 'cause I heard somethin' clankin', metal bangin' on metal, but didn't really recognize the sound. All the others did as told, and I hesitantly followed suit, thinkin' we were done for so I figured there weren't no rush. I covered up my head when I heard the first shot peel back the air 'round it and whiz just over my head. I heard the horses thunder the ground and I pictured them runnin' off across the field as in one of them movies where the wild mustangs gallop across the prairie. I got brave enough once to roll my eyes 'round to try to see what was happenin', and that was when I saw them men firin' away with their big ol' shotguns and machine guns (I weren't sure what kind of guns they was 'cause I'm not really a gun guy but a fishin' guy) so I figured the old feller was toast.

They didn't spend much time spewin' out ammo, 'cause after a few seconds they stopped and for some reason beat it across the highway and then into the woods, leavin' their horses tied up. I suppose if those horses could scratch their heads they would've, 'cause I was sure puzzled. Before I could say anythin' at all or even move I heard footsteps in the grass behind me close to my feet, and then the voice of the old man.

"You folks can get up now," he said, then he cleared his throat. "They won't be back for a while, but they left us a nice gift."

The air was kind of thick and smelled of gun powder and sweat.

It was kind of one of those times where nobody says anythin' but everybody's thinkin' really loud, so loud you can almost hear people's thoughts bein' projected right out of their brains. All of us stood up slowly from the ground and brushed ourselves off, but Ralph was standin' still, not a grain of dust on him, starin' off all quiet like, his face lookin' like he'd just smoked a heap of cigars. He was starin' at the old man like he'd seen some kind of horror from beyond, then his eyes wandered off toward the horses standin' in the field. They was grazin' again as if nothin' happened. I figured it was just shock from such a near miss, but Ralph stood there quiet, his mouth open, breathin' heavy.

"What did you...?," asked Ethan, pullin' small bits of grass from his uniform.

"We'll talk later," said the old guy. "Right now we need to take those horses and get on out of here before those guys realize what really happened and come back with a bigger army."

"Sure, yeah," stammered Amy. "I... I haven't ridden a horse since my Dad took me to a riding stable on my tenth birthday. Should come back to me."

Crossin' the highway, we all made for a horse, and I ended up ridin' on the back of Amy's horse because she insisted. I felt kinda awkward on the back of the horse with her, but not as awkward about what happened just a bit ago.

We all rode in silence, and after a while the old guy started singin' an old song about somethin' that sounded churchy. I didn't know, but I was thankful I didn't get massacred by them militia yahoos.

Ethan

We all rode the horses without talking for some time. I don't know when someone started speaking, but it must have been after traveling for nearly a day. We were all so puzzled by what had happened back at the horse pasture. We all rode in a line, me first, then old man Jacob, then Amy and Clayton, and that Ralph kid rode at least three horse lengths behind all of us. His face was really pale for a while until finally the color came back to it.

"You guys know where we are goin'?" asked Clayton. He was kind of like one of those kids that never really "got it" but somehow seemed to figure things out slowly, working them out in his mind.

"We just follow this highway to the river," said the old guy. I don't think any of us had asked his name. I decided to get some info.

"What is your name, sir," I said to him formally.

"Oh!" he exclaimed. "How rude of me. The name is Jacob Buckminster. And yours?"

"Ethan… er… Sergeant Ethan Farmer," I managed.

"You in the army, Ethan?" he asked.

"Was, sir. I suppose I was."

He chuckled to himself, prodding his horse with his booted heels and riding up beside me. He looked at me, winked, and suddenly I felt as if he saw right through my ruse. I changed the subject.

"I was too busy ducking and covering to see what happened back there," I said. "…So what…did… happened back there?"

He smiled that infectious smile of his and his eyelids squinted together to make his eyes almost disappear.

"I suppose they saw we were of superior number," he replied, his voice calm and soft. "Sometimes God does things that defy explanation as well, isn't that right, Raphael?"

Jacob looked off to my left when he said the name, but I certainly didn't see anyone. It was then that I thought that he might have spent too much time out on his own or had fallen and hit his head or something. I didn't know what to make of it, so I pulled back on the reins a bit and let Amy and Clayton catch up. Jacob rode on ahead and seemed to know where he was going. I felt like riding with someone who actually made sense when they talked, so I hit up the youngsters.

"You guys know what happened?" I asked. "I was covered up like a good soldier."

Amy shrugged, but Clayton couldn't keep quiet. He spoke in low tones as if telling me a dark secret.

"I can't explain it, but those guys opened up on the old guy. I could hear somethin' clangin' around but didn't dare look that way. All I know is them guys took off runnin' and the old guy didn't have a scratch on him. I can't figure it, unless he's in with those rough guys with all the firepower and this is all a trap, but I really don't think it's a trap. Man, I don't have a clue."

Yes. Talk to someone who makes sense. Not happening on this trip.

Just then we could hear Jacob singing, a rich baritone, some hymn or other I had heard somewhere before but couldn't place. There used to be this old, run down church next to my apartment building in McAlester and I'd sometimes hear singing coming from there on Sunday mornings, just when the hangover was wearing off. Those people couldn't sing well, but Jacob's voice was somehow beautiful in an old world kind of way.

"I dare not be defeated
With Calvary in view,
Where Jesus conquered Satan,
Where all His foes He slew;
Come, Lord, and give the vision
To nerve me for the fight,
Make me an overcomer
Clothed with Thy Spirit's might.
A victor, a victor!
Because of Calvary.
Make me an overcomer,
A conqueror, a conqueror..." and then he hummed the rest.

We rode on, and soon we came close to the river which lazily flowed under the highway bridge through the hills. We saw several multi-colored tents down at the water's edge, so we all stopped our horses to let them graze along the grassy shoulder of the highway. It was a quiet looking place, a ring of trees springing up along the beach cushioned from the sandy shore by a field of tall grasses and cat tails, and then woods beyond. I was thinking that we needed to proceed with caution. There was no telling what kind of people camped down there, hostile or friendly.

We dismounted our horses, all but Ralph who was still staring at the water flowing by down below, his brown eyes unblinking, his mouth slightly open. Amy walked over to him and waved her hand at him.

"Ralph?" she said, almost a whisper. I had to listen close to hear what she said next. "I think we are going to give the horses a rest and see if we can get to the river. What do you say?"

It took a second for his gaze to break. She touched the Indian kid's leg and he sort of jumped, then without much ceremony climbed out of the saddle as Amy led his grey horse over to the side of the road to graze. In one hand she held the reins and in the other Ralph's trembling hand. I thought they made a cute couple for whatever it was worth. Clayton, probably feeling like a third wheel, followed close behind and then Jacob joined us, pulling his white horse by the bridle. The old man let go and patted the horse's neck. It bowed its head and nibbled at the dry grass.

There was a steep incline just past the bridge and a small, well traveled trail that snaked its way through grass, on around a few granite boulders and emptied out on sandy gravel by the water's edge. Jacob shouldered his satchel, grabbed his walking stick and looked at all of us with a huge grin.

"Who wants to go down and visit with the locals?" he asked, taking a deep breath, filling his lungs with air.

"Jacob," I said sternly, as if speaking to someone with Alzheimer's. "I'm not really sure that's such a good idea. They might be hostile."

He laughed. It was a wheezy, barrel chested kind of laugh.

"Now," he beamed. "We can't go assuming everyone is a bad apple, now can we? How else will we get along in this world. We'll just ask and receive."

With that, he started down the path as methodically and quickly as his denim clad legs would carry him, walking stick stabbing the ground for support now and then. We all watched without a word. The only person to speak was Clayton.

"Maybe we should hide."

Kelly

I stood by the flowing river, the cool wet sand squishing up between my toes. Grant and Eddie, both wearing their dirty tank tops and ragged shorts were down by the shore, fishing poles stretching out over the rushing, sparkling surface of the water. I waved to them and they nodded back. We had become a small family here.

A few of the children, those who had survived the winter, had found two crawdads and were pitting them against one another like two gladiators in an arena. These little ones were all very dirty, the life of vagabonds not hard for them to live. They did not know they were living in a fallen world.

My first warning of something new was the familiar owl noises that Darren made when intruders arrived, but then I saw the old man, striding down the path to the river with a walking stick in hand, the ring of white hair around his head, the short cropped white beard covering his sun-weathered face. He held his free hand out, palm toward me, and I could hear him saying something, but could not make it out.

Julia and Mr. Coffman grabbed their rifles and ran out to stand on the beach in a threatening manner, and my eyes scanned the bushes on the other side of the river to see our scouts, their clothing sprouting twigs and leaves, training their lethal guns on the man.

Where was Gideon?

"State your business here!" growled Mr. Coffman, his days of being a high school principal giving him that

authoritative sound. School was so long ago. I wish we
were preparing for homecoming again. I knew what Mr.
Coffman was thinking. We wouldn't have room for them on
the boat. We must not let them see it.

The old man paused, a smile forming on his sun-baked
face.

"I don't mean any harm," said the old man calmly, his
voice strangely soft. "I am with a group of travelers who
would like to share resources. We will be building a raft to
get on down the river. We will not stay more than two
days."

"How many?" said Julia forcefully, strands of her blonde
hair escaping her pony tail, falling lightly across her face.
"We got troubles of our own."

Mr. Coffman lowered his rifle and put his meaty hand on
Julia's rifle barrel to guide her to do the same.

"Send your group down slowly," he told him, his eyes
scanning the top of the hill near the bridge. "Unarmed
would be the best way. Make sure of it."

I had never seen Mr. Coffman trust so readily, but there
was something about this old guy that just seemed...well...
fatherly.

After a bit of hand shaking and uneasy introductions,
four more people came down the path toward the river
camp: a girl, two young men and a soldier. I thought the
soldier had a kind face. Both of the boys looked confused
and the girl smiled when she saw Julia. After a bit, we all
kind of stand-offishly accepted them. It was only for a short
time, anyway, as they said, and they would be leaving.

I approached the soldier thinking about my husband,
long gone to war. He was a Ranger, too. But this man's

patches were… And his last name read…Farmer…and that was when I blacked out.

Amy

Clayton and I had helped lift Kelly from the sandy gravel and carry her to the waiting arms of some of the villagers. They took her inside a dirty blue nylon tent and lay her on a rusty cot. She had totally passed out, but not before her eyes opened wide, focusing on Ethan's name badge, that look of total fear in her eyes. I didn't really know why she did a face plant, but I assumed that she knew something about Ethan's past or possibly the truth of who he was.

I decided to keep my eye on him.

I'd found Ralph again, and we walked slowly toward Jacob who was talking to that large, broad shouldered Edward Coffman. I'd tried to talk to Ralph about what he'd seen, but he was so quiet. The guy was just not great with words. Words, however, were about to be exchanged, because Ralph was, like, figuring out that he had guts.

"What...," stammered Ralph, totally butting in on the two men. "What happened back at the field?"

Jacob turned and looked at Ralph and me, placing a large knuckled hand gently on the Ralph's shoulder. Ralph didn't pull away. Jacob only beamed at Ralph and chuckled gently, but in a way that didn't make us feel all third grade.

"I did what I had to," he replied softly. "I asked and I received."

"But who were those... Those men?"

"Excuse me a second, Mr. Coffman," said Jacob, and he turned to put his arm around Ralph who did not squirm away. I moved in on the other side of Ralph and he shoved his hands in his pockets as we all walked slowly away from the group.

"You saw what you needed to see," said Jacob, leading us away to stand near the water. "It is as simple as that."

"I..I don't think it was real," stammered Ralph. "But it looked real, and you walked away without a wound."

"Sometimes God allows us to see things that will convince us of his presence, but it never gives man the glory, only shedding light on his," said Jacob reassuringly, and I thought *here we go.* "Our unbelief files it away as coincidence or some other trick of the mind, but it is the maker of the universe that beckons to us on a daily basis. He desires a relationship with you both. He is showing himself to you in such a profound way that the mind often has trouble understanding. We live in precise times, and this kind of thing will become more common. We are in a war, son, and we are on the front lines. Do you choose to join with the master or will you be counted with the lost?"

"I don't want to be a part of anything," replied Ralph, folding his arms across his chest. "I just want to get some food, some supplies, and get on my way...and stop seeing weird stuff."

I'd seen this tactic many times in church growing up. After a couple of weeks in college I started doubting what my grandma told me about Jesus, and that kind of dumped out into a year of soul searching, and then that led to not really knowing what I believe anymore...but I listened.

Jacob only smiled. He placed his hand gently on Ralph's shoulder and his sky blue eyes darted back between the two of us. I suddenly felt really warm; not because of the sun, but because of something to do with old Jacob. I didn't really know what to think about it, but the X-Files moment we had back with the horses was creeping in on my mind, playing with my resolve.

"You have a choice," said Jacob. "And I'll be speaking to the group later about that choice. It is a choice that brings hope in this forgotten and downtrodden world. We'll see what you say after that. I hope you change your mind, or rather your heart."

Ralph looked at me, and I could tell from his expression that he wanted to go, so I took his hand and we walked back to join the others. Jacob simply smiled and let out a long sigh.

As we were walking away, I looked back to see him standing all stoic by the water , staring out across the shimmering surface, and then he bowed his head, closed his eyes and I guess he prayed.

Clayton

I was bound and determined to get Jacob alone so's I could talk to him.

It seemed as if people really liked him here at this camp. I don't think he'd ever really been here, but I figured he just had a way with people. Boy, was *I* shootin' in the dark. He had been given something much more real and turns out he weren't the only one.

I waited 'till he walked on down to the river to wash his face and that's when I joined him. At first I didn't think he noticed me, then he spoke in a real quiet voice but one that sounded very similar to my Dad's.

"I see you are a man of faith," he said. "Clayton, is it?"

"Yeah," I said, soundin' as I did when my Dad would get on to me for somethin'.

"God led me to you, Clayton," said Jacob, standin' from a crouching position and puttin' his gentle hand on my shoulder. His other hand held a staff made from a small hickory tree. I suddenly thought about when my grandpa grafted a waxed pecan branch into the top of one when I was a little boy. That big ole tree was prolly still there.

"God?" I asked.

"The Living God, our Father in Heaven. You have trusted in his grace. I can tell that about you based on the way you talk, the way you live."

"I try," I said, a little embarrassed. "I figure we just take one day at a time and don't worry 'bout nothin' and then he kinda takes care of the rest."

"Exactly. Except that reading your Bible every day and

praying every day isn't enough. It is a relationship that we have with him. It is a way of life that refuses sin and realizes that we have died to this world, that we have been crucified with him on the cross, that our old self is gone and that Jesus is now living out his life in this dead husk of a body."

"I trusted him with my life about a year ago, after I'd been wanderin' around in this crazy new world for a while. It's what's kept me from goin' outta my gourd."

He laughed a little funny laugh. It wasn't mockin' me or nothin', just kind of that laugh your Mom gives you when you mention some gift you want for Christmas and she's already bought it but won't tell you about it.

"Remember the story of Moses?" he asked, grabbin' his hickory walking stick with both hands and leanin' heavily on it. It looked as if he was holding up a lot of stuff on his shoulders and just needed a rest. "Moses was a man who was a murderer, a persecutor of his own people, a simple sheepherder, but God did amazing things through him. He used this simple flesh and blood man to part the sea, bring water from the rock, call bread down from heaven and many other miraculous things. All those things were done to show God's glory on earth to the unbelieving peoples around the Israelites. Those were extreme times. I would argue that we live in times just as extreme. The world is ending, son. The war is over but the battles are winding down and getting more and more intense."

"I can see that," I said, scratchin' my chin stubble. "I've seen some pretty bad stuff. Worse than most of the bad stuff that happened in the stories in hist'ry class."

"True," he said. "Many more bad things are coming. There is a power rising in the east that I have heard some speak of around camp fires. It is growing in strength. I was told to go there three years ago."

"The guy who told you this…was his name Gabe?" I asked.

He smiled wide and I noticed that one of his back teeth was missin', the others were kinda yellow. His eyes, as blue as the river used to be I suppose, glimmered and shined like the peace in my heart.

He knew.

"I have to go to New Orleans," he continued. "There I will find what destiny awaits me. I have heard that there is food and shelter there. Possibly if we go together, I can show you what I have learned about fighting the battle that is unseen."

"What do you mean?" I asked.

He turned and walked to the water's edge, placed a booted foot in the glassy water and flipped out a little of it, sprayin' some droplets across the surface. He turned and looked directly at me.

"Paul said we do not wrestle against flesh and blood but against principalities and powers of the air."

"Yeah," I said. "I read that part a few times. Are you sayin' this Gabe fella is part of that?"

"Yes," he said, as he walked toward me and put that gentle hand on my shoulder. He locked his steady, clear eyes on my face. "If you have enough faith, you can indeed move mountains, friend. God does all of it, but we are his children and he listens to a diligent child. If it is his will, and it *is definitely* his will to win, the battle belongs to the Lord."

He walked away from me then. I went back to find my old Targus backpack, dug through it and pulled out my

Bible. It was time to study it to find out what he meant.
I found it on page 1347.

Ethan

That lady knew something about me.

I could see it on her face when she looked at my shirt.

I knew that I had to put as much distance between myself and these people as possible and I had to do it soon. I thought I'd wait until nightfall, see what I could find as far as supplies and then split.

The people were shuffling around, some of them gathering over to where Jacob was standing. He had a small black book in his hand and he was waiting quietly, being patient for a good crowd to gather. I knew a con man when I saw one. The old man had a good game going. I decided to listen.

"Friends," said Jacob, his voice remarkably carrying a good hundred feet to the back of the crowd where I stood with my arms folded. "How many of you know the verse from the Bible that says 'I can do all things through Christ who strengthens me'?"

A few people raised their hands. A guy next to me let out a string of profanity that was eloquent and artful, expressing the desire to hang the old man. It made me chuckle. Jacob continued.

"Many people know Philippians four thirteen well," he continued, smiling. "But most people skip completely over verse twelve which says, and I'll read it 'I know how to live in poverty or prosperity. No matter what the situation, I've learned the secret of how to live when I'm full or when I'm hungry, when I have too much or when I have too little.' Now, what is that secret the writer mentions here? We've all been through some terrible things these past few years. None of us standing here today can say that they have not been visited by tragedy or some other horror, but you may be asking why we have to suffer all of these terrible disasters."

"I know why," spoke a tiny old woman with a stooped back who was near the front. "It's because we're being judged for our sin and because we as a nation turned our back on God."

There was a murmur in the crowd as several around her shouted agreement. That guy next to me just laughed. Jacob put up his hands to quiet them down, and they eventually stopped grumbling. He had a way of getting people to listen to him that was almost otherworldly.

"I'm sure that if you are a person of faith, you might think this," said Jacob evenly. "However, I'm sure the people who lived in the dark ages probably felt the same way. How about the people living during the black plagues that swept Europe? Do you not think that they assumed the world would soon end? Surely they did! As we look around us at the horrors that a final world war has brought, the devastation of an economic collapse, the abandonment of our government and the ravages of Volos, we must try to find some kind of peace in all of it, find some kind of hope."

"Hope is right here," shouted a burly man toward the middle of the crowd, his accent thick with that hillbilly drawl. "We got plenty of hope right here with our families and friends. We can start over!"

"What you have here is stable," Jacob replied, his ice blue eyes looking directly at the burly fellow, his smile kind and genuine. Something in those eyes started to speak to me until I remembered that this guy was running a con and snapped out of it. Man, this guy was good.

"That stability may not last, however," Jacob continued. "What if we are attacked by one of the militia groups or raiders? What if Volos gains entrance to this camp? Life is full of 'what ifs?'. The writer of this letter in the Bible said he had found the secret of being content, that he had been poor and rich, that he had been without food and had also experienced times when he had plenty to eat. His secret was that he had found peace in the salvation that comes through the blood of Jesus Christ."

"Preach on, preacher!" screamed a dirty, oily man to my left, so loud it startled me. "Tell us about how Jesus is going to come and take us all away from here in a rapture! Tell us about how he's bidin' his good ol' easy time to come and save us all! Tell us how we should give all our stuff to you and then go on top of a mountain to wait on his return! Tell us how he loves us so much he died for us! That we are in the boat we're in because we don't have faith! Tell us a million other *lies!*"

This stirred up the crowd. They started grumbling and shouting and it was as if all of them were venting out all the frustrations that came with living in the Bible belt and being told about the day when Jesus would come and take us all to happy heaven, but never seeing it. Back in Jersey we had no illusions, and not many evangelicals, either. These people felt as if they had been lied to, and they weren't far from the truth.

"Jesus, in chapter twenty four of the book of Matthew said there would be a great falling away," said Jacob, his calm voice somehow louder than the growing roar of the crowd. "Only those with true faith will find peace in this dark age. Just because your religious leaders bought into the lazy lie of the rapture doesn't mean you should give up on Jesus. He did not fail you. Your church leaders did. What I am talking about today is a way to have hope in this dark age. It gives me peace, helps me to face the evils of this world, and gives me purpose. I just wanted to share that with all of you, not convince you to follow some broken ideology."

"Can Jesus make the water stop being bitter?" said the old woman at the front. "We have to boil it, but it still tastes like copper. It's been this way for three days."

Jacob looked directly at her. His face contorted strangely and I thought for a second that he might actually cry. He turned, bent down and picked up that old hickory walking stick of his and walked toward a granite boulder that jutted out of the ground just a few feet from the flowing river. The crowd parted around him strangely, as if they were afraid to touch him, many of them still murmuring angry words of disbelief and hatred, the voices of nearly a hundred suffering people. Jacob looked around, muttered something under his breath I couldn't hear, and struck the rock with the end of his stick.

That's when things went all wacko.

The walking stick seemed to grip the granite for a minute and then the end of it, I swear, started sinking right into the rock as if the stone had become soft clay. Jacob gave a quick jerk on the stick and it came out, and what was left was a hole where crystal clear water started gushing out. I rubbed my eyes and looked again, and the people let out a collective gasp as they started gathering up their water buckets and canteens and going over to fill up. Jacob, looking a little tired, shoulders slumping a bit, walked over to a small rock about the size of a stool and sat, holding his walking stick out in front of him for support.

Pretty good trick.

The people drank immediately, many of them saying it tasted sweet and was cold as iced water. I waited in line and by the time I got up to the water, I noticed that the girl who had fainted when I entered camp was standing at my elbow.

Her eyes were full of tears, and she didn't look too happy.

Kelly

I felt like killing him.

I had to know why he wore my husband's uniform, but the words wouldn't form in my mouth. I just stood there next to him as he waited in line for water and glared at him. He finally turned around to see me and smiled a bit. It was one of those uncomfortable smiles my brother would give me when he had stayed out all night drinking again.

"Hey, lady," he said to me, stepping forward in line as everyone moved toward the miracle. "I don't know what your problem is, but.."

"That uniform," I growled, launching in. I could feel my teeth grind together as I talked through them. "Where did you get it?"

"It was issued to me, ma'am, when I —"

"Don't lie to me!" I shouted, and now people around me, people I knew, started staring. "That is my husband's uniform! He was in Ranger group first airborne! You stole it from him and I want to know what happened to him."

He dropped the little canteen he held in his hand and stared away from me, not able to catch my gaze. It was as if I was one of those mythological cockatrices and he was afraid I would turn him to stone.

"Look," he said calmly, still not looking at me, some of the others now staring. "I really don't know your husband. I used it to get out of McAlester. The guy who wore it had been dead for a while and I just felt like I could use it to get out safely, that's all."

I couldn't look at him any more. I stomped away, the

tears flowing out of my eyes. I didn't even go get any of the water, but went back to my tent to lay down and cry, to finally mourn the loss of my husband. This world was full of madness, cruelty and horror. I had to move on. To keep my sanity I had to move on. I hated that man, but couldn't really blame him. At least I knew what had happened to Edward. At least now I could move on. I would find a way to do that soon, but now I needed to cry, to release, and to think about what I would do next.

I lay there, staring up at the orange and white nylon roof of my tent moving like a flag in the soft breeze, looking through the mesh mosquito netting window at the ridge that ran along the road above.

I noticed right around fifty or so men on horseback, all of them pointing guns down toward our camp.

Amy

Standing a few feet behind Ethan in the crowd, waiting for access to the water that somehow poured out of the large boulder, I couldn't breathe knowing what that liar had just told that poor woman. Other people had heard it, too, and were moving toward him, all of them looking sour. I was just about to say something to him when I heard gun fire.

Everyone started putting their hands over their heads as if the sky was going to cave in on top of them, but then we heard a tinny voice over a loudspeaker. Mostly it was the sound of somebody clearing their throat. I looked up on the ridge where we had been earlier and saw a row of men on horseback, all of them holding black shiny rifles and automatic weapons, staring down at us. They looked sweaty and gritty and ugly.

One of them, a big, bloated cowboy wearing a military style shirt and a wide brim filthy white cowboy hat and mirrored glasses sat in the middle of all of them, his white horse chomping on the bit. He held a long shotgun and wore a thick mustache that was one of those handlebar types that spilled down the corners of his mouth like hairy gravy. All I knew was that he looked old and seasoned and scary. He held a battered red megaphone up to his fat lips and started into his speech.

"Good afternoon, little tent village. I'm Captain Waldeburg," he said, his accent sounding deep south. "Seems to me you folks have a problem recognizing authority with the welcome party you sent us. Well, Andy, Phil and Donovan send their regards."

Three bodies suddenly fell over the edge of the ridge and tumbled down like bloody scarecrows, some of them breaking small saplings on the way down…and they were missing their heads. The people in the crowd went ape. I felt something flip in my stomach and fought the urge to puke.

"I'll be keeping the heads out of personal interest," continued the leader, really gravelly like a wrestling coach I used to know. "Now, usually I just tell everybody to drop on the ground and nobody will get hurt, but today's not one of those times. What I need from you people is firstly half of your food stuffs 'cause of taxes and all, then a portion of your able bodied men will join my ranks, and…"

He paused just long enough for the megaphone to feedback a bit and I saw a camouflaged man run up beside the cowboy's horse and say something.

"Scratch that," he said with a grunt. "Looks like you guys got a wizard in yer mix. I just want that guy first so's I can deal with him. No offense to the religious types."

Most of the people around me were crouching down on the gravelly sand, but two people were standing, looking up at the men on the ridge: Jacob and Clayton. Jacob spoke, and when he did it was so loud I thought he'd managed to get one of those megaphones, too.

"I'll come quietly if you will leave these people alone, Captain. They have not done anything wrong and are simply trying to survive like you and your men."

I could hear a low noise along the ridge line as this band of scary guys all practiced their villain laugh.

"Now, now," said the cowboy as he adjusted his big rear in the saddle. "You are in no condition to make demands,

Jacob. What will happen is that you'll saunter on up here and git down on yer knees and pay for the havoc you've caused me and my men. I aint gonna tell ya twice. Once that business is over then I'll commence to taxin' these kind folks."

Jacob looked around and made a motion for the people to stand. Some of them did. I realized that I was standing with my knees slightly bent and my arms out. I straightened up and walked over to stand by Clayton. Ralph joined us as we looked into the face of danger, or rather the faces of danger. Jacob turned around as if in slow motion and faced Clayton.

"Clayton," he said calmly, his mouth parting to show his old man's teeth as he smiled a bit. "I'm going up there to turn myself over to those men. I want you to stay here and pray. You know how to do that. When you pray, I want you to believe that God is hearing you. Do not lose your way. Send your message directly to the throne of God. He is waiting to exact his judgement and his mercy all in one action, to show his glory to these unbelieving men. Remember that there is no greater love displayed than when a man lays his life down for his friends."

"Will they kill you?" asked Ralph.

The old man only spread his lips in a smile and cocked an eyebrow.

Clayton nodded his head and put his hand on Jacob's shoulder.

Ralph looked back and forth at Clayton and Jacob and shook his head in disgust. I just didn't know if this was the right thing to do, but the old guy was willing to sacrifice himself for the group. Why would he do that? He didn't even know us. My chest hitched in some air as I fought back tears. Jacob looked up at the man on horseback holding the shotgun.

"Captain Waldeburg," said Jacob, his voice booming. "I'll come quietly if you promise not to harm any of these people. Take some of their food, but take out whatever anger you have pent up upon me. I will bear it."

Jacob started walking, and then came another blast of the gravelly voice from the ridge.

"No promises. Just leave that stick of yours down there," he growled. "No need in bringing your magic with you."

Jacob somehow managed a grin considering the circumstances, and gave the hickory walking stick to Clayton. He then started walking through the crowd of silent, world weary people, many of them touching him on the shoulder on the way toward the path. One woman stopped him to tell him that she loved his message earlier today, that she would be praying for him. He simply said "do" and walked slowly across the pinkish brown sand to the trail that led up to the road and the ridge line. I just couldn't believe what I was seeing. This was so horribawful.

Two men, two Sasquatch men, met him halfway down to the shore of the river and each grabbed him by an arm, but he did not struggle or say a word. When he had disappeared from view, the Captain spoke again over the megaphone.

"You folks don't go nowhere," he drawled. "We got some fellas headed down your way to cull the herd. We need some able bodied men to swell our ranks. Place all foodstuffs out on the sand in a pile and we will be taking our portion. Do what we ask and no one will be harmed. That is all."

I heard a click and a whine of feedback, and the men on horseback began to back away from the ridge. As they sent their goon squad down the pathway to our small village of tents, I stared at Ralph's pained face. Even though we didn't really have words to say, our faces told each other of our helpless fear. Clayton did not look at us. He knelt on the ground, his eyes closed, his mouth moving, speaking words that I hoped were being heard by someone. I joined him, even though I'm not much of a person of prayer.

Faith of a mustard seed, right?

Gideon

I lay in the bush under my Dad's ghillie suit, listening to the whole thing.

All my friends were in boy scouts, but not me. Dad was a SEAL. I hardly ever saw him, but when I did we were running around in the woods out here learning all kinds of crazy stuff. Dad's form of boy scouts was hard core and just the two of us. Dad never let me slide. He never came back from the big one, either. I was pretty much on my own 'till I hooked up with these tent people. I wouldn't let them down.

I was about a quarter of a click outside the perimeter of camp, minding my own business when the other three guys got jumped. Amateurs. I had tried to teach them some stuff but they were just good old boys. Thought they knew everything about everything. My taste in food kind of annoyed them, too. Wasn't afraid to eat anything for protein. They were always looking for some canned stuff when there's plenty of stuff out here crawling around.

My thoughts were interrupted by the commotion just this side of the camp, some guy wearing Ranger tabs backed up through the crowd and ended up at the edge of the woods near my location, looking like he was about to vamoose. I decided to watch him. Figured he was a spy sent by them militia types and he'd be reporting back to his cronies. He confirmed this action by sneaking away, crouching low. I decided to make things interesting for him.

If he really was a Ranger, then this might not have worked, but I snuck up on that noob easily. Nope. Not a

Ranger. I put a sharpened stick through his left thigh without much effort and he went down with a thud. Would have started screaming if I hadn't covered his mouth and put the bloody shiv up next to his throat. He was going to spill his guts about everything until Kelly came out of the bush as well and started in on me.

"What are you doing, Gideon?" she whispered. "I hope they didn't see us sneak off. If they did, we're all dead."

"We're all dead anyway, ma'am," I whispered to her, holding this wannabe Ranger still, forcing his wrist to touch his shoulder blades, shoving his face into the dirt. "Them guys are gonna wipe us out and take everything we have. Do we have a plan?"

The fake Ranger tried to say something and I gave his wrist a twist. He shut up real proper like.

"I say we hide out here and make our move," I whispered. "I'll ditch this traitor to the human race real quiet and then you and I can figure out how to help our people."

I heard the pop-pop-pop of gunfire up the hill on top of the ridge and I figured that was the old man getting a mouthful. Saw the whole thing how he sacrificed himself to cowboy Buddha up there. Way to go, gramps.

Kelly told me that the guy under my boot was wearing her husband's uniform and all about how he stole it. That made me put my knee in his back and grind. She was kind of cranky about it, so I asked her what we should do with him, and she said that he'd probably just run away like a coward and that she didn't think he was one of the militia. I took out a zip tie and fastened the fool's wrists together. Impersonating an officer. That boiled me.

I left him laying there in the tall grass, took Kelly by the hand, and we slithered away like ninjas. I had to see what that gunfire was all about, so I had a back door up the ridge to check on the action.

Figured I'd see what I could get into. First I had to get Kelly at least to the boat and possibly out of here. She kind of reminded me of my Mom.

Then I'd have to figure out something to do about all this that would make Dad proud.

Clayton

I knelt on down in the sand next to Amy. Ralph stood still, watchin' us both. All I could do was pray, pray, pray.

If the prayer of a righteous man gets a lot done, then I figured I could get somethin' done even if it were a little bit. Right then we needed a lot, though.

I thought about Jacob who had given himself up to who knows what. I hurt for him, and could feel the hurt in everybody around me on this sandy beach. He'd talked to me about givin' everything up, about sellin' out to Jesus, about goin' all in and what that could cause to happen. He'd said this was like the days of Moses, that these people would be my sheep. I'd fallen into it, lettin' the Spirit fall on top of me like a ton of lead, and it felt good...so good. I had purpose, somethin' I hadn't felt in all of my short life.

Something was stirrin'.

I could see the men on horseback come on out to the edge of the ridge, pile down off their horses, and then start the careful walk down the steep grassy path to the water's edge. A whole mess of men from the tent village had formed a welcoming party, but none of them looked to be carryin' weapons. The militia men each had a weapon, most of 'em carryin' rifles while others carried machetes or cheap-o swords they prolly looted from pawn shops. I'd seen these types of grunts before, usually from a safe distance. One of them, callin' himself Captain Waldeburg, limped along the sand toward us, a large grin across his greasy face. They guy looked like some messed up Civil War general who'd wallered in a pig sty and then put on human clothes.

"Good to see you folks know when you're beat," said the growly voiced Captain. "I hate to have to waste bullets on people who have figured out who's boss."

He stuck out a gloved hand, a yellow leather gauntlet glove. I had the bad fortune of bein' close enough to see small spatters of black dried blood on the knuckles. Mr. Coffman, a burly fella with square shoulders and short whips of brown hair crossin' the top of his bald head, stood with his hands to his side. He weren't here for trouble, but he didn't like this none.

"We'll do as you ask," said Mr. Coffman, his voice shaky. "But please leave our men here. We need them to defend the camp."

The Captain chuckled, and I bowed my head and prayed, prayed, prayed.

"You mean like the bang up job those three boys of yours did?" hissed Waldeburg. "You need our protection. B'sides. All you have to do is pay your food and manpower tax once per month and all will be well. Givin' up the wizard was a good move—."

"—He gave himself up," Coffman interrupted. "We didn't have anything to do with that."

I looked up enough to see the greasy Captain look like he was thinkin', and wondered if he had the brains for that.

"Yeah, I suppose that's good," the Captain growled, spittin' in the sand at Coffman's feet. "But there's still the matter of the men I need to replenish my numbers. Lost a few back in McAlester to the regular army types. Their superior fire power kind of made quick work of my cannon fodder, but we won the day. Did we not, men?"

There was an ugly roar from the men around him and a

few snickerin' laughs. It reminded me of that Lion King movie I used to watch with my little cousin Judy, mostly the hyenas. There was then this awkward silence that I suppose happens in every conversation, but the Captain was quick to end it.

"I'll tell you what," offered Waldeburg, takin' off his mirrored shades to reveal a nasty deep hole where his left eye should be. I got a little sick. "Give us about three women to do with as we please and twenty percent of your foodstuffs and we'll come back in three weeks and see if you change your mind any. Think about it, that's all."

I could feel Amy shift in the sand, start to get up. *Don't run*, I thought.

Mr. Coffman looked to his left and then behind him where his eyes rested on his four year old daughter squattin' by the river's edge playin' with a muscle shell she had discovered. I instantly started to think about that little girl, started offerin' prayers up for her, thinkin' if this got ugly I'd put feet to my prayer and grab her up, get her to safety…if there was such a thing. Coffman turned back to the Captain, and just as he was about to open his mouth to speak, the single report of a rifle peeled from the top of the ridge behind me.

I jumped along with everyone else.

Captain Waldeburg's right shoulder flowered open, a red bloody rose, and that's when I saw that the tent villagers were not empty handed in the area of fire arms.

Ethan

My leg hurt so bad.

I didn't really see that kid at all but then he was on top of me. I just wanted to get out of there as quick as I could before I ended up on the menu. I was done with the soldier boy routine, but now I was tied up face down in the mud with my leg soaking this gritty sand with precious fluid. It felt as if I had a sharp rock in the wound.

I figured I'd start trying to crawl away, so I pushed with my one good leg to slide across the muddy gravel on my chest. Too bad I didn't take a knife or something because I could have figured out how to unbind my wrists. Got tired of scooting along and decided to roll over and sit up. Surprising how hard it is to do that with your wrists bound behind your back. I made the mistake of trying to use my bum leg to push myself over and felt as if someone shoved a hot poker in there. Hardest part was standing up. I had to bend my knees and cross my ankles in the dirt and then roll forward to get up, then I fell face first and smacked my nose on a rock.

That was when I saw the snake.

It was a big black one and it sat there, head vertical a few inches, its remarkably white mouth open, hissing at me. I didn't know what kind of snake it was but it looked dangerous so I lay there as still as I could and tried not to scream.

Then there was gunfire. First a shot, possibly a high powered rifle then there was automatic fire and screaming and shouting. I didn't dare move. The snake didn't seem to care that there were bullets whizzing by. It just sat there with its mouth open, hissing at me not two feet from my face. A bullet shot through the weeds and kicked up the sand to my left. This caused me to flinch and close my eyes and then I felt a sting on my neck.

The snake was gone when I opened my eyes but the bullets were still streaking around over my head. I couldn't feel my neck but it was throbbing something awful just like my leg and I figured if that snake was poisonous I was probably going to be a corpse soon.

What did I have to lose? I rolled over again, got my legs in a cross ankled position, bent my knees, and tried to ignore the molten steel feeling of new pain in my thigh. I rolled forward and sat up enough to see over the tall brown and green grass and all the slowly waving cat tails.

My eyes blinked a few times, clearing away the dust as I saw nearly a hundred tent villagers, many of them carrying their children in their arms, stampeding toward me, and my kneeling body was not going to slow them down one bit. I only heard the sound of their thunderous feet as they broke over me, crushing me into the gravelly sand, introducing a new kind of pain.

Amy

I watched the barrels of the guns rise up and level off at their targets after that fat Captain got nailed. Everybody started pulling triggers. I watched those automatics shoot flames out of their black metal barrels and people started falling down who stood in front of them. I got so sick. I felt as if I was watching things in slow motion, sort of like one of those old-fashioned war-for-independence movies, two lines of soldiers going all bang-chest-gorilla at close range. Some of the militia men and even more of the tent village guys were barely able to get their guns up before bullets started ripping through their bodies.

And the babies! The little babies! People started grabbing them up and running away toward the cat tails.

Ralph grabbed me by the arm and I turned to look at him, clenched teeth, my hair flying. Clayton knelt in the middle of everything, head bowed, eyes closed, and then he stood up, raising the old man's hickory staff in the air. His mouth was moving but I couldn't make out what he was saying, couldn't hear it. The villagers who didn't have guns had their kids and were burning up ground off toward the tall cattails and the tree line where the river disappeared around the bend. They totally stomped, pushed and leaped over their cook fires and tents, stirring up a noise that sickened my stomach as I helplessly watched them go.

I could sense a static electricity in the air as things got all trippy.

The guns stopped firing all at once and just jammed up. I can't really explain it, but that is for sure what happened.

Some of the men pulled out machetes and other scary weapons. One guy started across the sand with a large knife, breaking into a full run, only to trip over his feet and fall forward on his own blade. The village guys who were left standing fired off a few rounds and took down a couple of the militia guys. I saw one of the militia, a really fat guy wearing Roundhouse overalls, clutch at his chest and drop his automatic.

I was frozen, and it was only through the screaming sound of Ralph's voice that I was able to break the spell.

I finally got myself moving, and started following Ralph out with the rest of the stampede. Clayton passed by me, a little girl in his arms who was screaming and screaming, and that hickory staff in his fist somehow. His face was somehow calm.

"Don't worry about them," Clayton said as we ran. "Everything is in his hands."

Leave it to Clayton to start talking all Jesusy when the bullets start flying. We ran through the weeds and cattails with the sound of gun fire and shouting behind us, rounding the bend in the river to see that big mass of people thinning out around the river's edge, making a long line of quickly moving people all trying to get as far away as possible. I didn't see any of the crazies along the ridge looking down, because I half expected to, and for some reason the gunfire fell off to a few pops here and there. I figured we'd be cut off, but we weren't. We walked quickly, running again when we heard gunfire, skirting the river for quite a while before we came around another bend in the river where the path went toward an overgrown wooden dock.

"Would you look at that?" Ralph said, his voice

quivering, soft.

Sitting in the deep waters at the edge of a rocky cliff, where the edge of the river made a wide bowl, floated two large pontoon boats. On the side of the one closest to me I could read the words "Red River Tours" in scratched and faded paint. People were piling on, so I figured it would do us some good to do the same.

Time to get out of here on the dub.

Clayton

That's two prayers answered.

I stood on the bow of the boat and watched as several children gathered 'round me. Them militia guys hadn't followed us down river and that was a miracle. The kids sat in perfect silence. I think they was mostly scared out of their minds from the mess we just crawled out of and because even though we was tryin' to be quiet and all, a bunch of them tent village folk were hollerin' and gettin' all riled up at one another.

"If we take these boats back down river those militia will be waiting!" said a lady with beautiful dark skin and silver hair. She looked like she might have resembled Beyonce when she was young. "Those monsters will kill all of us if they get a chance."

"Now we don't know that," said a sort of long haired guy about my age wearin' a suit made of fake leaves and carryin' a rifle. "I took out their leader, so they'll be a little less brave."

I raised my hand, but they ignored me and kept on jawin'.

"We got plenty of guns here on the boat stashed for just this kind of thing," said a fella with a blonde Mississippi mud flap and a greasy red trucker hat. "We can get the women and children to lie down on the deck and then us men can take positions along the side and shoot anything that moves."

"Sure," said old Beyonce. "Just get us all killed in the process. We can take these boats up river and find a new place, a place where we can grow some crops. There's plenty of places along the Oklahoma Texas border we can settle."

I kept my hand up. They still ignored me.

"But what about that messenger we heard from six months ago?" growled red hat guy. "He showed us pictures of the plenty they got in New Orleans. If we just get through this one spot and then down river, we can join up with that group down there and the livin' will be much better, both for us *and* for our kids."

This caused a bunch of the people to start to arguin' and fussin', so I just kept my hand up in hopes that somebody would listen. I looked over and saw Amy and Ralph sittin' close on the other boat which was parked twenty feet or so away. Amy locked eyes with me for a bit, then cast them down. Ralph was talkin' to her and smilin'. I couldn't let it get me, though. All we needed was for the enemy to find some way to worm his way into my mind and heart. I decided to focus on the group of straggly people.

The guy with the leafy suit started in.

"I vote we take a few guys around to the east and flank the militia, scout them out at least and then meet up with the rest of you down by the camp where we can provide some support in case things get ugly."

"Well, things is gonna get ugly," I said finally, and then everyone kind of stopped chatterin' and turned to look at me as if I'd said a nasty loud cuss word at some fancy banker party.

I heard some of them mutter words like "he's got the staff" and "that's the old man's friend". I started gettin' all uncomfortable as if I was standin' in front of the class at school. I said a little prayer, started focusin' on God's will and what He wanted from me and from these people, and then the words just came out of my mouth.

"I don't want nothin' but the safety of this group. I got nothin' invested 'cept myself, I know, but we need our sneaky people like... uh..."

"Gideon," offered the guy in the leafy suit.

"...Gideon here to flank our sides or whatnot in order to help us along. Now, I know you people don't know me any better than Adam, but I vote to go on down river and see what happens. God is gonna get us through this, I know he will if we just trust him. Believe it or not, and I don't really care if you do or not, but God has his hand on us. This task we have to complete. The goin' back I mean, is a test of faith. Sure we could go on up river and prolly find a nice plot of land to settle on and live out a few good days, but I've heard about New Orleans, too, 'round campfires and in the scuttle butt and on the lips of wanderers. There's hope down south."

"I'm sure your faith is strong and all," said Mr. red cap, and the crowd murmured a bit. "But we pretty much gave up on God when he let our country fall apart. Them preachers, at least the one in my little country church my wife made me go to — God rest her soul — was always talkin' about how we needed to get God back in our country or whatever. Well, then came the war and then Volos took durn near my whole family and here we are runnin' from militia. I got kids to worry about, son. I'da taken these here guns and lit out a long time ago, but there's safety in numbers, and even though we don't really have much of a country anymore, I'll do what we always do around here.

That's put it up to a vote."

"Good idea," said Gideon, wipin' the grit from the scope on his rifle, then blowin' on it. "All of you who want to go up river, raise your hand."

I looked 'round and about three people, most of 'em older folks, cautiously raised their hands. I saw the dirty palm of an old man in the back of the boat, then both his hands were in his lap. He looked around to see if anyone noticed, we locked eyes, and his lips pressed together tightly. I saw his shoulders slump as he faced the floor and studied the wooden planks. I felt really bad just then, as if I'd started somethin' that the old fella was not willin' to do, and that ate at me. I didn't want to force anyone to do this, but I was going because it is what I had been told to do by someone who could see all points of time: present, future and past.

A few of the people started to bow their heads, and then more of them, and we all prayed for our welfare, for our children and for the trip down river that we'd all voted on, some of 'em prolly prayin' for the first time ever.

I looked across at the other boat and saw not a soul raisin' their hand to vote for runnin'. All of them except about three or four were younger, about my age and a little older. Some of the men were pullin' rifles and automatic weapons from a place out of view, somewhere down below on the deck. Gideon didn't ask for a vote about the other choice. It reminded me of when I paid attention in history class, like how the first rebels started gettin' ready to war against old King George.

We was goin' down river to New Orlean, but like the guy at the party who spoke his peace, but still had somethin' else, I had somethin' else.

"I know you all saw what God did with the rock and the water," I said, hearin' a groan from somebody in the back. "God has done these things to show himself to you, to prove to you that he is still God, to show his glory to you, not for just some cool trick. I will be prayin' for all of us as we go up river. Best thing for us to do who's not carrin' a gun is to pray with me. God hears our prayers, and he's gonna be with us along with a whole host of angelic warriors. I have found the secret of being content, and you can do this, too. Just trust him."

As the men cocked and loaded their guns, takin' up positions around the outside edges of the boats, I looked over at Amy and saw Ralph help her and a little girl to lie down on the deck of their boat. I turned and faced forward at the front of ours, holdin' fast to the hickory walkin' stick the old man gave me.

I would not be carryin' firearms.

The orange sun was goin' down, what sun there was to look at through that gloomy sky full of ash or rock or whatever that meteor had kicked up. The pilots started the diesel motors, and I caught a glimpse of Gideon and his crew stalkin' off through the woods before I squeezed my eyes together and started prayin' hard. Many of the people around me followed suit.

Prayer was all we'd need.

Amy

It's so strange how stressful stuff can make two people come together. Here I was in the semi-darkness, feeling like one of those helpless maidens in the stories my Dad used to read to me, laying in the bottom of this boat while Ralph and all the other men crouched near the edges with their guns all pointing outward into the darkness. It made this old tour boat resemble some redneck battleship.

I just lay there on the floorboards, holding little five year old Anya's tiny hand, whispering to her that her Mommy would see her again one day, and helping her not be afraid of the dark. I didn't really know the family situation of any of these people, but it seemed like many of them had lost loved ones they knew back at the camp when the shooting started and hadn't had time to process it all yet. What was I talking about? I hadn't had time to process these past few years much less the past twenty four hours. My heart hurt so much for little Anya, though, and caring about that seemed to take my mind off of everything else. She shivered so badly even though it was Africa hot. I was pretty scared, too, so I was quaking right along with her.

Now and then I'd glance up at Ralph kneeling next to me with his rifle barrel glinting in the faint moonlight, his broad shoulders squared off, his dark skin glistening with sweat. He started to warm up to me on the boat when the people were all deciding what to do and Clayton started preaching…go figure. What a time for that, huh? Little Anya was so scared and so we tried to be happy around her to put her at ease. I actually got him to smile once, but got the four-one-one that there's some really dark stuff going on in that head of his. He keeps the lid on really tight.

I think he had to kill someone once, and it turned him all moody.

I wondered if Gideon and those other three rednecks he bugged out with had any chance of keeping the crazies at bay while we slipped by the camp. No telling. Gideon seemed pretty confident that he took out the leader. That Captain guy was freaky. What a funkdafied old guy *he* was, with that hillbilly outfit and that bull horn? Wow.

I hoped, hoped, hoped he was dead because if I saw him, I'd just lose it.

The puttering of the diesel motor at the back of this boat was a soft, even sound. I looked at Anya and she had her little dark eyes focused right on me. Why would anyone want to bring kids into this world of ours? So sad. I didn't want to think about it.

Our plan was to slip by the camp in the dark. When we heard the engines shut off, then we knew we were close, and we were supposed to can it when that happened, and put our hands over the babies mouths. I hoped nobody would cut off their air. Ah, man. That's scary.

Anya shifted next to me and put her little dirty thumb in her mouth and then squirmed over closer, her small arm wrapping around my waist. I could feel her warmth by me and thought that all little kids kind of put off a lot of heat, probably more than adults. I brushed her sweaty hair out of her face and she groaned a little. So cute I almost forgot where I was.

I looked up at Ralph and just as he was about to return my gaze, the engine shut off and I knew we were near the village. Somehow I started thinking about that story I read in freshman comp, about the Scilla and the Charybdis or whatever. You know, that ancient Greek story where that guy I couldn't remember had to go between a whirlpool on one side and a big giant monster on the other side that would swoop down and gobble up his men. They made a cheesy movie about it, so I watched the movie instead. Don't judge. I was a pre-med major and didn't care about writing papers at the time. Anyway, I felt like the men in that Greek guy's boat but not all Greek and toga-like.

Ugh. It's just that my mind was trying to get away from what we were doing, that is all. If I didn't think about it, maybe it would all work out right. I think I started praying right then. I just started asking God to help us. I didn't know if he was listening or at that time if he even existed. I just didn't want to see Anya die. I suddenly didn't care for myself, but I prayed for her, focused on her, just let out a long , heart felt prayer for her. I prayed that she would make it out alive, that she'd have a good life, that she'd get to play on a swing again, that she'd get a new mommy, and that was when I started letting the tears flow and held her small warm head up close to my chest.

I missed Dad. I missed his smile even when I did something obnoxious and the smell of his aftershave. I wanted to go back to the way things were. I even wanted Mom back. I just gushed all over the place, silently, on the deck of that boat, praying to God that if he would just save Anya I'd do more for him and I'd get real about it. I'd stop playing around like I did in the youth group so long ago just before college started and I had waved goodbye.

"God help us," I mouthed silently. "Please don't let us

die."

Gideon

We humped it through the woods a ways. We found a lot of horse tracks leading out just as the sun was dropping down below the trees. We had to navigate by wits and starlight after that. Didn't realize we had trekked so far out from the tent village.

Found the militia camp almost by scent and accident. We fanned out until I gave the boys the all clear with a whippoorwill call. Looked as if the land pirates lit out about an hour before we arrived but not before doing something awful to somebody.

We found a tree in the center of their camp with nails driven into it and dried blood with flies blowing around and a few bits of teeth on the ground nearby. Figure they had their fun with the old man who they escorted up to the top of the ridge. We were scratching our heads until our fingers bled over the why and the how of their sudden disappearance when we heard something, a sound of crackling fire in the distance to the north.

It was off in the trees, getting louder by the minute, and making the hair stand up on my arm. I looked at Ryan and the boys in the moonlight and we all felt the same. That's when the clicking sound got louder and we heard some kind of buzzing as a cloud of kicking, biting, black hell rained down on us and caused us to light out of there like John Force in a nitromethane funny car.

We knew we had to get to the water to make the biting stop.

Amy

When the boat motors sputtered quiet and we were drifting along in the current, all our guys got their guns ready for action. Ralph was cradling a twenty gauge pump action Winchester loaded with slugs (so he said) and his left hand gripped the pump slide, his knuckles all white. Even though my eyes had adjusted to the darkness a while ago, I still wasn't able to make much out along the shore as I dared to get up behind Ralph and peek out.

I could see the bend in the river because what little moonlight that made it through the meteor dust glinted off the black waters. There wasn't much sound, only the lapping of the water against the shore and against the side of the boat. Clayton had told all of us to be totally quiet. All of the men had guns pointed out at the shoreline and the trees. Any movement and they were told to shoot first and ask questions later. I strangely wondered how you could ask questions of the dead?

I crouched right behind Ralph, and he'd glance down at me every once in a while, his eyes asking if was ok. Anya was curled up around my feet with her hands over her ears like I told her to. I just couldn't sit still, couldn't lay down in the bottom of the boat like the rest of them. No way. I watched the shoreline because I just couldn't think about Anya getting hurt, about anybody getting hurt.

We were headed toward the camp again, back to the scene of all the shooting, but I hoped…hoped…

My eyes strained between the men, trying to see the clearing. I could see shapes mostly, partly because before all this happened I needed to go see the doctor about my eyes, but mostly because it was so dark and strangely calm. The wind wasn't blowing at all, and the summer heat had not left the air yet, even though it was probably around midnight…not that time was important anymore.

Like I said, all the men had guns pointed out at the shoreline, except of course for Clayton. He just stood there on the front of the other boat sailing just beside us and ahead, that hickory stick in his hands, head bowed slightly toward the water, his mouth moving slowly and strangely. He refused a gun when some people tried to give it to him. Said his "faith would shore him up." He'd been coming out of his shell more and more lately, but now he was all serious and quiet.

I looked up to see the highway bridge overhead, but not a sign of the militia men, a few fires still smoldering orange on the beach. No people, no noise, no nothing. I saw Ralph put the butt of the shotgun on his shoulder and cinch it up tight. The place smelled like ambush. Ralph was all Custer's last stand. How is that for irony. I couldn't figure out for the life of me why the militia didn't just ride us down like grass when we were running up the side of the river toward the boats.

Out of nowhere I heard a noise, the sound of a forest fire in the distance just before it's raging all around your house. I didn't see an orange light of a fire over the top of the ridge, but the sound started getting louder, and that is when something dropped by the corner of my vision into the water, and as it went by it was burning. It hit the water with a loud splash and then I heard breaking glass on top of the fiberglass canopy covering the boat. I dropped down into the bottom of the boat and covered Anya. A red-orange glow lit up the darkness.

"There's bodies on the shore," Ralph whispered, his voice monotone.

Burning liquid dripped over the side of the canopy and caused Ralph to leap back and almost step on me.

I sucked in air and screamed.

That raging fire sound got louder as the bullets started hitting the water and the top of the canopy, some of them tearing through to strike at the women and children lying on the floorboards. A lady next to me took one in the right arm, her hand springing up to try and stop the blood that shot out of the wound, and she bit her lip to stay bravely quiet.

"Up there!" someone shouted.

We were being ambushed. Just over the edge of the boat I saw men coming down the side of the ridge with guns raised, their faces like demons lit in the faint fires of the molotov cocktails. Flashes of fire shot out of their gun barrels, and then our men started ducking down behind the small flimsy outer edges of the boats as the fire that was burning a hole in the canopy started to leak through and drip on the deck boards and on the legs of a small boy. He screamed in agony but there was nothing I could do. A lady next to him tried to pat it out with her hands, but got the fuel on them and she burned, too.

I had to turn away.

Ralph let loose with three rounds, his feet spreading out in the boat to take the recoil, taking out a couple of grubby guys creeping down to the water's edge.

"Get down!" he shouted, pushing at me with his hand before sliding the chamber back for another round.

I didn't listen, and I managed to look over at Clayton. In the faint light I could see him standing in the same spot, head bowed, face odd and contorted in the orange flickering light of the fire on top of our boat, and his mouth was moving, moving, moving.

I could see a hand reaching out of the bottom of the boat to pull at his shirt, but he wouldn't get down.

"Pick up a gun, Clayton!" I shouted over the noise of the rifles going off. I saw smoke and sparks flying out of gun barrels and men who only hunted once in a while fumbling with their rifles. The militia men were more focused, stopping, taking aim, taking their time, shooting guys off the side of the boats like that target game at Bass Pro.

Oh Ralph. Please not Ralph.

Something flew by my head that sounded like a bee.

The sound of that fire over the ridge got closer, and I saw the shapes of four guys almost leap over the edge of the ridge and start skidding down the steep embankment, their rifles raised, their legs working hard to keep from losing control and rolling down hill. Behind them came something that I could not really understand, a black cloud that clicked and crackled. It got louder and louder, and reminded me of nightmares I had as a child.

It moved, rolled, buzzed, and hissed, bubbling out and sucking back in, moving quickly down the ridge after the men who had just barely escaped it. The four men dived into the river and it swallowed them hungrily. The men on the shore didn't really notice this at first because they were too busy trying to kill us, but soon the cloud, the black cloud that didn't seem to have an end, fell all over the militia men and they started swatting at first and then diving into the water to get away.

Our guys kept firing. Ralph squeezed off a round into a guy who had dropped his gun and was flapping his arms, batting away at the black things covering his face, and that is when the things started moving toward our boats. I guessed the bugs were attracted to the fire raging on top of the canopy. A few of the men had buckets and were dipping them in the water on the opposite side of the boats from the enemy and then throwing the water up on top of the fire, but this was about as useless as a fire sale on ice trays. One guy fell in and I didn't see where he went. Ralph just kept shooting his gun, and I hoped that the militia on the shore would give up.

The bugs made a horrible sound, and I could see them in the air around us, but none of them got in the boat with us. Black grasshoppers as big as my hand flew around our boats, an insane cloud, and the militia on the shore had all but stopped shooting when Ralph grunted and I suddenly had blood on me. I looked down to see that his leg was bleeding pretty bad, and I quickly sat up, tore some of the material from the blanket Anya was laying on and tied it around his knee really tight. Like a trooper he hopped up and tried to grip his gun again, but it slid around in his hands. I was breathing really hard and couldn't focus, but those guys on the shore were all gone, some of them laying on the ground and some of them floating in the water.

Just then we heard shouts from the bridge above our head, so I plopped down next to Amy. I saw a guy fly past and hit the water which splashed up on the boat, putting out some more of the fire. Then came two more. I figured the bugs were causing the militia on the bridge to chicken out and run away as best they could, and that meant diving over the side for some of them.

I peeked over the edge of the boat to see Clayton standing on the bow, not a scratch on him, head still facing down, mouth still moving. The grasshoppers were flying around us, not getting in the boat at all, but swarming all over the shore. The ground was moving and writhing. I heard horses whinnying, a strange scream in the darkness overhead, and shouts and screams of someone having a horrible day. The gunfire had stopped, and I lay quiet for a bit.

"Do you think it's over?" I asked, taking Ralph's hand and squeezing tightly.

"I don't know," he said. "They aren't shooting anymore at least."

We both looked down at Anya, this little girl who had come into our lives by accident and because she didn't have anyone. She was fast asleep.

Clayton

We floated down river, our boat tied to the boat behind because one of them motors had been hit in the fire fight. This slowed us down considerable. I didn't pay it any mind 'cause we were safe from the militia for now. God had done a miraculous work and we were in the middle of his grace.

Gideon and his three buddies were pulled aboard once we made it past the bridge. Somehow they had managed to get underwater and then swim to us. That in itself was a miracle worth praisin' about.

We were usin' the motor sparingly so as not to burn it up. I thought this was a heap of wisdom. The river's current kind of picked up once we got down it aways. I stood on the front of the boat as I had been doin' all along. I prayed without ceasin' as the Bible taught me, and this meant that I had a constant contact with God on a personal basis. I'd been doing this now for about a solid three days, and there was some side effects finer'n frog's hair.

One thing was that he talked back.

I could feel his words not in the water or in the breeze or in the chirpin' of the birds but in a soft voice in my head that calmed me and made things seem so clear that was otherwise muddled by my fear and doubt. Back at the camp I had just decided that I wasn't goin' to be afraid and I wasn't goin' to doubt what God could do. It didn't enter my mind.

I began to share these words with folks in the boat around me. Found out a lot about these people who'd been thrown together by this broken down world. They was startin' to look to me for answers about stuff, but I pretty much just listened to God's guidance for them, told them to trust in the power of Christ, and even though some of them was soured out on religion, they warmed to the idea of God's grace guidin' us, even if they'd lost loved ones in the shoot out.

These people had been through a lot. Hope in Jesus was all many of them had left, and that was enough, I suppose.

I was glad Ralph and Amy was ok, especially the little girl they'd taken a likin' to. It wasn't long before the two of them had her laughin' and singin' little nursery songs. The three of them looked like a little family just cuttin' up and carryin' on. I figured that was a pretty good thing after all we'd been through, 'specially for that little girl.

We kind of wondered about that yankee Ethan, but I figured he'd lit out as soon as there was trouble. I didn't think he was a real Ranger, anyway. My uncle was in the army and all of them guys kind of have a way about them, and Ethan didn't seem to have that way about him at all. He reminded me of my high school track coach that wouldn't let me take a break to pee. I hoped he was ok nonetheless, and said a small prayer for him as well, and forgave him in my heart, askin' forgiveness for my dislike of him as well.

After we'd been on the water for a while, the blister in the sky we called the sun started to goin' down behind the hill, so we decided to anchor for the night and let the kids swim near a sand bar. We built a few small cook fires to boil drinkin' water and cook some of the cans of beans we had stowed. Some of the men stood as lookouts at the edges of the camp, and two of the braver ones like Gideon decided to scout out around the surroundin' woods for any threats. I figured that if they didn't have at least walkie talkies to communicate, then that was just plain nuts. Oh well, I can't tell people what to do. I just prayed for them.

Amy and Ralph came over to me when we got settled and they brought that cute little girl with them. Anya was such a sight. Her dark brown hair blowin' in the slight breeze made me think of my sister so many years ago. I didn't know if I'd ever see her again, but didn't worry about it. God had a plan.

Ralph had some questions. He always had questions. I gotta say the guy was kind of sweet on Amy, but we all were. I can't say I wasn't a little jealous, but God was workin' on that.

"Clayton," Ralph said once we had cut up a bit to lighten the mood. "I want to tell you that I'm sorry for being such a pain when we first met. I really feel bad about it."

"That's ok," I said, placin' a hand on his shoulder. "We've all been through a lot. Things are backards in the world."

They both laughed at my accent, and I joined them. If there's one thing it's good for is makin' people feel good and welcome. Prolly the reason Will Rogers was so popular. I happened to look at Amy and caught her gazin' at me, her green eyes lookin' so pretty in the fadin' light. I felt that something about her had changed.

"I just want to know," asked Ralph. "What was all that with the bugs? They didn't get in the boat. I just don't get it."

"Well, Ralph," I said, my voice takin' on a strange quality. "I suppose the prayers of God's children were heard. God hears the prayers of a righteous man, and since the only way man can be righteous is through the blood of Christ, Christ did all that through the prayers of the people who were seen by God as righteous through the shed blood of his son."

Ralph squinted at me, wrinkled his nose and his mouth formed a smirk. The Spirit didn't let me quit.

"Jesus said that anyone who has faith in him would do what he had been doing and that the person of true faith would do greater things than what Jesus did on earth," I told him, somehow feeling that I was not in control of what I was sayin'. "I am only able to do these things 'cause God is doin' them with or without me. I'm just a tool. Faith is what makes us strong, but only God gives that strength, and he is doing these things to show his glory to an unbelieving generation."

Amy and Ralph sat quietly for a minute, and one of Anya's little friends came over and asked if Anya wanted to play. They wandered to the river's edge and put their tiny feet in the cool waters.

"I always used to think that these Christians were nuts," said Ralph, his brown eyes examining the backs of his dark hands. "They used to ask me to come to their church services and I even went with one of them to camp one year, but all I saw there was a bunch of kids doing what they did in school: getting high, hitting on girls, looking forward to when they were going to prank each other on the last night they were there. It was a joke."

"Sure," I said. "I don't have very fond mem'rys of that, either. I was usually the butt of the joke."

We spent a few seconds in uncomfortable laughter, and Ralph continued.

"What I've seen here is truly a miracle," he said. "God is

definitely real. I want to have a part of that in my life. I'm so guilty of so much stuff, Clayton. I killed two guys in Norman and…I…I didn't feel a… feel a thing."

Ralph's face tightened as he got real silent. His shoulders started slumpin' and the tears started flowin' out of his eyes. We put our arms 'round him and held on to him, and he finally stopped cryin'. I told him how he could have peace about it by havin' a piece of God in his heart. All it took was a little faith on his part. He promised God to turn from his ways, die to himself, and asked for peace.

"It don't have anything to do with all them miracles," I told him. "That's just kind of the icin' on the cake. The real deal is to have the God of the Universe takin' up residence within your heart, guidin' your steps, helpin' you along the way, and bein' there for you when that final day of your life comes a knockin'. Miracles are just God's way of showing his glory."

Ralph did want God. His face changed almost immediately, because two thousand years ago God put Ralph on the cross with his Son and that day Ralph died. Today was his new birthday. We walked to the water, waded down to waist level, and baptized him right there, 'cause that's what we did in my Momma's church and so I figured that was ok.

I was spurred by somethin', somethin' that made me open my mouth and speak. People began gatherin' around and out it came.

I told them about the sin of man, about the love of God, and about the saving grace of Jesus Christ. I'm not sure exactly what came out except that I felt like I was sittin' there with all of them as they gathered around to listen. In many ways I suppose that little speech was a bigger miracle than Jacob bringin' water outta that rock or the locusts or anythin' else.

It wasn't long before others joined us, some of them cryin', some of them laughin'. A small group of them stood outside the group and just watched.

I didn't judge 'em. I loved 'em all just the same, wanted them to know the peace of Christ. I didn't really know where the journey would take us, but I was sure that God was in control and that he would not let us fail even if we died tryin'.

I stood there laughin' with Ralph and Amy, them pretty shocked I'd given such a sermon (I guess) when out of the woods came the scouts and then Gideon followed by two of the men who were with him, and then came Jacob, limpin' along, bein' helped by the other scout in Gideon's group.

People recognized him right away, and he was mobbed with shouts of welcome and greetin', and his appearance caused many of the group to question as to whether or not there was anythin' to this Jesus stuff, so more of them started comin' over to talk to me and Jacob about it.

Several people got reborn 'cause of it, and Jacob let me dunk 'em, and a few of 'em wanted to be sprinkled with the water 'cause of the way they was raised, and it was all the same to us. It was all a picture of what they had done, anyway.

We knew what they did. Family's family.

Ethan

A pecking crow was my alarm clock.

Actually several crows. I opened my eyes and craned my head around to see one pecking at the wound on my leg.

"Get off me, you bird!" I screamed, and I guess he figured I wasn't dead, so he flew off along with all his other buddies.

I think I fell into the river at some point and then tried to get up on my knees when the current took me. I don't remember what happened next, or how my hands got free from the zip tie which was still wrapped around my left wrist, but all I knew was that I was further down the river and didn't really know where that was.

I sat up with some effort, propping myself up with my arms, then I stood cautiously and winced at the pain in my thigh. I swore that if I ever found that kid, I'd pop a cap in him. I'd have to kill those two other kids, too for leaving me as they ran out of there, bullets zipping by. I reached up and felt of my neck. It wasn't bleeding anymore but it was sure swollen. I coughed a bit and used the water to wash my face. It tasted bitter and coppery.

I realized just then that I was on my own with no gun and no hope of finding that group again. I swore that if I did, I'd cap all of them for leaving me. They were all freaked out by the militia group, but that was no reason to do what they did. I had yelled right at that Ralph kid and he just kept moving. I swore I'd strangle him.

I figured I'd walk on down river to see if I could find those boats they were talking about. Man, I'd love to get on one of those boats, or any boat for that matter. I'd heard about New Orleans being a safe place, but had to get there somehow just like everybody else. I found a long stick floating in the water and used it as a crutch. It sort of helped with the pain in my leg. I'd have to get it looked at by a doctor.

"Sure," I laughed to myself out loud. "I'll just stop at the next town, call nine one one and get some help immediately. Maybe they'll put me in a hospital room and feed me three squares a day. Then that cute nurse will come in and fluff my pillow if you know what I'm saying."

A horse snorted.

I looked up and saw two hillbillies wearing camo, sitting on black horses. Each of them had a gun and it was pointed right at my face. If I ran, they would probably shoot me, so I did what I do best.

"Gentlemen," I said as calm as I could. "I got lost from my unit when we were attacked by some militia men, and am in need of assistance."

"Shut up, army," said one of them, spitting tobacco juice, the liquid making a fine arc that fell a few feet away from his horse. "Get on yer knees and put yer hands up on the back of yer head. Don't make me tell ya twice."

I did as I was told, my face trying to keep from flinching into a wince of pain as I knelt down, dropped the stick and did as I was told. The two of them dropped to the ground, walked over to me and put yet another zip tie on my wrists. Before long I found myself wearing part of a burlap sack for a mask and positioned helpless on my stomach. I lay across the back of one of the horses after they zip tied my ankles together as well. The horse bobbed along a path for a while, on pavement where the hooves clop-clopped along, and then I was pulled down and thrown on the ground, my hood pulled from my head. It was dark so my eyes didn't have time to adjust. I sat face to face with a wild haired man with mirrored shades, a greasy grey mustache that grew down on his cheeks, and a yellowed grin that looked every bit the same as a great white shark right before it bites down on a helpless seal.

"Good day to you," he said calmly as a young man sitting beside him unskillfully sewed the skin of the Captain's right shoulder together.

The Captain did not wince at all, focusing that predator gaze on me, waiting for his prey to make a false move. The young guy, his blue ball cap on backward and his tongue sticking out of his mouth in concentration, looked as if his life depended on the quality of each stitch.

"Good thing I found you, Ranger," said the Captain, placing his sweat stained white hat over his tousled gray hair. "Y'see I lost a group of people that owe me quite a share of taxes, and Tully here tells me that you were in cahoots with them all."

Tully repositioned his rifle enough to give me a short wave of his hand and a grin full of teeth that had seen better days. The glint in his eye made my stomach drop into my shoes.

"No," I said as calmly as possible, realizing the word was not spoken to this guy very often. "Well, I just kind of fell in with these people just a few days ago. We were trying to get some food and water from them when you guys att… I mean came to collect your due. I just happen to know where they are going. I help you, you help me."

This sentence caused them all to burst into raucous laughter, and it was only then I noticed just how many of them stood around us in this makeshift campsite. I felt a cold finger run down my spine.

"I'll tell ya what, son," said the old Captain, his voice the sound of gravel dumping into a quarry full of dead bodies. "I'll bargain with ya, but you prob'ly won't like what I have to offer you in return for your...services."

This caused more laughter from the group, a raucous hyena sound from one of those National Geographic documentaries.

"You're gonna take us to where they are going to let out and then we'll set up an ambush there. Hopefully they won't have mother nature on their side this time. I'm tired of these people slipping our grasp, so to speak. Won't happen again, will it boys."

A mumble of approval chattered through the crowd of men and he continued with his speech.

"Now in return, you get to serve this fine outfit until we see fit that you have earned your term of service. Since you're a Ranger already, then we'll put your talents to good use."

I played along.

"Yes sir," I said as firmly as I could, straightening my back. The motion made my leg flare up and it was just too much to bear. I let out a little yelp that could not be taken back. The crowd found it amusing.

"Looks like this boy's in need of some doctorin'!" he shouted, producing a long bladed knife and cutting the string that the young man had tied into a knot. "Doc! Fix this boy up. I'll be in my tent drinkin' Jack. It's gettin' late."

"Yes, sir," said the young man. They cut me loose and I went with the "doctor" to get "fixed up." Three tylenol and a branding iron later I was nearly as good as new. Doc was out of thread.

Keeping up the act of being a soldier was more than I cared for.

Kelly

Gideon got the engine running somehow. I don't know anything about mechanical stuff. My husband always did that. We were on the water early in the morning and soon we were floating down river on our way to New Orleans with the wind at our back and the sails full as Gideon would say.

I cozied up next to him as he stayed back near the engine and adjusted it when it needed adjusting. He was glad to see me again.

"Hey Kelly," he said, a strained smile on his face. "Everything alright?"

"Yeah," I told him, though things weren't. "I guess I just needed someone to chat with. It's so hot and sticky out, huh?"

He laughed again, that strained laugh that a boy left on his own to fend for himself would tend to have. Gideon's Dad went to war some years ago and never returned, but Gideon never really talked about that. He would just sit at the edge of the tent village in the reeds, wearing his leaf covered gillie suit, trying to keep us safe. He'd come in to eat once in a while, and when he did he'd come to my tent for meals.

He could have been my son.

I turned around and sitting next to me, his legs crossed over one another, his blue eyes looking serenely out toward the shoreline passing by, was Jacob. I didn't really know what to say to him. He'd sat next to me when we started out from the sand bar and hadn't said a word since. I just hate uncomfortable silences, so I spoke up.

"Are you alright?" I asked him.

"Right as rain on a hot day," he offered, turning and focusing those kind eyes of his on me. I didn't feel intimidated or even the strangeness of meeting someone for the first time. It was as if we had known each other forever.

"What happened to you? I mean, what did they do to you?"

"Nothing that can't be forgiven, Kelly," he said through a genuine smile, and then put his hand on my arm. I noticed that there was a nasty puncture wound on the back of his hand. He didn't seem to be bothered by it. "What transpired was a work of God, none else. I take zero credit, but give it all to he who made it all. My time is soon, but there is much work to be done before then."

He turned and closed his eyes, his mouth moving in a prayer that was silent and only known to him. I felt a warmth that came from him, a springtime sunshine warmth. It was a good feeling, and I wanted more of it.

I looked toward the front of the boat. Clayton stood at the bow, his face lowered, his hands firmly grasping Jacob's hickory walking stick. I pointed in that direction.

"Don't you want that stick back?" I asked.

He laughed a laugh of one who knows a secret, a wonderful secret.

"No, dear," he said calmly. "I don't need that where I'm going."

He slowly stood, using my shoulder for a slight brace as he did, but I didn't feel much pressure. He limped slowly to the front of the boat where he touched Clayton on the shoulder. They sat down on the bow, Clayton facing out, dangling his feet over the edge, and talked about something I could not hear. They spoke in low tones, their voices sounding like whispers in a cavern. After a while, their conversation seemed to come to a close. Clayton's face was drawn and sullen when Jacob finished, but the old gentleman placed a reassuring hand on Clayton's shoulder and the young man managed a smile even if it seemed forced.

I didn't know what they talked about, but Clayton seemed changed after that. He stood up in the front of the boat again, head bowing toward the water, hands firmly grasping the vertical hickory stick, and the old man sat peacefully gazing out toward the shoreline as it lazily passed by.

Amy

The sun was it's usual dim self since the meteor hit. I guess that debris wouldn't be falling out of the sky any time soon. At least it cooled things down a bit. On the bright side the sun wasn't directly burning our skin. The canopy of the boat, even though it had been burned pretty bad in the last fight, provided some kind of shade for us.

I sat next to Anya as she hummed a little song she had heard sometime in her little life. It was a pretty tune, but I didn't know what it was. She was probably making it up. Ralph sat on my other side, his hand holding mine. I felt so happy to spite all the horribleness of the world. He would look over at me once in a while and smile, something I hadn't seen him do much in the short time I'd known him. There was a peace in his heart now, and all of us could sense it. The fact that his eyes were so gorgeous didn't hurt, either.

We rounded a bend in the river, and I could see a bridge or an overpass or something going over the water. Another highway, I guess. A pretty big city was on the right toward the south, but these days cities kind of blurred together as most people had either left them or found out that they were breeding grounds for Volos.

I heard a sound of what I thought was a firecracker, like one of those bottle rockets my Dad used to get illegally from other states and bring them to Oklahoma when he'd go on business trips in the summer. Jacob yelled from the front of the boat.

"Look out!"

I heard a thump in front of me, and then something

exploded between our boat and the bridge in mid air. When I looked up to see the fireball I thought I saw a man floating in the middle of it, his arms outstretched, his wispy gray hair waving in the wind, and then it was gone, and Jacob was falling into the water. I screamed as the bullets started buzzing past us like little deadly bees.

All of the men reached down and picked up their rifles, steadied their guns and started firing at a line of militia men on the bridge. My stomach turned over and I almost hurled. I grabbed Anya and threw her down into the bottom of the boat where she curled up in a ball and covered her head. There was a lot of shouting as the men and some of the women fired off rounds at the bridge. I looked to the front of the boat and Clayton was laying on the bow, his torso almost completely over the side. Oh no, was he dead? No! He was reaching for Jacob's body as it floated by us in the water. He missed it, screamed, and just as I was ducking down behind Ralph, I saw Jacob float by on his back, his arms outstretched, his wet shirt full of blackened holes, his eyes closed in peaceful slumber.

I knew he wasn't asleep.

Clayton was freaking out. He ran to the back of the boat, almost stepping on Anya and everyone else, bullets zipping through the canopy, one of them striking his shirt, grazing his ribs. He ignored it, looked out the stern and shouted after Jacob, but Jacob was gone, sinking beneath the water. I felt someone's warm hand on my shoulder, and I somehow knew what to do.

"Clayton!" I shouted. "Pray!"

Clayton looked at me as if I had slapped him. He nodded his head and then knelt down in the bottom of the boat next to Anya, his eyes closed, and he seemed to get calm. I heard a grunt and suddenly felt someone bump into me. I turned to see Ralph slump down next to my legs, a gushing wound in his chest. He looked up at me, those beautiful brown eyes of his seeming to ask me a question, his mouth moving to try to form words, and I lost it.

I flipping lost it.

As tears welled up inside my eyes making everything blurry, I picked up Ralph's shotgun, aimed at the first militia man I saw and unloaded. The guy fell off the bridge into the water. Then another, and another, and another. I just kept shooting, and heard someone screaming and realized it was me.

"No!" was all I could shout as the men fell off the bridge or sagged down out of sight. I would not be the victim. I would make them pay.

We floated on by, the sound of the rifles dying off, some of the people lost, some of the people wounded, but Ralph was not moving, not breathing, only laying there in my lap, his blood all over me. I dropped the gun in the water and just lay there on the floor of the boat, cradling Ralph's head in my arms, holding him close, feeling his lifeless body get heavier and heavier.

Nothing mattered. Not a thing mattered.

Ethan

When the two boats sailed on down the river and moved out of sight around the bend, I listened to the curses spewing from the lips of Captain Waldeburg. He had untied me when I convinced him that I was through with the villagers and wanted them dead. I sort of lied, but was coming around to pretty much hating them.

I felt sick. I could see the blood in the water and the bodies floating down the river, bobbing ugly corks, and I felt like throwing up. I looked down at the rifle in my hand and realized how useless I had been. I fired at the water, fired at the trees and at the shore line, and generally froze up, until I shot one of them and realized that it was Ralph.

Many of the militia had been killed and lay like bloated crash test dummies all over the bridge. Some of them were sticking dirty fingers in wounds that wouldn't heal. The Captain had taken one in the hip but was still walking around barking orders and screaming, a fat angry baby, his mouth always moving, his mirror shades on crooked so you could see that dead eye socket of his. He didn't realize that I was not completely on his side, so when I pointed my gun at him and pulled the trigger four times in a row, his face looked funny, all quiet and still and shocked. He fell down on the hot pavement and made a gurgling sound, drowning in his own blood. I put another one in his head for good measure, at close range, and blinked when some of his blood went in my eye.

I figured someone should give me a good hand or a pat on the back for offing the guy. Human waste.

After I whacked him, the rest of those guys just stared at me. They didn't have the guts to retaliate, I guess. I don't know why I did that. Mostly to shut him up. I didn't think about it as I dropped the gun on the broken road, walked to the railing and then jumped over the side. When I hit the water it felt cool and good and welcoming. None of those rednecks did a thing when I bobbed to the surface and started swimming. I was a good swimmer in high school back in Jersey. I just plugged along the river, swimming like a boss, ignoring the pain in my leg.

I saw my friends the crows, flying down to peck at the faces of the dead, and I climbed out of the water onto a small dirt road that came down by the shore, probably where some country bumpkin used to fish and bathe in the water and probably attempt to make babies with his sister.

After about an hour of limping along, I found a little house out in the middle of a wiped out field. There was a truck parked near a boarded up and sagging house at the end of a long gravel driveway. Didn't see anyone around, so I hobbled up to the front door of the house, up on the stoop, and looked in. Not a single sound. I turned around and coming around the house was an old redneck guy wearing overalls, a shotgun leveled at my head.

Time to do what I do best.

Clayton

Amy didn't sleep for about two days after Ralph died. She just sat in the boat and cried and held little Anya who didn't really understand what had happened. We stopped down the river a ways after we was sure them militia guys was gone. We had ourselves a burial for the ones that didn't fall out into the river when they died and the ones we were able to grab along the way. I said a few words, but Amy stood silent, her face lookin' pale and worn. A lot of the people were really shucked out at God that so many lost their lives. I did my best to love on them and prayed earnestly for their faith.

We camped out after travelin' down river another day or two and that's when Amy finally came over to sit by me on a big ol' log. For a while she just moped there all quiet, her right foot diggin' in the soft sand, diggin' up little muscle shells, their little pearly insides exposed.

"Why Ralph?" she asked, not really lookin' at me. "Why did Ralph have to die, Clayton?"

She then turned and looked at me with them beautiful green eyes of hers, her mouth carvin' out a terrible frown, and if it were solely up to me I would have caved, but it wasn't solely up to me.

"I hate it, too, Amy," I said, my voice somehow calm in the storm of all this. "Ralph was doin' what he could to keep us alive. I know it don't make no sense, but sometimes things happen and we don't have a reason for it. Sometimes things don't seem to have a reason for us, but God knows the reason, and since he sees past present and future all at once, I choose to trust him with it."

"But…" she managed, her chest hitching in air. "Ralph was a good one. He was a good guy who had just given his life to Jesus, and he… It has to make sense. God owes me that."

"I think about Job," I said to her. "Job was pretty much at the bottom of a hole with no ladder. He'd lost his land, his family, his health, and everything, but he didn't hate God for it. It doesn't make sense right now, but it will someday. God said in the book of Isaiah 'For my thoughts are not your thoughts, neither are your ways my ways. As the heavens are higher than the earth, so are my ways higher than your ways and my thoughts than your thoughts.' God made Sarah barren in her youth so that he could speak to her in her old age, he denied Moses' right to be a prince so that he could return as a shepherd and lead his people out of Egypt, and he took Daniel out of sweet and pretty Jerusalem so that he could be a blessing in ugly ol' Babylon."

"Don't get all preachy on me, Clayton," she said, but I knew that was the enemy, so I prayed a little as she continued. "What kind of God would let Ralph die? I mean, I went to church and all, but this is just too much. God is a good God, right? I just don't get it and I don't care."

"Sorry, Amy," I said, lowerin' my voice a little. "Just think about it this way. If you believe that Jesus died for you, and you have faith in that, I mean really have faith in that, then we'll see Ralph again one day. This world is cursed, has been since the fall. Evil things happen. I hate it, but that's the truth. No sugar coating. I will see Ralph again."

"But I want to see him now," she sobbed. "I want to see

him now! I don't want to wait. Why was he taken from me when I was just learning to love him? I loved him, Clayton, and now he's gone. There just isn't any churchy answer for this."

She started to crying most terrible, and I just let her, but she didn't lean on me as before. She put her hands over her ears and pulled her head down by her knees and sobbed. A wailin' came from her that was all too common on this broken earth. People started to look, but I just let her get it out of her system. As my Momma used to say, sometimes you just have to shut up and let a girl feel, so I did. She finally looked at me after a while and frowned, closed her eyes and sat up, her face looking up toward the darkenin' sky.

"I guess my faith isn't very strong right now, Clayton. Nothing really matters to me anymore. I'm just tired. So tired. I guess I just never really had much faith."

I didn't answer her. I thought about Jesus and how his friends came and told him about Lazarus dying, but he stayed away knowin' that God was gonna to do a great work through Lazarus's death. Jesus raised Lazarus from the dead to show the world not what faith could do, but to show his glory. That's why I knew in my heart that Ralph was gone for a reason, that Jacob was taken for a reason, a reason that was not readily available to me at that time even though I think Jacob was tryin' to tell that to me just before all this happened. I just trusted that God knew, and left it at that. If he wanted Ralph to come back, he'd let me know, I'm sure. If he wanted to, God could make Ralph walk right up out of the river and eat dinner with us, like nothin' happened.

Amy walked away from me and toward the cook fire.

Beans again. Oh well. I figured when we reached New Orleans there'd be steaks and baked potatoes for everyone. At least I hoped there'd be.

Gideon

About a week after the ambush we started getting closer to a bigger city. Didn't know at the time, but it was Shreveport. We could see the busted up skyscrapers from a ways off and knew that either things would be dangerous or deserted, either one...probably both. We were also running low on supplies and really needed to stock up.

As we got closer, we saw several bridges that had fallen down by either natural or unnatural means, and from the looks of the powder burns on the concrete somebody had set a good helping of explosives on the bridges and blown them down. We passed by a few cargo ships grounded on sand bars, some of them partially sunk, and we had to watch carefully so as not to tear open one of the pontoons on the scuttled ships in the river. The river was much wider and deeper here, but there were still dangers down under the water.

The weird thing was that all of the campfires were on the west side of the river and the people standing around those fires seemed pretty harmless, but then so did most maniacs. We took our time floating along the river until we saw a campfire with mostly women and children standing around. We got close enough for shouting distance.

"Ahoy there!" I said as official as I could. "Is there a place to get supplies here?"

A woman about the same age as Kelly looked at me and nodded. She waved us in, and so I turned the boat in her direction to pull up to the dock. The campfire was built just outside what I guessed was an old loading dock, and I figured that these people might have more than they were letting on.

All of our men had their guns at the ready just in case, and the women and children were laying down on the deck like normal, so I decided to be brave and step out onto the concrete dock and put out a hand of friendship. The lady came closer, her yellow and blue dress covered with dirt and grime, her hands nearly black, and she was smiling at me, some of her teeth missing.

"You say you got some supplies for us?" she said when she got closer. "We've been waiting for weeks. You from New Orleans?"

I stood up straight and cocked my head to the side.

"I... I think there's been some mistake," I said to her softly, all apologies. "I was asking *you* if *you* had any supplies for *us*."

"Aw, no," she laughed. "My hearing isn't what it used to be. Sorry, fella. We're totally out of food, and nobody has the guts to go cross river to get it."

"What do you mean?"

"Something is over there," she whispered. I saw a grimy little boy peek out from behind her dress, then disappear again. "We don't go over there cause of the wildlife. We hear sounds at night clear across the river."

I handed her a can of tuna and got back into the boat. Had to pay her for being nice even though some in our group didn't look very kindly at giving up some of the last of our food. We poked along the river a ways and then stopped by a section of sunken bridge near a sand bar to talk it over.

"You heard the lady," I said to the murmuring group.

"Some kind of wild animals over in the city proper, but she said that's our best bet at finding food. We can hold out for the week or so it will take to get to New Orleans or we can send a scouting party into the city to find supplies. What do you think we should do?"

Mr. Dillon spoke up from the back, his shoulder wound was healing nicely it seemed.

"I figure we could send a few of our best shooters in and see what we can find," he said. "Anything is better than nothing."

"What does Clayton think?" said Mrs. Edwards, her eight year old Timothy on her lap. "Our kids need to eat more than I do. I can go without if they get food."

Clayton sat at the bow of the boat, his face toward the water again, praying to God or whatever. The group kind of saw him as some kind of Moses or something. I don't know. Clayton had yet to pick up a gun and help us during a firefight, but he usually had some pretty good ideas about what do to, and the people trusted him. I was surprised that such a dork had survived this world for so long.

"I'll go with anyone goin' into the city to get food," he said, standing up. "But I'll do whatever the group decides. We just wanna get to New Orleans as safe as possible, and I can't bear losin' anyone else."

That Amy girl looked over at Clayton when he said that. I used to think they were pals, but here lately she was all sulled up. Losing the Indian kid was kind of a blow to her. You know, Clayton talked a lot about God and what he did for us, but where was God when Tommy Fuller took one to his lung and drown in his own blood? I'd seen some weird stuff, some down-right unexplainable stuff, but like Clayton

I didn't want to lose anyone else, either. Deaths are always hard, but I guess people sometimes fall on religion to get them through. I just sucked it up and moved on, but the strength for that was starting to bleed out of me.

The people discussed it a while, and finally decided that we should send a scouting party, and since it was my idea I decided to lead it. Clayton tagged along and so did Amy even though young Moses protested. She just picked up that Winchester 1300, chambered a round and stared Clayton down. She did take out about five guys on the bridge by my count and that was cause she was all venomous over the death of her lovey. She had a cool head, though…and wasn't too bad to look at.

Rick Young and Ryan McKinley, a couple of scouts I trusted, old time hunters, took our people over to stay with the nice lady in the yellow and blue dress. I told them to share what provisions we had with her group. The fellas rounded up a little bass boat from the locals and took us over to the other side. Wasn't too much trouble to step out onto shore once the boat let us off.

The city was eerily quiet, as if we were in one of those horror movies where the monsters are asleep in the buildings. We went in at night so as not to wake the monsters up. Kind of wished we'd not gone in at all because of what happened.

I still get the shivers thinking about it.

Anyway.

Waiting until dark probably wasn't the wisest choice. Clayton walked right behind me, and then Amy came right behind him. Two of my best guys, Hanson and VanLew walked to our left, shotguns at the ready. Amy had been carrying that Winchester since Ralph died and it had become almost an extension of her arm.

As we passed through the deserted streets, the glass windows of the buildings looked down on us like great jagged eyes of giants. Paper and other trash blew around the lamp posts and gutter drains, and abandoned cars sat still, their tires low or flat, typical wasteland stuff. Some of them had been turned over and some of them were burned out hulks of steel and re-hardened rubber. There was a smell in the air, an acrid smell of burning trash and I knew that eyes were watching us, the eyes of something left over and neglected and feral. I pressed on, knowing there'd probably be a fight soon, but supplies were needed.

The job had to be done.

An H.E.B. drugstore built into one of the storefronts loomed ahead, it's rounded red letters faded and full of bird's nests.

"That's our objective, people," I said, chambering a round in my bolt action rifle and then slinging it to pull out my .45 pistol, readying it with a pull of the slide. "Be ready for anything. If it moves, give it a mouthful of lead."

We moved closer, stopping just outside the smashed glass of the front door. Dried blood was all over the ground and smeared on the glass of the store front. There were black hand prints and smelly streaks all over the walls and even on the concrete smash and grab barricades in front of the store.

Not a good sign.

I stood outside the shattered glass door for a few seconds, my pistol in both hands pointed directly into the darkness of the store, and then I let one hand free to motion everyone inside. I stepped across the threshold first, and that was when I heard the low growl of several savage animals.

They came at the us, five of them, teeth flashing, mad eyes wide, a group of gnashing dogs, some of them biting each other, some of them biting at us. We all opened up on the store, our empty shells bouncing all slo-mo Clint Eastwood on the shattered, glass strewn pavement. One of the dogs, some large shaggy mound of hair, it's matted fur clinging together in clumps, pulled at Clayton's pants leg, writhing back and forth. Clayton beat it away with his walking stick. After we fired several rounds, the big animal dropped to the sidewalk, and the other dogs ran away creating a slowly growing vacuum of sound. Amy spoke up, and I could tell she was stifling a scream.

"Anybody bit?" she asked, voice a high vibrato.

"M' pride is a little worn, that's all," responded Clayton, unusually calm. Guy was a real hard-case when he wanted to be.

"Good," I said, pressing my boot on the neck of the dead animal. "This one here's got rabies."

Man, I hate rabies.

"Let's just get the stuff and get outta here," Clayton agreed.

All of us crept all ninja into the H.E.B, our guns at the ready, our pride a little shaken by the repulsive greeting we had just received, because we all knew that in this crazy world stuff happens like lightening.

The store inside was a mess. All of the shelves had been toppled over and what looked to be useful items at first glance seemed to be gone. We started scrounging around, a practice that had become second nature to most of us, I guess. We started picking through the remnants of the store and did so for an uncomfortable time, two of us always keeping guns pointed out toward the street in case more trouble arose.

It did.

I kept my gun trained on the door as Amy shoved several cans of random foodstuffs from vienna sausages to aspirin into her bag, and then a noise started to build in the street outside, a sound of a strange crying in the distance, then growls and barks and gnashing of teeth and then sharp, high pitched yowling. Apparently the dogs we'd took out were only a scouting party for a larger pack of maddened mongrels. I stared at them from the broken window of the store front, and watched them circling around in the street, their glowing eyes reflecting the cold glow of the moonlight.

"God protect us from the evil of the enemy," said Clayton. "We put our lives in your hands, oh Lord."

I didn't know about God's protection or anything, but I had a piece of steel at the end of my arm that only spoke one language: hot lead.

Amy

Gideon and his two buddies opened up with their rifles into the swarm of dogs that ran into the store, the monster's eyes red with disease, mouths foaming something awful. Clayton jumped in front of me to bat a medium sized nearly hairless dog away with his walking stick. The stick made a sound like when we used to go to baseball games and the guy would hit one out of the park. This time, though, it was a nasty dog whose feet slipped and tried to gain ground on the slick tile floor between the two lifeless checkout counters.

"Don't just stand there," Gideon screamed. "Shoot at something!"

So I did. Oh gosh I did. I shot at several of the dogs and started crying at the horror of it all as the powerful shotgun kicked my shoulder. Their faces were not the lovable faces of the dogs I had owned throughout my life, but the twisted, diseased faces of rabid beasts. As I fired off the first round, catching one of them along the side and dropping it to the cold floor, I had a flash memory of Chewy, my Labrador who got out in the woods and was bitten by one of those skunks or raccoons or something. He came home with a bloody wound and because my Dad was away so much forgot to get his rabies booster that year. Before long he was a growling brute under the porch who had to be put down. Well, now there were a hundred or so growling brutes out in front of the store biting at each other and darting in and out, some running away - at least the ones fearing the gunshots.

The loud bangs of the guns were not making most of them run, the brave ones growling and whining and snarling at us. One of the bigger ones darted in and had one of Gideon's guys pinned to the ground, and then another group of the dogs fell on him, tearing and biting as he screamed and screamed and finally stopped screaming.

I saw Clayton out of the corner of my eye as the dogs began to swarm us, and he said something kind of under his breath and then I saw something so strange. A man appeared just between us and the dogs, his arms outstretched, and hot light was pouring out of him, a light that caused me to look away. It was so startling that my gun went off in his direction, but the blast went right through him as if he were a ghost. His shaggy hair floated around his head as if he were under water, and he hovered just a foot or so off of the floor. The light beaming from him caused all of the dogs to run in fear. The whole lot of them skittered across the floor and slid on the tiles, falling down and stumbling on one another, biting the ones that got in their way, and then the bright man was gone, a floating mist of bright little particles.

"Let's go," Clayton said to the rest of us, and we followed him without a word, our bags of canned goods slung over our shoulders, our legs pumping hard as we shuffled down the street to the sound of the dogs way behind us barking and carrying on. Whoever or whatever the guy was who appeared in the store needed to come back because those dogs started running after us again, their barking getting louder and louder. Gideon and his crew didn't bother firing backward as we bounced out of there so fast hearing a few precious cans drop out onto the pavement. The dark waters of the river were right in front of us.

No boat. Where was the boat?

I could hear my heartbeat thumping in my ears as we rounded a corner near the dock and heard the squeal and growl of hundreds of those dogs on our heels. I didn't look back, but jumped right off the pier and into the water, joined by what was left of our group who splashed in right behind me. The current was so strong. I didn't think about that at all.

It was so hard to hold on to the heavy sack of cans. It weighed me down so much. I thought about letting go of it, and as I came up for air I heard Gideon shout from behind me.

"Ditch the guns!"

I heard heavy breathing and grunting as the men and I swam hard against the midnight current, and me trying so hard to hold on to the sack of cans and medicine I had managed to get. It was so dark, and the people from the village were too far away to hear us. I started screaming when I came up for air again, but my lungs just wanted to breathe, and I wasn't going to let go of the supplies because everyone was so hungry. Little Anya was so hungry.

I started getting tired, my legs feeling like they could boil the water around them. My lungs sucked in air and I tried to keep above the water, and that is when I felt a hand pulling on my right arm, right up into a boat. It was Ryan and Rick, the two guys who Gideon had ferried us over. Ryan, a tall guy with dark hair, and Rick a shorter stockier fellow with a peppery grey van dyke mustache, pulled us all up into a metal boat. My eyes caught the words "Bass Ackwards" painted on the side in big green letters, glimmering in the faint moonlight.

"Are you guys ok?" asked Rick, his voice a welcome

sound.

Gideon heaved his body into the boat, and I noticed that he didn't have his bag of cans. In fact, no one had their bag of cans except for me. Gideon gave a thumbs up, and then looked at me and started breathing out a wheezing laugh.

"Looks like you guys got showed up," laughed Rick, his elbow arching upward as he worked the engine's pull rope. "This little girl here brought home the bacon."

Several of the dogs scurried around the dock, some of them jumping helplessly into the water, and three other guys who were with me lay in the bottom of the boat, some of them with their limbs hanging over the side, and I heard weakened laughter all the way back to the two pontoon boats waiting near a sand bar.

I just kept thinking about that guy who died, but I guess Gideon and the others were just calloused about that after all they'd been through, all except Clayton who sat on the edge of the boat and looked out toward the city, his face looking old and worn.

Clayton eventually brightened up, and took to calling me "hero" for the next few days. It started out kind of funny, but then he ran it in the ground and I had to ask him to stop. He only smiled and said he would, then winked at me like he knew something I didn't. We all had a pretty good meal that night, and as the morning sun came up over the skyscrapers to the east, I thought more and more about the glowy guy in the H.E.B. I could just see him there, floating above the floor, but after a while I had to think real hard about what he looked like, kind of how I had to think real hard about what my Dad's face looked like or what he sounded like. It was like the memory of it was fading away faster than normal, and pretty soon I stopped thinking about it all together.

Weird how I am talking about it now. Now I remember it, but then it kind of passed away from me, gone on the mists that hovered over the waters of the river at sunrise.

Kelly

The river sent us along, and we just went along with it. Amy and Clayton sat near each other but they didn't really speak much. I suppose she was still pretty upset about all the people she had lost, mainly Ralph. Anya climbed up into Amy's lap and she put her arms around the child.

"Hey, Amy," I said, plopping down next to her.

"And you're…" she managed.

"Kelly," I said, and we shook hands awkwardly.

"Hey," she said, trying on a smile.

"Anya's really taken with you," I told her, touching Anya's soft hair. "You should consider yourself pretty lucky. You're really the first person she's been close to."

"Yeah," she laughed, genuinely, her eyes watering. "It's a lot of responsibility, really. Who knew?"

We sat there for a while, the water passing by the boat, listening to the banter of the others next to us as we puttered along. I guess she couldn't stand the silence.

"Remember Chic-fil-a?" Amy said.

"Oh man," I said, turning to look at her. "They must have put an addictive chemical in their chicken because it was so good."

"That stuff was crack," Clayton said, butting in. "Oh man! Remember Five Guys?"

"Oh," said Amy, her face getting stern. "It's a competition then. I've got two words for you: Pei… Wei…"

"That place never had enough seating," I said, laughing. "We always had to sit outside during lunch hour."

"I know what you mean!" shouted Amy a little too loud,

catching herself and laughing.

From behind us, out of nowhere:

"Marble. Slab. Creamery," said Mr. Jackson's deep voice, smoothing his son's soft black hair as the dark eyed boy sat between his feet. We all laughed again as the rest of the boat started shouting out their favorite indulgence back before the war and the world going sour.

"Starbucks!" said Gideon. "And Bass Pro! A Starbucks *in* a Bass Pro!"

Someone at the front of the boat started singing: "I got two all beef patties, special sauce, lettuce, cheese, pickles, onions on a sesame seed bun!" This started a round of jingles sung by everyone in the group, and people could probably hear our laughter for miles off.

Mr. McKinley, steering the boat along, told us about missing his favorite movie *Ghostbusters*, and started quoting lines from it at random. It turned out he could quote the entire movie from beginning to end, and we listened as he recited it for us. We all lost it when he did his best impression of Bill Murray saying that the apocalypse would consist of "dogs and cats...living together...*mass hysteria!*" You just never know what some people have in them, even if it's weird stuff.

As the people were laughing and discussing more things they missed about the world gone by, I looked at Amy and she had grown quiet. Clayton sat next to her and held her hand as they looked out at the water and the shoreline rolling slowly on. They missed Ralph. We all missed the people we had lost.

"I miss my husband," I said, my voice cracking. "I miss his voice."

Amy looked at me, her eyes closing, squeezing out tears. She took my hand and we just sat there on the edge of the boat crying. Clayton put his arm around Amy and reached out to touch my shoulder, and I could hear him mumbling something to himself, almost a whisper. Anya climbed down to the bottom of the boat and sat with her hands around her dirty little knees.

Somehow — and I'm not sure how — I felt better after that. I still missed my husband, but I felt ok with it. I felt as if I could move on. Amy, however, was just beginning her journey of grief. I decided I'd do what I could to help her travel it.

Clayton

Once we got on down the river a ways we found that there were boatloads of people with the same idea we had. I suppose they heard about the same stories around campfires lit in places I had not traveled. I heard accents from all over, mostly the south, but pretty much from everywhere.

I spent most of my time in the front of the boat just prayin' over the people and our safety. We had lost so many, and I figured we prolly wasn't out of the woods yet, so to speak. There could be militia, dogs, or other crazy nonsense before we got to New Orleans. I got a message to make friends and so that's what I did.

I looked across the water at the boats around us and hollered on out to them, startin' up conversations which made them float closer to us and share their stories and what food either of us could spare. I met people from all over the U.S., some of them from Canada. Their story was pretty much the same as ours even if there were some minor differences. All of us was headed to New Orleans because we had heard that there was hope down there. I met Moms and Dads, cops and criminals, bankers and homeless people, even though I suppose all of us was pretty much homeless.

The river started widenin' out, and as we floated along we saw people walkin' or ridin' horses along the banks of the river, some of them crossin' the roads that went along bridges that we passed under. I looked around at the faces on my own boat and noticed that even though things had been hard for all of us, people started smilin' again and laughin' with each other, just cuttin' up and havin' a good time. After a while a couple of guys in the back of our boat broke out a deck of cards and started playin' Texas hold'em. I didn't know nothin' about that game so I kept to myself.

I just smiled and realized that I was doin' what Gabe had told me to do, and that was get to the coast. That, he said, would lead me to Jerusalem. Whichever way that was supposed to happen, I didn't know, but I figured life was an adventure with God, and he hadn't let me down yet, and wouldn't. His word was pretty clear about that, and I had seen enough of his grace and power to know that he would be helpin' me along where I needed it.

He was there when I got robbed all them times, there when I felt alone, there when I dropped my sack of cans in the river, but also there when I heard bullets whizzin' by my head, there when them big grasshoppers came, and there when we was about to be torn to shreds by them dogs. He will never leave me nor forsake me. I guess forsake means like when Judas did what he did.

Yeah, that. He'd never do that.

Gideon

New Orleans was a lot bigger than I had originally thought, and as our boat started getting closer to the city, I started noticing a lot of heavies standing around in body armor and helmets holding mint new Mossbergs and Bushmaster AR-15's. There was a great big docking area along the river where people were pulling in with their boats to tie off and disembark. Everybody was all giddy about the fact that the lights were on in New Orleans, run by some kind of elaborate generator system, probably off of military hardware. I wasn't giddy at all. I was always cautious about new people, and just smiled when I had to and said "yes sir" an "no sir" but mostly "yes sir".

Ryan and Rick steered our boats over to the dock once it was our turn, and I jumped from boat to boat, tying off the lines real official like while six toughs, all of them shaven and showered from the looks of them stood on the concrete dock armed to the teeth. There were about five suits, two women and three men, walking up to our location to help us unload our gear, but one of them had a bull horn and was barking orders.

"Welcome to New Orleans, everyone," he said, his voice really pleasant and soft. He had a funny accent I couldn't place. "You may disembark from your craft carefully. Let us help you with the children and the infirm first. Please leave all firearms and other weapons on the boats. You will not need them at all. Your safety is secured by the best of professionals. Your days of fending for yourselves is over, and a new chapter of your lives is beginning."

The guy had a big smile and I could see his white teeth. He had access to a tooth brush at least, and when I got close he smelled clean, not a guy with years of body odor like everyone else. I fought the idea of having a shower and a home-cooked meal, and walked up to the bullhorn guy, my Bowie knife carefully stowed in the waistband at my back.

"What if we don't want to give up our weapons just yet?" I asked calmly, in a quiet voice that only he could hear.

"It's policy," he said, placing a hand on my shoulder. It felt weird, him touching me like that. I let him. "We just feel that it's easier if we can get people off the boats without too much…trouble. I assure you that your weapons are not needed, but if you feel that you want to keep them, I can place them in the storage hold of the vessel you are assigned and you can retrieve them at your leisure."

"Vessel?" I asked. My arms folded on cue.

"Oh yes," he said. "It will all be explained later. Just let's get all of the people off of these boats, proceed to processing where you will all receive a hot meal, access to showers and barracks where you can enjoy a good night's rest. I'm sure you are very tired from your long journey. God has seen fit to see you here safely. Let us take it from here."

Yeah, the last part was weird, but I don't really judge a guy's religion. I decided to do what was right and just bide my time, and after all of us had made it to the "processing area", I soon found that what the squirrely guy said was true. They did have a hot meal, they did have nice hot showers and they did have a warm, soft bed to sleep in.

Our people ate it up.

As I lay in my bunk later that night, I stared out the window of my barracks at a flag flying over the camp, all lit up with spotlights. It was not the flag of the U.S. of A, that's for sure. It sort of looked like the United Nations flag, but there was this weird symbol in the middle kind of like the symbol for a hurricane. A map of the globe made up the center, a perfectly round shape, but coming out of the north and the south east and south west sides like points on a compass were three curved lines all turning clockwise.

Even though I was dog tired, I didn't sleep very well, and when I did sleep, I dreamed about being chased by a beast in the desert.

Amy

Oh, it was so good to finally have a shower and sleep in a bed. And *air conditioning*! I had forgotten how good it felt to sleep in a cool room with no crazy people outside trying to steal my stuff. Anya slept in the bed next to me. They told us we could all stay together, and that we were going to be bussed over to the Mercedes Benz Superdome for a "briefing" before loading up on all the ships to go to a new city.

The ships in Quarantine Bay were so many and so big. From our barracks we could see aircraft carriers, battleships and a cruise ship or two. I was hoping that if they planned on putting us on any of the ships we would get to ride on the cruise ship. I just thought the others would be so cramped and a bummer to ride in.

More and more people were coming to New Orleans every day by raft, boat, horse and on foot. They fit all the people in our group on a Greyhound and after a short ride we were getting off the bus in front of the giant domed structure. I felt like we were all going to a game or something, but I kind of felt weird with all the armed guards, their faces all intense. They didn't talk at all, and Gideon told me that they wouldn't even joke around, kind of like those guards you hear about out in front of Buckingham Palace.

Creepy.

Well, we all piled into the stadium where there was a stage set up down on the field and the lights had been turned on. Some of the bulbs were busted out and the place smelled kind of musty and it was sticky hot in there. There was trash littered all over the field, but in the middle near the fifty yard line someone had set up a small black stage. They didn't keep us very long, but the buildup took a while. Some guy I couldn't see really well walked up onto the stage and grabbed a microphone.

"Attention," he said, and I could see that he was wearing a suit and tie. "I will keep this short, but this is the best place we could come up with to get a message out to all of you at once."

The crowd started to get quieter, and there was a dull roar of voices that went away. All of a sudden you could hear yourself breathing it was so quiet.

"Thank you," he continued. "I am so glad to welcome all of you to one of the ports we have set up to transport the rest of humanity to the shining city of New Jerusalem. I am sure you have many questions, and we have representatives of our new government aboard every sector of every ship that are now preparing to take you to your new home. Many things have happened in the time since the war. We have seen a decrease in cases of Volos as God has provided a vaccine that is being distributed at the ports just outside of New Jerusalem. We are also able to feed more and more people each day with new advances in food production. The human race will indeed rebuild and thrive. We are here to inform you that these ships in the harbor will take you to your new home where you will enjoy a peaceful, carefree existence, a life of prosperous wealth and opportunity thanks be to God. The busses outside will take you to your destination at the ports. If you have any belongings that need transport, we have already made arrangements for them to be packaged and carted aboard. If you have any questions, feel free to ask the governmental representatives on the section of the boat to which you have been assigned. Thank you, and peace be upon you."

And that was it. Pretty much it. They then started herding us back to the busses and I noticed that the guys with weapons were standing in lines along our path, all of them quietly looking at us, no expression at all, just quietly looking Scooby-Doo spooky.

On the bus ride to Quarantine Bay I sat next to Anya who was giggling and laughing as Clayton made faces at her. Gideon sat in the seat behind me, and when I turned around he was sitting there all stoic and quiet, his dark hair falling in his eyes.

We heard music as we got off the bus, and it was the first time I'd heard music in so long I didn't really know what to think about it. It was light, classical ye-oldie stuff. It kind of caught me off guard and threw my mind into a spin. Clayton started dancing, sort of. He can't really dance. This caused Anya to laugh and giggle again and it took my mind off the fact that we were about to board a boat to who knows where, but there would be peace and prosperity and God knows what else. We lined up to get our ticket, a little metal disc that had the name of a ship on it.

Please be a cruise ship. Please be a cruise ship. Please be a cruise ship.

It was an aircraft carrier.

Clayton

All of us formed a line leadin' to a long bridge that went out over the water and onto a large deck. At first it didn't resemble a ship, but when I looked closer and actually stood on the pavement I realized it was the loadin' elevator of an aircraft carrier. The ship was huge, as big as a skyscraper layin' on its side. The elevator we walked across was lowered down to let us on, but was actually the deck where the planes used to be lifted up so they could take off. When the elevator was down, it emptied out into a hangar bay inside the aircraft carrier that was ever bit as big as a football field. Turns out there was three of these inside, lined with cots and privacy tents.

They had gone to a lot of trouble.

Speakin' of trouble, I sort of felt strange in my spirit about the whole thing, as if I was bein' watched or somethin'. I could also sense that Gideon was kind of bothered, but then again he always looked like that, sort of sulled up and bothered. Amy and Anya was hittin' it off. That little girl was somethin' else.

Amy kept goin' on and on about the showers and the beds and the good food, even though I was sure she was upset we weren't on that cruise ship. Accentuate the positive, I guess. I had heard that them cruise ships was top heavy anyways, and was glad to be on such a big stable boat. The Reagan had been cleaned up and repainted I guess, 'cause all the evidence that this used to be a United States vessel was gone. I kept seein' this flag painted everywhere that was like a globe with three curved lines comin' out of it and didn't know what to make of it. I supposed that humans had to have a government, and just hoped that this one wouldn't fight with its neighbor if we had one.

Wasn't long before we was drawin' anchor, and the captain, a fella with clean cut hair and a big bushy mustache, let us go up to what he called the folk-sill and watch. That was the biggest chain I had ever seen, all covered with grease, the sea water beadin' up on it.

Amy was the picture of happiness. She sidled up to me once we was underway and put her arm 'round me. She didn't smell so bad no more and neither did I. That was a blessin', somethin' we take for granted when we have a nice warm bed and a roof over our head.

"Thanks for your help," she said in my ear, and I could feel her warm breath blowin' on my neck.

"No problem, Amy," I said. "What did I do?"

She laughed and hugged me up, and I hugged back. Gideon had Anya on his shoulders and they were playin' some kind of game I wasn't sure I knew about. I guessed that he was settlin' in, but could see a glimpse of his bowie knife handle when he turned 'round, and when he looked at me it was as if he was tryin' to tell me somethin' dark even though he was smilin'.

After the boat headed out, I climbed several flights of stairs and went through several bolted doors to get to the flight deck. Them armed guards was everywhere, but I payed them no mind. I thanked God for bringin' me this far and sendin' me to Jerusalem even though it was now called New Jerusalem and was supposed to be some kinda emerald city from the Wizard of Oz.

The sun, all faded and weak-like, was shinin' down on the water, and I heard a voice speak to me inside my heart. God told me in no uncertain terms, right there on the deck of the former U.S.S. Ronald Reagan, to be sure to pay attention to the man behind the curtain.

I caught His drift, and decided to do just that.

Ethan

I woke up on a bed.

"Just lay back," said a woman in white. "You've had some nasty gun shot wounds but you are fine. Just lay back."

I felt darkness take me, washing back over me after that old redneck did what he did. I made him pay for it, that's for sure. Made him pay.

I could see the ceiling far overhead, lights that might have been stars on the white ceiling. Is that salt I smell? It's getting so dark.

"Shhhhh," came the voice of the woman again, but I was not able to move my arms or my legs, and there was some intense pain in my stomach where Farmer Joe shot me.

"You did good, soldier," said a firm voice in my ear, a man's voice, a voice full of gravel. "We'll talk when you get well. Until then take a breather."

I felt the world slip away from me then, and I could see the shape in the darkness of someone standing over me, his slender face grinning, his wild dark hair billowing in a wind that was not there, and I realized that he was...

...darkness.

Book II:
The U.S.S.
Ronald
Reagan

Clayton

The ship had lawn chairs. They were the recliner kind with them rubber bands that formed to your body and made you feel like you were pampered.

We sat real quiet, right smack dab in the middle of the runway gazin' off at the other ships of all makes and models sailin' along with us. I saw all kinds from cruise ships to navy vessels from all countries. One of the crew pointed out that there was a few Russian ships in the fleet and that they had to learn the language to operate them. We was goin' to Jerusalem…or New Jerusalem…whatever.

We'd hear noise over the loudspeaker now and again tellin' us that it would take about a week to get to that city, and that we would have plenty to do once we got there. I wondered what kind of job they had in store for me. All of it kind of made me feel weird inside. When I prayed about it I would get the idea that God had different plans, which was a little strange since I was supposed to go to Jerusalem.

Amy sat next to me in her lawn chair, a cool plastic cup of water in her hand, shades on (don't know where she got 'em), starin' ever so quietly at the big ol' cruise ship floatin' just a few thousand feet away. I looked at it, and it too had that strange flag flyin' over the top most part of it, a weird globe with three curved lines comin' out and turnin' around toward a clockwise direction. Our local representative of the new world government, a Scottish fella name of Mr. Mark Knight, said it represented all of the world comin' together under one banner. They'd finally licked war and poverty and all that other stuff that made humans bad.

It was all just plain weird. That prolly worked on Star Trek, but not in the real world. I remember watchin' that show with my mom years ago and all the while thinkin' that Federation of Planets stuff was absolutely impossible. If everythin' was so great, how come they was always havin' to bust out the laser beams and torpedoes? We'll see.

"You think I could, like, trade in my chit for a trip on that cruise liner?" asked Amy to no one in particular. "I mean. It's worth a shot, right?

"Amy," I said to her without lookin' at her, my eyes fixed on the tiny people walking around on the sun deck, watchin' one of them take a big dive off a diving board into their lovely blue pool. "I just don't think it's gonna happen is all. Don't ya wanna hang with me 'n' Gideon?"

She turned and looked at me, raised her shades so's I could see her pretty green eyes, and smiled a halfway smile.

"Where *is* the lone wolf?" she asked. "I haven't seen him in a while."

"Said he had some business elsewhere," I said. "Don't really know what that's supposed to mean and don't think I want to. The guy's had his undies in a bunch since we got on this here boat."

"He's a weird one anyway," Amy laughed. "He's all 'area fifty-one'."

I looked up and Gideon was standin' next to me. Didn't even hear him approach. I guess a few years runnin' from militia will do that to a guy.

"Better cautious than dead," said Gideon, his dark hair hangin' down in front of his even darker eyes.

Amy brightened up a bit, her body language shiftin' over to soft and warmin'.

"We were only kidding," she giggled. "Me and Clayton think you're pretty cool. We only rib you 'cause we like you."

Gideon said nothing. He had a lawn chair in his hand, and after opening it with some difficulty, sat down on the other side of Amy and scowled out across the water.

"Kelly don't have time for me no more," said Gideon, his voice so low I almost didn't catch it. "She's found somebody to pass the time who's more her age."

Amy looked at him, reached out, and took Gideon's hand. Gideon looked back at her, and for a moment I saw what he probably looked like as a little boy before all this nonsense started.

It was real peaceful lookin'.

Gideon was the only one of the three of us who didn't flinch when the side of the cruise ship facing us blew outward in a great big fireball, sending little pieces of deckin', glass and people parts across the glimmerin' water.

I felt an ache in my gut, all them people dyin' pressin' down on my heart like a stone, and then ever'thing got all slo-mo.

We all three scrambled to our feet, me knockin' my lawn chair over as alarms started goin' off all over the place and the soldiers ran across the deck, orderin' us to get on down below to the hangar bay where we slept. There was shoutin' and screamin', guys with guns runnin' up on the deck and then fannin' out around us. Just as I was herded past the bulkhead at the base of the control tower, I turned to see two or three black zodiac boats loaded with black uniformed soldiers skippin' across the waves to the burnin' ship, oily smoke roilin' out of the side of it from a massive flamin' hole.

I started prayin', and trusted that was gonna be enough.

Ethan

I woke up because somebody was sticking my arm with a needle.

I could smell rubbing alcohol and iodine, so I knew I was still in the infirmary or hospital or whatever place this was. I could see florescent lights far overhead on a grey ceiling, and that told me I was at least in some place that had a power source. My stomach felt like it was on fire.

The person sticking that needle in my arm was this cute brunette. She had on scrubs that fit her in all the right places and the way she was smiling at me told me she was on my side…or at least being paid a lot to help me.

Do no harm.

"Hey, doll," I said, grinning at her and winking. "What's your name?"

"Not Doctor Doll," she said, her accent foreign, laughing that laugh girls laughed when they were turned on. "It's Doctor Angela Schiff, actually, and you seem to be doing much better since you arrived here."

"Where is here, Angel?" I asked, keeping that charm going.

"Just Angela," she smiled, the accent definitely German. I was still in. "You are on what was formerly the U.S.S. Ronald Reagan and what is now the flagship of the New Jerusalem fleet, and it has not been named yet, so we simply call it the Reagan. Now it is time for you to lie back and rest."

I started feeling a little nauseous just then, and had to lie back down on the pillow and when I blinked my eyes that hot little angel had vanished. I thought about getting her number, but then remembered I hadn't seen a working phone in, well, forever. The pain in my stomach canceled out everything else.

"I have plans for you, Ethan," said this deep voice in my head. I thought I was going crazy until my eyes blinked open and a guy was sitting at the edge of the bed next to me. He had the strangest eyes, two silver ball bearings sitting in sunken sockets. He was surrounded by a haze as if I had just opened my eyes for the first time after being in a coma. There was a kind of dreamlike quality about him and he was all fuzzy around the edges.

"Who..." was all I could get out before he cut me off.

"Name's Morax," he said, his long skinny fingers playing with the I.V. tube of the patient next to me. "You and I have the same goals. You'd like to see the blood run out of the people who wronged you, and I'd like to see them ruined. An arrangement is in order."

Weirdest thing was that his black hair was moving around his head, a tangle of writhing snakes, but there was no wind.

"Where are they?" I asked, my voice cracking. These drugs were good.

"Here. On this ship. They are not aware of you. I want to hand them over. Serve them up. Slice and dice."

"Sign me up," I told him, my blood throbbing in my head, making the overhead lights dim and brighten with each beat of my heart.

"Hold still," he said, and then he came to me, stretching out his frail looking arms and raking claw like hands across my shoulders that felt like cold steel on my skin. I felt heavy, then warm, then the air got really thick and I could hear music, soft music that drew me down…down…down….

It's so dark here.

Amy

The security guys were all buggy about the bomb going off, and I guess they had good reason. I was too young to really remember 9/11, but I heard a lot about it in school. Went to New York one time with Dad and saw the memorial, but was only twelve, so I was too busy being boy crazy and checking my Twitter feed to care much about all that. Terrorism was an awful reality for a lot of people for a while, I guess, until they had the final war that ended everything.

Turns out terrorism didn't have anything to do with the end of the world, just good old human greed.

We all got patted down by a couple of butch looking ladies who really needed to tweeze, and then we were sent to our assigned hangar bay where our cots were, each section separated by privacy curtains that were just about useless. We had only been at sea for two days and things were already getting tense.

Clayton was his usual praying self, his head bowed down as he walked along, holding that hickory stick in his hand. I was surprised he didn't trip over the bulkhead thresholds as we were herded into the hangar bay. I think I saw tears in his eyes a few times.

Gideon found Anya and she came running to us, her brown hair whipping out behind her, her face all drawn down in fear. The way those security goons were marching around made the whole vibe of the place get all oobie-joobie. If you ask me, the biggest fail was the government representatives who were talking over these bullhorns and telling everyone to "remain calm" and "we have things in hand" to a crowd of people who had watched their own government fall apart and disband, a government that no one would ever think could die.

Gideon wasn't buying the official line.

"Something big is going down," he said to me, his voice really low and quiet. "There's just something about these New Jerusalem guys I don't trust. I can't put my finger on it, but I just don't like them."

"Gideon," I said, putting my hand on his arm. He didn't flinch. "We lived on our own for so long, and it's probably normal to not trust authorities. Give them a chance."

He smiled at me, probably the first time I had ever seen his face do that, and it was kind of cute. Then he sniffed and cleared his throat.

"Nobody gets a chance," he said cryptically. "Not anymore. I survived for a dog's age in the middle of militia hell and it was because I was smart. Watched out for number one."

He started to walk away from me when Anya grabbed his hand and pulled.

"A pony ride," she said to him.

Gideon broke his strange expression and suddenly got all picturesque dad as he scooped Anya up and placed her on his shoulders. Their play was interrupted by Mark Knight who stood toward the outer doors of the middle hangar bay and raised a bullhorn to his hard, chiseled face.

"Everything is under control," he said, his voice even and without any obvious stress. He sounded (and kind of looked like) that guy on that movie about the Spartans. "It seems that there is a terrorist in our midst and this individual is being hunted as we speak. There is swift justice in our society, no longer allowing the criminal to go free or live when their victims die a senseless death. Rest assured we will soon have this perpetrator in the hands of our justice system, and he will suffer the fate of all criminals in our new world. Please relax, as the galley is making preparation to feed everyone staying in the hangar bay a lavish buffet. Thank you for your cooperation, as we will not be allowing any more civilians to roam freely about the ship for obvious security reasons. In a few days we will reach our new home, and it will more than compensate you for your inconvenience."

Wow. I guess due process is out. Sometimes I forgot that justice is dealt out differently in other parts of the world. I wondered what kind of justice was "swift" and what that might look like. I thought Gideon might start getting all paranoid about that kind of justice, and when I turned around to ask him about it, he was nowhere to be seen and Anya was taking my hand, asking me for the pony ride.

Clayton

Old Mr. Chalmers was sittin' on his cot, the one next to mine, and he was tellin' a knee slapper of a story again. Never coulda guessed he'd lost everything he'd had or everyone he'd known. He was a livin' miracle and never let you forget it. He was all animated, his large calloused hands clawin' at the air in front of him, his white bushy eyebrows raisin' now and again for emphasis.

He always kept us in stitches with his crazy stories.

We mostly sat around talkin' about the way things used to be and he would tell us how things used to be before that.

"Me 'n' my wife, God rest her soul," he'd say. "We had us a nice little house on some land there in Nebraska, see. Well my Dad died and left us some money so we opened up a money market account with the credit union. Well, our homeowner's insurance was comin' out of our checkin' account and then all of a sudden they was takin' it out of the money market account. We kept transferrin' money over to it and then one day it was all gone and the check bounced and we lost our insurance. The best we could get after that, 'cause of the black mark on our record, was some cut-rate insurance. What burns me is that we spent all that money over all them years, dodged several tornadoes and floods and bad storms only to watch the world end and that money disappear."

"Might as well have set that money alight," I said. "I guess they couldn't insure the end of the world. I guess insurance ended up bein' a result of people havin' no faith in God."

Chalmers laughed at this comment as did many people around me. We'd all spent thousands of dollars on insurance only to have the bottom drop out of the world economy. Crazy that.

I'd spent a lot of time with ol' Arden Chalmers the last two days. Met him when we boarded the Reagan and found our bunks. He was a good story teller and kept us all on the bright side o' things. I figure that was needed, and it was like God had sent this old codger into our lives just to brighten the mood. We was in lockdown, couldn't go nowheres, was pretty much cooped up in this here hangar bay with nothin' to do but talk and cut up. We's gettin' stir crazy even though it had only been a day or two.

We was used to wide open spaces, mostly fresh air, somewhat stale water and, well… I guess things was better here.

B'fore long it was lights out, and I had a little LED flashlight I'd bummed off one of the guards who gave it to me so's I'd shut up mostly. I pulled out my Bible and started readin' it again. After a while the kids got quiet, then there was whispers, then all talkin' eventually stopped. My eyes started gettin' all blurry so I shut off the light and then drifted off to slumberland.

Somebody bumped me a bit later. It was one of them guards and they was roustin' ol' Mr. Chalmers out of bed in the dark. I looked around and noticed that they was gatherin' people up. I poked the guard and he turned around real fast, shovin' a gun barrel in my face, and I jumped, puttin' my hands up out of habit.

"Dude," I whispered. "No harm comin' from me. Just wanna know what's up."

The guy looked bothered, but he looked at me with steely eyes as he put the gun away helped Arden to his feet. Arden looked sorta dead, his old bones creakin' from the early mornin' wake up call.

"We're taking the elderly to a quarantined area," he said, his words soft but full of authority. "There's a Volos outbreak on one of the ships and we have found that the elderly are more susceptible to the disease. Don't worry. They'll be well taken care of."

I felt somethin' flip inside my stomach just then. I can't really explain it, but my radar went off or somethin' and I just got really scared. I dropped down beside my bed and started prayin'. I didn't know what else to do.

"Dear God I praise your name for all that you are. I long for your presence. Please walk with Mr. Chalmers and the others. Keep them safe on their journey. I ask for your protection for us all, keep us from falling into the hands of the enemy. Thank you Jesus in advance."

If Volos was on the loose, it was bad news for everyone, but somethin' in my heart told me that this was all wrong.

All wrong.

Gideon

They didn't see me sneak through the starboard hatch.

Even when security is locked down there are always ways to slip past the most wary guards as I had discovered when stealing food from militia groups in the early days of the end of things. Most of these guys were rent-a-cops, but some of them, very few of them, were heavy operators. Once Mr. Knight started in on his little speech, I gently pushed Anya over by Amy and then slipped through the crowd, ducking in and out of the tight clusters of people until I worked my way over to the hatch. Strangely, the guard's line of sight was not tracking my way, so I made it through the hatch and down a ladder before any of them were the wiser.

After going down a few ladders and through a few dark corridors, I managed to climb up into the ceiling and lay down on a row of steam pipes that snaked along. I waited there for what seemed like hours as the steam, a byproduct of the reactor, slowly warmed me through my heavy clothes. I wondered if my sweat dripping down would alert any guards that patrolled beneath me along the hallway, but nothing ever came of it.

I had to find out what was going on with the cruise ship. Things with these New Jerusalem types were all out of whack, and they were tight lipped about it.

Pretty soon I heard a commotion down the hallway back the way I came and then down the hall marched a column of guards slowly leading some elderly people along. They passed under my position, guards making up about less than five percent of their number, so I waited because as per protocol there usually would be a guy at the very end who was back there because he wasn't that good at his job.

Sure enough, that's what happened.

I jumped down all quiet and was thankful that my tactical boots didn't make a sound on the hard, thick painted floor. I crept along in the dark behind the group, my fingers brushing the handle of my pig sticker just in case. If these amateurs had not found my knife, then they probably wouldn't figure out I was missing for a long time, either. I never saw any of them count us. I had to find out some info.

I followed the group until they went up a few ladder stairs and then out a port hatch and onto a balcony that ran along the port side of the carrier, then up some stairs to the flight deck. It was night, and they were using flashlights and spots. I decided I would hang by the hatch to the balcony and hope I could hear something important. That's when I heard a voice speaking loudly, loud enough to be heard above the waves, but not loud enough to need a megaphone. The accent was unmistakably Scottish.

"We have determined that your existence will be a drain on our resources in New Jerusalem. We are sorry that we must do this, but you must now walk off the bow of our Lord's ship. May he have mercy on your souls, but it is for the good of the young that we must ask this sacrifice of you."

I heard moans, a scream, and then the unmistakable sound of an AR-15 being fired. As I was trying to process this and figure out what I was going to do, I was grabbed from behind and a couple of strong arms wrestled me into a side room where all I saw were wires and tubing and a closing hatch before I was thrown to the cold hard floor.

I jumped to my feet to see at first a Ruger stainless P95 pistol and behind that a black knit tactical mask. All I could see was dark eyes and onyx black skin.

"We gotta do something about those old people," I told him, my fingers clenching to form fists. I wondered if I could get to my knife before he could pull the trigger.

I'd done it before.

"Ain't nothin' we can do about it," he said, his voice calm, his dark eyes trained on me. I could see them looking at my center of mass to see what I would do, not at my face. This guy was trained...and an American from the sound of it.

"I take it you don't like it," I whispered. "Well I certainly don't, and when the people on this ship find out that the guards just threw the elderly overboard, they are going to have a major mutiny on their hands."

He looked at me, then looked at his gun. The pistol was motionless until he looked at it, a lethal instrument that was an extension of this stranger's arm.

"No," he said, still holding the gun on me but pacing around. "I can't really do anything to help them, and if we do, we run the risk of losing our own lives. These guys are ruthless, and will stop at nothing to see to their agenda. You were stupid to follow them out there. They probably saw you through cameras mounted in the ceilings."

I folded my arms and put all my weight on one leg. He lowered the gun, but not enough to no longer be a threat. He was sizing me up.

"Call me...Austin," he said all short and to the point. I sensed something about this guy that was good, but didn't

really know how to take him. Figured I'd let him explain.
Keep him talking. Maybe he'd make a mistake.

"Gideon," I said. "Look man, I don't care if you try to
shoot me, I gotta do something about those elderly. Those
monsters have to pay for it."

"They will," he whispered. "I can't really go into it right
now, but if you will be patient, I'm part of something…a
resistance…that could do some good. Let's just say the
United States is not done. I've been watching you and your
friends for some time now, just planning my move. Saw you
duck out and figured it was time for us to meet. Right now
you need to lay low and not let on you saw me. Soon we
will be triggering a pretty big strike, but if you don't know
about it I'm afraid you will probably just get in the way. I'll
contact you when we are ready to move. Can I count on
you?"

"If you are against these goons then I'm your man," I lied
to him. "Just say the word."

With that, he opened up the hatch door, looked around
cautiously.

"Don't get yourself caught, kid," was all he said before
disappearing into the darkness. I beat it over to the door as
soon as he lit out, but he was long gone. Guy knew how to
move.

I made it back to the main group without much incident,
hiding when I had to until one of the noobs saw me. Played
like I was lost. That usually did it anyway, and worked this
time.

At least I knew there was a resistance against the happy
town goons, and meeting Austin…or whatever his name
was… told me that the official hard cases weren't who they

pretended to be. I didn't say a word to Amy or the others. Figured I'd just bide my time, map the defenses of the New Jerusalem stiffs like I had already been doing, and keep an eye out for Austin.

Kelly

It was so late, almost morning.

I couldn't believe we were on the deck taking a moonlight stroll after all the violence and the lockdown, Mark rousing me from my bed as he made his early morning rounds. It was so strange. He was so nice to me, made me feel safe, spoke to me with a voice like silk, his Scottish accent rolling his "r"s in a lovely way.

It didn't hurt either that he was so easy to look at.

I'd met Mark at the camp in New Orleans. He'd approached me rather abruptly and struck up a conversation, and I didn't know about his importance with the New Jerusalem government until someone came up to him, saluted, and reported some information about the need to feed another thousand refugees who had arrived on foot. After the frightening ordeal with the cruise ship, he was quick to find me and the look on his face told me that he wanted to make sure I was safe and unharmed. It was a look of fear, but something told me he would be able to handle it.

I didn't really see the cruise ship they had told me about. I think it had fallen behind because of the damage. I was only assuming this because every time I'd ask Mark about it he would change the subject. He was kind of evasive about government matters. I was used to this kind of thing being married to a Ranger, but Mark was kind enough to deflect my questions politely and carefully so as not to hurt my feelings. All he would say is "we have matters in hand."

So confident.

I walked to the edge of the runway on the flight deck and looked out across the water, the faint light reflecting off of the tips of each wave. There was a haze in the air that obscured the stars but allowed the light of the full moon to shine through as if it were a flashlight behind a thick piece of gauze, and it was beginning to sink beneath the waves. I felt Mark's strong hands gripping my shoulders and I melted, longing for that feeling again, falling willingly into his steely arms, weary from those two years of not knowing and then the awful sadness that I wished would vanish from my heart.

"Things are so much better where we are going," he said, his voice smooth, a beautiful song in my ears. "You will see, lass. We have all but eliminated hunger, disease and war, the three things that brought our world to its knees. We have a strong government under God's guidance. He is helping us every step of the way, and has been influencing all of our greatest discoveries. So many achievements have been realized through his guidance."

I was never that religious. I went along with it. At least he believed in something beyond himself. It's what I loved about my husband. It was the thing that kept him going even in the thick of battle, but I had lost that faith when I no longer heard from him.

"When will we get there?" I asked, turning to face Mark, a smile forming on my lips that I could not help, could not hide anymore. He took my hands in his. Big, strong, warm hands.

"In about five more days," he assured me. "We will be seeing the lights of the new city as we sail in under a blanket of darkness just as this. After our voyage, the people will be given new homes and new lives in the government. No one will have to earn money or make a living because we have done everything to ensure that people's lives are pleasant and happy. We will find work for everyone, because everyone has a special service they can offer."

I smiled wide, and he returned the favor, his beautiful dark eyes gazing into mine.

"What would be my job?" I asked. I hadn't felt this way since my husband and I met so many years ago.

"What would you like to do?" he responded, pulling me by the hand to walk along the edge of the deck, his other hand brushing the railing as we went. "There are many jobs. What are you qualified to do?"

"Not much but to be a doting wife. My husband's pay took care of both of us before the war. Thought about going back to school. I haven't really considered…"

And he kissed me, held me close to his surprisingly muscular body, and I gave in, my body melting into his embrace, my heart pounding.

"I want you to be with me…," he said softly. "If you will have me."

I did not say anything. I stood quiet, feeling the guilt of my dead husband's memory for a moment, but then seeing Mark's kind eyes gave me solace for that. It was time to move on.

"I'm not being too forward, I hope," he explained. "It's just that in this new age we do not have time for cultural hindrances."

"Oh, no," I said, my face flushing. "I…I don't mind. I'll have to think about it, though."

I followed him down below decks to a door marked

"officer's quarters", and then he led me to a room with one of those bulkhead doors, but inside was a queen sized bed with a beautiful green bedspread and a porcelain and stainless steel personal bathroom decked out with all the niceties I had before the war. We stood at the door, kissing, embracing, and I could feel his heart thumping in his chest. I gave in.

"This will be your quarters from now on," he told me. "Feel free to tell the porter if you need anything at all. These are hard times. People need each other, and I'm glad you have considered being a part of my life. I would only ask that you stay here as a gift from me."

"Sure," was all I could say.

"I have to go to a meeting now," he told me, lightly kissing my forehead. "I will come back and we can talk later tomorrow. Until then enjoy this room."

He walked away, and I closed the bulkhead door and lay back on the feather soft bed, my heart racing, my head spinning pleasantly. After a bit, I took a shower in the well stocked bathroom and borrowed one of the white fleece robes I found in the bathroom closet. I lay back on the bed again, and I didn't think I would be able to sleep, but remarkably I did.

Peacefully and dreamlessly.

Howard

The phalanx of ships sailed in the night, the black ribbons of evil visible only to my eyes. The decision to scuttle the cruise ship was not known to the passengers riding on the other ships, and they had purposefully placed passengers with people they knew in order to minimize this in case of Volos outbreaks, but it was still beyond my capacity to understand how one group of humans could so carelessly write off the lives of other humans.

I hovered above the scene, wishing I could do something about the elderly floating in the black salty water, few of them still hanging on, trying to tread to the surface, using the dead ones as flotillas, but failing horribly. I asked the Maker to take them to their rest.

We are not capable of tears, of human emotion, but we are indeed capable of becoming indignant, agitated when injustice has been committed. It was all part of the curse of this world, the evil brought about because one of my brothers decided that he wanted to be in charge, wanted to be worshipped in place of the Most High.

Judgement is being passed on him, but his evil must play out in order to redeem all that our enemy has chosen to undo. I had always marveled at the ability of humanity to embrace the Most High from their fallen state, to find peace and grace and then hold fast to it in times of tragedy, the mystery that knitted them to the Most High even when the cursed earth struck back at them.

I rose to the deck of the U.S.S. Ronald Reagan, a ship that once saw grand service in the hands of a now fallen nation, a ship now being used as a ferry to a city of the damned. My charges were being allowed to discover for themselves what the world had become. I was ordered to let it happen. I knew my place. Everything in me vibrated with the anguish that came with waiting. I was to only observe the enemy for now, to discover ways to thwart their plans when commanded.

I found Kelly in her new state room, sleeping peacefully. How I had worked to help her grow close to Gideon, but now the enemy was luring her away. I moved into the hallway where Kelly's new friend Mark leaned against the outside wall, his arms folded casually as he smoked a cigarette. He was lost in thought, and I could see the fallen beings writhing around him as worms squirming under the heat of a hot coal.

He turned to go, flicking the spent cigarette into a nearby waste bin. He then twisted the ball of his booted foot to stride sternly away from me. I followed him down a cold hallway, up a shiny ladder and realized that I was passing into the enemy camp, several of my fallen brethren sitting around on the walls, hanging from the ceiling, spewing foul words and flinging obscene gestures at me as I went. I did not fear them.

We passed into the forecastle where several of the government officials gathered. I could hear their singing down the hallway as we entered the foreword compartment. The great chains attached to the anchor ran in two rows on the outside of the room, and someone had erected a podium toward the front of the ship where a gray headed old man in a black suit was directing the crowd in a song of praise.

A mighty fortress is our God,

a bulwark never failing;
our helper he amid the flood
of mortal ills prevailing.
For still our ancient foe
doth seek to work us woe;
his craft and power are great,
but armed with cruel hate,
on earth none are his equal.

They had changed the words. They had changed the words to Martin Luther's song. The enemy began to gather, thick like bitter bile. They hung from the walls, rose from beneath the bulkheads, drifted down from the ceiling, and sang along, a chorus of voices once used to worship the Most High and now repurposing them for praise of their leader: a destitute, failed, unholy general.

Soon, the fiery eyed old man began to speak of the advancements of New Jerusalem, how their leader had created a place for them that was free of war, disease, heartache and intolerance, his speech accented by drops of spittle that flew from his mouth like that of a rabid animal. They all chimed in with "here-here's" and other agreement at each key note in the address. At the end, the old man, a wry smile on his face, took two steps backward and pulled on a cord, causing a large tapestry to unroll from the ceiling with the face of a man printed on it, his angular features smooth and pleasing to the eye, his dark hair combed perfectly, his swarthy eyes staring at a point above and just out of frame, causing his chin to rise slightly, a sign of superiority.

And the entire group, Mark Knight included, dropped to their knees, bowed to the deck plating, and worshipped a name.

"Asher....Asher....Asher...."

C l a y t o n

I kept on askin' about the elderly people, especially about old Mr. Chalmers. Them guards kept on tellin' me that we'd be sailin' in to New Jerusalem in about four days and we'd all be reunited with them by and by.

I didn't believe a word they said.

Somethin' was just plain off about all the secrecy, the way they shuffled us around from place to place, off to the galley to eat a hearty meal, off to the aft hangar to play volleyball and all sorts of games that I wasn't good at. Plenty of nonsense.

Mostly I spent that time readin' the only thing that had any answers, and askin' God to shelter us from the comin' storm.

I started lookin' around for any sign that these guys were up to no good, but the only thing I felt was just uneasy. It was all them guards. They just stood around all silent like a bunch of kevlar jacketed statues, just like the heavily armed agents in that *Matrix* movie.

If there was one person who was not snowed at all it seemed to be Gideon. He stayed close to me and Amy after the bombing and once in a while I'd look up and he'd be gone. Don't know where he'd get off to, but one day I looked around and he and Amy were both gone. I wished I was in on their little secret, but I figured they might just be sneakin' off to get some alone time. I guess she was kinda sweet on him. I didn't mind none.

We headed on off to the galley again for dinner. I looked down at the floor and there was all these stars with famous people's names on them, kind of like that street in Hollywood. We got in there all orderly and fine due to the hard work of them guards. This time we had chicken fried steak and mashed potatoes with white gravy. I hadn't had that in forever and considered it an answer to prayer. It's the simple things really.

I sat on down by myself 'cause I couldn't find Gideon or Amy nowhere and Kelly was even off somewhere, too. Little Anya had taken to a couple of little girls her age and was havin' the biggest time. If it weren't for my content heart I'd be lonely. I'd been readin' through Philippians lately and if Paul could be content after bein' beat half to death, I suppose I could, too.

Halfway through dinner, I finished off my paper cup of cool water and was shakin' the excess out on the floor when I noticed somethin' written on the bottom in pen. I pulled it up close to my face and read the words "Don't drink the Koolaid."

I couldn't help it, but I chuckled a bit, and then started scannin' the room as if the message was meant for me. I noticed a couple of folks had found a message on the bottom of their cups, too, and was startin' to look around as if they was also gonna find the culprit.

In the process of lookin' around, I caught the gaze of someone starin' right at me, his coal black eyes burnin' holes right through the back of my skull, his lantern jaw grindin' away at his food. I could feel the heat comin' off of him, as if somethin' filled with poison and hate lived inside his heart.

It was Ethan, and he was a long way from bein' dead.

Amy

The guards stood in a little group over to our left, one of them telling a story in a language I didn't recognize. Every once in a while they would get a little lax and Gideon would start getting all jumpy. Gideon stared at me, his dark eyes looking into mine, his right hand gently grasping my left wrist.

"I'm going to dart in here," he whispered, pointing to a hatch. "You count to ten and then follow. I'll make sure you get through ok."

"But…"

"Shhh. Just follow, ok? It's a big hole in their line."

I nodded, and he waited for the crowd to sort of cluster up and then he was out of sight, the guards not even close to seeing him, all of them laughing out loud, uncomfortably loud. I hoped they wouldn't look when I tried the disappearing act. Gideon said they wouldn't, as if he just knew. It was all just freaky how ninja-like he was.

I counted to ten, looked around me, and saw that the guards were looking off in opposite directions. Like he said: "A big hole".

I shot out, staying low, weaving through the crowd, and found the hatch unlocked. Gideon was waiting on the other side.

He closed the hatch.

"We have to talk," he whispered, breathing heavily. "I knew something wasn't right from the get-go. C'mon."

I followed him down a ladder and into another darkened room. The light was really dim down here and it was a little humid, not like the air conditioned hangar bay. He lit a lighter.

"Where'd you get that?" I asked, keeping my voice low.

"Don't ask," he grinned. "Let's just say there's one guy on this ship who just quit smoking…like…permanently."

He pulled on my arm and I followed. We walked down this dark hallway that smelled strangely like an electrical fire and we turned a corner and then into a small room. When Gideon lit the lighter again, I could see that this was a broom closet or something because of all the mops and there was a little sink. Pipes and wires ran up all the walls and it was humid hot. I wanted to go back to the hangar so bad.

"They killed all the old people," said Gideon, the blue light of the butane flame dancing across his stern face.

"They what?"

"You heard me," he said, his voice at the top of a whisper as if he was trying to yell but trying to keep quiet all at the same time. "They marched them all up on the flight deck and forced them off into the water at gunpoint."

"That's crazy, Gideon," I said, reaching back to find the door handle. "Why would they do that? Did you actually see it?"

"Heck if I know, and no I didn't actually see it," he said, his eyes wide. "All I know is that I followed a line of them out there but just as I was about to get a look I heard one of the guards fire his gun and then I heard screams. That's when some guy grabbed me and we had it out. Said his name was Austin. I think he's the one that blew up the cruise ship."

My two hands shot out to shove at Gideon's chest on reflex.

The light went out.

"I could have been on that ship, you dork!"

"Yeah," he said, his voice strangely quivering. "Me too."

He lit the lighter and shook his head, his longish black hair falling in his eyes again. He then clicked the lighter shut and got real quiet, and I could feel his warm hand cover my mouth. I didn't resist him, but I heard footsteps outside in the hallway clank by, heavy booted footsteps. After they got distant, I shook free of him.

"Gideon," I said to him, trying to keep my voice down but failing somewhat. "What do you think this terrorist guy wants? Is there a reason he just revealed himself to you? Why would he do that, especially to a complete stranger?"

"I don't know," came Gideon's steady voice in the darkness, then the lighter flicked on again. "I was going to let it play out and see what happens. This guy hates these New Jerusalem guys for sure, and after what I… experienced… I don't blame him. The guy was American and said something about how the U.S. isn't finished."

"So did the guy have, like, a social security card or something? How do you know he is who he said he was?"

"I just do," he said, his eyes darting around nervously in the flickering orange light. I'd never seen him this way. "I just have a good feeling in my gut and that has never strayed me wrong."

I folded my arms.

"They said they were taking the elderly to a quarantined ship because there was a Volos outbreak," I whispered. "You said you didn't see them get killed, so how do you know that someone didn't just get scared or something. Some old people, heck some young people, get scared, you know. Did you ever think that maybe this Austin guy is nuts?"

"I don't know, but it's just not right," said Gideon. "This is all just not right. I can't put my finger on it, but I don't trust these utopia government guys. I've always been pretty good at sizing people up. I'm letting you know that I'm going to try to seek out this terrorist and see what he needs, maybe help him."

"Probably would be a good idea if you found out what really happened to the old folks."

He closed the lighter and then I felt him place a hand on each of my shoulders and squeeze. It was strange talking to someone in the total darkness.

"I'm gonna do this, Amy. I can't explain why. Something stinks around here and I'm going to find out what that is if it —"

The lights came on, really bright.

"— kills me."

There was a loud clang and the bulkhead door burst open and three armed guards with black jumpsuits, bullet proof vests and those German style helmets came stomping into the small room where we had been hiding. Before we knew it, our wrists had been zip tied behind us and there was a mousey little guy in a suit standing in the doorway. He was holding a cigarette between his thumb and index finger, his hair was all slicked back with what had to be lard and he had a grin on his face that didn't look friendly.

"Don't you know you are not supposed to be out of the quarantine area in the hangar bay?" he said, swirls of white smoke rising out of his mouth.

I didn't know what to say, but neither did Gideon. I thought he'd at least fight this, but I guess he knew when he was supposed to shut up and take it. I turned to look at him, my eyes watering over, and I could only say one thing.

"I believe you," I whispered.

Ethan

After a full day of orientation and lies about my abilities, I found myself in the galley with a full plate of food and a hunger for meat. The galley food, however, was not really anything to write home about. Mostly high protein starchy fare that made you feel like you was about to gag. Didn't care about that really. Mostly I cared about the fact that it was just so crowded and smelly.

Some of these people hadn't figured out that there was such a thing as a shower, even if it had been handed to them on a silver platter. I took advantage of all the amenities, that was for sure. Since I had been drafted into the welcome arms of the New Jerusalem squad without so much as a look at my real credentials, only a little oath of allegiance to some guy I never heard of and it was three squares a day, meds for my aching stomach and all the booze I could handle (when I was off duty, of course). The uniform had saved my skin more than once.

I was minding my own business when I heard that voice again, that raspy voice that sounded like my grandpa, except it was coming from inside my head.

"He's here," it said. "That do-gooder that left you for dead is here."

I looked down at my half empty tray and then looked up and sure enough, there he was, that little punk Clayton. He was moving his fork around in his mashed potatoes with one hand and was holding his paper cup upside down for some reason, his thin little eyebrows furrowing as if he were reading a book. I kept on staring at him until he looked up and we locked eyes.

Wanted to jump up, knock over the table and fill him full of hot lead, but I'd left my gun at my station because I was off duty at the moment. I just glared at him and he looked at me as if he was looking at a painting in a museum. Didn't even bat an eye.

Do him. Do him in.

I stood up, left my tray sitting right where it was, walked calmly over to him. He saw me coming but he just looked down at his tray and closed his eyes. The fool was praying again and something got real hot inside me, a furnace of fire and hellish rage.

Stop that praying! Stop that!

I moved a little faster, as if being pushed, until I was standing right behind him, my hands behind my back all casual but wishing they were around his throat.

Not here. Not here.

"That water was cold," I said, my voice a black vapor rolling out of me. "Cold like a grave."

He didn't say anything. He was ignoring me. The scrawny rat was ignoring me. I poked his shoulder with my right index finger and it probably felt like a piece of rebar, wished it was a knife.

"I made it," I said, whispering, almost growling. "I made it even though you probably thought I was dead. Well, you're going to wish that I had drowned."

Just then he turned around, but his face was all wrong, his face was like someone else and I felt so sick at my stomach I almost puked all over him. He stood up and looked at me, and it was bright in the room like I was staring at a welding arc. I felt something clawing to get out, something clawing at my insides. That kid was saying something to me but I couldn't make it out behind the white hot stare of his eyes, eyes that saw through me like Superman in the comics, and there was a roar like I was standing next to a drag racing engine.

Had to get out of there, so I ran. I ran away and by the time I made it into the hallway outside the galley I vomited chicken fried steak and potatoes all in the floor. Got yelled at by a superior and had to clean it up.

I'd be back. I'd have to. Payment must be made.

Gideon

I was somehow in school again.

I could see the fine tan wood grain of the desk when my eyes finally opened, and I had made a little drool pool there, but I was at an awkward angle, my back hurting something fierce. My hair was in my eyes, but when I went to brush it out like normal I realized that my hands wouldn't move.

I blinked a couple of times, wondering why this dream about being back in school wasn't ending. That's when I saw the skinny guy in the white button down shirt and black pants standing in front of a mirror on the opposite wall and realized that the reason I couldn't move my hands was because they were shackled into some kind of cold metal rings that were built into the scarred up wooden desk top.

I sat high up off the floor, high enough to see that I was about eye level with the skinny little guy. This weird school desk they had slapped me into was up off the floor enough so that my bare feet dangled down, and even though I couldn't see my feet, I felt that they had two more rings that they had clamped around my ankles, attached to the front legs of the chair. My eyes could see well enough through my hair to notice that at the front edge of the wooden desk, just beyond the shackles, someone had used what had to be their fingernails to make very noticeable scratches in the surface. The room was all white except for that mirror on the other side of the room. I could see everything from my knees up in the reflection, but I couldn't see my feet.

Hang on, soldier.

"I'm glad you are awake, Gideon," said the rat-like man,

his voice speaking with some accent I couldn't place. He scurried over to me and then his head was just below mine, just even with the front edge of the wooden desk. I wondered where my boots were. My feet were getting cold, but I was afraid that wasn't all they were about to feel. I wondered who was behind the mirror watching all this. I was going to give them a show, but if I could, something unexpected.

I tried to sit up a bit, but my back popped because it was in such an unnatural position. Looking down at the wooden desk in front of me and the weasel's head just beyond, I could see only the despair of my situation, but I had to stay strong. I wondered where Amy was. Now was a chance to test my resolve. I looked at the little rat man, the lackey doing the dirty work, and narrowed my eyes. He didn't smile, only squinted back, and so I focused on the mirror and sneered at it. Just let me out of these shackles or get near enough to my teeth and I'll have a little surprise for you...

"I understand you had a meeting with someone just near the entrance to the flight deck not long ago," said the weasel, his little pin hole eyes like tiny ball bearings. He stepped up close to the front of the chair and his hands dropped out of sight, but I could hear metal clicking. "We want to know who he was and where we can find him. It is urgent that you cooperate with us."

"Yeah," I said. "I think I remember his name. It was go get—"

And that was when my left pinky toe felt like it burst open and the little rat grinned at me. He had a silver tooth.

Didn't see that coming, but I figured it had to start at

some point.

"That was your first warning," he sneered, placing a blood smeared scalpel on the desk in front of me with dainty little hands. Didn't even wear gloves. How unsanitary. "You will give up the name of the man you met or I will be forced to do something else. Each time you don't, the punishment will get worse."

My foot was on fire, but it just made me more angry. I had only read about this kind of thing. Dad told me about it once, too. I was not going to give up, but everything in my body wanted to start crying like a baby. I just got more angry, used it, kept my breathing normal as I could. I sucked up as my torturer walked away from me, turning his back and standing feet slightly apart as he wiped my blood from his hands with a little handkerchief he had pulled from his back pocket. In the mirror I could see myself, see that my face was sullen, see that the blood was trickling from between my toes.

"Yeah," I whispered, and it surprised me I was whispering. "I saw that guy but he didn't really give me his name. He just about killed me, though. You aught to go catch him, bro."

The little guy spun around, darted over to me and snatched the scalpel away. He smiled at me knowingly and then sunk below my vision just below the edge of the desk.

It was so quiet.

I braced myself, but had to grunt when he shoved something into my right calf muscle.

Yeah, probably the scalpel. Not good. When he backed away, I saw that it was indeed the scalpel.

I saw the top of his head, then his little steely eyes, and

then his thin nose and crooked mouth, and I could see myself in his shiny silver incisor tooth. I could hear something dripping, splatting on the floor, and wondered how long I had until I passed out.

"I'm going to leave this in for a bit," he said as that spot on my leg started burning. "I'll go out for a little while and then come back when you remember more. Try not to go to sleep."

As I started to wonder how bad my leg wound might be, he spun around again and headed for a door to the right, almost executing a dance move. The incandescent bulbs in the ceiling caused a soft haze. He went to the door and someone else let him out and then shut it behind him. I heard the sound of someone talking outside, a language I did not recognize, but wished I spoke.

That's when I saw the light come on in the other room beyond the now non-reflective mirror and Amy sitting in a chair, her wrists bound behind her, a large beast of a woman standing near her. Even though I couldn't hear her I knew that she was screaming.

Ethan

I was late to my post.

Playing this soldier part was getting old. My C.O. was from somewhere in England and the thickness of his accent messed with the meaning of his sentences. He was pacing back and forth in front of the men when I shuffled in there. He looked right at me and his nostrils flared like a bull.

"Wha'?" he shouted, his voice straining. "Decide to bounce ou' o' bed, eh? Ge' ba' in line yank! This boat ain't gonna patrol itself!"

We all stood at attention. I did my best to fit in. Basically I was seen as a sad example of American soldiery. Everybody's army was always better than yours. They didn't know that I'd never been to boot camp, never trained. They just saw me as a sloppy soldier was all.

"Right," growled Sergeant Ames. "Davis an' Phillips. Get down to the engine an' patrol the 'allways. We got a terrorist on board an' we don't want 'im muckin' about in the works. Bailey an' 'arper! Get over to the armory and make sure 'es not got off with any o' our little toys, eh? Jus' guard it, then."

He turned and gave me the stink eye.

"Jenson an' Farmer. Right. Go to the flight deck 'an aide the mates up there with the patrols. Load your gun this time, Farmer. Don't blow your face off, eh?"

They all laughed, mostly uncomfortable laughter. I was waiting for an opportunity to kill this sack of manure. I snapped to attention and said "Yes sir" low like a growl.

"*Kill him*," said a voice from within my head. I was

hearing it more and more now. At that moment I chose to ignore it.

"On your way, then," said the Sergeant, and Jenson and I left to climb several ladders and stairs until we popped out on the flight deck. Even though I'd been up here a few times since we shoved off for New Jerusalem, I never really got over just how big this ship was. You could probably lay the old Empire State building on top of it and it would stretch from end to end. It was like an airport at sea.

"Got any entjie, bra?" asked Jenson. He was a thick guy with marble black skin who used a razor to shave his shiny head. Jenson was from Africa, and when he spoke English, I could tell it wasn't his first language. I knew he wanted a cigarette, so I fumbled around in my front shirt pocket and pulled out a pack. These things were precious, but I didn't care. This guy hated the superiors, too.

Actually, what I found out was that most of these guards were former prisoners. They were hired because they did dirty work and didn't ask questions. I didn't care. It was a job.

We walked across the flight deck, shouldering our weapons, smoke curling about our faces as the salty cool air blew around us. Even though the meteor had caused the sun to get weak in the sky, there was a large thunderhead spreading out on the horizon. I wondered if it was one of those hurricanes. Hoped it wasn't.

"Ag man," he said, his voice a permanent rasp. "You gotta stop that bossies behavior in front of that Khaki, bra. He gonna run you up the yardarm for sure."

"Don't worry about me, mack," I told him. "That guy's gonna get what's for one day. Mark my words."

Something exploded in the sky just then. It sounded like when those jets from McGuire used to fly over Trenton and break the sound barrier. Soon there were more of them, banging, thumping, so loud that they felt like they were slamming me on the side of the head with a baton.

"Get below," came a voice inside my head, and I turned to run when a noise like a shotgun blast rocked my ears and Jenson lit up like the fourth of July. Bright bolts of lightening were dropping out of the sky like daggers of light and for some reason they were hitting not just randomly, but at the people standing around on the deck.

I bolted, feeling the air get thick with static electricity. My hair stood out on end and there was a smell like somebody left the toast on the stove. I dove down the steps on the left side of the boat and just as I was running inside, a bright flash of lightening struck the door, and I could feel the white hot energy flow into my body, looking for a place to exit.

As I blacked out, I saw the shape of a man in a long black coat, his frazzled black hair circling his pale, gaunt face. He was reaching out, his fingers tipped with razor sharp claws.

"Time to act," he said.

Kelly

Something was making a horrible racket above me. It sounded like something several decks above was exploding enough to cause the metal in the walls to rattle. The lights started flickering on and off, and I heard shouting outside my door and people running.

I sat up on the bed and walked over to the door to find it locked. This sent me into a panic. I couldn't believe Mark locked me in here. Why would he do that?

The booming continued, and I wondered what had happened to Mark and if he was going to come back for me. Why did he lock me in here? It didn't make sense. If I was truly someone he trusted, then why lock me in?

Perhaps he was trying to keep me safe and there were secure places nearby that I wasn't allowed to see. I knelt down over by the bed and covered my ears with my hands. The booming noises continued and I could hear yelling out in the hallway.

I ran over and pressed my ear up against the heavy metal door and it felt cold on my skin. Someone was running down the hallway because I could hear the deck plates banging outside with their footfalls. Two men stopped just outside the door and began shouting.

"Sir," came a young man's voice. "The electrical storm has claimed the lives of eleven guards on the flight deck and three on the bridge. Went right through the windows, sir. It's playing havoc with the electronics. I've never seen anything like it!"

"That's strange," said another voice, older, harder but

familiar. "It's like it's targeting people who are exposed. Keep everyone below decks until it passes. We have to get someone up to the bridge to check on the status of the instrumentation. Good thing for failsafes or we would be adrift. As you were."

I heard the deck plating bang as one of them ran away and then the door to my room was being unlocked.

I stepped back, and there was Mark wearing a black uniform that looked like a Navy dress outfit. It fit snugly on him and accentuated his rugged features.

"Sorry I had to lock the door," he said, knowing what I would ask. "I had to ensure that you were safe. There is a terrorist on the loose, you know."

All of the arguing I had planned in my head melted away when he smiled at me. I put my arms across his shoulders and then let my fingers play with the back of his head, his black hair slipping through my fingers. We kissed, a kiss that lasted for a long, breathless time.

"I have to go, love," he said, his eyes blinking. "There has been an emergency. Stay here where you'll be safe."

"When will you be back?" I asked.

"Soon, lass, soon. This is a minor inconvenience, I am sure. I will ensure our safety, and then I will be back with you."

He kissed me one more time and then shut the door behind him and I heard him lock it again. I slowly walked to the vanity and sat in the soft backed metal chair, let out a sigh, and gripped my shoulders when I heard more loud noises overhead.

When Mark came back the lights were still flickering. I walked to him, but he caught be before I fully left the chair, holding me close, kissing me again and again. The noises slowly subsided, fading away until there were only a few echoes now and again.

I was sure someone was taking care of it. We didn't care, caught up in the moment, as if the two of us were the only people on earth.

Amy

I screamed.

The big blonde broomhilda who stood guard over me only glanced at me and grunted. I think her mom was a Russian bear or something. I sat in a wooden chair and they had zip tied my wrists together behind me. My ankles had the same treatment.

I started praying.

I didn't know what else to do. I hoped that God would hear me, knew that He had to. At least tell Clayton so he could get his mountain of faith on the job.

I had watched the awful little man slice at the web between Gideon's toes with that scalpel and then stick it in his leg and walk out of the room. Gideon sat there now, staring at me. Oh how I wished I could just break these bonds and get over there. What could I do, though?

Nothing.

Nothing at all.

Oh, God, please help us. Help Gideon, please God. Help Gideon get out of there before they kill him. I was staring at Gideon when I was praying this and saw that he had dropped his head down and was looking at the desk top. Was he praying? No way.

"Gideon!" I screamed. That big bertha looked at me again but stood her ground by the door, blocking the light from the hallway coming through the small round window. Good grief she was big. Then Gideon looked up and right at the glass between us.

He winked at me and smiled.

Show off. That guy amazed me.

I had a thought to rock back and forth and fall over, busting the chair maybe like in the movies, but when I did, I fell over and the chair almost landed on my wrists, pinching the skin on the back of my right arm just above the elbow. I closed my eyes, bit my lip, knowing that that big lady would come over and set me back up, and I prayed for Gideon, for Clayton, for little Anya who I felt I would never see again.

"Roust," said the gruff voice of the she-bear. "Aufstehen."

Whatever *that* meant.

I felt two heavy hands grip my shoulders and then as I was being lifted to an upright position, there was a noise outside and above us, a great booming sound like a bunch of cannons going off. I got plunked down on the floor again, closed my eyes and started praying, asking God that He would just spare me, spare Gideon, spare Anya, spare Clayton.

That big heavy door opened up.

"It appears that her friend won't tell us anything," said the thin voice of someone in the hallway. "He is perfect for Asher's needs, however ill advised, but I suppose we will have to ask the young lady a few questions about any conversations she may have had with the young man…or eliminate her altogether. She is not part of the plan."

Broomhilda stomped over to me, and I could feel her clammy hands grabbing at my shoulders, setting my chair up. I dare not open my eyes. An involuntary squeal came out of my throat and escaped my lips. I heard a thin laugh.

"Open your eyes, dear," said the squeaky little voice. "No one will harm you if you cooperate."

I opened my eyes and that guy who cut Gideon was inches from my nose. I could smell cigarettes and some cheap aftershave. Old Spice? Oh, it was Old Spice. Of all the aftershaves to survive the apocalypse.

I couldn't speak. I couldn't make a sound. My lips were still quivering out the mouthed words of my prayer. The creepy little guy only smiled. I couldn't see the big man-lady. She must have stepped out. I clenched my fists behind me.

No way I was going to tell this little guy anything. I didn't have anything to tell, anyway. I didn't know anything about the terrorist guy Gideon met because he didn't really tell me anything. That didn't matter anyway. He probably thought I knew something or he would have let me go. I figured I'd give him a bunch of useless information and maybe, just maybe he'd treat Gideon's wounds.

"Do you have anything to tell me?" asked the little guy. I saw a little speck of blood on his collar. That might not come out.

It took me a bit to answer. My lips wouldn't move. My voice was trapped in my throat.

"I... I think he told me he met some guy in one of the showers," I managed, lying. "I remember because it was so creepy the way he told it. Guy wanted to get him to help with the resistance or whatever."

"Yes," said the little weasel guy. "Go on."

"Well, he said that he was planning to take out the engine and needed Gideon to cause a diversion so that he could get down there."

"I'm sorry," said the little man, his face twisting into a dark smile. "I don't think that is the real story. Do you realize how hard it would be for someone to, as you say 'take out' the engine on this vessel? It is manned by former American sailors who have informed us that it is nearly impossible for a person to sabotage the engines or the reactor. Your story does not ring true, young lady."

I was caught. I could see the warped wheels turning inside his head as he thought of untold horrible things. Most of them probably had to do with me or Gideon and how he would hurt us further.

"I...I'm sorry. Truth is I don't know jack about the terrorist. You know, wrong place at the wrong time and all."

He sneered at me. Oh, how I wanted to break my bonds and get away. I looked up and saw that the light in Gideon's room winked out and the lights in my room flickered with the booming noises far above. It was like a signal or something because the little dork was grabbing me by the elbows, slashing the zip ties and lifting me out of my chair. He had a little pistol, a shiny black pistol and he was grinding it into my temple and telling me to 'get up'.

"Tell the guard to get the young man," said this surprisingly strong little guy with the gun to my head to Large Marge. "We will see how he responds to the death of his friend. It will cement his hatred toward us."

This could not possibly get any worse.

Clayton

Somethin' was bumpin' around up on top of the ship. I could hear it. Shoot we all could hear it. Sounded like when the hail would hammer down on my house back when we used to have tornadoes all the time, 'cept it was much louder and had them guards runnin' around like chickens with their heads cut off.

They was so frantic that they kind of left the bunch of us people in the middle of the hangar bay and scattered off in all directions. I couldn't see Amy or Gideon and didn't know where they had got off to. I sat next to that little girl Anya who had so taken a likin' to Amy and she put her little arms around my waist there on the cot and started crying. The noise was freakin' the little one out.

"I'm scared," said her mousy little voice. I grabbed her up and held her tight against me and she pulled me even closer, hangin' on to me like I was a life raft and she was seein' nothin' but wide open ocean.

"Let's pray," I said. And I did, but the words spilled out of my mouth as if I wasn't really sayin' them at all.

"God we ask humbly for your grace in this time of need. May you guide us and keep us in this time of trial and watch care over our friends who are not with us. I want to pray a special prayer over Gideon and Amy wherever they may be, and ask that you would send your mighty angels to protect them right now. I am powerless to help, but know that You, the God who parted the waters, who saved the first born, who was our safe place in the middle of the locust swarm and who helped us escape the militia men are our rear guard at this time as well. Give me wisdom for the days ahead, and help me to be your servant as I pour myself out to you as a living sacrifice for your will. Not my will but yours. Thank you Jesus for your grace and mercy. Amen."

I opened my eyes to see that several people had gathered around me and they was prayin' too. All kinds of people youngest to oldest was mumblin' out prayers and so I bowed down my head again and agreed with all of them. I knew that even though we was here in the middle of the Atlantic Ocean with all kinds of terrible things surroundin' us, the God of the Universe was listening' to our concerns, and he was answerin' them yes or no, dependin' on his will.

That was fine with me no matter the outcome. I figure if I died, then I'd be home.

Gideon

I heard that banging noise topside and wondered what on earth.

The scalpel started to really throb. It burned and pulsed with every beat of my heart. I started wondering how much blood I had lost. I wasn't dizzy yet, so I suppose my body's ability to clot wounds was kicking in. I don't think the little waste of skin who stuck the knife in my leg planned to leave me here this long.

I could tell that the little guy wasn't the head of this organization because he looked like he was just doing a job. I really wasn't going to tell him anything at all about Austin because there really wasn't much to tell. The guy didn't say anything to me other than he was part of some resistance movement or something...and then there was the part about the U.S.'s final hurrah.

At that time I was not privy to any information about anything really.

All I could think about at that moment was the fact that Clayton would probably be able to work some kind of magic and get out of this if he was here. I thought about all the times on the river, the locusts, the militia launching that RPG that didn't take out the boat, the way the guns of those militia guys failed on the beach.

So I started to talk to God for the first time in my life.

"God," I said aloud, my voice echoing in the small room as if I were talking inside a soup can. "I swear I don't really know if you are real or not, but I've seen some pretty crazy stuff recently. If you are real, then I really need you right now. I don't know anything about you and I haven't ever read a Bible or anything, but I just want you to know that I'm thinking about it, ok? So…If you could help out…"

Nothin' to do but wink at Amy and smile. She'd hopefully feel good about it, but her look was kind of puzzling to say the least.

I looked at the wood of the desk that my wrists were shackled to and noticed that the varnish on it was faded and the wood was pretty old. After all, it was wood and not steel. I started wondering if my chair would scoot around. I rocked sideways, ignoring the searing pain in my calf. I had to flex it to get the chair up on two legs, but then it came back down again on all fours with a bang, causing the scalpel to fall out and clang on the floor. Wasn't in too deep.

I waited.

Nothing.

Then there was a bang somewhere topside and the lights went out in my room.

I rocked again, this time throwing my upper torso into it and the momentum took me sideways. I lifted my head in the opposite direction of the fall and tightened up as best I could given the fact that I was so contorted…and the wooden desk part splintered into a mess of fire wood. My hands were free, but my back muscles would be feeling it tomorrow.

I still had the pieces of wood attached to my shackles, but I could move, and I immediately checked out my leg and felt like it wasn't all that bad, the wound more for pain than death. I was able to feel down to my bare feet and noticed that the shackles on my wrists and ankles were only held on with wing-nuts and after placing the scalpel in my mouth I unscrewed them with some difficulty in the dark. After I did this and my legs were free, I limped away just as the lights started to flicker on and off.

I went over to the glass window that was now darkened and wondered if Amy was alright, and that was when I heard someone outside the door shuffling around. I hobbled over to the door just on the hinge side and waited, scalpel at the ready. That little guy was going to be shorter when I got through with him.

Time to do what I do best.

The door opened slowly, and I held my breath. It was a bigger guy silhouetted by the hallway light, but I hid behind the door as he came in. As soon as I had my opening I put one forearm around his throat and my good leg in between his legs to hook his right foot in, slamming the door behind him. The scalpel went for his right ear and nicked it.

"You feel that?" I whispered. "You peep and it goes in your ear canal."

He did as he was told.

"Drop your weapon," I growled. "This thing wants to slice your throat open, pal."

He did as he was told. Smart one, this guy.

"Now. I'm gonna let you loose, and I don't want any trouble. If you're good, I'll let you live. If not, I will make it slow and painful."

He nodded, his breathing shallow and quivering somewhat. I slowly let him go, making sure to keep the scalpel close to his right eye so he could see it, the handle firmly grasped in my fist. I struck the goon at the base of the skull with my elbow enough for him to slump to the floor unconscious.

"Take a nap, bro," I grunted, flashing the scalpel. It still had my blood on it.

I stood sideways toward the door and undid the latch. The door swung open, and there stood Amy, her face white with terror. Standing behind her was the little runt who had tortured me and he had a small pistol pressed directly at Amy's left temple.

"Drop the gun if you know what's good for you," I growled.

"I don't think you have any room to negotiate, Gideon," said the little weasel quietly. "I seem to be holding all the cards."

"That's such a cliche thing to say, toad," I said, and that was when the lights winked out again.

I darted forward, and the gun went off. I could see the muzzle flash in the dark and it deafened me, a loud ringing sound. The bullet bounced and landed into someone because I heard a grunt. I grabbed at greasy hair and went to work with the scalpel. As the rat-man fell limp in my arms I could hear something soft and faint like shouting from a distance.

"Amy?" I said into the darkness. "Amy?"

No answer.

Kelly

I was only able to doze off for a while before someone was banging on the door of the officer's quarters. Mark went to the door. He was in the bathroom getting out of the shower and wore only a white towel as he answered the door.

The young man standing just outside in the hallway saluted and Mark told him "at ease". The young sailor stammered over his words a bit before speaking.

"Sir," said the young ensign. "Your presence is requested in engineering as soon as possible. There seems to be a problem with one of the cooling pumps on the compressor and..."

Mark put his hand up to stop the dark headed young man before he could finish his sentence.

"That will be all, ensign," said Mark, his voice taking on a strangely confident tone. "Wait outside and I will join you within moments. Radio down to engineering and tell them that I will be bringing a guest and that she is to be cleared to accompany me."

"Aye, sir," said the ensign. He saluted and darted off down the hallway outside and I could hear his boots thumping along as Mark shut the door.

"Guess I better get ready," he said sheepishly. "And maybe you should, too, Kelly. You're coming with me."

"What?" I asked, hoping the grimace on my face did not stun him too much. It didn't. He only smiled that gorgeous smile of his and returned to the bathroom.

I rose from the bed, pulled my hair back into a pony tail

and put my old clothes back on. Mark popped his head out of the bathroom. He had a toothbrush in his mouth. He started to say something, but it was blocked by the toothbrush. He removed it quickly, some toothpaste still on the corner of his mouth.

"You'll find a dress or two in the closet there," he said. "I had the ensign bring up some things while you slept. I asked around the female staff for any formal wear they might have on board and got lucky. I think they will suit you well. Had to guess at your size given what we had available."

He popped back into the bathroom and I moved to the closet to find some beautiful dresses — clean dresses! They were so colorful and wonderfully made and in several sizes. I found one — only one — in my size, but it was an adorable blue made of virgin wool. Even though it was a little shorter on the thigh than I was used to, it felt soft and sheer on my skin and smelled so much better than the clothes I had been wearing. I found some shoes as well, shoes that really didn't go with the dress because they were some of those slip on numbers like water shoes, but they did the trick. My feet thanked me.

In a few moments, Mark came out of the bathroom dressed in his dress uniform and tie, his jet black hair combed perfectly, his smile sending me into a dreamlike state.

"Shall we go?" he asked.

I did not say a word, but took his arm as we went out the door and down a few ladders and very steep stairs until we reached a doorway where two young men wearing black uniforms with black bullet proof vests, each carrying large shotguns, stood guard. When they saw us approaching, they turned to face each other, the doorway in the middle, and they opened it for us. We passed through without a word from them and on into another area that seemed to be warmer and more humid than the rest of the areas on the ship.

The room was full of energy and excitement as three men approached Mark all at once, each having something to say.

"Report," said Mark, his voice taking on a strange tone, one that I had not heard him speak so far.

"Sir," said a young woman, her olive skin glistening with sweat, goggles pushing her hair out of her face. She held a small box in her left hand with wires coming out of it. I did not recognize its purpose. "We discovered this on a water pipe just inside the main coupling on the condenser pump. It's filled with a shape charge designed to punch a hole in the coolant water feed line. There was another one on a power conduit just starboard of here, but it detonated before we could find it. Power was restored to that section of the ship in a matter of moments."

Mark took the device from her.

"This one has been deactivated?" he asked, turning the device over in his hands, examining it.

"Yes sir," said the woman, her eastern European accent coming through. "It appears that we have a mole in the organization. I recommend a full security lockdown immediately."

I suddenly realized that the three subordinates were looking directly at me. I smiled at them, but they didn't return the favor. Mark looked at me, smiled softly, and then turned to look at his people.

"I think that is a splendid idea," he said firmly, and I noted some sarcasm. "Perhaps we could question every person who works in engineering. Obviously *someone* knows something."

"Sir," said one of the others, a burly fellow who had a thick red beard. "We have monitored the security logs and have gone through the DVR system, but someone had access to the cameras in order to place the device, which means there had to be more than one infiltrator. We also think that the attack on the power conduit was a diversion to take out the cameras so that the saboteur could plant the shape charge on the more important target."

"Of course," said Mark, evenly, coldly. "I think we may have some kind of infiltrator on board, but this person is not working alone. I have someone in custody and am about to pay a visit to them to see what they know. Major Toht has been interrogating him and should have some answers when I arrive. Mayles, please take Miss Farmer here back to my quarters."

He turned and looked at me and took my hand, looking into my eyes.

"It won't be long now, Kelly," he said. "I will be with you shortly, and then we will be in New Jerusalem and we will have peace. No more war."

Mayles, a stern looking young man with a lantern jaw and flat top haircut took me by the arm and gently asked me to follow him. I obliged. When I finally reached Mark's quarters again and the door was shut behind me, I started thinking about the way Mark had referred to me: *Miss* Farmer.

I hadn't been a *Miss* for a very long time.

Miss Farmer.

It was Brooks anyway… Kelly Brooks. I was Kelly Brooks when my husband sat next to me in that bar in Coach's overlooking the Bricktown Ballpark in Oklahoma City and asked if the seat was taken. He had looked at me with those wonderful green eyes of his and smiled. He'd been on a particularly dangerous mission, a mission he could never talk about. He told me about it much later just before going off to fight in the war that claimed him.

I sat on the edge of the bed, this virgin wool dress not feeling so comfortable anymore. I squirmed out of it, put on my old clothes, the t-shirt Clark had bought for me so long ago. He had bought it to replace the soft cotton tee he accidentally spilled chocolate syrup on when he leaned in close to kiss me with his sundae in his hand.

I started crying again.

Howard

I stood next to Clayton as the people began to gather around him in prayer. The light emanating from the Spirit would have been blinding if the humans would have been able to see it. They were praying much like the saints in China used to do, all of them voicing prayer all at once, their voices sounding to the untrained ear like a cacophony of rabble, but in actuality it was all being deciphered and translated into perfection before reaching the Throne.

It always amazed me. I was so taken with it that I almost missed the sound of footsteps next to me as Gabe appeared, still glowing from being in the presence of the Throne, his heart heavy with news from the mouth of He Who Created the Universe.

It was not the best news, but the plan must be followed.

"These next actions are not to be interrupted," he said, his deep blue eyes looking into mine. "It is to be done, and we must not intervene. It has been ordained."

"A test," I managed. "A test of their resolve...their faith."

"Indeed," said Gabe, his voice lowering. "The faith that He gives that is reciprocated back to Him. A mystery."

We both knew how to wait, to obey while saints were tested. We had done this countless times, watching as children of God were set upon by the enemy yet we were told to stay at the ready just as human armies are often ordered to do when the strategy calls for them to "stand down."

It did not mean that we liked doing this. It was difficult to wait and watch as believers went through horrible things

all as a test of their faith, but we knew as seen many times
before, that this test caused something to break within the
believer and they came out stronger on the other side of it…
or they are claimed by the enemy for a time. Sometimes we
found that they were never really serious about their
commitment in the first place.

Life for these humans was indeed a threshing floor.

We watched as the enemy began to fill the room,
surrounding the shining group of saints who prayed and
prayed, who voiced their concerns, and there stood Ethan at
the front of them, possessed by the demon Morax, my
former brother's twisted shape fading in and out behind the
human's face.

He winked at me, and I could only scowl.

Mark

In the somewhat deserted hallway just outside the two interrogation rooms I noticed someone slumped in the floor with their left shoulder propped up against the wall, their hands and feet splayed out in every direction, chin against chest, and I realized it was Major Toht.

Blood pooled out around the dobber's gangly body.

I had given him the simple task of interrogating the prisoners, of testing the subject to see if he would be a worthy candidate for Lord Asher's plan, but Toht had taken to his usual theatrics. His bungling had not only claimed his life, but it looked like the life of the one female guard I trusted, a strong German woman who had been at my side through the thick of the early days of Lord Asher's rise to power.

Bile rose in my throat.

"What happened here?" I asked to no one in particular. The private snapped to attention near me, rubbing the back of his head, and stated the obvious, for which I gave him the worst tongue lashing before ordering him to start cleaning up the mess. Gerta, not dead after all but bleeding from her side, grunted something and then started rising to her feet. I kicked them out from under her and she went down with a satisfying plop.

"I am sorry, Magistrate," she pleaded, rolling over and raising her hand in defense, her other hand holding her side, her eyes filling with unforgivable tears. "I don't know what happened. I was overcome."

"You?" I mocked. "Overcome? Gerta, an earth mover

couldn't overwhelm you. Now get up and help dispose of poor Major Toht."

She rose, coughing, holding her superficial wound, ducked as if I were planning to hit her again, and went to work beside the private. They each took an end of the unfortunate and clumsy Major and carried him away, his head lolling backward in a rather unnatural manner, and for some reason it was only now that I noticed that the private was barefooted.

It would only be a matter of time before the two prisoners were found. I was certain of that. I pulled my handheld from my pocket and clicked the receiver a few times. Mechanically, the voice of Captain DeWalt answered with robotic precision.

"Two young traitors have escaped our interrogation room. One is a young woman, long red hair, the other a young man with a mop of dark hair wearing military fatigues of American design. They probably are making their way to a lifeboat. Send a search party immediately. Find them, Captain, or I will find a use for you that is messy and unpleasant."

"Yes sir," came the dutiful Captain's gravelly voice. "Consider it done."

I hated when they said that. When they failed it made for such a waste of words. I clicked twice on the receiver button and put the communicator back in my pocket. Stepping over the pool of blood in the floor, I decided to ascend to the conn and see first hand the workings of this crew.

I was determined to find these terrorists. Asher's plan would not fail, however ill advised or strange. I had to trust him. Our safety and security depended on it. I would not fail Asher.

Ethan

I walked into the holding area where everyone was huddled together like cattle. They all were standing around Clayton, him leading them in prayer. I fingered the trigger of my rifle. I smelled their fear and it was like warm spun sugar. Our men circled in, all of them ready, all of them on orders to do what was necessary.

The people were singing and it hurt my ears. I couldn't stand it, as if the words they were singing were trying to push me back through the wall. I resisted. I was after Clayton, wasn't going to back down until I had him at the end of my gun. He stood in the center with his stupid wooden staff and his preachy voice and his hot, burning face turning to look at me.

He knew.

He saw me right through the crowd of soldiers, and his gaze was hot and burned me but I moved on.

"Come with me," I said. "You must come with me."

And the people around him got those puzzled looks I'd seen a lot in my life and they clawed at him with their useless hands and they said whiny things like "why?" and "why him?" and "what has he done?"

"It is ordered," I lied. "It is ordered by the…" I hesitated and then found the words "…the regional government of New Jerusalem. He is only wanted for questioning, that is all. His friends have been arrested for terrorist activities."

Clayton raised his hands, holding the stick in one fist.

"I will go with them," he said, so calm, so uncannily calm.

His calm gave me chills of rage.

All of the sheep wondered why as Clayton was led away from them, and I fingered my trigger again, so glad I was getting to finish the job I wanted to do in the galley not long ago. Oh how I wanted to kill him here, but not here…not here… I wondered if the preacher boy knew what would happen.

He was somehow dangerous. I resolved to watch him closely. I listened to his every word, watched his every move.

I felt like I was being pushed onward by something I couldn't explain, and I liked it. I ate it up. Something powerful coursed through my veins.

If I took him up to the deck and shoved my rifle barrel in his face, would he give up? Would he get all weak kneed like all the others, like the farmer who took me in before I took his life?

I could still see the farmer's eyes tearing up as he knelt before me.

I'd see to it that Clayton shared the same fate.

Gideon

"If I remember right, it's down here," I whispered.

I remember thinking this would all be a lot easier if Amy knew basic tactical hand signals. I figured I'd probably have to just take what I could get with her, but she was sticking close to me, probably the safest thing to do. I could hear her breathing more and more as it shook out of her lungs, and sometimes she'd just bury her face in my chest when we stopped to wait for guards to stroll by in the dim hallways. The interrogation messed her up pretty bad, but I used it, let it create adrenaline.

We stopped somewhere safe where we could rest, in between watching for the rent-a-thugs to roll by, and that was when she asked me a question I couldn't answer.

"What about Anya?"

I stood there in the dark, trying not to look away from those green eyes of hers, but all I could see was the unkempt edges of her red hair backlit by a security light. For some reason the ship was conserving power, and I couldn't figure that one out at all. I decided to reassure her a bit. Had to keep her going or we were both dead. Anya was safe with Clayton. He'd take care of her now. Me and Amy were headed down a dark road, one that little Anya could not walk.

"I'm sure Clayton will keep her safe," I lied. I really didn't know, and I had to keep her on the move or we'd be found and I liked my toes right where they were — shoved into that rent-a-cop's boots. They hurt my feet (and my wound) something fierce, but I wasn't going to let on.

Couldn't help the limp, though.

We took the opportunity of quiet to move a little further down the hallway.

When I was a teen, my Dad flew me out to San Diego, to Coronado Island, where I got to tour this very boat with a large group of gawking teachers and parents. I was under the care of a boatswain's mate who owed my Dad a favor and who took me on a grand tour, all cleared by the Captain of course. It had come in pretty handy for our current purposes once I got on board and found out that the people in charge weren't really all that friendly. The plan was to make it to a life raft and then find a way to shore. I figured we were close enough to land that we could probably make it if we used the stars…if we could see the stars. Otherwise I'd figure it out.

Survive at any cost. That was my motto, and it had kept me alive.

I pulled Amy down the hallway, through some bulkhead doors that had been left open, and once we were in another utility closet, I closed the door until just a crack was open so I could see outside. I heard footsteps again and this time there were more than just two. For whatever reason, Amy decided this was time to bother me about stuff I couldn't change.

"I really want to go back for her," she whispered into the dark humid air. "I'm worried about her, Gideon. If we can get to just outside the hangar bay, I'm sure…"

I reached out and touched Amy's face intending to put my hand over her mouth. She got the idea and stopped her mouth from moving just as three guards came around the corner and started down toward our position, flashlights shining around the walls and floors. They didn't talk, but their boots tap-tap-tapped away on the hard floor and I got the scalpel ready. If they came in here, they were going to get the business end of a bad decision. Wasn't about to use the little weasel's pistol shoved in my waistband. Too loud.

The soldiers stopped just outside the door and one of them started barking orders.

"You two check down there," said an older one. He sounded like he'd had some experience. I so wanted the other two to stay. At least the noobs would be more easy to take down if something went south.

"Yes, sir," said the both of them in tandem, and they stalked off the way they were going, leaving the older guy, the more experienced guy. I hoped he wouldn't hear us breathe, hoped his ears weren't as sharp as they used to be.

The old guy stood out there and I dared not look at him through the crack in the door. He was just on the other side of it, and I could hear his feet shuffling, clearing his throat. His flashlight shone around the hallway, a white splash of light that lit up every corner bolt and hinge until he shined the light across a reflective surface.

The door to the head across the hall was open and there was a mirror on the wall over a sink, reflecting back the light on my eyes. I blinked, and before I could do anything the old guy flung the door open behind him and he was on me.

I shot out a string of sailor words as we hit the floor, and the old guy was pretty tough, 'cause I had jabbed the scalpel in his ribcage as soon as he tackled me to the floor, but he was still giving it the old college try. He grunted, and in the darkness I hoped that Amy was doing something constructive, but she wasn't. I could hear her high pitched wheezing breath from somewhere to my left, so I figured it was up to me, but this old guy was like an anvil sitting on my chest. The useless gun dug into the small of my back between me and the floor.

For some weird reason I started thinking about the wrestling matches with my Dad, and could hear his voice in my ear, whispering through the sweat and the blood, saying I wasn't cut out for the real game. It made me fight harder. It made me roll the old dude over onto the scalpel and let it drive up deeper into his lung until he coughed and spattered something wet and warm on the floor.

He lost his grip, and I spun over on him just before something whacked me on the back of the head. I saw stars, but then Amy was pulling me up saying she was sorry, sorry, sorry.

"I couldn't see," she confessed. "You both looked the same in the dark."

"That's alright," I managed, wincing, wondering what she had used on me that hurt so bad, but then not caring. "We better get going. Those guys'll be back soon and we don't want to be around."

"What about him?" she asked, gesturing at the old soldier. "Won't they know we were here?"

"They know we are here," I told her, trying to smile, and I could taste blood on my teeth. "We better beat it to the life raft. There's no going back for anybody. She'll be safe, a lot safer than with us on the run."

"I know," said Amy, her voice shaky in the near-dark. "I just have to have faith about that, I guess. Clayton is so right."

We snuck out of the door and down the hallway in the

opposite direction that the guards went. I tried to remember which way to the life rafts, and the intersection ahead looked very familiar. It wouldn't be long now and we'd be home free. Getting the life raft down and into the water would take a distraction. I thought I'd figure that out when I got there. There might be something to this faith stuff after all.

"Amy," I whispered. "If we get out of this, you have to tell me more about what Clayton knows about God."

She didn't say anything, but took my hand as we shuffled down the dark hallway.

What I saw on the deck made me wish for a miracle.

Clayton

"Step along over there," said Ethan, his eyes fixed on me as if he were one of them hypnotized fools at the fair. I knew what was up with him, that he weren't quite himself, but I figured it was all part of the plan.

I did what I was told, followin' the orders and going out in front with my hands over my head. I held on to the hickory stick for good measure, and guessed it wouldn't do much as a weapon against them guns, but then again, my weapons are not forged from metal or wood or anythin' a person can really see.

We walked out onto the flight deck of the old Ronald Reagan after a long climb up some stairs that were mostly like a bunch of ladders. Ethan told them guys to wait just inside the door of the exit onto the flight deck while he "interrogated the prisoner." Things was gettin' bad in a hurry and I was on the business end of Ethan's gun which didn't feel very good pressed into my back. When I looked back at him he had a desperate look in his eye like some guy who'd run out of options, but I knew who was really in charge, and knew that if I was going to get out of this it was gonna be God and no one else who did it. Out of the corner of my eye I could see the lights of a city a ways off along a shoreline, so I wondered absently if we was nearin' our destination.

"Get out to the edge of the deck, Clayton," said Ethan, and I could hear somethin' growlin' behind that thick Yankee accent of his. It was angry and feral, like some kind of monster. I could see somethin' under his skin, livin' in there, just wantin' to bust out, but I wasn't afraid of it.

I backed up until I could see the railin' just behind me in the twilight of the mornin'. Sun'd be comin' up in a bit I figured. At least the storm had let up.

"You guys left me there," Ethan grunted, his teeth grittin' and grindin'. "You left me on the shore to rot while you rode off without me."

"I didn't know you was there, Ethan," I said as calm as I could. "If I would have known I would have stopped to get ya, I promise."

I noticed the end of that machine gun of his had a special barrel that was long like a smooth black metal pipe with a little hole in the end where the bullets would fly out without much sound. His intentions were purt near known to me at that point. I just closed my eyes and started prayin' hard, askin' for whatever I was gonna get that it would be quick, that God would take care of little Anya and Amy and Gideon and all the rest of the innocent people God had put in my care.

Just then I had a thought that ever'body visits a funeral at some time in their lives and that was just natural.

A thump shook the deck platin' under my feet, and then the sirens started goin' off, and even though the other guards started scramblin' around Ethan didn't pay it no mind, just stared at me with that crazy look of his.

It was at that moment that some things were revealed to me in such a way that can't right be explained with any amount of words. I felt the barrel of that gun press up against my breastbone. The deck, bein' wet and all, slipped away beneath my feet and I fell backwards over the rail, my shoes squeakin', the hickory stick thwackin' on the metal railin' makin' a loud ringin' sound. I heard the gun go off, a surprisingly pretty noise like a bird chirpin', and then came a far off scream of someone who sounded familiar.

I felt like I was fallin' just like in a crazy dream, and when my eyes opened, all I could see was black.

A m y

There was a loud thump somewhere in the ship, and the guards standing near the life boats ran off to the left. Sirens began to wail. Gideon chuckled a bit, putting one finger to his temple and tapping gently. He said that Austin probably just launched his first offensive.

Gideon ran over to a large object wrapped in a tarp and pulled a lever that released an inflatable boat that was long and black. It fell over the side and hit the ocean below. He told me that he would jump first, and once he made it in I was to dive in after him feet first, crossing my arms in front of my chest. I was shaking all over, thinking about Anya, thinking about Clayton, my teeth chattering due to the sudden coolness of the sea air. Wherever we were, the sun was just coming up and I could see far away the outline of a city along the shore, the skyline a jagged hazy shape on the horizon.

Just before Gideon jumped, I heard another loud thump deep within the boat, and it seemed that the alarms got louder, a whine that sounded like one of those air raid sirens you hear in the movies. All Gideon could say was "there's our diversion" before he jumped overboard, following the inflatable boat to the dark sea below. I couldn't see him splash down, or hear him, but I just had to go on faith and follow after.

Right before I was about to jump, I looked up along the long deck railing along the side of the ship and saw two figures in silhouette, one of them pointing what looked like a rifle at another, and the other person carrying the unmistakable shape of Clayton's hickory walking stick. He held it in the air above his head, and then he slipped, and I screamed as Clayton fell end over end through the air and into the blackness.

I couldn't move.

The sound of the alarms echoed in my ears as I stood near the railing and watched as the figure who pushed Clayton fired his weapon, causing a bright yellow burst to light up his features. I couldn't see him clearly, but he wore a uniform, one of the uniforms of the guards. I hurled myself over the railing, putting my hands over my chest in a cross pattern and stiffening up my legs, pointing my toes, all the while thinking of Anya and what might happen to her.

I'll have to go back for her. I…and the water took me, the cold, black water. Then I was struggling to breathe, kicking hard to the surface, wondering where Gideon was, wondering if he had made it.

A hand grabbed my arm and then shot around my rib cage.

"Clayton?" I gasped.

But it was Gideon, pulling me toward the inflatable boat, then into its safe, somewhat dry interior, where I lay on the bottom as Gideon paddled with the oars, paddling away from the dark, hulking shape of the U.S.S. Ronald Reagan. A fire burned on the other side of the ship, and I could see the yellow caps on the reflective waves as we rowed away into the darkness.

I mumbled Anya and Clayton's names as the burning sun peeked above the waves to the east.

Book III:
Babylon
the Great

Kashif

It was very hard for my family.

I had heard that there was a new city in the east that could provide shelter and food for all of us, but the way was hard, and the sun was, lately, much more hot and oppressive since the veil that covered the sky had lifted. Not only that, we had heard about the horrors that the war had brought upon the people of this region. So many had returned with horrible burns and sickness beyond what my nightmares could conjure.

One of them was my brother Hassan.

He came to us after the war had ended, and we were so excited that he had returned to us, but he was not well. He was riding a sickly camel which collapsed not far from our little farm. My mother and sisters ran to help him, and he called for water, his face covered with scars and blisters, his clothing charred and burned.

We cared for him as best we could, but it was not the burns that claimed him. His thick, course hair fell out in clumps in my hand and then came his teeth. My strong, handsome brother had been reduced to a frail old man, his eyes blinded by the sun, his skin scarred from the heat flash of a terrible weapon.

We buried him in the sand.

Mother felt that Hassan had brought something with him on the wind, for something in the air began killing our goats one by one, and soon our food source dried up like a puddle of mud in the desert. We heard that there was help near the mouth of the Nile and after much debate, made the journey,

my mother being carried most of the way on a cart we used
for transporting grain. My two young sisters dressed as
men, leading us along. We covered their faces with scarves
so as to hide their beauty.

My family and I had found our way to our ancestral
lands, the lands of the Ja'alin which lay on the sea shore near
the Nile river valley. The cities had been laid waste, the war
consuming all things that would be called civilization in a
great conflict that lasted for over a year. Old machines of
war lay scattered around, some of them covered with
blowing sand, their hard metal hulls smelling of sulfur and
death. We hid, mostly, trying to stay away from the deadly
gangs of bandits. I could not bear to lose any more of my
family. I vowed to keep them safe, somehow, even if the
world was dark to me, but that vow became a curse.

We found shelter near the Nile river in a small village,
but soon the people began to bicker and argue over who
should eat and who should be sent away and my family,
being new to the group, were told to leave. I could not bear
the thought of spending one more day in the desert, of
becoming a mound of sand like my brother Hassan. I stood
my ground, arguing with the old men who would force my
family to die in the desert, and when one of the elders
offered a compromise by saying he wanted to violate my
sisters, I ran at him, and in the struggle, lost the rest of my
family.

That seemed like so long ago.

I could smell meat cooking somewhere near me, and the
hot desert sun beat down on my skin. I felt around on the
ground and found my small burlap sack with my few
crumbs of bread stored away inside. I was so hungry. I

licked my blistered lips and scooted back across the dirt until I felt the wall behind me again. I held out my hand.

"Please," I said. "Please I am so hungry."

I heard laughter and muttering somewhere in front of me but could not see through the cloud of darkness that had been my vision since birth. I heard someone speaking another language, a language that sounded like English and then I heard footsteps approaching toward me across the hard, gravelly ground.

I felt warmth as a hand was placed on my shoulder, and I cringed away from it only to hear a calm voice speaking Farsi.

"Do you want to see again?" he asked. I normally would have shoved him away, but somehow I felt safe.

"I want to eat," I said. "Please, can you help me?"

I felt a hand on my wrist, and then something was placed on my palm, a metal dish holding something soft, warm and greasy. I could smell the mutton, seasoned perfectly and roasted over a fire. I began to eat. Oh, it tasted so good. I thought of my mother then and the tears began to fall down my face.

"Thank you," I said, my mouth full of mutton, nearly choking on it and I felt the hand pat my back.

"You are welcome," said the voice. "Do you want to see again?"

"I do not understand," I managed, my hands trembling as I ate the delicious meat. "How? There is no *again* for I have been blind since birth."

"I was told to help you, that you would be my guide in this place," said the voice, his Farsi having a strange accent I could not place. "But you are blind and Isa wants to make you see, to prove to you that he is who he said he was."

"Isa?" I asked. "Has Isa spoken to you? I do not understand."

"Do you want to see?" said the voice with a slight laugh, a laugh like my mother would utter when I was a small boy and did not understand her. "All I want to know is do you believe that Isa can make you see?"

"Isa did many wonders," I said. "Perhaps he could do that if he wished. I do wish to see again, but I do not know if Isa can do that."

"Isa has brought me here to you from far away, and I have much to do in his name. Will you help me?"

"I cannot. I cannot help you because I am blind and a beggar."

"Do you wish to see?"

"Now you are mocking me. Of course I wish to see. Why do you mock a blind man? You are cruel and should be punished."

"The forty ninth verse of Imran says that Isa can bring the dead to life."

"I suppose it says that," I growled. "What does that have to do with me?"

"If he can bring the dead to life, then surely your sight is a small matter."

I heard his voice raise above where I was sitting, so I stood now, bracing myself against a wall, my legs shaking with fatigue and lack of nutrition. I reached out and touched his shoulder and he did not pull away.

"I must believe the Holy Quran," I said. "If it says this, then I must believe it."

The man did not speak, and I felt his hand touch my

wrist again, but he was gentle, holding me slightly and I could feel him moving, could sense his face close to mine.

"Then believe that Isa can heal your eyes and he will do so. It is the first of your tests today."

I do not know what happened then inside my mind. I suddenly wanted to see, all of the memories of being teased as a child, treated unfairly by others, having to live with my mother for all of my life, my sisters tending to me, my anger at the universe for making me this way. All of it faded away. I wanted to see, and if Isa could provide that for me I would believe. I would believe that Isa could do that.

"I want to believe that Isa can heal me," I told the stranger. "Can he?"

"If you believe on him, he can do much more than that."

I hesitated, and I felt as if I would fall down from fatigue, but somehow the strength of the stranger held me fast, would not allow me to fall.

"I believe," I said, trusting only a little that it would work.

I felt the stranger take my hand from his shoulder and hold it gently, and then I felt him reach along my arm and place something soft and wet in my other hand. I knew right away what it was.

It was mud.

"Put this on your eyes and go and wash in that pool over there. I will guide you."

I laughed, but that little grain of faith that I had in what he said did not falter, for I was desperate for something real. I was desperate to see, and somehow I knew it would work.

I was led to the pool, and with my hand I smeared the mud on my eyes, feeling it burn as the grainy, fine sand scratched at my eyelids. The stranger placed my hand in the water and I washed the mud from my fingers, listening as the people around us began to laugh at what they rightly saw as foolishness.

As if in defiance, I plunged my face into the water, feeling the coolness of it washing over my skin, soothing my cracked lips and blistered flesh. I rubbed my eyes twice before someone pulled me out of it, complaining that I was contaminating the drinking water.

And that was when I opened my eyes and saw a round man with a grizzled beard and a wide brim hat staring at me. His bushy eyebrows were angled down in the middle, but I could not read his expression.

He backed away from me just as all the others near me were doing, all of them not speaking, a few of them muttering to one another about something I could not hear.

Only one person stood close to me, holding my hand, and that was a white man with lighter colored hair than everyone else, eyes like the color of the water and strange clothes.

"Clayton Delroy," said the stranger, shaking my hand. "I'm glad you can finally see me."

Amy

I had to reach up to pull my eyelids apart and my tongue was a roll of sand paper. Gideon was slouching sideways in the raft, his lips all cracked and blistered from the horrible sun that beat down on us every day. I guessed that whatever the meteor had kicked up had finally fallen to earth.

We had been afloat for a while, our strength giving out after some kind of weird current pulled us out further to sea. The waves were barely choppy but the constant rocking and swaying of the raft made me want to hurl, and there was a smell in the air that caused me to think about rotting fish and disgusting sea life.

"Do you think we will find land soon?" I asked Gideon, my voice cracking in my throat as I swallowed more dry air.

"I don't know," he managed, almost a whisper. "I think if we hold out one more day we might see a bird or something and that might give us a direction to follow."

I lay back against the soft, inflated black rubber of the boat and listened to the water lapping the side. If only we could get some shade or a rain cloud or something. It was just unbearable. For some bizarro reason I kept thinking about some story I'd read in high school about a Spanish conquistador who landed with three hundred men in Florida only to stagger into Mexico City some twenty years later with only one faithful companion.

I guess that would be me and Gideon…if we made it.

Just then Gideon moaned something, and I opened my eyes to see him pointing a drooping finger off in the distance. I raised up enough to see the long blue green horizon of water before us and off in the distance a small speck of something bobbing up and down in the air. It got closer, and the little black blob looked like it was wobbling in the air, a small football of a thing.

It was a bird. A precious, wayward little bird.

Gideon mumbled something that sounded like the words "let's row", and that was all I needed to motivate my action. I pulled on that oar like there was a midnight sale at Abercrombie, moving that boat toward where the bird was headed.

There had to be land where it was going.

We rowed on until we couldn't move our arms, which in our sapped out condition didn't take that long. Soon that hell-spot of a sun went down and it got really dark, the stars winking on and off as if to mock us that the bird had gone. We really had no hope of catching it, but Gideon said that it should be heading toward land. He charted the stars, and I dozed off while he tried to row the boat toward that star he'd marked.

It seemed like moments and he was waking me, shaking my shoulder and sounding all frantic. I opened my eyes with some difficulty again and he was smiling at me with his yellowing teeth and his cracked lips splitting open...but he was all jazzed about something.

I sat up in the boat and saw that we had run aground in the night and there before us lay mound after mound of sand, huge dunes that stretched off over the horizon, and the brutal sun rising up behind them.

"Water?" I asked, the physical taking over the desires of my heart.

"No," Gideon said, shaking his head sadly. "I didn't find any water, but we found land. There has to be a settlement near here or something...there just has to be."

If there was one thing Gideon was, it was Captain Optimism. I don't know how, but it seemed like he had just taken one of those five hour energy drinks. He was all bouncy and full of life, pulling me out of the boat and onto the shore. It took me a second to stand up without falling over, but I got the hang of walking on solid ground again with Gideon's help, wobbling around like a toddler learning to walk.

"Looks like we've come from one wet hell to a very dry one," I said, my voice cracking. "Now what?"

Gideon started to smile, but then looked past me at the top of the hill, the joy draining out of his face.

Five soldiers stood on top of the dunes, staring down at us like a pack of wolves.

Howard

I found Clayton and his new friend Kashif just outside a small village on the northern coast of Africa, somewhere near what was left of Cairo. They were talking to one another not in English but in Farsi, and for someone who had never taken a class in the language, Clayton was doing an amazing job of speaking to his new friend.

It was the Spirit.

Clayton had been transformed a little over a year ago, but the recent events of his life had pushed him over the edge of something that could not be explained by even those humans who would consider themselves extremely religious. Clayton had found the key to the relationship, something that those of my kind marveled about, but could never fully understand. His fall into the sea had been a baptism of sorts, and now he was renewed, moving in a straight line toward the Father's mission for him. I hadn't seen a human behave in this manner in a long time. For a time that was undetermined, The Most High had broken the barrier of language for His own purposes.

"Can you speak English?" asked Clayton with a smile.

"Only little," Kashif responded, crouching, looking at his hands, bending to take a handful of sand and examine it. "I can speak…understand some. Do you wish to speak in English?"

"Well," Clayton said, seeming visibly tired. "I suppose I'd prolly prefer that. B'sides. I don't know how long I can keep this up. It's like the knowledge is leakin' outta me like a sieve."

The Egyptian scratched his head and looked hard at Clayton, looked at the hickory staff he carried, and smiled.

"I can be guide for you? I speak languages you do not, yes?"

"That's pretty much the idea…why I'm here…why Isa led me to you. I know the way…I just need…help."

The two of them stood there looking at one another as strangers walked cautiously around them, some of them staring at the man who had been given back his sight. An elderly woman approached them wearing a black dress that covered everything except her hands and wrinkled face. She handed them a small bag with provisions inside and a canteen of water.

"Itfaddel," she said, her voice soft with a little nervous laugh, her eyes bright.

Clayton took the bag and the canteen and thanked the woman, bowing slightly to her. It filled me with wonder to see how the Spirit could bridge cultural and language boundaries. I knew then that the purpose must be very dire.

"Where we go?" asked Kashif, his heart ready to repay this young man who had given him sight, not realizing yet that Clayton had nothing to do with it.

"Well," said Clayton, hesitating somewhat. "We're supposed to head to New Jerusalem."

All of the chatter around them suddenly stopped at those words as if Clayton had said something horribly offensive. In seconds some of the older men in the crowd began to mutter words of fear and foreboding. One of them, a frail looking man, his skin dark from a lifetime of toiling in the sun, his beard long and white, his teeth nearly gone, darted out of the crowd to hold out his hands in a pleading gesture.

"Please," he said in Farsi. "Do not leave us. Stay and live in peace."

Clayton held out his hand and took the hand of the elder, and the elder smiled, holding fast to Clayton. Apparently Clayton had lost the ability to understand Farsi.

"He wants you stay with them," said Kashif, translating. "They want you help their sick...ones."

"I'm sorry," said Clayton, placing a hand on the elder's shoulder, tears suddenly forming in his eyes, his compassion for these hurting people evident. "I hafta go. I have a mission to get on with down the road and I need you to go with me, Kashif."

"You gave eyes to me," said the young Egyptian. "I follow you anywhere."

"Not me," Clayton said softly. "Not me."

Clayton waved at the people as the two of them gathered up bedrolls and the small supply bag and canteen and started off toward the East. They did not carry weapons or goods, only what would sustain them for the journey, and soon the calls of the villagers grew ever faint, blending in with the sound of the wind blowing across the desert.

Gideon

These guys were heavy operators, for sure. I noticed at least three autos and the rest had the usual bladed weapons. They all wore ratted out desert camo, turbans, had full beards, but the beards weren't your usual black and silver of the native variety.

These guys were warmongers. From Europe or hopefully the good old U.S. of A, but then again...

I pulled a handkerchief from my back pocket I keep for such occasions and waved it around. It used to be really white, but I'd used it for a tourniquet once and had blown whatever cold germs into it and hadn't had the time nor the means to wash it. I hoped it was white enough for a surrender flag.

Two guys started down the dune, their booted feet making little flows of sand that poured down and made me think of water. I saw a canteen swinging back and forth on a belt on one of them. Mostly I just saw the big guns they carried. Standard issue G.I.

I let out a breath, but then...

"You two look tired," one of the men said, his teeth inside that grizzled beard something of a forgotten enterprise. "Where did you come from?"

Yep. Americans.

They stopped at twenty paces, guns slung over shoulders but cradling them in ready position. I decided to make my intentions known.

"Ship wrecked on it's way to New Jerusalem," I said, hands out in front, palms facing them. "We're lucky to be alive."

I think I said something wrong because both their faces hardened. They were already pretty hardened but something I said caused them to go all steely and get the thousand yard stare.

"No, no, no," said Amy stepping forward and waving her hand at me like I was a little child. "We didn't want to go to that city. The place is all creepy weird. I have no intention of going there at all."

"Looks like you two are at odds," said the other man, his gun relaxing a little. "So which is it? You two headed for New Jerusalem or not?"

There was a long pause, us standing there listening to the waves slapping the beach. I wished Amy would have just kept quiet. Didn't know what answer would get us killed or get us safe.

"We'll let you talk to the Colonel," said the first. "He usually has a way of sorting things out."

With that, they got real with the weapons and held them on us, marching us up the sand dune to the top. It took a bit of work after sitting in that raft for so long, but when we crested the dune we saw a small camp made up of desert brown tents, a few burned out Chenowth Scorpion dune buggies, all sitting around the blackened hulk of an old Abrams. The tank was missing its turret and had long been left for dead. Someone had mounted a fifty cal on top of it and surrounded that with sand bags. One bearded guy wearing a tan tactical helmet and goggles spun to face us and then aimed the fifty directly at my head.

I smiled at him, keeping my hands up, but he didn't smile back. Not a good sign.

We were led to a tent on the outside edge of the camp where a short old soldier, a block of steel with a tattered Marine Corps flat top hat, stood with his hands on his hips, smoking a fat cigar.

Where on earth did he get one of—

"Colonel Snyder," came his gravelly voice. He stuck out his hand and I hesitantly shook it. "Seems you washed ashore right near my bivouac. Would you like to tell me the truth now, or wait until I beat it out of you later? Your choice."

The old guy squinted his eyes, and that was when I noticed the horrific scar across his left cheek. Looked like he'd spent some ugly and lonely days without a corpsman. I decided to weigh my options.

"My name is Gideon," I said firmly. "This is Amy. We escaped from the Reagan just a few days ago and managed to make it to shore and keep our pride, but we really just need water and some food if you could spare it and we'll be on our way."

He looked at me again, his steely eyes studying me, and I put my hands back up as he came uncomfortably close.

He laughed, a sort of grunting, growling laugh.

"You two don't look like much of a threat, and you aren't local by any means. Seems to me you two are lost."

I thought about the militia I'd eluded for years in the U.S., how many close shaves I'd had when on my own, but now I had Amy to worry about. I started thinking about a way to get us out of here, but nothing came to mind. I stood still, for the first time in my life with nothing to say in answer to a possible threat.

Colonel Snyder then broke, his face cracking open in a

laugh that thundered across the dunes.

"I'm just funning with you, son," he laughed, his cigar chomping in the corner of his jaw. "We Americans must stick together. I have given up all hope of seeing my beloved country. It has been a most brutal time, my young boy. There are not words to express my grief over the loss of my armies. What you see before you is all that is left of my proud devil dogs. We refuse to give in to the power to the east. It is out of principle."

Amy smiled at the old man and he took her hand gently, and in an old world way planted a kiss on her knuckles like some old general from the civil war.

"Sergeant," grunted Snyder. "Gather what provisions we can spare and help these two to a meal. It is good to have guests who are not trying to erase us from the earth."

"Aye, sir," said one of our bearded escorts. "Right away."

"Oorah!" growled the Colonel and he stooped to go back into his tent and sit on a metal foot locker, pull out a pistol he had holstered and proceed to take it apart and clean it.

I wondered what we would have to do to repay these men as I was led to another tent which sheltered us from the blistering sun, and was served a type of meat I did not recognize and luke-warm water from a filter canteen. The soldier who slopped the provisions on our small metal plates did not seem too bothered that we were eating their food, but the other soldiers seemed to be avoiding us.

While we ate, a man with large goggles strapped atop his bushy head approached us with a small medical kit. He wanted to check us out "for health reasons", and proceeded to draw a little blood from us. I let him simply because I was so tired. Amy was a little freaked out by it, but went through with it once she saw that the needles were sterile and in their own little blister packs.

After dinner, Amy and I were then led to another tent where we were allowed to use two cots that were set up for us. There were torn and well used sleeping bags but we slept on top of them until the sun went down and the desert became cold.

In the dark, I could hear Amy's chattering teeth and when I asked her if she was cold, she darted over to me, climbed onto the cot beside me and I put my arms around her for warmth. There was nothing romantic about it at all, only necessity to keep from freezing.

Any use of feelings at this point would only complicate things.

Kelly

We disembarked from the U.S.S. Ronald Reagan with some fanfare. It had limped into the port after the attack, and we were all glad to finally place our feet on solid ground. The ship had been making some awful sounds, and for a time had been taking on water, but the engineers managed to salvage her dignity.

There were people of all nations at the port, a sea of faces arriving to greet us and welcome us to New Jerusalem. I had watched some of the early fighting of the war on television and on the internet until it all went down. I had never been to Israel, but I had heard that most of the cities, most of the bigger ones, had been leveled.

They started grouping us together by age, the parentless children like Anya being gathered together by a young woman with a soft voice who looked everything like a preschool teacher, but who wore a black uniform with a black cap. I watched Anya go with her new little friends, and assumed that she would find happiness finally. I hoped she would be adopted by good parents. I was grouped in with the adults, a very large group, but soon I was being shuffled around by more official looking people, and they seemed to know me by name. I didn't see the elderly people being grouped together, but then the crowd was so large that I couldn't see much but what was immediately around me.

The docks in the harbor were made from something resembling concrete and there were shiny metal railings everywhere. The city beyond that was massive and resembled many of the port cities I had visited in my lifetime and on vacations with my husband. There were larger skyscrapers toward the center of the city, with massive cranes standing near the skeletal structures of others being built, and all of them made from what looked like gold frosted glass. Some kind of gigantic, thick cables stretched up into the sky in several places all around the city, their movement barely visible. I could not see where they went, and shielded my eyes from the burning sun to follow them but they disappeared into the haze.

It was so strange to see things entirely new. Not broken, dirty or burned.

"How are you?" asked Mark, his accent so lovely. "Taking it all in?"

"How did you manage to build all this?" I asked, my voice cracking.

"In due time," he smiled. "I will take you on a full tour soon. Today you will be taken to your living quarters. I have arranged for you to stay in my building near the center of the city, near the old temple mount. I hope you will enjoy your new home."

I couldn't really say anything. I only nodded and he took my hand, leading me down the stairs to the docks, surrounded by thousands of others who were leaving our seven day home on the Ronald Reagan. The air smelled clean and somewhere there were flowers releasing their fragrance on the wind.

At the end of the stairs we entered a security area that resembled the TSA security lines of days gone by, but with an air of cold efficiency. Black clad officers with strange red armbands searched each embarking passenger with a wand and then had us stand in a scanner to take pictures of us. I was told that it was only a precaution, and that it was for the safety of everyone.

I couldn't help feeling a little disturbed by the guard's emotionless faces.

Once through, Mark led me to a waiting four passenger electric car that looked more like a souped up golf cart, the doors removed for ease of use. It was still very hot out.

"Kelly," said Mark, indicating a woman with short cropped red hair wearing a black ball cap and black uniform. "This is Emiliana Budzyński. I simply call her Emmy. She will be your personal assistant today. Emmy, please take Kelly to her new apartment and then stay outside her door until I arrive."

"Yes, sir," Emmy replied with a thick Slavic accent. I didn't like the way Emmy smiled.

Mark indicated that I should sit in the passenger seat, and Emmy saluted Mark, climbed into the driver's seat and after Mark banged on the top of the car a few times with his hand we were scooting down the newly paved road toward the center of the city, electric powered buses ferrying people around in a strange, nearly noiseless quiet. The only noises heard in this city were the sounds of people's voices, an occasional car horn and the whine of electric engines.

"Where is all the power coming from?" I asked.

Emmy sat quietly, her slender fingers, nails cut short, tapped on the steering wheel.

"It is wind turbines," she said, and I could feel the frost from her nearly canceling out the heat of the day. "High above, attached to these cables you see around city. Asher's idea."

"Who is Asher?"

She turned and smiled at me again, that strange toothy smile. I felt like a mouse looking at the fangs of a cat.

"Magistrate may take you to see him," she said. "He is great. Bring all of us together under peace and prosperity. It is good."

We passed a row of shops. Shops! I couldn't believe my eyes. I hadn't been shopping in forever. There were huge screens at every intersection of every street, and on each one I could see two men shouting something loudly, but I only caught bits of it as we rushed through each intersection. It looked like a news program with a black ticker bearing white letters running at the bottom.

"What is that?" I asked, but Emmy was not speaking, focused on driving through the busy city streets.

Before I knew it we were stopping before a huge high-rise, its golden frosted windows reflecting the glaring sunlight and the image of our little weird golf cart as we approached.

"Come," said Emmy. "I take you to new living quarters."

I didn't say a word, only complied with her wishes. The steeliness of her face and the small pistol strapped to her belt made me uneasy, even though I was supposed to feel safe now. I had made it to the great sanctuary that was New Jerusalem, and it seemed like everything was so wonderful here, but something in the back of my mind ate at my resolve like a cancer.

We entered the building lobby, shiny black ceramic tile beneath our feet and fresh white paint on the walls. We passed two armed, muscle bound guards who nodded at Emmy as if they knew her well. A group of guards were having a meeting over toward the back of the lobby, and a woman was talking to them about protocols and other words that I couldn't hear completely. After boarding a shiny chrome elevator, Emmy typed in a key code onto a touch screen and we climbed higher and higher to an unknown floor. There were no indicators above the door to tell me where I was going.

The doors opened swiftly like on Star Trek and I followed Emmy down a plush, green carpeted hallway to a brushed steel door at the end with the number 2004 stamped on it at eye level. Emmy produced a small device resembling a credit card, swiped the lock and the door clicked. After opening the door for me, Emmy motioned me inside with a flick of her wrist and that strange smile.

Inside was an amazingly huge space. My hand went to my chest as I looked out on a view of the city that was literally breathtaking. I turned to tell Emmy something about it, a reaction really, and found her to be gone, the door closed, and only my own reflection in the mirror that was mounted to the inside of the door.

I looked old.

Turning from my own image, I walked through the apartment, examining the king sized bed, the fully stocked kitchen, the living room with the...television?

I looked around the black leather couch and nearby on the glass coffee table I found a silver remote control. I pressed the red power button and the television winked on, a standby message held in the middle of the screen for a few moments, and then what looked like a live news broadcast.

A ticker of information scrolled at the bottom of the screen, but no voices could be heard other than the voices of two men who stood at what looked like a large mosque...the

Dome of the Rock. The men were dressed in robes, looking like something out of that Ten Commandments movie. They both had long gray beards and one of the men was bald.

I could hear a static that interrupted their voices periodically, but one thing came through perfectly clear.

"Repent!" they said.

Ethan

The city looked nothing like what I imagined. So pretty and shiny. Nothing like back home. These buildings were all new, golden, clean.

I wanted off that stupid ship. There was a big gaping hole torn in the side of it from the explosion, and if I had not listened to that little voice inside my head I would have been in the wrong place at the wrong time, if you know what I'm saying.

I wanted a different duty, and since my commander (God rest his sorry carcass) got burned up with a couple dozen other slobs, I was now under a different command who was completely unorganized. It was so off the mark that I walked right off the ship and through the gates with not much trouble. I was able to convince the rookie stiff that I was supposed to pull land detail, and before long I was down on the docks where I found a recruiting officer looking for security squad for the high and mighty.

I used my security badge issued to me when I signed on to this outfit, but it didn't get me much further. Once I got to the docks, things got sticky. Some little blonde headed kid with nearly white eyebrows looked me up and down and asked for my identification. I gave him my card.

"This will do," he said, all official. The urge came to snap his neck, but I resisted it for good measure.

"Where is my detail?" I asked, trying to sound like I had experience with this kind of thing, smiling from ear to ear.

The kid scratched the back of his neck and looked intently at my identity card.

"Looks like we need some *detail* over at the executive plaza," he said. "Nothing big. Just lobby duty. Pretty easy really."

"Lobby duty," I said, my smile fading. "What does *that* mean?"

He laughed, ran a hand held scanner across my identity card and handed it back to me.

"You watch a lobby, make sure the people who come in the building are supposed to be there. Simple as pie."

Such a stupid expression. I grinned at him and snatched the card out of his hand.

"Just go over and get on that flatbed," he said, pointing at an electric powered truck with a few security guys sitting on it, all of them carrying weapons. "That truck will take you where you need to go. You can meet your new crew along the way."

I put the identity card away, walked to the flatbed, sat toward the back bumper so my legs hung off of it, and soon we were whirring down the street toward the biggest building in the city. It towered over everything, its gold tinted windows reflecting everything around it. We passed by large gated structures that looked like giant u-bolts, and rising from those were these thick cables as big around as fifty gallon drums extending up into the sky toward something I couldn't see. I shielded my eyes from the sun to look but couldn't really see anything.

It was all kind of surreal.

I hadn't seen civilization in an awful long time, and hadn't seen people who were this clean, either. Everybody was showered and shaved and not smelling like the back end of a horse. It was kind of nice...orderly...efficient. I remember thinking that a guy could get in a lot of trouble in a place like this.

It was time to find my place.

The truck dropped us off in front of the golden building and we entered the lobby where we were met by a stocky brick of a lady who wanted to see our identity badges. We gave them to her, sat in some chairs to the back of the lobby, and she started in with her speech after giving the identity cards to an assistant for scanning. She then tugged on the bill of her black ball cap and folded her arms.

"You will be the lobby detail for this building. No one is to enter or exit without being carded. You are to check the floors and make regular rounds. Duty schedules are posted in the break room over there, and I expect you to follow them. Any questions?"

She then began to explain some procedures to us as the assistant passed our cards back to us, and everyone was listening intently, and that was when I heard the front lobby doors whoosh open and I turned to see that veteran's widow walk into the lobby following close behind a young red headed woman wearing a black ball cap and matching uniform. I spun back around quickly, hoping she wouldn't recognize me and blow my scam. In a few seconds I got the nerve to look again only to see her disappear into the elevator and the chrome doors close behind her.

"One more thing," said the commander. "I need a detail of three men to come with me. There is a special service that Asher himself requires of you."

I stepped forward without asking, strangely as if I could not help it, as if I was being pushed forward for this volunteer position.

"Come with me," she said. "We will have one more security verification before we ascend to the top floor."

I got real nervous then. They'd check me out for sure and I'd be found out. She took our identity cards and scanned them through a little black device on the wall with blinking lights. All three cards blinked green and not red. I thought that red might be bad.

She got this weird look on her face and motioned for us to follow her. We entered a freight elevator down the hall and it moved us up at least a hundred floors where we came out into a large room that took up one whole floor of the building. I could see the skyline of this new city that was still being constructed, all the large cranes lifting materials to great heights.

Standing near the window was a tall man wearing a pair of jeans and a green t-shirt, his feet bare, and just then some kind of switch flipped on inside my chest. I felt energized, and I had a bounce to my step when I walked in lock step behind the commander. I felt like I had to meet this dude. He seemed important, and it felt like that importance echoed out from him like some kind of radio waves.

When he turned and looked at me, it was like he was looking into the blackness of my heart and his eyes saw all the things I had done, but instead of being repulsed by me, he was drawn in.

"Hello, friends," he said, his accent somehow foreign but something I couldn't quite put my finger on. "Welcome to your new home. I am Cain Asher and I am happy to meet you. Is this my security detail, Ilsa?"

"Yes, my lord," she said. But yes. He was our lord. I could sense it. Something stirred inside me that told me that he was our lord, our master, our leader. This man was more than just a man. He asked for our names and we told him, and I offered my name to him as well, all fear melting away.

I started to kneel down, unable to prevent myself in his presence, my inward self recognizing the power he wielded. I wanted it. I wanted all of it, and if I followed him he would give it to me. I could hear that in my head. He stopped me, told me to stand up.

"You will never kneel again to anyone," he said, his voice soft and steady, collected and reserved. "You will serve me well, but you will not be my servants."

"Asher has selected you three for a special task," said Ilsa. "He will explain."

Asher walked across the black tiled floor to some couches arranged in a circle. He sat at one and asked us to sit across from him. I did as he asked, and he put his elbows on his knees, folded his hands together, and began to tell us of the enemy.

"Two men have been preaching at the temple mount for some time. I did not want to stop them because they have developed a following. It will be your task to find a way to remove them from our fine city. Religion is a thing of the past. We need peace to heal our world, not division and intolerance. Many of the people have been confused and frightened by them, but they have not responded to any peaceful negotiations. Please, can you help us?"

"Yes," I said, a voice rising up within me and spilling out of my mouth. "I will help you. It will be done."

"Good," he said, sitting back, sinking into the couch. "I will expect results soon."

We then enjoyed drinks and food served to us by a host

of waiters and waitresses, and a grand party was had by all. I was denied nothing…by no one. It was fabulous… decadent.

Later that night, as the party raged on, and the liquor flowed, Asher had a meeting with a man, a slender black man, who spoke to him quietly, but the music flooding the penthouse was nearly deafening.

I think I heard the words "assassinate" and "worship", and when I moved a little closer, Asher looked at me and smiled.

"I grow tired, Ethan," he said, giving a flick of his wrist to the man he was just talking to. The man nodded and started to leave, then turned back to face Asher.

"I'll see you after the plan has been executed, then," said the man. "Are you sure this is what you want?"

"Yes," said Asher. "How else will they follow if they do not have faith? They must have faith in me."

The man had a strange look just then, a look as if he was about to see Asher for the last time. I felt a little sad.

The man left us, and the party continued, and soon I forgot about what they talked about, and when I woke up the next morning, two strange women in my bed, a hangover using my head as an anvil, I decided to get busy with the task Asher had given to me.

Amy

I barely slept.

There were all kinds of crazy noises out in the dark during the night. Freaky weird ones.

When the sun, somehow stronger and brighter here, peeked out over the horizon, the camp was already full of activity. The soldier types, most of them rough and grizzled from not shaving (or bathing for that matter) roasted something over a fire that at least had four legs but I didn't really want to ask about it. Just ate it.

I was handed a cup of cool water and offered some camouflaged clothing that was meant for someone much larger than me and, like, a dude. I was shown to a latrine where I could change, and was glad to at least have some clothes that were a better choice for this dry ugly climate, even if they were ill fitting. The sand was blowing around so much and was so powder fine that it got in everything and chafed something awful.

When I left the latrine, I found Gideon sitting on a footlocker next to the old colonel dude. They were laughing about something, probably some soldier joke, when Gideon finally noticed me. The old guy hopped up and offered me his seat and I took it after hesitating for a second or two. He grunted as he took a knee in front of us on the sand like some rickety old football coach.

"Gideon and I have just been talking about New Jerusalem and what could be expected," he said, his voice all gravelly and hard. "He mentioned that you'd like to get in and find a little girl you lost. I don't want to rain on your parade, but as I explained to him, that's not the best course of action."

"Why so?" I asked.

"Well, there's been a great horrible heap of ordinance been fired off in that region. There's nomadic bandits that have resorted to cannibalism. They'd soon roast you as look at you, and we've had our share of run-ins with those brigands. We've been picking up transmissions out of New Jerusalem that seem on the surface to be all roses and caviar, and several of our ranks have gone to join them, but my old soldier's heart is untrusting."

"How did you get a working radio?" I asked.

"Strangest thing. These radios hadn't worked since the big EMP's that wiped out all electronics and then one day they fired to life. Lieutenant Jacobs seems to think that power is somehow being sent wirelessly from somewhere, possibly a satellite or a broadcast tower. Said something about Tesla or whatever. I don't know. I'm not an engineer."

"I've crossed swords with the New Jerusalem people," said Gideon, his voice taking on a quiet, almost whispering sound. "I watched them march a whole herd of elderly off the deck of the Ronald Reagan right into the sea. Anya's not safe there, I know it."

"That is not the first time we have heard this kind of thing," replied Snyder as he looked at the back of his grimy hands. "I hear, and this is only rumor I tell you, that people over the age of forty are not welcome in their city. Something about rebuilding the world in a new image of man. I don't know. Anya might be safer there than you think, but I also hear things coming out of that city, mostly about two old men who are keeping the authorities there on their toes."

"What do you mean?" I asked.

"Listen for yourself," he said, producing a small black, handheld radio.

He twisted a knob on top of it and it crackled to life. At first there was nothing but static, but he held up a finger as if to bring something out of thin air, and then a voice could be heard behind the hiss, a vowel sound here, a consonant there.

"...Es...di...pro...of the lord of hosts commands you to turn from your wickedness and accept his son, a gift offering for the sins of all man from the beginning of time to now and to the near ending future. A warning to the man who would call himself god. For he has offended the most high god with his blasphemy. A reckoning will come soon for the---"

And he switched it off.

"That's all it does. It's like when I was young and they used to have preaching on the radio. Can't get any other transmission and can't broadcast out. My men can't use the radios to communicate, and for all I know this is some kind of weird trick to get people to come and see what that New Jerusalem is all about. I have heard stories about two old men near the temple mount spewing fire out of their mouths, burning up entire columns of soldiers with something the consistency of napalm."

"What if you help us get there?" I asked. "Your men seem more than capable of escorting us."

The old guy laughed, but not like he was making fun of me, just one of those knowing laughs.

"Ma'am," he chuckled. "You two are welcome to swell our ranks, but you must know that this is a dangerous place you have landed. Not three clicks from our position rests probably one of the nastiest nomadic human filth I have ever seen. They eat their own children. It would be a high risk to all of us to travel to New Jerusalem."

"But sir," replied Gideon. "I don't trust the ones in charge of that city. I've seen what I've seen."

"That may be true, Gideon," said the Colonel. "But think about it like this: if we go toward the city, we'll face daily dangers. All I have heard is rumor about New Jerusalem. At least if you are living in or at least near that city, you will probably have food and shelter and a modicum of safety, but getting there is the problem, and then we don't know what kind of people are running that place. Volos has made many people do some very strange things in order to prevent its icy tendrils from spreading to the rest of the populace. Perhaps what you saw on the Reagan was a culling."

"A culling?" Gideon asked.

"Yes sir," he said, now sitting in the sand, his knees popping with age. "I participated in a culling of fifty of my own men who showed signs of Volos. It is by no means completely gone. Why do you think we drew blood from you when you arrived? If you showed any trace of the virus I would have put two bullets in each of your brain pans myself. We cannot take any risks."

We sat quietly after that. Things were kind of awkward as the men buzzed around doing soldier tasks, saluting one another and locking and loading I guess.

"I apologize," said the Colonel, grunting to his feet. "Talk of your...demise... is rude and unbecoming of an officer. This desert life has dulled my manners. Please forgive me."

"None needed, sir," Gideon managed. "I have done some things I'm not proud of, as well. All of us have."

"This world is hard, son," said the Colonel, his gray bushy brows looking all angry face. "It is only to harden further, but I had kids back in the world. Let me think on your situation. You spend the day at your leisure. If you still want to swell our ranks you are welcome if you can wield a weapon to our liking…or I guess we could train you. Perhaps if we can find a way into the city we'll help you get there. Here."

The colonel produced a large knife sheathed in a leather scabbard and handed it to Gideon. Gideon snatched it up and stuck it in his belt.

We then heard a shout from outside the camp. Our peace was interrupted by gunfire.

Kashif

So strange, the journey had been.

We had walked for many kilometers in this desert, and it was so wonderful to be able to see all of it. I did not need anyone to lead me around or use a stick by which to feel for things that might cause me to stumble. I had felt faces and through my sense of touch had been able to imagine what people looked like but only now did I discover the cracks and lines and shapes that made up an eyebrow, a mouth, an eye, a nose, a chin.

All things were new to me again.

My friend had quit speaking Farsi some time ago, and we had agreed to speak in his native tongue even if his command of English was full of slang and strange pronunciations of his region. I had to often stop him and ask him to speak slowly or to repeat certain words, and I was learning American slang by the minute.

"Where might we get us some food in this desert, Kashif?" said Clayton. "Y'know…in case we's to run out of what we got."

"As my people say," I responded, laughing. "What coming is better than what gone by in past."

"And the meanin' of that is…?"

"I merely trying to make you happy."

He laughed at this, and I patted him on the shoulder for comfort. It is good that I did so, for as we topped a hill we looked upon a sight that still haunts my memory.

Stretching far out in the distance were the remains of hundreds of abandoned vehicles, their metal burned so black that the stench of it was still floating across the wind even after years of being idle. I saw many white sticks lying in the sun, and when I stooped to pick one up my hands immediately told me that they were the bones of the dead. The hot wind inhaled and then blew sand at us.

"Heavens," Clayton managed to say. "Looks like somebody had themselves a whopper of a battle here. Nothin' left but the machines and the bones. I ain't never seen so many tanks in one spot."

"The war," I said. "Many men died here. It is this way for long distance to north. We be careful here."

I attempted, in my broken English to tell Clayton about my brother and his horrible burns. I believe he understood too, despite my problems with his language. His eyebrows raised and the corners of his mouth turned downwards, and I took this to mean that he had become very sad. I think it was the first time that he had faced the war in such an ugly sense, even though he had experienced much hardship in his own country.

"I'm only alive 'cause of the guidance and protection of the Most High God," he said. "It's by his grace alone I walk, Kashif. It's that grace that gave your sight to you and it's that grace that helps me when I need it most, no matter the problems I face."

"What of my brother?" I asked. "Does grace save him?"

"I don't know, man," Clayton replied. "I didn't know yer brother, and can't judge him yes or no. Not my place. I pretty much worry 'bout myself and that's it. I just tell people what Jesus or Isa did in my life and let others make up their own minds. The fact is, I came to you for a reason. Nothin' happens 'cause of some coincidence or random game of roulette. I was put in your life right at the most needed time, to tell you about Jesus's love and to see if you would accept it. It's because you accepted his healing power that you can see."

"I am man of peace," I said, placing my hands on my hips. "I am grateful for healing. I am in your debt."

"No," Clayton said, laughing and squinting his eyes. "It's not me who healed you, bro. It's Jesus of Nazareth. You call him Isa."

"The Holy Quran says that Isa heals blind by Allah's leave. He can do this, but there is only one God and his name is Allah, and Muhammad is his prophet."

He put his hand on my shoulder, and I did not feel that he judged me, but instead he had a look on his face that I could not readily interpret. I could not explain it, but I knew it to be love — pure, holy and powerful love.

"Walk with me, Kashif," said this strange American. "I know you're tryin' to fulfill some kind of debt to me, but you hafta know I don't hold ya to it. You can leave anytime you like. I ain't gonna keep ya, but I was told you was supposed to come with me."

We stood in silence, looking out across the horrible destruction that this war had caused. Even though this man confused me, I did not feel like leaving him. We did not share cultures, this man who was alien to my world. I decided to walk with him, even if it was to help him survive. I would see what he believed and what else might happen to us both, to keep an open mind.

"We have other saying," I said to him, walking toward the horizon, trying not to step on the bones of the dead. "il-mo'men muSaab, which means 'the believer is afflicted'. You have dangers to face, so I go with you."

"Dangers. Of that I'm certain, Kashif," said Clayton, his face set like flint. "I know we will, but I will walk through the valley of the shadow of death and fear no evil."

We walked across this valley of death for nearly a day, all the while wondering when we would see an end to the broken tanks, their treads laying in pieces, the large black holes in their now useless armor, the guns and other weapons littering the sand. All the while, Clayton hummed a beautiful tune, and when I asked him what he was singing, he said he was giving praise to the Most High God. I offered to sing one of my people's traditional songs and found him to be a quick study of music.

We would face much danger, but we would face it together like brothers.

Kelly

I left the television on. It was like watching one of those televangelist programs back before the war. However, the two men standing in the center of the screen were not wearing suits but the long, almost nightgown like shirts that men wore in this region of the world. Both of them shouted in unison, as if scripted, and both of their speech patterns sounded like they were from the former United States.

Puzzling.

How could they be from back home? Even weirder, the way they spoke sounded much like the way the people spoke around my home town.

"This is the end of days," they shouted. "Turn back from the wickedness of man and embrace the loving kindness of Jesus of Nazareth! He is coming again soon and his voice will be like a two edged sword to the nations! Judgment is soon upon this earth!"

I thought about all of those people who had given their lives to Jesus on the river, all because Clayton and Jacob had said that they should. I didn't say anything because so many people were following along, but I felt like that old way of thinking was in many ways what had led us to this terrible place in human history. The Muslims hated the Christians and the Christians hated the Muslims and they picked up guns and fought over oil and ideology and other nonsense.

After changing into some fresh clothes that I found in the bedroom closet, I decided to see what was in the refrigerator in the kitchen. I walked across the soft, green carpeted floor and opened the fridge to find a wealth of fresh vegetables and frozen chicken. Investigating further, I found a pan, some olive oil and a knife and soon I was chopping garlic, onion, zucchini and some of the chicken I had thawed in a bowl of warm water. Before long there was a new aroma in the not-so-modest apartment, an aroma I had not smelled in years.

And it tasted better than anything.

Just as I was scarfing down fork loads of sautéed chicken and veggies, the television changed over to another channel with some difficulty, flickering back and forth between the two old preachers and the chiseled face of a handsome young man, blue eyes, dark hair combed perfectly, his chin slightly raised as he stared lovingly out toward the masses.

He thumped the microphone attached to the podium in front of him.

"People of New Jerusalem," he said, his accent strange. I couldn't place it. "We have made much progress these last few years since the war ended. We have rebuilt this mighty region in our own image, making it the peaceful, clean and enjoyable place that any human of any culture can feel welcome and safe. It is what makes us all commonly human, the desire for a place to live in peace, have food in our bellies, and safety to raise our children as we see fit. I am so proud to be a part of bringing all of us this glorious city, and I am only happy to be a part of it."

Who was this guy? I couldn't take my eyes off of him. I was only able to glance away enough to notice that my fork held a skewered piece of chicken and onion that had not made it to my mouth.

"There are threats that must be dealt with, and they are

being dealt with I assure you. Rest easy. These two invaders who have upset the balance of our fine city will not stay for long. I am working on a way to neutralize the situation. Trust in me. I have never let you down. If you trust in me, I will surely eradicate the threat within the week. Any images you see of them or messages you receive from them are not being filmed by us, I assure you. There are no cameras or recording devices of any kind in their location. It is the work of something else. I am only—"

Static. The image of the two men appeared again, the word "blasphemer" was heard, and then there was more static, and then the image of that handsome man appeared again.

"—only trust me, then the combined work of all of us will manifest in their destruction. I never lie. My citizens, my friends of the world, we will not have to endure this nuisance much longer. Asher is only here to help."

The static appeared again, and again the image of the two men flashed on the screen. They were a bit more animated now, walking back and forth, shouting into the cameras, cameras that according to Asher did not exist.

"He speaks with the tongue of a serpent! His children are the living dead but they will soon consume no more! No man can serve two masters! Asher is the one who will be sealed away in fire! —"

And I shut it off.

But I could still hear it faintly, though. When my husband was home on leave one time, we had a bad season of tornados. He bought one of those weather radios that would go off when there was a tornado warning and the mechanical voice would then give us information about the weather and where to go in an emergency. I slept within a few feet of it, however, and it would broadcast that voice ever so quietly, just out of the range of my hearing. My husband couldn't hear it at all, but I could, and within a month I had yanked it out of the wall.

I could hear the voices now, as if in my head, shouting about the end of the world, the repentance of nations, the voice of evil. I looked all over the apartment. Perhaps there was one of those weather radios in here.

I didn't find one, but made a huge mess in the process. If Mark came back he would probably think I was nuts.

The fourth wall of the apartment was nothing but pane glass windows and there was a balcony just beyond the large sliding glass doors. I turned the latch and then slid open the door to feel a blast of warm air flood into the room and push small objects around the coffee tables and cause the large hanging curtains to billow. I stepped out onto the balcony, shutting the door behind me and moving over to the brass railing to look out over the city, the newly created, shiny modern city.

And I could still hear them, echoing up from the ground from far off, from the temple mount near the center of the city. There the shining gold Dome of the Rock stood, tarnished a bit with war and time, a massive hole in the side of it. A roaring crowd of people surrounded it, looking like a colony of ants from this distance, but in the middle of the crowd stood two small dots. These two small dots I knew were the two men I had seen on the television, and I could hear them as clearly as if they were standing on the balcony with me.

"Turn from this evil blasphemy! Give your lives to Jesus

and he will set you free from bondage! It is not too late, but soon, time will be no more and there will be a new heaven and a new earth!"

Clayton

I suppose most people'd think choosin' a blind guy, well, a former blind guy as my guide through the Middle East would be kinda foolish, but God had his reasons...always did. Good grief, look at all the folks he chose for his purposes in the Bible - murderers, adulterers, weaklings and simpletons. B'sides, I knew which way I was goin'. Couldn't explain it. Just did. Kashif was along for other reasons.

Howard was with us. I didn't let on that I could see him but I figured I'd just let things go. I'd been allowed to see a lot of things 'cause it was pretty much the end, I figured. I'd never had the notion to speak to him 'cause I figure he had a mess of other stuff to get on with. Mostly I was concerned with the faith of my new friend Kashif.

He was a happy fella. Mostly 'cause God had healed him of his blindness. Pretty cool thing, the healing'. I don't think I had much to do with it since I was just doin' what I was told. The part about the mud was 'cause I'd read about Jesus doin' that to some blind guy. I didn't spit in it first, 'cause I always figured that was Jesus's way o' breathin' life into the guy and that wasn't my place.

I kept on talkin' to him about Jesus and I suppose the verses just came to me. I used the old testament a lot 'cause I figured that was what the Bible and the Koran had in common, but Howard kept whisperin' stuff in my ear for help. Wasn't about to tell Kashif about Howard. Didn't think he'd understand.

Ol' Kashif really loved Jesus, but had trouble seein' him

as savior of the world. I figured I'd give him time and just love on him and see what happened. Can't make decisions for people. You just gotta tell 'em your heart and they just kinda figure it out on their own, and one day the Spirit gets through. I's prayin' the whole time.

We'd camped out for the night at the far end of that terrible burnt out battlefield, takin' shelter inside the back end of a little square tank that prolly held a bunch of troops for transport at some point in its short life. It was all black and greasy, and the sand had crept up on top of it with help from the wind. Made a real cozy little hut and was sealed off enough so's we didn't fear no bandits in the night.

Man, did it get cold in the desert at night. Kashif didn't seem to pay it no mind. He said if we built a fire them nomads might come and eat us for dinner. I tended to listen to what he said.

"Why you choose me?" he said. I wished I could still speak his language. I figured there was a time and place for everythin' under heaven, and the time and place for me to speak Farsi was long gone. He knew enough English to get by and he was teachin' me his language so I figure we'd meet somewheres in the middle eventually.

"I chose you 'cause God told me to," I said. "It was faith led me to you, friend."

"I blind my whole life," he said. "I led around like small child. How I lead you to New Jerusalem?"

"Look, Kashif," I told him, placing a hand on his shoulder for comfort. "I was led to you for a higher purpose. I figure you got some kinda talent I don't know about or the Most High has a plan for you or something or other. I already know the way to New Jerusalem. I'm just doin' what I'm told. I don't question the will of the Most High."

"Yes," he said, smiling a bit. "I do not question the will of Allah."

"We'll see," I told him, smiling back. "At least you can see now, right?"

He laughed, sensing my humor, but then he hugged me up. I expect that was some kind of cultural deal. I didn't mind. He told me during the walk across the death field that his people practice a thing called a 'life debt' which as far as I can tell is kinda like he's bound to me until he pays back his gift of sight. I told him a couple of times that it wasn't me that fixed his eyes and he didn't owe me nothin', but he kept on and I figured I'd insult him if I kept at it, so I dropped it and we talked about other stuff.

He told me that this whole area had been burned out by the war, and that most of the cities in the Middle East had been shorn off like tree stumps. Pretty much nothin' looked the same anymore, at least that's what he had been told. He'd hear people talkin' about it as they'd walk by him back in the village and he'd also hear word about gangs of former soldiers and tribesmen who had gone all crazy with radiation or a messed up form of the Volos virus. I's hopin' good ol' Kashif would be able to steer us away from that sort.

The next mornin' when the sun started climbin' up the sky, the debris from the comet's impact no longer dimmin' it out, we looked around for anythin' we could scavenge from the tank. We got lucky and found some MRE's and a half-full canteen. Well, I say that, but there ain't no such thing as luck.

I winked at Howard and he made the funniest face.

That was when we heard it, the sound comin' from somewhere back where we had been, the sound of voices ever faint, tinny little voices. Kashif and I turned to each other and at the same time said: "You hear that?"

He headed off, bent real low and cockin' his head to the side like a bloodhound and then he stuck his hand down into the sand and pulled out a silver shiny object, and when he brought it to me I immediately knew what it was.

"An iPhone six," I said, rubbing the sweat from my forehead. It was made out of one piece of machined aluminum and had a glass screen that was cracked, but now I could hear the voices even louder, and it sounded everythin' like preachin'.

"Turn from the evils of this world! Give your lives to the son of the living God! He has paid the price for all of your transgressions! Fall on your knees and worship his name!"

Kashif turned it up, and even though the screen was all cracked and spider webbed, we could see an image of two men, two old men, shoutin' about Jesus, shakin' their fists, holdin' out their hands, pleadin' with us to turn from our wicked ways.

"This is trick," said Kashif. "How could we get signal way out here? And how is powered?"

"Dude," I said. "I'm not doin' it. It's gotta be the power of the Spirit doin' this…or somethin' else."

At these words, Kashif dropped the phone on the sand, let out a yelp and his eyes got real wide. I think I said the wrong thing.

"No, no!" I said, smilin' and puttin' out my hands toward him. "I mean it's the work of the Most High. How else could an iPhone owned by a dead solder from a war that has been over for three or so years be workin' way out in the middle of the desert?"

I reached down and picked it up. Kashif folded his arms, his dark eyes glarin' at me. I felt like that time I convinced Johnny Devlin to sneak on them people's land and hunt doves. He was about as happy with me as Kashif was at the moment.

The phone kept talkin' and I tried to turn it off or turn it down, but I think that part of it was broke, and didn't seem like it was gonna turn itself off. I put it in my back pocket, which muffled the sound a bit, and we started on our way east again.

Gideon

I heard shouting. Sounded like the gates of hell had opened up and a horde of beasts poured on out.

The Colonel's face looked like an anvil, immovable, not seeming to be bothered at all.

"Get these civilians to the hole," he growled. "We got company."

One of the men pulled at my arm and I shook free.

"Sir," I shouted. "Give me a gun. I can help you."

The Colonel squinted, turned toward me, his head on an iron swivel.

"Son," he grunted. "No time. Maybe after you've been proven."

I felt another arm grab at me and turned to see that it was Amy. She bore her teeth and was saying something through them, her eyebrows squeezing down over her eyes.

"Do what they say!" she commanded. "Let's go!"

No time.

I heard a bullet whiz by my ear, the singing sound of lead. They were getting close. We followed a bearded soldier, crouched down, his arm flapping up and down to tell us to stay low, and I could hear that fifty cal start up, streaking tracer fire over my head as the bearded soldier leading us opened up the trunk of a burned out car only to reveal a tunnel that went down into the dirt beneath.

"Here!" he shouted, un-shouldering his AR-15 and pointing at the hole.

Amy didn't hesitate, climbing down into the trunk of the car with little effort, and soon I followed after. The trunk lid was closed behind us to leave us in near darkness as we climbed down a ladder into the pit. Almost stepped on Amy when I reached the bottom.

I pulled out my lighter and flicked it on — then promptly closed the lid when I caught a glimpse of what was down here: mounds of C4 and semtex. Could be dynamite.

"Turn that back on," said Amy, the sounds of gunfire and shouting coming from above us. Man, I wished I could get up there and take some guys out.

"No way," I said, putting the lighter back in my pocket in the dark. "Did you see what they got stored down here? The C4 and Semtex is safe, but if they got dynamite...or gunpowder..." I made a sound like an explosion.

She got it.

We listened to the gunfire and the shouting. We could hear Farsi then English and then just random shouting. Once, it sounded like someone fell against the metal trunk lid or maybe it caught a stray bullet.

After a while I couldn't stand it anymore.

"I gotta get up there," I said, reaching in the dark for the ladder.

Amy reached out and grabbed a fistful of my shirt.

"No way are you leaving me down here!" she shouted, a little drop of spittle landing on my cheek. She was close. "Just stay down here and keep out of it. It's not your fight, Gideon. I can't make it to New Jerusalem alone!"

I listened, shut my mouth and listened, but held on to the ladder with my right fist. I went against better judgement, pulled out the lighter, and lit it. Shielding it with my right hand, I could see that there were also several rifles down here and several boxes of ammo. These guys were ready for anything, I guess, or had been raiding others for this arsenal. I decided to see where the tunnel led.

"C'mon," I said, and Amy followed in the blue light of the butane as we walked carefully through the stacks of supply boxes, ammo boxes and other items. I saw a sweet PSG1 laying on top of a footlocker with a couple of loaded clips. At the time I ignored it. From the look of the rusty metal walls, it looked like they had buried a big supply trailer down a few feet under the sand. Where they got it, I couldn't say, since the PSG wasn't normal G.I. stuff, but in my experience guys like this who had supplies like this in this day and age were not on the up and up.

They were usually bad. Really bad.

The fighting seemed to be dying down, and I heard less and less gunfire from up above. Wasn't long before I didn't hear anything at all, and that was when I started getting nervous and that little guy inside my head that always kept me safe started to scream at me to duck and cover.

A shaft of light appeared over the ladder.

"You two ok?" came the gravelly voice of the Colonel. "You two can come up now if you like. We're all clear."

I hesitated. Using the faint light, I dug in a box near me and pulled out some smoke grenades and a — SCORE! — 1911A pistol with full mag, except it was heavier than normal.

"Yeah," I managed, stuffing the loot down my pants and in my cargo pockets. "Are you sure we can come up there? I mean, is it safe and all?"

"Sure," he shouted down. "Come on up."

I put out the lighter and saw Amy climbing up the ladder bathed by the dim light from above. My mind started fighting the idea of climbing out (*would they search me?*), and then I reached up and grabbed her ankle and she looked down at me with that look on her face that said she'd pretty much had enough.

I did the best with my expression to let her know that things were not squared away with these guys. I think she got it, and let me climb up first. When we reached the top the Colonel helped us onto the solid ground above. Took us a bit to catch our breath before the old guy winked at Amy and smiled. It looked like his yellow teeth were going to grate together.

"So you two saw my secret supply stash, then," he said, a little out of breath.

"We don't want anything," I said. "We just want to move on, that's all. No worries."

That was when I saw the carnage.

There were bodies littered everywhere, mostly tribesmen wearing their galabia, the long sleeved long shirt that stretched to their ankles. The blood soaked the sand and the remaining soldiers dragged the bodies out of the camp and over the nearest dune.

"They were after what you just saw," said the Colonel. "If they get their grubby hands on it, then this whole region will fall to them. I'll protect it with my life, and use it to eradicate any hostiles in this area."

He stood up, and when he had reached his full height, his face exploded out all over me in a mass of blood and bone.

"Sniper!" someone screamed, and the whole process started over again. The Colonel fell against me, then lay on the ground, motionless, blood spilling out of a red crater in his forehead.

Amy screamed, and I grabbed her arm and pulled her to the sand where we crawled under a burned out Hummer but not before I had whipped out the 1911A. Amy lay in the sand, face down, hands over her head, her feet kicking slightly, the fear taking her.

If there was one thing I knew, it was sniping, and if something wasn't done the little bugger would pick off everybody he...or she...could see in this camp.

Something had to be done.

As the fifty cal started in on the dunes, and the remaining soldiers, probably twenty strong, crouched down behind anything that was metal, throwing out smoke bombs, I started to think of a plan.

Kelly

I sat in the apartment, surrounded by luxury, feeling utterly alone. Even though I had gone to bed that night and had shut the door to the balcony, I could still hear the voices of those two men far below, somehow reaching me here inside this sealed apartment. I even heard them when I'd wake periodically throughout the night.

Morning came early, so I went to the kitchen to prepare some breakfast, showered, thinking the whole time how many things I had taken for granted before the world fell apart. I sat on the couch to let my hair dry, basically staring at the darkened glass screen of the television, and I didn't like the reflection of the woman there.

A knock sounded at the door and I jumped.

I ran to the door and looked through the peep hole to see Mark looking to his left. I opened the door immediately and he held a lovely bouquet of purple orchids, little droplets of water glistening on the pedals.

"Oh," I stammered. "I...I haven't seen flowers like these in so long. Where did you get them?"

"I have my methods," he said. "I have come to take you to see Asher. He is anxious to meet the woman who stole my heart."

It was cheesy, but I didn't care.

"Really," I said, my mouth curling into a wry smile. "Asher wants to see me? Why?"

"He and I are very close," he said, his face suddenly looking as if he hid great sadness. "I have been with him since the beginning, since before the war. I suppose he is like a brother to me…in a sense."

I had the strangest feeling, as if my stomach was trying to claw its way out of my mouth. I dismissed it as nervous jitters and tried to smile, but Mark sensed my uneasiness.

"What's wrong?" he asked, his Scottish accent rhythmic. "Is there anything that you need? I can have anything brought up here. Just say the word."

We moved into the apartment and sat on the couch, his hands smoothing the hair out of my eyes. He kissed my forehead so gently, his lips soft and warm on my skin. I tried to smile again, and I teared up, lost it, my husband's face rushing back into my memory.

"It's just…" I managed to force out. "I…miss my husband so much and I…I found out about his death so callously, from a horrible man who ran away like a coward when we were attacked at the tent village. I know I should be mourning my husband, but I want to have a life with you, too. It's the guilt. I know he's dead, but I'm just not able to move myself past it. I just need some time, Mark."

He moved aside, sitting a distance from me, but placed his hand on my shoulder. He smiled, and then let out a deep sigh.

"I suppose we moved rather fast," he said. "For that, I am sorry."

"Oh, no, no, no!" I said, taking his hand, moving closer. "I…I just want to move on. There is so much life here in this city, and I want to experience it all. I want to get on with my life. Let's…Let's go meet your friend. Maybe meeting Asher will help me shake all this off."

He laughed, but not condescendingly.

"You are a strange puzzle, lass," he chuckled, his

informal country accent bleeding through. "I cannot wait to introduce you to Asher."

I was glad that he was not speaking so formally anymore, and for a second I saw that young boy that he spoke to me about when we first met, that boy that wanted a better world to live in.

I put the flowers in a vase of water and placed them on the black marble table, still clean and never used. We went to the elevator, and after going up a few more floors the chrome doors opened up into a large room that took up the entire floor. Glass windows surrounded it in every direction, looking out onto the entire city around us. The floor was of a black marble that was flecked with tiny pebbles of gold that glimmered in the soft light coming from the recessed lamps in the ceiling. Some kind of tranquil, stringed classical music was playing, rolling out from speakers I could not see. Several beautiful leather couches and chairs were arranged in a circle near the center and a large marble staircase descended down near the middle of the room, a brass railing curving outward from the center, elegant and yet industrial. Black marble columns supported the ceiling which was at least fourteen feet above our heads.

A tall man appeared on the stairs. I had not seen him when the doors first opened. He wore a loose green t-shirt and a faded pair of jeans and was barefoot. He was the man I had seen on the television earlier. When he saw us, he spoke.

"Mark," he said, his voice rich and soft, a smooth sound of silk. "I was wondering when you would bring your friend with you. I have heard so much about you, Kelly, and am glad you have come to stay with us here. These beginnings are the spice that make our lives rich."

I felt as if I were in a dream. Mark and I approached him across the spacious room and he reached out with his hand to take mine. I felt like I had met him somewhere before. His smile had nearly the same effect on me as two glasses of wine.

I wanted to love him.

Mark did not sense this. He simply smiled and, oddly, took Asher's hand and kissed the back of it.

Asher laughed.

"Oh please," he said, his thick eyebrows raising. "There is no need for that, my friend. Kelly will think you strange."

"But...," said Mark. For the first time I saw what looked like confusion on Mark's face.

I looked at them both, a little puzzled. Asher made a motion with his hand, waving down toward the floor. Mark made a short bow at the waist and turned to go.

"Make us some drinks, would you Mark?" asked Asher, a smile spreading across his face.

Mark, somehow looking like a confused pet, jogged up the stairs and before long I heard clanking glasses and...ice?

"I'm sorry about all that," he said as we ascended the stairs to another spacious apartment. "I was the founder of this new city, and I developed all the technology that has kept it running, not to mention reactivating all of the electronic devices on the planet, so some people seem to think I have some kind of place with the gods. Silly, that. All I wanted to do was get the word out to all the remaining people of the world to join us in this city, and it seems that nearly everyone who has heard our message have responded in kind, flowing to our new sanctuary, their only purpose to better the human race. All of the ships we commandeered to gather what is left of us have made port after their year long journey, and at last nearly all of us are in one place…to rebuild."

I looked into his kind eyes, and as we sat in comfortably plush leather chairs, I started to understand the scope of this man's abilities. He was a charmer, an inviting soul who only wanted to see people happy and secure.

I sank deeper into the chair, the view through the large windows overlooking the beautiful city of New Jerusalem, and as Asher sat across from me, his well toned arms falling across his lap, he began to tell me the story of his success, and his intricate plans for the future.

Kashif

"So you would *eat* that?" I asked, the bile rising in my throat.

"Of course!" Clayton said. "Man, when you don't have nothin' to chew on 'cept your own tongue, you get kinda creative."

"Rodents forbidden by law to eat," I said, my eyes wide. "They… unclean."

"Well," he said, laughing. "I prayed over it, and I ain't dead, so I suppose I'm fine."

Something cracked in the air and we both jumped as the echo resounded over the faint wind.

"You ok?" Clayton asked.

"Yes," I replied, making a thumbs up sign. "Ok."

We heard more gunfire, some of them larger than others, echoing over the hills toward us. The desert had a strange way of carrying sound, making it difficult to judge the distance of the things making them.

Clayton crawled to the top of a dune.

"Down there," he said. "Looks like a camp is under attack. No tellin' who or what the trouble is about. We gotta go 'round it."

I crawled on my stomach to peek over the dune myself.

"What is happening?" I asked.

"Looks like a bunch of these here tribal folks have some soldiers pinned down. Can't really see too good, but them old vehicles look like they's made in the U.S., and that dead fella slumped over in the seat of that fifty cal is prolly an American or European. Who knows? Looks like a mess we should avoid."

"How?" I asked. "We must walk long distance around conflict. Many tribesmen in this area. Very bad. Heard many people speak of them. Their land is very very big."

"Then we'll hafta go 'round 'em," said Clayton, his set, his eyes focused. "I ain't gonna risk our mission no how."

"I am not a guide," I exclaimed. "I only know the people, and these people are bad. You wanted me tell you when people bad. Now I tell you, but you go anyway. Why?"

We lay on the side of that hill for a long time, listening to the sound of gunfire and shouting. We started to crawl on our bellies around the outside of the ridge, hoping that they would not hear or see us. I prayed for our safety, hoping that we would make it out alive.

Clayton prayed, too. I could hear him speaking his language, speaking to God, but in his prayer not once did he pray for himself, only for me, for the well being of all the fighting men, for both sides. I had never heard such a prayer, such a careful prayer that seemed more like a conversation than a prayer in reverence or fear.

What was this strange Christianity he had? It was nothing like what I had been told.

Kelly

"So what do you think of this city, Kelly?" asked Asher as Mark sat down next to me after serving glasses of an iced whiskey, something I was not used to at all.

"It's very remarkable," I said. "I was expecting—"

"A heap of radioactive slag," he said, laughing, finishing my sentence. "Yes, I suppose that is what you would think after seeing the war on television…at least what you were allowed to see."

"I am amazed that you have rebuilt the city this much," I said, taking a sip of the whiskey, my eyes growing wide with the strength of it.

"Yes," he replied, his gaze dropping to the floor, smiling. "It was very hard, but we managed to exceed all expectations. This city will now be a beacon of hope for the world, a place to rebuild our glory, unhindered by past superstitions and fallacies."

"What do you mean?" I asked.

Asher stood, swiftly, in a blur, and I was amazed at his speed. He walked to the large plate glass window and looked out at the city below, his hands clasped behind his back.

"It is a grand plan," he said. "Do you know that it has been in operation for many years, at least three years before the war began. Kelly, my dear, do you remember what caused the war?"

"It was," I stopped, thought, framed my answer, then set the glass of whiskey on the small glass table in front of me. "It was because of the unrest in this part of the world. Most said it was because of the oil and that it all ran out. I do remember Iran's involvement in Syria and the nuke that went off in Gaza, the unrest in Ukraine, and then the Russians and the Chinese joined forces, and then my country got involved along with Europe."

"You are partly correct," said Asher, his face becoming sad. "I would say it began in twenty thirteen in the United States, at least the beginning of the end, but it goes back much further than that. Do you remember the 'H two' missionaries?"

"Vaguely," I said. "Weren't they the ones who called themselves 'coffin missionaries', the ones who sold all they had to go to the middle east and other so called 'unreached' places of the earth to spread the Christian message? But... what do *they* have to do with anything?"

"Ah yes," he said, clapping his hands together twice. "*They* came here mostly, to Damascus, to Tehran, and were killed for their message. Poor things, beheaded as examples of the intolerance of infidels. This only caused the hatred between Muslims and Christians to explode. But do you sense the pattern here?"

"Not really."

"Religion, Kelly. Religion. It is the one thing that has kept the human race from reaching its zenith, from reaching to the stars and beyond, from evolving to our true potential. If we had a world free of religion, we would have a place free to explore, to treat each other with respect because we are all together human. Think of it! What we could accomplish if we use this opportunity to rebuild, to fashion our world in our own image: a place of peace and good will to all mankind...to use a well worn phrase."

I felt a little strange. My mother was very religious, took me to church every Sunday, told me about the golden rule, and even though church wasn't really for me, I still saw it as sacred. Something not to be messed with. I went along with it for now. I wasn't sure how to react. At least he wasn't pointing a gun at me.

"I have a surprise for you," said Asher, his face lighting up. "Mark."

Mark rose and went to a door on the far end of the room, opened it, and within I saw brightly colored walls, a mound of stuffed animal toys, and little Anya running toward me laughing.

"Oh, thank you!" I shouted, so glad to have her back.

"She missed you so much," said Mark. "And she didn't take too well to her new adopted family, so we decided we'd place her with someone whom she knew."

Anya ran to my arms and I caught her just as she jumped, holding her close to me.

"Come see what I made!" she shrieked.

I followed her into the brightly colored room and she proceeded to show me several works of art she had constructed from paper and crayons. How did they get paper and crayons?

For a moment, while Anya was playing with a small plush rabbit, I looked out of the room to see Asher and Mark talking to each other, saying something I couldn't hear, and somehow I thought about the horrors that the militias had brought to my country, the awful disease out there, the frightening plight of those still trying to survive this hostile world.

I looked at Asher, his eyes flashing back and forth

between Mark and myself, and wondered what was going on inside his head. Deep within my mind, somewhere on the back side of my heart, I was deeply afraid.

Amy

The stupid sniper had friends. Bullets were whizzing all around us, pinging into the side of the Hummer and breaking glass, some of them causing little dust clouds in the sand just to my right.

Gideon lay next to me under the Hummer, face down like me, and then he rolled over and lay on his back, his fists up near his chest, clenching and releasing. He looked at me.

"Stay here," he said. "I've got a plan, but you've gotta trust me."

"You what?" I screamed. I'd *had* it. "Let's just stay under here and try to be safe. Maybe they'll quit and we—"

But he was gone, and he, like, kicked sand in my face when he skittered out and didn't so much as say he was sorry.

Great.

Just great.

Left me there under this Hummer. I was starting to think about what would happen to me if he got shot dead. Those grubby tribal people would make me a wife in some gross *old* guy's harem or something or they'd just behead me because I didn't wear the right clothes or whatever.

No telling.

Oh man, what if they made me a slave and I ended up in some caravan like in the movies. Just shoot me *now*.

And then Gideon popped back in under the Hummer right beside me, his face dripping with sweat, his black hair sticking to his skin in long wet strands.

"Listen," he stammered, the sound of gunfire popping all

around us. "When the smoke rolls up under this Hummer, I want you to head toward where your feet are pointing and you will find that car with the fake trunk. I want you to get in there and climb down to the bottom. Get yourself a gun and when you see some light you shoot whoever comes down there…unless they drop my shirt…then *don't* shoot, 'cause it'll be me."

"What the heck, Gideon?" I screamed. "I'm not gonna get out from under this truck, you hear?"

"Stay under this truck and you're dead. Do what I told you and you'll be safe."

He left me again, more sand.

I grit my teeth, and could feel sand grinding around between them. I was so mad, so angry that he left me, and the gunfire didn't stop. It seemed like it got worse when Gideon left that second time, and I could hear shouting. Some of it I understood, but other words were in a language I couldn't place, probably Arabic. No telling.

I lay there for what seemed like forever, bracing myself, ready for rescue, but it didn't come. The Arabic foreign jibber-jabber got closer, and then I could hear something hiss and drop in the sand near the back of the Hummer, and my nose sucked in the acrid smell of smoke. I couldn't see anything at all, and my eyes stung and watered, but I climbed out from under the Hummer not because I was doing what Gideon said, but because I needed fresh air, my lungs burning. I ran to the back of the hummer, felt around and found the old car trunk totally by accident, opened it and climbed inside just as something struck the lid and shot something into my hand.

When I reached the bottom, sliding down some of the

rungs, my hand was all wet and slimy and I fumbled around in the dark for a gun or something just like Gideon said but it was so *dark*. My hand hurt something awful and finally I barked my shin on a box, and opening it, found a rifle of some type. I hoped it was loaded because I hadn't the faintest idea how to shoot it.

I pulled the trigger but it was not working.

Just my luck.

Found a gun but no bullets.

And a shaft of light poured down into the hole illuminating the ladder.

Somebody was coming down here.

Gideon

I couldn't worry about Amy right now. She was a big girl. She could handle herself...at least I hoped so.

I shot out from under the Hummer the second time and came under some heavy fire from the top of the dune. Ducking back around the back bumper, I tossed a smoke grenade to my left and then another one to my right. They started coughing out smoke immediately and this gave the soldiers defending the camp a little help as they lay down cover fire on the hill, but the death of Snyder had been a terrible blow to their organized effort. I darted around the fifty cal emplacement, the poor sap in the driver seat all slumped sideways with his memories all splattered on the seat. I whipped out the 1911A and when I went to cock it back, wondered if I was tripping because it had two barrels.

Oh man. Didn't notice that when I picked it up in the near darkness of the bunker. I'd only heard about one of these babies.

Sneaking around the ridge line, the smoke spilling around me, I ran for cover outside the edge of camp and dropped down below the crest of a little hill. I could hear the sniper fire just up the dunes in front of me, and from the high pitched sound of the report and the fact that the shots were too close together to be a bolt action, I figured he was using a Dragonov, a nasty little gift left behind by some dead Russian.

That made me sick.

If the guy was using a bolt action, there would at least be a few seconds for reloading the weapon and sighting back in, but since it was a Dragonov, that gave me no time between shots. I'd have to follow the ridge line and hope that nobody gave me trouble along the way, or hope that he had to pop in another clip.

Sucking up my resolve, I stayed low and trucked it around the ridge, and when I got out of the smoke, that's when it got ugly. Some dude who thought he was better than me shot out of a hole and went at me with some kind of pig sticker. Don't bring a knife to a gun fight is all I have to say. The 1911A's double barrels kicked so hard it almost jumped out of my hands, and it did double the damage to the assailant.

It wasn't long before I could see the sniper laying on the top of the ridge, his gun barrel sticking out like a black stick. He didn't have a spotter, so this meant he was probably an amateur, so I dropped down and belly crawled toward his position, my shirt filling with itchy sand. I reached around with my free hand and pulled out my knife to then place the blade between my teeth pirate style.

This guy wouldn't know what hit him.

That's when he took one to the head and I rolled down for cover just as a bunch of bleach white dune buggies topped the hill, all of them raining death down on the hostile tribesmen from the opposite side of the camp. I decided to stay low to keep from being mistaken for a baddie.

When the shooting stopped, there was a loud voice on a speaker mounted on one of the vehicles. They were speaking Farsi, and so I didn't really take the time to pop my head up for fear of reprisals. Most of the tribesmen skittered away like spiders, running past me. I popped my head up to see our boys coming out to meet the new party guests.

When I saw that, I stood up only to have a few guns point my way, but they had scopes so they saw that I was one of them. When I finally made it down the hill, I noticed that one of the upper command mercs was chatting it up with an African, but when I got closer I recognized the voice.

It was Austin from the Reagan, the guy who nearly bested me right after those New Jerusalem goons killed those elderly people, the guy who helped us escape from the air craft carrier...in a round about way. He wasn't African at all, but part of a larger resistance movement bent on bringing down Asher, and as I later found out, part of a remnant of the CIA.

He brought me in on the debrief, mostly gathering whoever was left and mustering them for an all out on some guy with designs on being another Hitler. There was talk of atrocities, of germ warfare to cull the weak, but mostly we was glad we hadn't been killed by the tribals. Grateful to be alive, I guess. Austin came over to me when he was finished with the main debrief, put a hand on my shoulder and smiled, a little laugh rising out of him.

"What's up, Gideon," he said. "Ready to join the resistance?"

Heck yeah.

Ethan

"We've tried nearly everything to disrupt the message of the two preachers," said commander Nellis, hanging on to the rail built into the ceiling of the transport van. "but we quit after so many attempts had failed."

We were headed down the main strip through the middle of New Jerusalem, the road a little bumpy for a new road. I think it was all the hills. I couldn't really see out of the van as it was one of those transport panel vans without windows. We were trucking pretty fast, and the electric motor that powered us there didn't make a sound, which I had always found to be out of place.

Engines needed to be noisy. I had trouble selling fully electric at the lot because they didn't have that "vroom" that most Americans liked.

We had spent about thirty minutes loading up our weapons, and we were only going to the temple mount to, as they said, "run crowd control", but I had a better idea. If these two preachers were causing so much trouble, I figured that the guy who whacked them would be moved up the food chain in the New Jerusalem organization, especially since Asher had pretty much given us license to kill.

It was worth a shot.

"Commander," I offered, raising my hand and steadying myself with my other as I sat on a bench with the others along the outside wall of the van, rifle clipped to my tactical vest. "Permission to speak freely."

"Go ahead," he said, his thick eyebrows raising.

"What tactics have been used against the two men?"

I heard a soft chuckle from some stiff across from me, and fought the urge to glare.

"We originally tried reasoning with them, but they are so deep into their dogma that they have been deemed unreasonable. We tried sending in a negotiator, but the minute the two men realized that the negotiator was not going to convert to their belief, the guy shriveled up like a prune before our eyes. Autopsy said that the water percentage in the negotiator was at something like ten percent. His skin was like soft mud.

"We then took more drastic measures because they'd basically declared war, and sent a sniper to sit on the building across from them and take them out. From the comm traffic, I heard the sniper (a good guy, from my old outfit) scream through the headset that he'd been made, and before he could squeeze off a shot, fire rained down on him from what he said came from above and burned him up before he could get out another word.

"We laid off them for a while, but then they started converting people, and so things got a little more delicate. Since then we've been working on a way to take them out without making too big of a scene, but they just won't leave that spot. I don't think they sleep or eat, because we've had them under surveillance now since a little bit after they appeared, and they just don't stop.

"The last group we sent up there came back with some kind of boils all over them. All of you are volunteering for a very dangerous mission, but you will be well compensated."

I thought about this for a few seconds, and started doing what I do best: worry about myself. I looked around the van at the other poor schmucks who were sitting here with me. I wasn't about to be cannon fodder. Something had to be said.

"If it's all the same to you," I said. "I figure the best chance I got in this deal is to come out with guns blazing. If all of us fire at once, then we can probably take them out."

"You are out of line, sir," said the commander, but the rest of the men in this van were all grumbling in unison, and the voice of the commander was being drowned out.

Yes...shoot them. Shoot them both. Don't give them a chance to do anything. Who cares about their followers. Shoot them, too.

It was that voice again, leading me, that voice of the man with the jet black hair and the long coat with the strange hands. I was going to do it. When these doors opened, I was going to shoot those two preachers dead, and if that commander got in my way, I was going to shoot him, too.

Josiah

Crowds are sometimes a strange mystery.

This crowd, for example, had been standing at this spot, here on the temple mount just outside the gates of the old temple for weeks. What was more amazing was that all of the devices we had so depended on that went silent with the great war suddenly worked again, but annoyingly all that was visible or audible was the voice and images of these two men who stood before me.

One of them, a tall muscular man for his age, barefoot, was dressed in a loose maroon tunic that fell to his ankles. A long grey beard and wild white hair, he had. The other wore the same beard but was bald except for a ring of white hair that wrapped around the back of his liver spotted head. The bald man wore a tunic like the other man, but his was of a woolen off white color.

What was astounding to me was their boldness. They cried out to the crowd to "repent" and "turn from evil", to "fall on their knees before Jesus the Nazarene." I had seen missionaries in Jerusalem before the war, before Gaza and the war tore apart the city of my birth. Now I had returned to find a shining new city, but in the heart of it now stood an example of the small minded dogma that threatened our way of life.

Standing next to me was a young woman, about twenty I suppose, pretty blonde hair she had, who smiled and nodded when I spoke to her. She indicated with the one English word she knew that she did not speak my borrowed language. I tried Hebrew, but she did not respond to this either. I noticed, however, that she was listening intently to the two old men.

Strange, this was.

I heard them speaking plainly in Hebrew, but she did not speak the language, so was her interest in these two men purely out of curiosity? I noticed her nodding now and again as if she understood them, and when I looked around, I saw many people from many parts of the world standing in the crowd, listening carefully, some of them rolling their eyes, but some of them seeming to follow the message of the old rabbis.

I had heard rabbis many times as a boy when my father would take me to the synagogue, but oy gevalt were these men well *versed*.

The two men's knowledge of the scriptures, astounding it was, spouting out verse after verse to support their message about Jesus being the true Messiah. It was insulting to most. Many of us felt this way, but none of us dared act on our impulses here. Several had paid the awful price for trying to stop them.

I remember it well. A year or so ago, when they first arrived here, a man with security personnel tried to tell them to cease and desist their loud noise and the taller one, the one with all of the hair, turned to spray a stream of fire *from his mouth*, engulfing the young man in white-hot flame. I wouldn't have believed it if I hadn't seen it myself, and I think that is what has drawn this crowd.

They want to see what next the two men will do.

Others who have tried to remove them from their night-and-day perch have met with similar fates, but the public had grown restless. There was a faction in this city to make a more concerted effort to remove them, but then there were also some within the city who had heard their message and "converted" to their paradigm, many of whom had off to the outer world gone to spread this message. Everything I had ever believed told me that these men were somehow fooling everyone, that they had become the wolves in sheep's clothing.

But how could all of these people understand Hebrew? As a skeptic, a professor of rhetoric in my time before the horrors visited our planet, I wanted to know. I wanted to ask them how they were able to do what they did. I wanted answers.

I gathered courage and stepped through the crowd, pushing my way forward past the dumb onlookers and sycophants who would give these men audience. Stepping out of the masses, I approached the barricades set up after the first of the incidents and even though I could feel my heart thumping in my chest, spoke out, I did.

"You there," I said, trying to be as kind as possible, wondering if my flesh would also be boiled away. "Why are you doing this?"

I fully expected some retribution, and the onlookers began to gasp as the bald one stopped, turned, and with purpose strode over to stand before me, his off-white tunic somewhat dirty, looking very healthy for a man of seventy as I guessed it, but also since no one had seen these two men eat or take any sustenance at all for almost a year.

Stared at me, he did…an uncomfortable stare.

He had the most wonderful brown eyes, eyes that seemed like they had seen so much. A wide smile parted that scraggly white beard of his, and he reached out to place a hand on my shoulder. He was a bit shorter than me, and had the look of a man that had spent his life herding sheep rather than working strange and horrible miracles.

"I am here as a witness to you about the Most High God," he said in Hebrew. "He is, was, and shall ever be holy, holy, holy, the Lord God almighty. You have abandoned the Lord's commands and have followed the false gods of this earth, the god of your own mind, of knowledge. How long will you waver between two opinions? If the Lord is God, follow him; but if your mind and your knowledge are God, follow them. You know from your youth the hundreds of prophesies that told of Jesus written thousands of years before his birth. Who else could they be referring? He would be of the line of David, he would be crucified, raised on the third day, heal the sick, feed the poor, give sight to the blind, yet you do not believe."

I had not been struck by some strange plague or fire, so I asked another question, a more daring question.

"But could the Christians have gone back and re-written those verses to support Jesus as Messiah?"

"In the valley of Qumran, the truth was found," he said, his eyes narrowing. "Near the Dead Sea, the scrolls determined that these verses were written by the prophets, proof to all Jews and Gentiles...thousands of years before Jesus walked this earth. Stop doubting and believe."

"They are planning to take you far from this city," I said to him. "Why do you not leave, for your own safety and for the safety of your friend."

He laughed.

"You do not understand the power of the Living God,"

said the man. "We will fall to earth today, for it is ordained, but like our Lord we will rise again. Look. Even now the wolf comes to eat the bones of the sheep, but he will choke on the marrow in three days time. Our day has come, the day that the Lord of Hosts will allow us to die so that all will see the power of the blood of the Lamb. Watch, child of David. All will be revealed."

I heard vehicles approaching, and the magistrate of the city stepped out of one of them. He carried a bull horn and was surrounded by an army of armed men in kevlar vests, helmets and riot gear. They were making one final assault.

"You will cease and desist this outrageous diatribe at once," he said in English, his Scottish accent thick and rolling. "It has been the judgement of this government that your intolerant message is disrupting our way of life, and you must come with us for transportation out of the city."

"We will return," the rabbis said in tandem. "for our lives are in the hands of Jesus of Nazareth, the one who rose from the dead, the perfect lamb who was slain for the sin of all mankind. Our message will not return void. Many have believed here in this city that has become Babylon, and many have gone out as witnesses to those who would be called to him. Their voices will be heard —"

And then the sound of gunfire ripped through the air as a spray of lead shot out from the many rifles of the security officers, puncturing large bloody holes through the tunics of the two men, their lifeless bodies falling like rags to the ground. People screamed and panicked and I was knocked to the pavement as the mob pushed and kicked and scurried away from the gunfire.

But when the smoke cleared and I was helped to my feet

by a concerned young man, I saw a crowd of security officers holding back the swelling crowd who only wanted to catch a glimpse of the two dead men, the two men who had haunted our city for so long, who had spoken their message of repentance and warning to millions of people here and who knows who else since their message seemed to be the only thing able to be broadcast on any electronic device.

Who had they reached?

For the first time in my life, I questioned my own beliefs.

Amy

Some smelly creep was climbing down the ladder, and he left the trunk to the car open enough so that all I saw was his outline in a turban and some kind of shabby old robes as he climbed down after me.

I braced the stock of the gun against my shoulder and pulled the trigger.

Click.

I hissed through my teeth.

I didn't know how to work the thing past pulling the trigger, so I guessed it was useless now. The guy turned around and saw me, and I threw the gun at him which he batted away as if it were a fly or something.

Great.

Just great.

I backed up into the darkness, looking around for something to use as a weapon that I didn't have to load, and there just wasn't anything at all. That's when the dark skinned little freak grinned at me and in the dim light I could make out that he probably never brushed...ever...and he had a gun.

Just then I heard a noise and somebody slammed the trunk lid closed on the bunker and it got really dark. I felt behind me, and kept low, trying to find a small place to hide between some of the metal boxes.

"I wouldn't shoot your gun," I said aloud. "Lots of stuff goes bang in here."

Note to self: when in a dark room hiding from a bad guy, avoid the urge to smart off. I could hear him walking toward my voice and I bit my lip, feeling around for something, anything that would be a weapon.

There.

But then he was on me, and his breath was hot in my ear. I kicked at him and something got near my face and I bit down on what was probably his cheek because he was trying to hold me down and kiss me or something gross like that. He shouted and put his full weight on top of me.

I struggled, and then I heard a loud bang.

Clayton

They were dead.

I couldn't believe my ears. They gunned the two of them down while they was tellin' every soul on earth (I guess) about the love and power of Jesus Christ. It was a message of peace, but I figured these people who lived in this here city, this city of New Jerusalem, were like the people of Ninevah in a way.

I'd been reminded of that story time and again as I traveled along, listenin' to them two guys talk about the love of God. There was a whole heap of urgency to their voices, and it had been beautiful to listen to. Sometimes they spoke in unison, sometimes apart, but through it all it sounded like the most pretty music you ever did hear, like the time I went to that family reunion in Tishomingo and my two old uncles got up and sang them hymns.

"Why they kill them?" asked Kashif. He looked ever so sad.

"I don't know," was all I could say. I was kinda speechless, really. I knew that I was to go to New Jerusalem, but was this supposed to be what happened to me as well? To live is Christ and to die is gain, I supposed. I wondered how old Jonah felt when he had to go to Ninevah. I mean, I knew what he did, but more and more I felt like that old guy. I wasn't about to spend no time in no whale…much less anything else like that.

I was goin' no matter what.

I said a prayer for Amy and for Gideon, 'cause I didn't 'spect to know where they was or what had happened to them, and I asked God to take good care of my good friend Kashif. He was so downtrodden and straight up homesick. He kept on about losin' his momma and his brother and sister. I felt a heap bad for him, even more than I let on. Sometimes this ol' world, as broken as it was, got a hold on you like some kinda pit bull and wouldn't let go.

We'd been out of water for about three days, and we was powerful hungry, too. We's livin' on little bits of that flatbread we got when we lit out of that village, and we hadn't seen hide nor hair of any friendly folks since we skirted 'round that skirmish back there a ways.

Durin' my prayer, I felt that still small voice tell me to look over the next hill and I'd find what I was lookin' for. That made me move a little faster even though my legs was rubbery, but when I topped the hill, all I saw was a great big rock about the size of a Volkswagen Beetle.

"It is rock," Kashif laughed. "Perhaps we eat it."

I walked up to the rock and put my hand on it. It was hard and sandy, and in the glarin' hot sunlight that was sinkin' down toward the horizon, that rock was a little warm to the touch. I had a notion, and put the lower end of my hickory stick right on the rock, but it was hard and unforgivin', sittin' there on the sand as if it was a laughin' at me and ol' Kashif. I sat down on the ground near it, and started to get real sleepy.

"Camp here tonight?" asked Kashif. "We must find food soon. We are to die here."

I nodded at him, and lay down on the sand in the growin' shadow of that rock, takin' out a small cloth from my satchel to ball up and lay my head on. Kashif sat near me, leanin' against the rock and layin' his head back against it. It wasn't long before the both of us was knocked plum out.

I had a weird dream that I was swimmin' in my grandmother's pool, that I was gettin' wet, but the water was runnin' over me and I was in my clothes. I woke up to find that I wasn't that much far from the truth.

The early mornin' sun was comin' up, and in that faint light I could see water pourin' outta that rock like a water hose all over the sand. I nudged Kashif, and he woke up with a funny snort and as soon as he saw that water he grabbed his canteen and started fillin' it up. I was gettin' gulps of it myself just as Kashif was cappin' off his canteen. That's when he shouted and let out a string of strange words that didn't make any sense to me.

"al-Mann wa al-Salwa!" he said, pointing at the ground, 'cause covering every inch of the sand around us was some kind of fluffy stuff that looked like cotton candy but it was white as snow. I picked some of it up and smelled it and suddenly got a memory of my grandmother's kitchen when she used to cook home made bread. One taste and I was hooked. The stuff tasted like that honey bread we used to get at Golden Corral…but better.

We gathered up as much of the stuff as we could get for the trip, and Kashif said that we aught not take what we did not need. I agreed with him, 'cause both of us had read that story.

"God is good," I said. "He's provided our meal and our water. Can't get much better than that, huh?"

Kashif smiled at me, his mouth full of that awesome bread.

"You may be on the path that is…God's," he said, his face

lookin' like those words were hard to say. "I will listen more to your faith story. Come, we will walk and I will listen to more of this."

We headed on over the next hill, on our way to New Jerusalem. I didn't know when or at what time I'd reach that city, but I figured I'd at least tell Kashif about the grace of Jesus before we reached there, and hopefully we could share together in that grace.

Kashif

Our supplies were running low again, but the bread we had found on the ground filled our bellies with only the smallest morsel. When I opened the bag to sate my hunger, it smelled like fresh bread from my mother's mud brick oven, but with a sweet quality that was beyond description.

Clayton was singing, as he did often. The songs he sang were unfamiliar to me, not having grown up in America, but they were always praising "the Most High God" as he put it. The songs were beautiful, even if his singing voice was much to be improved upon.

I decided to introduce him to some songs of my own, and he listened intently as we walked, and he tried to learn them. My songs were songs of praise as well, taken directly from the Psalms of David. He loved them, and wanted to learn more of my language just as I was trying to learn more than what I knew about English. I had learned to speak his language from listening to the television. My brother loved American television until he fell in with the zealots.

We walked down to the bottom of a wadi, and the outside cliffs started to rise up over our heads, but it provided some shade from the sun which was unforgiving and brutal. Clayton had told me the story of when they had seen the comet race over their heads toward the Pacific Ocean and we wondered if it had something to do with this horrible heat. Somehow, though, it seemed that the sun was a bit hotter than I remember it for this time of year. Even the shade was difficult to bear.

As we reached a spot where the floor of the wadi rose a

little, I noticed a small boy standing at the top of the cliff and he was looking down on us. The wind started to pick up bits of dust and dirt and blow them around, and I shielded my new eyes from the glare of the sun. Yes. It was not an illusion. It was a small boy standing there.

He seemed to be smiling.

I turned to Clayton to tell him about the boy and noticed that he had seen the small one as well.

"Do you see that?" he asked, his hand shielding his eyes from the sun.

"Yes," I replied.

At that moment, the boy started to shout "Down there!" in Farsi and pointed, his face a wide smile.

Clayton and I looked at each other, and then when we looked toward the boy again, we noticed that he was not alone. Several men, all of them armed, appeared on the cliff edge above us, all of them wearing ragged, dirty clothes.

"Whatever happens," Clayton said. "the Most High God is in control. This may get ugly, but we will be delivered. You must trust Him."

As the men started climbing down the rugged cliff face, some of them sliding and some of them nearly falling, I started to say a prayer for us both, but Clayton knelt in the dust, holding fast to his walking stick, head bowed, eyes closed, offering a prayer to the Most High God.

The next hour was extremely painful.

Hafiz

I had found a nice plot of land to graze my goat herd. It was becoming harder and harder to do this, since after the war the desert had become even more inhospitable.

If it were not for the words on the radio, I would have lost hope. I had lost nearly all of my possessions in the war, and some of my family, all of them so young, going off to fight the Americans and the Westerners. They would not listen to my wisdom, their father's wisdom. That war was not ours, not our people's.

My smallest daughter, my two young sons and my wife were all that was left of my family. They had followed me through this broken land trying to find any water, any food so that we might feed our goats and feed each other. They are our entire life now, and we prayed each day that the bandits so frequent here would not fall on us like jackals.

One day as I stood among the goats, using a small stick to keep them together, I noticed a wavy image of a man approaching. I could see parts of him, his image distorted by the heat waves rising up from the desert floor. I placed my hand on my knife, and told Rija my wife to take the little one to the tent. My sons were prepared, each of them reaching for their blades as well.

The man approached with his hands raised, and stood on the other side of my small herd of goats. My sons looked to me for guidance, and I put a hand out, pressing down at the air as a signal for them to remain calm.

"Do not be afraid," he said. "I come in peace."

I could not speak. Something was familiar about his face,

but I could not place it. He looked like my brother, but my brother had been killed in the war.

"There are two men over the next hill, down in a wadi, who need your help," he said, pointing away from us into the desert. "It is the will of the Most High that you go with me."

I had recently found hope in the words on the radio. I never thought of Isa as anything more than a prophet, but lately I had allowed the prophesies of old to speak to me. I had broken with tradition, and changed my mind. My heart followed. It seemed that this man spoke with the same voice that I had heard, and I looked toward the tent and shouted at my wife.

"Rija, stay with the herd. We will return shortly. Someone needs my help."

Rija, a good wife, knew to trust me and that trust had been given to me on the day of our wedding so long ago. My oldest boy, Iqbal, went with me while the younger Fawzi stayed with the herd. I knew that the herd was in good hands, that our daughter would be safe. I cannot explain why. I just knew.

"Take me to them," I said, and I took my satchel with my water skin, some bits of food and a bottle of iodine that I used on the goats when they developed infections.

We walked for some time until we crested a hill and looked down from the edge of the cliff of a wadi to find two young men lying face down in the sand. Quickly, Iqbal and the stranger descended to the bottom and covered them with blankets from my satchel and did their best to quickly carry them out of the wadi. The stranger's agility and strength were amazing, as he scaled the cliff on the way out carrying one of them over his shoulder like a sack of grain. We brought them back to our tent where we did our best to clean and dress their wounds.

Rija cared for the young man with the broken arm by tying on a splint to set his bone while I dressed the wound on the westerner's head. It was bleeding terribly, and by the time I was done I had to change my clothes, for his blood was all over me. When I finished working on them, hoping that this goat herder's skills were enough, I knelt and prayed over them. I looked up to ask the stranger if he wanted anything to eat, and he was gone, vanishing on the winds which brought him to me.

It was hours before the westerner awoke, and when he did he moaned and coughed, and I hoped he did not have any serious injuries that would require more attention than I could humbly give. The other young man was asleep for a long time, nearly a day. We prepared what food we could manage to spare, and the next day the westerner sat up and looked at us, and then he smiled.

He spoke to me in his language, probably English, but I could not understand him. I did not speak the western languages. He pointed at his friend and I told him that he was in much pain and needed to sleep, but he did not understand this. He only moved to sit near his friend, lay his hands on his arm, and mutter to himself. I knew he was praying, so I knelt beside him and offered my own prayer as he prayed in his language.

That night was difficult. Fawzi had first watch and heard noises coming from the north, the sound of shouting and gunfire. I stood watch the rest of the night, and the stars were beautiful. It seemed that the clouds were beginning to clear, and the strange haze that blocked the sun and night sky from us for so long had been swept away by the hand of the Most High.

I thanked Him for the coolness of the night air, for the health of my family, for the health of my herd and for the quick recovery of my new friends. We would care for them as long as needed. I would do what I had been taught to do as a small child: care for the helpless.

I wondered what happened to the stranger, and the stars in the night sky gave no answer. Perhaps he was malaak Haaris, their guardian angel. I decided that I and my family would be the malaak Haaris of these two young men.

When Kashif awoke, he wanted to know how he was rescued, and I told him of the stranger and the way he carried him out of the wadi. Kashif told me that when he was being carried, he awoke for a moment and saw that the hands of the man who carried him were deeply scarred as if pierced with a nail. He said that Isa had rescued him, and now he was in debt to him.

"You are not in debt to anyone," I told him. "Your debt has been paid by the man who carried you. All you have to do is accept it. It is a free gift."

"Then I do," he said. "I have seen much on this journey, and so I must accept my savior's...free gift."

We laughed together for a few minutes, and then he asked me:

"Does this mean we are becoming Christians?"

"Oh no," I told him. "We will not be drinkers of alcohol, eaters of pork or to become part of a different ethnic group. We will follow the teachings and life of Jesus the Messiah, free of worry about offending the Most High God, for we

have supped at His table."
    "Oh good."

Kelly

I had been shopping, but really couldn't call it that since everything was on Mark's credit chip. I picked up a few new dresses, but all the talk wherever I went was about the two men who had been killed at the temple mount. I went back to my apartment, and after getting a briefing about Anya's day from her sitter, said goodbye to the young girl as she left. She had been watching television, and it was up a little too loud.

"In a daring display of courage, seven security personnel gunned down the two radicals when they tried to unleash their powers on them. We have Asher to thank for this. His men were victorious, and this three days have been filled with partying and revelry. A massive crowd has been dancing and singing around the bodies of the two men, this plague on our way of life, and I don't think it will stop anytime soon..."

I turned it off.

Anya played with some blocks. She had built a small house out of them and was talking to a doll she had found.

"This is your new house," she said, her little voice kind of squeaky. "Nobody can take you out of it. You live here forever."

I wondered what she had been through and I could only imagine the horrors she must have witnessed in her short life. We had been through the boat ride down the river, and in that escape we had lost her mother, and her father was lost in the war. I doubted she even remembered him as she was probably only a newborn when he left.

So much heartache. So much terror.

At that time I had much hope that the world had finally calmed down…at least where we were. The city seemed a peaceful place if not strange. The two men had been killed for — what? — sharing their religion?

"Why did they shoot those men?" asked Anya.

Her question was so sudden that it completely caught me off guard.

"I…I suppose it's because they were kind of dangerous. I don't know."

"But they talked about Jesus," she sobbed. "They said that Jesus loves us."

She stood up, dropping the doll on the floor, and big tears began to flow down her cheeks. I grabbed her up and held her close as she cried so hard that she didn't make a sound, and I wondered if she would ever start breathing again. I kissed her face, tasting the saltiness of her tears, and that's when I joined her and we both sat on the floor and sobbed. I couldn't explain it, but I felt terrible for those two men. Yes, they had killed many of Asher's men, and Asher felt that they were a threat to this new city they had built, but the reporter on the television was so blatantly happy that they were dead, and the people dancing around the temple mount were in such a frenzy, like some type of primal orgy.

It was like some strange dream.

I took Anya into my bedroom, pulled back the comforter, and covered her up. I kissed her forehead and she put her little arms around my neck and pulled me close. We lay there like that until she fell asleep. I then sat up, wiped my eyes, and walked back into the living room to turn on the television. It looked like the ball had dropped on Times

Square on New Years Eve.

People were shouting and screaming, a band had set up and was playing music, and not only that, I could hear people through the walls of this apartment reveling and carrying on. I felt like the girl who got left home when everyone in the world was partying, but somehow I didn't really care, somehow I felt very sad about all of this.

This was all wrong. I realized that the two men had done some terrible things, and strangely no effort to remove them from the temple mount had succeeded, all of the attempts until now ending in someone being harmed or killed. I could see the sense in using deadly force, but somehow I was saddened by all of it.

I should have been glad they were dead, just as all the people in the shops were, but something in the back of my mind said that this was all wrong.

I sat on the couch, watching this giant party continue as it had been continuing for three days, when there was a flicker of static, and then I saw what looked like a wave of light explode outward from the middle of the crowd, knocking everyone to their feet, and roaring the speakers on the television so loud that I was sure they would break. The pane glass windows of my apartment vibrated as well. I looked back at the screen to see the camera bobble a bit, lose focus, then it tried to zoom in on what was going on, to see what had thrown the band members from the stage like rag dolls and knocked every person to the ground.

It was the two preachers, standing - no - floating just above the ground, their arms outstretched, their clothing brilliant white, shining like a welding arc.

"Judgement is coming," they said in unison. "His

winnowing fork is on the threshing floor, and he will separate the wheat from the chaff."

The camera followed, impossibly, as they rose into the air, becoming smaller and smaller, two white glowing orbs in the sky, and then they were gone.

"Bye bye," said a little voice, and I turned to see Anya standing in the doorway to the bedroom, her little hand waving as if seeing off a friend.

Gideon

"It's good to see you again, Gideon," said Austin, taking off his tactical gloves. "We've been checking out the new relay stations as part of cover, but we've been meaning to join up with Colonel Snyder for days."

"He bought it in the initial exchange," I told him. "Guy was a tough old soldier to the end."

"Well, at least his men are mostly intact. We need them to mount the rebellion against Asher. This is the last contingent to be gathered. The rest are mustering just outside of New Jerusalem."

Just then I remembered that I had told Amy to go hide in the bunker.

"Sir," I said, "I need to go grab Amy. I told her to hide and just wanted to check to see if she was o.k."

"Sure," he said. "Take your time."

I left him and sprinted over to the old car, and when I raised the trunk I yelled her name, but didn't hear any answer. I climbed down into the darkness, and took out a small mag-light I had liberated from an enemy. I twisted the end of it.

A dust flecked beam of light shone around the bunker, but I didn't see anyone standing up. Maybe she was hiding.

"Amy!" I said, a little louder, but no response. I started toward the back of the bunker, shining my light around in even sweeps, and then I saw her, lying under a tribesman, a large circle of blood soaking into the dirt floor.

I grabbed at the tactical vest that the tribesman wore over his robes and pulled, dragging him off of her, and she was covered in blood, eyes closed, didn't seem to be breathing. I knelt down and put my ear next to her nose and could feel her breath and that was when she grabbed me and held me in a vice grip and started screaming.

"It's ok, it's ok," I said, her clothes soaked with the blood of her attacker, some of it getting all over me, but I didn't care. I had her back. She was fine if not a little freaked out.

"Gideon, that man…he…" and she started sobbing, the weight of everything we had been through crashing down on her mind. I sat her up and helped her to her feet even though her knees knocked together a little and her hands were shaking, one of them with a nasty cut on the palm.

"You did good," I said. "Let's get you to the surface. We have some new friends."

Just before we ascended the ladder, she placed her hands on my shoulders, then reached up with one hand to place it gently on the back of my head, went up on her toes and kissed me. I gave in, and we kissed over and over, my heart racing, not caring about the dirt and the grime, just giving ourselves to each other in a moment of innocent love.

Before it went any further, she stopped and took my hand.

"Thank you, Gideon," she said, a faint smile crossing her soft lips, her eyes fluttering in the soft light from above. "I hope that wasn't —"

"Weird?" I said, laughing a little. "Naw. Not at all. Was wondering when my dogged good looks would draw you in. But…You're worse for wear. Gonna have to get that blood off of you so you don't look like Carrie."

She laughed, and it was good to hear that laugh. It was worth all the pain somehow. We climbed the ladder and when we reached the surface, the sun seemed brighter somehow and the desert air smelled sweeter. One of the men handed Amy a wet rag and a change of clothes, and when she came out of the latrine she looked so much different. There was a look on Amy's face that made me want to go on, to finish this task once and for all.

The world would be a better place.

Clayton

We waded down into the shallow pool near Hafiz's camp 'cause we had to go and baptize Kashif, bein' really careful of his broke arm, of course. Kashif said he was a follower of Isa and that he would be happy to go with me to New Jerusalem to tell others about His love. He was so bold, and I found out that Hafiz and his whole family had become believers just three weeks ago. They really loved Jesus, and would talk about him every chance they got.

Hafiz told us that there was a caravan headed to New Jerusalem and that his oldest boy would take us to meet it in the mornin'. I was glad God had put such a nice fella out here in the desert to help us out. We ate goat meat, some flat bread and had water that he'd boiled from the little spring-fed pool just outside of camp. His wife was so nice. She just went about cookin' up food as if it weren't no trouble even though I know they didn't really have a lot. I took what they offered and ate, and it was so good to have a home cooked meal and a warm bed to sleep in even if it was a little thin mattress lyin' on the dirt.

The next mornin' we said our goodbyes — well, Kashif said goodbye for me — 'cause all I could do was say "MA'a salama" and "Alhumdulilah" which were two phrases Kashif taught me. The old guy waved and bowed toward us, smilin', so I suppose it worked. I really did appreciate Hafiz's hospitality, and wished we coulda stayed with him.

Hafiz's son Iqbal took us along a northerly path by the sun and soon we saw a long line of old broke down cars that had been hooked up to teams of black horses and a few camels. There was several guys on top of the cars who had rifles and they had a bead on us before we even noticed 'em. I hoped Iqbal knew what he was doin', 'cause them guys looked pretty mean and all.

There was a heavy set guy who sat on a camel who kicked the sides of it to lope on over to us with his own rifle out. He had it pointin' at Iqbal's head, the tatters of his robe blowin' in the hot desert wind. Iqbal started in talkin' his language to the guy and Kashif put a hand on me to reassure me that everythin' was o.k., but I couldn't help but feel a little uneasy. The fat fella was all unwashed and had a beard down to the middle of his chest, and I think there was some little critters livin' in it. Least he was eatin' good so he might not be as cranky as a starvin' fella.

Iqbal handed the guy a bag of somethin', Kashif said it was goat cheese, and the guy looked in the bag and then at us and then made a motion with his hand.

"We are to go with him," Kashif said. "This caravan ends at New Jerusalem. These men going there to stay."

"Well I'm game if they aren't gonna kill us or eat us," I said, smilin' at the heavy guy just for good measure.

The heavy guy smiled back and that's when I noticed that he had about three teeth to his name and they was all yeller.

Wasn't long and we was wavin' bye to Iqbal and ridin' in the caravan, sittin' in the back of an old pickup bein' towed along by some really shabby lookin' horses. Kashif thought the transportation digs was pretty keen and I guess I was just as keen about it. As a matter of fact, these fellers were about the nicest bunch I encountered throughout all of my travels. Along the way we met more people who would sidle in next to us and move along the path we was on, and as we got closer to New Jerusalem we noticed that the amount of people in our little caravan started growin' and growin' until we looked somethin' like the people of Israel in that Ten Commandments movie.

I always thought that Heston fella was too over-dramatic to be anywhere near the real Moses.

One day on the road, Kashif pulled out that iPhone we found in that field of tanks and there was a broadcast comin' in from New Jerusalem of a party goin' on that was somethin' to behold. There was a whole mess of people dancin' in the streets 'cause them preachers had been shot dead. Then somethin' happened and all them people was knocked down flat on their faces by a huge blast of something, and then we seen them two guys who was once dead stand up and glow brighter than a star on Christmas, speak some choice words about judgement and rocket off into the sky. Me and Kashif was really excited about all this but the people around us who saw it was a little puzzled. It gave us a chance to talk to them about Jesus, and one of them got on his knees in the bed of that truck and gave his life to Him.

After a few days travel and a few nights campin' out under the stars, we started to see a little of the wreckage left behind by the big war. Old burnt out tanks and crumbled down buildings and lines and lines of rusted out old cars sittin' with sand all over them and weeds growin' up in the windows

Everywhere were signs of great battles and death.

Off in the distance we started to see it: the shining golden city of New Jerusalem.

It was like a big ol' gold dollar shinin' in the sun, its yellow glass towers all reflectin' the light of the sun somethin' spectacular. As we got closer, we noticed more and more of them security people with the kevlar vests sittin' on top of brand new white armored vehicles that had that symbol on them. It was that same symbol I saw on the flags in New Orleans and on the side of the U.S.S. Ronald Reagan. It was a globe with three curved lines coming out of it in three different directions, all curvin' off clockwise on a white background.

I also started to get kinda sick to my stomach, but it weren't because of the food I was eatin'. It was the place, the presence of the enemy. It weren't no enemy of this earth, though, but an enemy that was in the air, surroundin' everythin' like some kind of black fog that hung over us, taintin' the very ground.

"Do you feel it?" asked Kashif, his face lookin' drawn down and poor.

"Yeah," I said. "Feels like someone died here, like I 'spect the crows to come pick the meat off the bones."

"Why do you wish to come here, Clayton?" he asked.

"I don't know," I said. "I suppose that'll rear its ugly head soon, and when it does, we'd better be ready for it."

I mean, I came all this way. Might as well see what's in store.

Amy

Gideon sat next to me in the back seat of the dune buggy as we sped across the desert, the bumps jarring us something awful. The engines put off some nasty stink that probably was biodiesel or something like that. Austin sat in the front passenger seat, his afro looking kind of nappy, his dark face shiny with sweat. He twisted toward us in his seat and explained Gideon's role in the big plan to take down Asher.

"There is a pretty large force in Turkey waiting for our orders. It's made up of what is left of the European forces and the Americans who survived the big one. Asher is in league with the Russio-Chinese hegemony, and he is planning to consolidate that power into a final push to take over all that is left. He has managed to somehow gather enough resources and personnel to take over the better part of what was Jordan, Israel, Syria, Iraq and Iran. It's the old Persian empire all over again. The fact is that we are kind of low on spec ops at this point, and need your skills, the skills you demonstrated on the Reagan, to infiltrate the city and eliminate Asher."

I felt my stomach flip.

"How?" asked Gideon. "Why me?"

"We will get you in, and you will need to shave your head. They are expecting that mop of yours and the facial hair has to go as well. We have a set of clippers if you want to do it, but we also have a guy here who can accommodate you. Once you do that we will dress you up in the security officer garb that is common in the city."

"Again," Gideon repeated. "Why me?"

"Gideon," Austin explained. "You were sneaking around on the Reagan right under the noses of some crack commandos, some of them loyal to our cause, and we didn't even know you were there. However you learned this amazing talent of yours is not important. You are a valuable asset to your country, and as a former intelligence operative, I can tell you that we use any talent that is readily at hand. We simply do not have anyone like you at our disposal. The security guys know all of my men. They don't know you. You are the best choice for this."

"Once I'm inside, what do you suggest I do? I'm not like flipping John McClane. I'll need some help."

"You will," Austin said. "Now that the two preachers are out of the picture, Asher is looking to consolidate his support with the people of New Jerusalem by giving a big speech and throwing a huge party. We want you to position yourself on a scaffold just across from the podium, use a breakdown weapon that we will provide for you, and assassinate Cain Asher with extreme prejudice."

"Why?" I said, putting my hand out as if I could stop any of this machine that was clanking along. "What makes this guy so bad other than his supposed connection with the Russians and the Chinese? I thought the Chinese were done after Volos and the nukes ripped through there."

Austin looked at the road in front of him for a minute and then turned back to continue.

"Everybody thought that the Russians and Chinese dissolved their alliance after the war ended, but that is a lie. That's really the small of it, however. Did you know that there are not any people living in New Jerusalem under the

age of forty? Asher systematically gasses the elderly. The
guy is like a David Koresh or a Jim Jones. He's got people
believing he is some kind of god or something…and he has
fanatical followers. Once they managed to kill the two
preachers at the temple mount, they quietly arrested all of
their followers the next night and took them to who knows
where. We still don't know what happened to them. There
is also the matter of some very powerful and experimental
hardware that Asher is rumored to have. It could tip the
balance considerably. Something has to be done about him.
If we cut off the head, the snake will die."

Gideon sat next to me looking out at the rushing
landscape and Austin stared at us, his face a weird
expression that I couldn't really read. All we could hear was
the sound of the loud engine and the wind rushing into our
faces.

"I'll do it," Gideon said, a soft chuckle bubbling out of
him. "Yippy kay yay."

"Good," Austin said, a smile spreading across his face.
"We will brief you further once we reach the safe house."

We sat in silence for most of the rest of the way, but the
more time that I sat there, the more I started to worry. Before
long my worry turned into just straight up anger. I folded
my arms and looked at Gideon, but he was looking out at
the rocky desert that blurred by us and wouldn't look at me.

I knew why.

We started seeing burned out buildings pretty soon and
then larger ones, most of them crumbling and burned from a
horrible fire. I had heard that there were nuclear bombs
used in the middle east during the war and started to get
worried about radiation. I wondered how close a person

354

had to get before they got sick from the fallout.

"That's it," said Austin. "Just ahead. The first checkpoint. Just act normal."

We slowed down and soon we saw a white army tank with a huge, weird looking barrel sticking out the front. Two men sat on top of the tank, and there was a large gate that went across the road. Piled up on either side of the dirt road were huge chunks of blackened concrete and debris from some wrecked buildings, I guessed. There were a couple of dune buggies like the one we were in sitting on the other side of the gate and two men approached us wearing the uniforms I had seen on the Ronald Reagan.

I saw several dusty white skulls laying in a pile near the front of one of the tank treads.

"Identity please," said one of the men, his accent sounding foreign, probably French. English was not his first language. "Give ze card to us."

Austin pulled out a card and handed it to the guard who looked at it, scanned it with a little hand held thingy that looked like a cell phone and then handed the identity card back to Austin. With a nod, the other guard lifted the barrier and we drove on through.

Beyond it was the golden city that so many people had told us about. Its buildings were bright and shone in the sun as if they were made from pretty jewels. Oh, they probably had shops.

But who cared, really. Austin and his goons were going to take Gideon away from me and make him do some god awful stunt that was probably going to get him killed. I started thinking about Ralph just then, but he was always in the back of my mind somewhere anyway. Gideon would not be another Ralph.

Once we were through the checkpoint and zooming toward the city I turned to Gideon and let him have it.

"Gideon, why on earth do you think you can make a difference in this thing, anyhow?"

He looked at me, put his hand on mine and smiled, but it was a really uncomfortable smile like it hurt his face to do it.

"I have to, Amy," he explained, his voice softening. "If I don't then they won't have anyone to do this job. I fit with these guys. I never liked those New Jerusalem phonies for one second — knew they were bad news — but now... Amy you didn't see what they did to those elderly on the Reagan. This has to stop, and if it can stop by taking out their leader, then I'm going to do it."

"But I can't lose you, Gideon!" I shouted, tears blurring my vision. "I just can't! I lost Ralph because we just *had* to fight. Just *had* to go and put ourselves in danger. Can't we just go away from here? Find some place where it's quiet, someplace where there's no threat of death all the time?"

"And where is that, Amy?" said Austin, butting in. "It's everywhere since the war. People are without hope. This man, this Asher, is trying to strip all hope from humanity. He has to be taken down, and Gideon is the only one who can make that happen for us. All of our other allies are being compromised as we speak. I don't even know how long my identity card will last."

"What do you mean?" I asked.

"They are on to us," he said, his voice suddenly getting all shaky, and it wasn't the road. "It's only a matter of time before every person in our organization is ferreted out. For some reason Asher is very adept at espionage. I think he was with some kind of shadow organization before the war or maybe was the head of one, and the war has made him insane. It's not Hitler we are dealing with here, but someone worse, someone who sees all other views as nonsense before his grand plan of world domination. He is a genius, has figured out how to activate every electronic device on the planet to send out his message, is always one step ahead, and seems to know what we know before we know it."

We sat in silence for a little while, and Gideon reached out to take my hand and I let him. I was still mad. I didn't like this at all, but then I started to think about what Clayton said to me back on the river bank, about how things happen and we "gotta trust God with it". Well, I was pretty much tired of worrying about Gideon, about everything. I decided to start praying like I did back on the boat when we were going up river and all the freaky militia guys were trying to kill us. I closed my eyes and asked God to help us, to help Gideon so he wouldn't leave me, and that was when I heard it.

It was a small voice, almost like the sound of the wind, and it was speaking my name. It was calling to me, asking me to trust, to give in, to just have faith.

We stopped the dune buggy just at the edge of the city near what looked like a broken down warehouse. Two men were waiting on us. They looked mostly friendly, but I felt kind of uneasy about the whole thing, and Gideon was set in stone. He got out of the buggy and then helped me out.

"These two men are Hajid and Lawrence," said Austin, introducing me. "They will care for you until Gideon has done this task for us, and then they will ensure that you and Gideon, Lord willing, get out of this city before our forces in the north start their assault."

The two men looked tough enough, their kevlar vests on tight, their guns slung over their shoulders. They looked all gung-ho about it, but I was not liking it one bit. I was still sure I could convince Gideon not to be their Lee Harvey.

"Can we have a minute?" asked Gideon of Austin.

Austin nodded. "Say what you gotta say, but we have to go soon."

Gideon took my hand and we walked to the edge of the clearing and stood near another one of those piles of concrete chunks. I could see another skull, but I didn't want to ruin the mood by pointing it out.

"I'll be fine," he said, putting his arms around my waist. I wanted to resist, but didn't. "Don't worry about me. I've been through a lot. You know that. I survived by stealing from the militia for a long while before I found Kelly's group. My dad would climb out of his grave and kick my butt if I didn't help these people."

"Let him kick your butt," I said. "I'd rather have a beaten and bruised you than a forever dead you. I just can't take losing another person, Gideon."

"I know," he said, wiping a tear from my eye. "It'll be ok. You stay here with these two grunts and I'll be back soon…then we can go get that little house you were talking about. I'll even marry you or something."

"You wish," I said, laughing, feeling a little better but not really. "If you don't come back to me, I'll hunt you down and kill you myself."

He laughed, that strange crooked mouth laugh that was so cute to see. I bet his mom probably loved that once.

Gideon kissed me for a long time, but not long enough,

and then he was on the dune buggy and gone, leaving me to make uncomfortable awkward small talk with two soldier types.

They were so boring, and terrible at cards.

Kashif

Clayton was very determined to get to the Dome of the Rock, but I did not feel the necessity to do so. We had come so far, done so much, but if our journey was to go to New Jerusalem for the purpose of dying for our cause, then it was a foolish purpose.

As we neared the main gates we slowly found the remnants of what the war had done to this region. Large chunks of concrete, blackened by fires and destruction, lay scattered about surrounding many of the ruins of what used to be a great city.

As a boy, I had traveled here to fulfill a pilgrimage to the Dome of the Rock. I did not see it, but the smells were familiar except that they now also smelled of decay and putrid garbage.

Before we reached the first checkpoint at the entrance of the city, Clayton became agitated and grabbed me by the arm as he told me to tell the driver that we would be "getting out here". I did as requested, and we left the caravan to find ourselves standing in the middle of the road with New Jerusalem just out of our reach.

"Why must we stop here?" I asked Clayton.

"We have to try to get in another way," he said, his hands gripping and twisting on the bark of his walking stick. "There is something we must prevent. God will guide us from here."

We stood there for a while until the caravan passed through the first checkpoint and the sun began to go down behind the hill. It would be dark soon, and I did not like the look of the ruins around us. I was new to these eyes, but I knew danger when I saw it.

"Come with me," Clayton said, and he walked around one of the burned concrete walls and pulled on a rusted old sheet of plate steel to find a small four wheeled vehicle with two handlebars and a seat big enough for two people.

"What is this?" I asked.

Without a word, Clayton climbed on the vehicle, turned a key that had been left in the ignition, and then pressed a button. I heard something whine and then the old thing coughed to life, apparently still holding fuel of some type. I sat on the seat behind Clayton, and he pressed on a lever on the right handlebar and we were off, bumping and bouncing along the rocky ground, finding paths here and there and eventually we had skirted completely around the checkpoint and were racing toward the city.

But we were not going there.

The gas ran out just outside of a warehouse with broken out windows and dirty rags of cloth hanging from one of the flagpoles outside. We heard shouting from within, and the sound of a girl screaming. We raced into the open doorway to find two soldiers pointing their guns at a young woman with long red hair tied in a ponytail behind her head. She wore baggy military clothing, and she had her hands on her head and was on her knees. One of the men was shouting in Farsi for her to get on the floor, but the woman was refusing, shouting back at him with a shrill voice that was making him lose his temper.

Clayton did not stop, did not slow his stride, but ran over to stand just ten or so feet from the men, and pounded the end of his walking stick into the hard concrete floor, and it echoed somehow from the broken walls of this building.

"In the name of Jesus Christ I rebuke you!" he shouted.

They turned to fire at him, and when their bullets exploded from their guns, I saw the strangest sight. A man appeared, flying horizontally just in front of Clayton, catching the bullets in mid air, and then vanishing or rather fading away. The attackers fired again and this time the guns were removed from their grasp and thrown across the room by the mysterious disappearing man…and then he reappeared and went to work on the attackers.

Their screams echoed off the walls as they ran from the building in terror.

Once the men were gone, I saw the mysterious defender no more and the young woman turned and noticed Clayton. Her face red with the tears of her near demise lighting up with an expression of joy.

"Clayton!" she shouted, bounding from her knees to throw her arms around Clayton and nearly squeeze him to death. "I thought you were dead!"

When she let him go and he could catch his breath, he lay his walking stick on the floor and hugged her close.

"I ain't dead, Amy," he laughed. "There's still too much work to be done."

After this, he introduced me to Amy Lawrence, and I found out that she had been with Clayton from the beginning of his journey. So strange how they had been reunited after so long, and so far apart. She had some unfinished business.

"Clayton," she said. "Gideon has gone off with some resistance group to assassinate Asher, the leader of this city. I couldn't talk him out of it, and he feels like this is important to the world…at least that's what Austin was saying."

She filled us in on all the details of the attack, about the armies to the north, the Chinese and the Russians, and everything else.

"The thing is," she said. "I just don't have any peace about this at all, and I just know he's headed into a trap. These guys you just ran off were supposed to be taking care of me, but instead they decided to, you know, *take care* of me — in the mafia sense. If these guys were bad, then what about Austin? He told us that this Asher guy was in the process of ferreting out his organization. What if they got to those two guys who tried to kill me…or what if they got to someone else close to Gideon?"

Clayton stood still for a moment then raised his hand to his chin, closed his eyes briefly, and then spoke.

"There's probably a lot of stuff we don't know, Amy, and if those guys were dirty it might mean that the rest of 'em are…but what would they be up to if they plan on knockin' off this city's biggest war-chief?"

"I…I'm just so worried," she said. "Gideon is headed for something really bad, Clayton. We have to try and stop him."

"We will pray, Amy," said Clayton. "God brought us together right here in this place even though you thought I was dead and I didn't think I'd ever see you again. That's important and can't be ignored, 'specially how I found you. But if we go headlong into that city we're liable to get *ourselves* taken care of."

We knelt down right in the middle of that old burned out building and started to pray. We asked for guidance, protection, and help. We prayed for peace and comfort, for our hearts were heavy. I knew that the Most High could hear us, for I could feel his presence in and near us, floating around us, penetrating us, pushing out all the evil spirits who would cloud our minds or strike our hearts with fear. That is when Amy broke.

"I want peace, Clayton," she said, tears flooding her eyes. "I want the peace of God in my heart, the peace that you have. I've lied to myself for too long. No amount of going to church or following the rules can do it. I've...I've never really had a relationship with God, just thought I was good because I was so involved or that I led a good life. I need to know that I am ok with God."

Clayton put his arm around her as they sat on the floor. I was compelled to raise my hands in praise of the Most High who is worthy and is rightly to be praised.

"All you gotta do is ask him to save you, to trust in his grace to save you," Clayton said, his voice very soft. "If you do this, then you will have peace. He wants you to be his child, to hold you in his arms and carry you through the storm. Give your life to him and he will never leave you nor turn his back on you."

I watched as Amy bowed her head and mumbled a prayer that was private between her and the Most High.

After we had spent some time in song, praising the name Isa, Jesus, Lord of all creation, we set about planning what we would do about Gideon.

Gabe

I saw the two witnesses, Moses and Elijah, the messengers of the Most High, ascend back to heaven, their job done, their warnings bestowed on the world for one last time.

Judgement was about to come.

There was a whirring sound that emanated from a satellite near me. I turn to look at it, a piece of technology that had not been in operation for a few years now. Today it activated as the monster set in motion one of the wheels in his grand plan.

I descended through the stratosphere and deeper, lowering down past the large balloons concealing giant propellers that generated power from the wind. Below this was the city of New Jerusalem. This was not its real name. A more appropriate name would be Babylon, but this city was far more spectacular than that ancient city, full of people who were just as foolish. They shook their fist in the face of the Most High even though he sent his only Son to save them from their pain and anguish, their sin, so that they could sit at His table and be called friend. It is a mystery to us, to those of my kind, as to why this must be, how this must be.

It seems impossible to us, as strange as when a human being looks at the vastness of the universe and marvels at its workings. I suppose we have that in common, the misunderstanding of mysteries. This misunderstanding has allowed this monster of a man to deceive millions.

There was a celebration in the middle of the city of death.

I saw the swirling black cloud of the enemy surrounding the stage and the crowd of people who had gathered there. The monster stood at the podium, his voice heard by all of the reactivated electronic devices upon the earth. It was not the power of the Most High who activated them all, but the monster's. We simply used his evil for our good.

Now he was using it, spewing his filth to every corner of the globe. He railed against all religion, saying that he had discovered a cure for the plague, and then used the plague as a metaphor to speak of all religions of the world. He shouted about the coming of an age without religion, where humans would reach to the stars and beyond, building a world in their own image. He said that the war was caused by religion, beliefs in that which cannot be seen.

It was about to be seen.

I reached for my weapon, the hilt warm in the palm of my hand. It was time for the great war, the war to end Babylon the Great, the war to end all wars…and once and for all the Lamb would silence the roaring lion.

Kelly

"I get a seat of what?" I asked. "Why?"

"Honor, Kelly," said Mark, his eyes lighting up. "You get a seat beside me on the stage with all of the dignitaries. This is a great day, my love."

We rode to the temple mount in style, as stylish as a four seater electric car could be, I guess. At least I had on a nice dress. When we arrived, there were several scaffolds that had been set up to make a massive arena where a standing room only crowd had gathered numbering about ten thousand by my estimate, and people were so glad to see us...or rather Mark.

They had several questions for him, and he stopped and took his time with most of them, carefully answering all of their concerns. Most of the questions had to do with new policies implemented by Asher. I didn't really understand it all, but Mark took my arm and the security personnel soon parted the way for us as we moved through the crowd to ascend the stairs and sit in chairs facing out toward the masses. A large lectern stood in the middle of the stage and the white flags of New Jerusalem flapped in the warm evening breeze.

Some of the people in the crowd started singing something, and before long it was like one of those concerts I used to go to with my husband, the people swaying back and forth, a young girl being lifted onto the shoulders of a young man to gain a better view of the stage. All they needed was a giant beach ball being passed around by their outstretched hands to complete the image.

A band, set up on a smaller stage to my right, hard to see through the glare of the spot lights, started playing a song that I did not recognize, but it was more of an instrumental number for guitars and drums, with a rock feel to it. Everyone started clapping in unison, and as the crowd started dancing within the limited space of the arena, Asher appeared to my right and walked out onto the stage.

The crowd went crazy, screaming out Asher's name, a rhythmic cadence of: "Asher, Asher, Asher".

He held up his hands to quiet the crowd, and amazingly they silenced themselves.

"People of New Jerusalem," he said, his voice rich and evenly managed. "I come not to you today to praise the two preachers, but to bury them."

The crowd roared again, and he again put his hands up to quiet them only to stay in that position while they cheered and laughed and shouted out profane curses toward the two men who had mysteriously vanished two days ago.

"Ah yes," he continued, the crowd noise subsiding. "I feel the same way."

It was strange to see this man, standing before this crowd, directly in front of me, wearing a green t-shirt and jeans, strangely barefoot. He looked back at me, smiled, and I felt like something crawled down my back. Part of me was glad Anya was back at the apartment with her new nanny.

"Today is a new day," he said, turning back to the crowd, gripping the edges of the lectern. "Today we celebrate what it means to be human. Today we shall end the oppression that is religion, that nasty old man who nearly ended our world with its prejudice, its bigotry, its intolerance. Today we will bask in the glow of the new world we will create for ourselves."

Some movement, something out of place at the back of the crowd caught my eye, and I noticed some people standing on what had to be a raised platform, possibly chairs, holding signs that read "REPENT AND BE SAVED" and "JESUS CHRIST IS LORD OF ALL". Moments after I noticed these people, I saw them yanked down from their chairs by security personnel who then pulled out nightsticks and began beating them, knocking them out of my view. I saw the nightsticks rising and falling, rising and falling, until I could no longer look. I looked at the back of Asher's head.

"Too long," he said, his voice reaching a higher pitch. "Too long have we allowed the small minded people of the world to talk and talk and talk and never get things done! I know they say that Rome was not built in a day, but look at what we have built together in only a few years! Look around you. No crime. No limits. No hunger. No disease. We do not need a heaven when there is heaven right here. We have eliminated pain and intolerance and the nonsense that made the human race flawed. Welcome to the new world that will one day reach the stars and beyond. We *will* rebuild this world in our own image. Who needs God anyway when we can be gods."

I started to look again to see if I could see the people who had been beaten by the security personnel, and that led my eye above to the flood lights that topped the scaffolding across the arena from the stage. Just out of the range of my vision, I caught a glimpse of someone climbing the scaffolding, and for an instant I thought it looked like the outline of someone I knew, someone familiar.

Gideon.

Gideon

Yeah so these guards were true rent-a-cops. Not a single one noticed me sneak back behind the security line with my little package and climb the scaffolding. Probably helped that I'd shaved my head so they didn't recognize me.

The platform at the top was the perfect spot. The flood lights just above shielding me from anyone who would look up and see me pointing a rifle at the giant swelled head of Asher.

That guy was really full of himself. All I heard once I blended in to the crowd was them talking about how awesome he was. All I saw was just another guy who figured something out and now wanted all the glory. The song remains the same, I guess.

I pulled the long black box out of the satchel that I had lugged up to the platform and then started assembling the rifle. It was sweet, too. It was a takedown version of an AR-7, the kind pilots packed in their planes in case they got shot down and needed a good rifle. It would make quick work of Asher.

As I was putting the rifle together, I thought about my dad the first time we went to the shooting range. "Aim, exhale, squeeze" he would say. All he taught me was about to come into play. If I wanted to see Amy again, wanted the remaining allied armies to have a chance at peace, I would take care of business and get myself out of here before the rent-a-cops were any wiser.

I meant what I said about marrying Amy.

Where would I find a justice of the peace?

No matter.

After I had assembled the gun, I loaded a few rounds into the clip and slowly set it in its place just in front of the trigger guard. Laying down on my chest, I braced the butt of the gun on my shoulder, and looked down the scope at a blur. Adjusting the scope, I then judged the wind speed and direction, making...

Did he just look at me?

It looked like he looked right at me through the scope and winked. No. It was a smile or something. I thought he looked at me for sure and I started to sweat.

No time.

Had to do it.

Amy. Just think about Amy.

Aim, exhale, squeeze.

The report was louder than I expected.

Josiah

The best spot I could get was right at the back of the crowd. The stage looked long and skinny from here, a long black platform rising up like an altar before the sea of people.

A young man picked his girlfriend up and sat her on his shoulders just in front of me, so I moved again, trying to get through the thick mass of spectators, but found myself pressed against a fence at the back near a tall scaffolding where many spot lights were mounted.

Whatever Asher had to say I would have to hear it from the back of the crowd.

After some time, a band began to play some music that had a rock beat, a few men who before the end had been quite successful in the music industry. They were older now, but still young, playing the music that made them famous.

Asher approached the stage as the music reached a crescendo. He wore not a suit or a tie but a green t-shirt and a pair of jeans. It took some time for him to quiet the crowd as they screamed and cheered, the woman on the young man's shoulders in front of me raised her arms and laughed, then screamed loudly, then put her fingers in her mouth and whistled.

Asher began his speech well, speaking about the end of an era and the beginning of the new age of enlightened progress and change. That is when I noticed the young man near me reach down and pick up a piece of plywood, painted white it was, and written across it in black lettering the words "JESUS CHRIST IS LORD OF ALL".

A woman on my other side knocked me over, nearly.

"Excuse me," she said with a smile, touching my arm gently. "Sorry."

Then she grabbed her sign , a bright red one with white letters that read "REPENT AND BE SAVED"...and there were others. They began chanting, standing on chairs, shouting loudly about Jesus of Nazareth, the Messiah, they said. Screaming it, they were.

The young woman who nearly knocked me over looked at me and laughed as if she were a college freshman playing a prank, but these people were serious, converted by the two rabbis, I supposed.

As if by magic, I suddenly saw a line of security personnel brandishing nightsticks and heading toward our little group. I put up my hands and tried to tell them that I was not with these people, but they did not listen, and one of them hit my left cheek with the end of his brutal weapon. I was knocked to the ground, and the rest of the protestors were kicked and beaten with the nightsticks in a way that was beyond a normal crowd control move.

Murder in the guards eyes, there was.

The young people did not put up a fight, and I heard the young woman who had apologized to me.

"Lord," she said as one of the security personnel, a large, burly man with a mustache, beat her across the back. "Please forgive them, and let this man beside me hear the truth of your gospel though I go to my rest."

And then she was knocked unconscious...and then she was being beaten even still by the security man, the baton in his hand getting covered in gore.

I tried to crawl away, but I was being beaten on the backs

of my legs, and I was sure that I had broken some ribs because I could feel the sharp pain when I breathed. I put my hand to my side, and felt someone take my other hand. When I looked up, there was a man pulling me to my feet, a man who looked vaguely familiar, his beard thick and his hair long and dark, with eyes that broadcast love to all around him. I could see the back of his hand and the deep scar there, but my mind became clouded with the terror of what was happening to me.

"Come," he said. "Follow me."

I stood, pain shooting through my chest, my legs feeling like rubber, and I followed the man into a swelling crowd of onlookers as if following the edict of a king, escaping the painful nightsticks and the eerily silent security personnel.

When I managed to reach the outside of the crowd, find the man who had helped me I could not. I looked around and did not see him anywhere, so I sat upon a curb trying to rest from my ordeal, and that was when I heard the gun shot.

Ethan

Guard duty.

Yeah, it was a joke.

I stood at the back of the crowd, and our guys had just taken care of a bunch of punks who decided to try and rain on Asher's parade. I stood with my rifle shouldered and a fresh cigarette dangling from my lips.

From the chatter in the earpiece, the protesters had been "dealt with" if you know what I'm saying. Wished I could have watched that.

I didn't really see Asher get hit but I heard it, the report echoing around the large banners and outer effacements of the arena. As soon as I heard it, I pulled my gun out and then heard the scaffold next to me start to ring and shake as someone was flying down the ladder on the outside of it as if he were covered in grease.

When he dropped down to the ground not five feet away from me, I knew who he was even though he'd shaved his head.

"Gideon," I mouthed, wrapping my fingers around the pistol grip of the AR-15. "I've been waiting for this."

"Ethan," he said. "I don't —"

But I had him. I put the gun up to my cheek to squeeze off a round, end this dirtbag who left me for dead, who stuck a sharp stick in my leg, who —

I didn't feel it at first, but looked down to see the handle of something protruding from my chest. How did he do that? How...

"Sorry dude," said Gideon moving close, pulling the

knife out, his eyes looking so sad...sad. "Nothing personal."

I sank to my knees as he ran away, and as I fell down to the ground, the warmness flooding out of me, things went black...darkness like I had never seen flooded over me.

And then I was standing in a dark place with countless others.

Kelly

It was warm and sticky and I couldn't breathe, and it took a moment for things to register.

Asher's head had exploded all over me.

Some security men wearing their thick kevlar and their black helmets grabbed me and pulled me from the stage, rushing me, carrying me away to a waiting car where we sped away so quickly, I did not have time to process what had happened.

I looked at my hands, my blood stained hands, and I thought about Anya who had been left back at my apartment with the young woman who had been hired as a nanny.

I tasted copper and I spit out a bone fragment, a piece of Asher's skull, and then I started crying and looked around the four seater electric car and there were not any familiar faces.

I was paralyzed. My heart racing, my face contorted in a bloody frozen mask of fear.

What will happen now? What will they do now that he's dead? Will Mark be in charge? Will this place break apart like the rest of the world? I couldn't think about it. It was just too much.

And I knew it was Gideon. I had seen his silhouette as he climbed to the top of the scaffold. Just before the shot I was trying to see if it was really him, leaning back and forth and trying to see around Asher, but the light was so bright and I couldn't see…and then I was blinded by Asher's—

We were taken back to Asher's building, the golden glass

reflecting the mess of my face, hair and clothes as the security guards rushed me, carried me, into the building, down three flights of stairs to a large room that looked like a parking garage, all concrete with large round pillars supporting the ceiling. I was shown to a bathroom by a female officer…oh it was Emmy…Emmy with her short red hair and her face that looked strained and yet trying her best to make me feel at ease.

"Go in there and wash up," she said. "I'll have someone bring you some fresh clothes."

I barely heard her, and as I walked into the large cold bathroom with its wide black tile squares and stainless steel walls, I collapsed in the corner when I got a good look in the mirror. I had chunks of gore in my hair and on my face, and my dress was soaked in sticky blood. I staggered to my feet and shot to the sink, where I gagged and vomited up what I had eaten that evening. I ran the water to wash it down, then went to the sink to the right and turned on the water there, trying to wash the stains from my skin and the gunk out of my hair…Asher's blood.

Gideon.

Why had he done this? What was the reason? I just didn't understand. Asher had done much to try to bring humanity back together. I thought about filling the sink, holding my face under until I couldn't breathe, and that was when a woman came in with a bundle of fresh clothes.

"Ma'am?" she asked, a petite blonde woman wearing black military style fatigues. "Are you ok? Do you want me to call the doctor?"

I lifted my head from the water, catching a glimpse of the red mess flowing down the sink.

"No," I managed. "Just trying to…" and then I lost it, and the girl ran to me and held me as I sank to the floor, sobbing.

"Ma'am," she said, helping me to my feet. "I have to get you cleaned up. They have brought Asher's body and the Magistrate needs you there to support him. He told me himself. He said he just can't do this without you."

I tried to smile, but the expression on the girl's face made me think I had grimaced.

"I'm Debbie," she said. "I'll help you get fixed up. I have some shampoo and some makeup in my kit and we can get you looking nice in no time. Come on."

She helped me to my feet, and we went to the sink to finish the sloppy job of washing all of Asher's remains from my hair and face. In about thirty minutes or so, we had washed it all away, and Debbie helped me get dressed and put on makeup, brush my hair, and I did my best to cover the fact that I was about to fall to pieces again.

We exited the bathroom and there was Mark. He ran to me and took me in his arms and kissed me. I melted again, and he nearly carried me to the center of the parking garage where a crowd of twenty or so people circled a medical gurney with a blanket over it, a soaking red stain on one end.

A man with a stethoscope around his neck checked his watch and pronounced Asher dead. People were crying, many of them moaning in despair and pain. Mark was one of them, and I guess he decided that now would be a good time to reassure everyone.

"Friends," he said, his voice almost a whisper, but strangely audible in this large space. "We must carry on with Asher's dream. We will dress his body and allow him to lie in state for a few days as were his wishes should this happen. The people will have one last look at him before he is cremated. We will then spread his ashes about the streets of this city he built."

Mark raised one hand and wiggled his index finger. Three security personnel appeared near him, and I felt suddenly surrounded by power. Mark turned to his lieutenant, a tall African-American man wearing black military fatigues.

"Find who did this," said Mark, his voice a growl. "We will make an example of those who would upset the happy balance we have created here. And call in all assets. It is time for plan B."

"Right away, sir," said the man, who ran toward the door with his two troopers in tow, and I suddenly felt like someone walked over my grave.

Gideon

Had to duck down an alleyway after I took out that soldier poser. To see him there at the bottom of the scaffold was...well...all kinds of wrong place at the wrong time.

Guy had it coming, though.

I slipped in the side door of a shop that I guessed had closed for the day, slipping in behind some large crates with shrink wrapped cases of bottled water. I took my knife out, wiped the blood from the blade on my pants, and slit one of the packages open to grab a bottle, get a drink. The water felt good on my throat even if it was lukewarm. No telling when I'd get another chance to hydrate.

I could hear the people running by outside, screaming, shouting about the death of their fearless leader. Austin said that I'd be doing the world a favor taking this guy out, but somehow there didn't seem to be that much of a celebration outside.

I started to feel sick.

Never done anything this...big. Squirreling around outside of militia camps and stealing food was nothing like what I had just done.

I knew that I had to get out of the city and pronto, but Austin said that he would meet me in the ruins and Amy and I could scoot off somewhere to have peace and quiet... after they had won the war, of course.

Austin probably wanted the city for himself, but I didn't really care about all that. Seemed like a guy could get pretty far out in the nothing in the middle east if that guy knew his way around.

I'd figure it out. I always did. Start fresh with Amy.

I had to ditch the rifle. Threw it in a dust bin as soon as I got away from the main complex. These security rent-a-cops were still unwise to my shenanigans. I wondered for how much longer.

Got my answer when the door bumped open all sudden like and a goon shot into the room, AR sighted and cocked, and spun around on me before I could spit.

"You there," he said, this big player with a marshmallow face. "Come out of there with your hands up."

I dove, he popped a few suppressed rounds off, and the water shot out everywhere, leaking all over the floor. He didn't hit me, but I made a noise like I was, and he came over to investigate and found me in a kneeling position on the floor.

"Get up," he said, his voice kind of soft for a big guy. I did as he said, keeping my arms at my sides as I did.

"Now put up your hands," he said, and I did as I was told, but was already thinking about my risky move.

I'd done it twice before. The first time the gun went off, a near miss. The second time I took a nick to the chin. Third time's the charm.

D. Chavez, as his name tag said, let go of the gun enough to reach for his shoulder CB and I shot both hands out to grab the grip and then pushed the butt of the rifle into D. Chavez's nose. This made him let go of the rifle enough for me to take it from him, spin it around and immediately point it at his left eye.

"Drop your hand, bro," I said. "There's no shame in saying uncle."

D. Chavez tightened his lips and squinted at me,

sputtering out his disgust with some choice Spanish phrases. I took the zip ties from the passant on his shoulder and tied up his ankles and wrists with two of them, then I ripped off a piece of his shirt and shoved it in his mouth, clocking him out with the butt of the AR for good measure and then shot through the store out the back and down another alley to drop down into the sewer after fiddling with the man hole cover.

Those things are really heavy.

Once I was down there I pulled out my trusty compass from the hilt of my knife and navigated south toward the ruins using the sunlight from the storm drains to guide my way. I hit a dead end though because some of the sewer had caved in.

Looking for an exit, I found another ladder leading to a man hole cover which came loose with a little shove, and after listening for traffic, which sounded like the normal citizen noise, I popped out to see a middle eastern lady staring at me.

I was in some kind of a market just at the outskirts of the city, and there were people everywhere. I ditched the gun, not wanting to raise suspicion, and rose out of the hole.

A couple of other burka clad women joined the lady in the staring contest, and then two men came by and ushered the women away, but the crowd was thick enough for me to blend in, especially after I grabbed a scarf from a nearby street vendor and wrapped it around my head. All of them were talking about what had just happened, all of them heading to the safety of their homes.

"Get off the street," said a woman near me. "There is a killer loose in the city."

"They will find him," said another man, carrying a sack of groceries. "He cannot escape security."

I decided to look for another alleyway, and soon found one off to the left, heading toward the ruins. I had to get to Amy. I had to get us out of this city and far away where no one would trouble us. No militia, no more killing, no more running.

"In here!" came a familiar voice. It was Austin, sitting in one of those electric cars. "Let's get you out of here."

At last! I dove in to the front seat and when I did, Austin pressed the accelerator and we started to drive through the crowd, the people parting ways in front of us and forming ranks behind us when we passed.

"You did well, Gideon," said Austin, and I turned to see two more men in the back seat, both of them wearing black fatigues. "You did exactly like we had hoped. I would like to say that Asher thanks you for your service, but he is not here to do that...perhaps in a few days."

I turned to him, my hand going for the door handle to barrel out, but they had locked it.

"Oh no, don't try to leave," he grinned. "You did exactly as Asher planned for you to do, and he needed a patsy, an outside enemy to take his life in a most spectacular and public way."

"But he's dead," I said, my voice feeling cold in my throat. "What does it matter now?"

Austin laughed, and I thought that I was in some strange dream, but knew full well that I wasn't.

"Not for long," he said. "Soon he will rise from the dead and lead us all to a greater tomorrow. You played your part well, Gideon. We have been observing you since the

Reagan, and much has been orchestrated to see the plan come to fruition."

"You guys are I.D. ten tango," I said, almost a whisper. I was planning my next move. "You mean to tell me that the whole Reagan bit was a smoke screen? That the bombs and the rescue and all the rest was a set up?"

"Exactly," said Austin. "Planned by Asher himself. How do you think you managed to sneak around on the ship so easily? Our men and women represent some of the highest trained special operators in the world. Do you really think a self trained survivalist like yourself could have outsmarted all of our security to assassinate Asher without help?"

"Well, your guys really are a bunch of dinks, man."

They got silent, too silent, and even though most people in my situation would think they were dead and done, I never thought I was really done.

"We will take you back to the Magistrate," said Austin calmly, coolly. "And then we will plan a more suitable end for you now that you have served your purpose...unless of course you wish to join us."

I sat quietly for a bit, and the two men in the back were fumbling with something. I didn't dare look.

Now or never, bro.

I shifted my weight toward the door, striking with the back of my fist to attempt to shatter Austin's larynx, but something went around my throat and I got my fingers in there just in time to stop a garrote from tightening on my neck. I pulled my knees up to my chest, and then put both of my feet past Austin and through the driver's side window, sending little shards of safety glass all over the street outside.

The guy behind me tightened the garrote, and I pulled one hand free to find his face and then drove my thumb into his squishy eye socket. I felt something bust, the guy shouted, and Austin put on the brakes, which made the now sightless thug to let go of the garrote enough for me to push off, slide through the open window past Austin, and give him a smack with my elbow and a few choice words about his mother on the way out.

We were in an alleyway, and there weren't many people, but I felt the door swing open into my back, knocking me face down on the pavement. I spun over, just in time to see the guy I hadn't injured bound out of the rear driver side door, jump on top of me and drive his knee into my stomach. I fought the urge to pass out, hearing my father's voice in my ear screaming "Weakness! Weakness!" and I crab walked backward to stand on my shaky legs, the dust swirling around me.

This was going to get out of hand.

Had to take care of this guy quick.

Flat top was squaring me up, a brick of a soldier, getting into some kind of stance as Austin piled out of the car, his nose a bloody mess, nightstick in his tightening fist. I could hear the other guy in the car screaming about his eyes. They didn't want to kill me here. Someone else wanted to see me die. I was determined to get the heck out of dodge, but better to stand my ground than go on a futile chase and get shot.

I shook the groggy out of my vision, put out my hands and made fists, drawing Flat Top in. He shot his fists out, connecting a couple of crushing blows on my ribs, and I purposefully leaned in too far and let him get me in a

guillotine headlock. With one bump from my hands to
loosen his grip, I took a chunk of meat out of his forearm
with my teeth and when he backed up in pain, I spat the
bloody mess in his face and kicked him with the ball of my
foot square in the chest, knocking him back into Austin.

Don't pass out. Don't pass out.

I could see Austin dropping Flat Top to the ground and
coming at me with the night stick, and little stars danced in
the air between us. The knife was in my hand like magic,
and I waited for him to advance, letting him swing the stick
just inches from my nose as I staggered backward, but he
was so quick. He came back around and jarred my hand as I
used the blade to block a blow directed at my head. I kicked
out to take his knee and he sidestepped and then jabbed
forward with the end of the stick, catching me on the
cheekbone.

Lights were going out. Had to deal an ace.

I dropped my assault, fell back, let him come. Because I
was so groggy, he grabbed my right wrist and struck my
forearm, trying to get me to drop the knife, and I heard
something break, felt the pain of it, drank it in, pulled him
close feeling the bones in my forearm separate, and with my
other hand I shot in with my fingers and grabbed his right
ear in my fist, twisting until I felt something tear.

Austin screamed as I pulled down and my fist left his
head with a piece of his ear, a spray of blood shooting
toward me. I dropped the ear, hot blood in my eye, and I
managed to hold on to the knife enough to drop it to my
bloody left hand and then drive the blade under Austin's
ribs as deep as I could plunge it.

He dropped to the ground, his last words masked by

gurgles.

I stood, legs shaking, arm throbbing, darkness surrounding me, and then staggered to the electric car where the man in the back seat lay moaning.

"Get. Out," I growled, and he did as he was told.

Steering with my left hand, my right arm on fire, I drove out of the alleyway into the street, wove through the crowds of people being evacuated to their homes, and drove through an intersection before I blacked out.

Amy

We went into the city on foot, which to my mind was just freaky stupid. Clayton said that we'd be fine, and I just had to trust that he knew what he was doing. Once we got past the ruins we found this, like, huge market or something with people crowding around large displays of fruits and vegetables that made me so hungry.

We stopped at a fruit stand, and Kashif picked up three apples with his good hand, and then spoke to the man in his language, but Kashif started looking all puzzled in the face, turned to us and said: "This is all for free."

I didn't understand the why and didn't really care. We were famished. We just munched on the apples as we walked through the crowd, looking for some clue as to where Gideon got off to. Clayton kept saying that we would "know it when we see it" or whatever that meant, and every now and then I would see him turn to talk to someone next to him, like a stranger or something in the crowd, but then he wasn't really talking to anyone at all, so I thought that maybe he was losing it a little.

Man, that could be really bad if he went all one fry short of a happy meal.

We rounded a corner in the market and stood in an alleyway that was a little less populated. I just looked at all the different people strolling by, all of them seeming to be really happy and unbothered by the fact that the world had taken a nose dive. It was like they didn't know what was going on outside their walls. Like they were all content and that things were actually normal again.

"We'll wait right here," said Clayton, nodding his head, holding on to his walking stick. "Things are gonna get interestin' real soon."

I didn't like the sound of that. Even though I trusted in Clayton and his feel for what God was doing, my faith was still, like, really small. As Clayton had taught me, I started to give all that over to God again, just leave it. But doubt clouded my mind again, and I thought about Gideon. I worried about him...*loved* him. Where was he? What was he doing? I just felt sick when I thought about him.

I knew Gideon could take care of himself, but this place, even though the people seemed all happy and the food was...well...free, there was a sickness that I couldn't put my finger on. Everything just kind of felt weird like they were all walking around in slow motion. It was like when you have one of those days when everything is going right, but the pessimist inside tells you to wait for the other shoe to drop. I suppose I should have been happy that the food was free and that everyone looked happy and adjusted for the most part, but somehow I felt like the place was all wrong like that movie where all the kids run the town and they feed people to the thing in the corn field.

I suddenly heard music, like that fanfare in those Hunger Games movies, and above us was a screen mounted to the wall where I could see a crowd and a stage and a podium all made out of black cloth and metal. Standing at the podium was a man who was way too good looking to be real. People stopped all around us and started staring at the screen, some of them munching on food, others of them with arms around each other, but weirdly I didn't notice any old people. Everyone here were all twenty something, and there didn't seem to be any kids. They looked at the screen all wide eyed, many of them with huge, satisfied smiles on their faces. This dude had a way with people, I could tell. He had like a really cool sounding voice, like Morgan Freeman or George Clooney.

He started into a speech where he talked about how awesome everything was in this city and then started in on religion, basically that it was what was stopping humans from reaching their full potential, and then his head sprayed all over...Kelly?

No way. Was that her in the background?

People started screaming and backing away from the screen, and I suddenly knew what was up with the dead guy: Gideon. Gideon had followed through with the job those guys wanted him to do. I just felt sick. I know Gideon had a checkered past, but I knew that he had it in his head that if he could just do this one thing he could save the world or whatever.

I was tired of trying to save the world. The world was dead, and those guys who had sent Gideon off to be their errand boy had also tried to kill me after he left.

Clayton suddenly reached out and grabbed the two of us and then Kashif and Clayton started praying in this alleyway, so I joined in, doing my best to agree with everything.

"Lord," said Clayton. "We don't know what's happenin' to Gideon right now, but we ask in your mighty name to bring him to us. We can't find him in this big city, but you know exactly where he is right now. Give him strength, Oh Lord. Help him find his way out of this mess. We don't know what you have in store, but we trust you to guide us and lead us."

We left it there, and when we looked up, there were people crowding all around us, watching us. It was kind of creepy. Clayton turned and looked at the crowd, and then he smiled at them and started talking.

"Hello ever'body," he said, that silly drawl of his so pleasing and comforting, like coming home. "I come to you today to tell you about hope that ain't a wish. This city is pretty nice, but there's a better city waitin' for those who choose to accept the free gift of grace…"

He continued on, sharing the gospel with these people who had stopped to listen. I was blown over by his ability, his boldness, to talk to complete strangers about the grace of Jesus Christ, offer it out there as a free gift, and then let people take it or leave it.

"Is this not…beautiful," whispered Kashif, leaning over to get close to my ear. "Clayton's Farsi is perfect."

If I was a cartoon, a question mark would have appeared over my head.

"What do you mean?" I asked. "It's that stupid southern Oklahoma English of his. It's not Farsi."

Kashif smiled, then looked at me with tears.

"It is happening again," he said. "Praise be to the Most High."

I walked away from the gathering crowd, my mouth a huge smile, and watched as people started to get on their knees and accept the free gift, the gift that reconciled them to the God of the Universe. It was so weird that in the middle of all the chaos of people reacting to the death of the man on the television, this small group of people listened to Clayton and found peace in the storm.

We spent some time with them, these new believers, and some of the people left without accepting the truth. We were all able to understand one another without an interpreter for some time, and in the middle of a conversation with a young woman and her two sisters, I looked up and saw an image of Gideon on the screen, an image of him climbing down a ladder or a scaffold or something, with the word "fugitive" flashing in red underneath. It was so bizarro to see him without hair.

Clayton and Kashif found me, and their faces were all business and urgency.

"We have to wait right here, I'm sure of it," Clayton said. "Can't leave this spot."

"But Gideon is somewhere in this city and he needs our help. We have do do *something*," I said, my voice strained. "We can't just stand around and do nothing at all."

"Hide and watch," said Clayton, and he winked at me and smiled.

This did nothing to make me feel better, but I decided to let it play out.

We moved to the alleyway again and stood looking at the people standing in little groups discussing what had just happened, some of the people were moving away. The screen above us was running a message just under Gideon's picture that told people to go to their homes or whatever, at least the part that was in English. People were starting to do just that.

"What if he...?" I said to Clayton, and Kashif put his hand on my shoulder and tilted his head, his face drawn down in a sad smile. The guy was really empathic, and I could hear him speaking something in his language...Farsi, I think he said. We stood there for some time, my fears boiling over as I watched the screens, watched as Gideon's face was plastered all over every digital device, and I wondered if I would ever see him again.

Clayton only looked out into the market, leaning on his hickory walking stick, his new tribal robes on over the clothes I saw him in when I first met him back at my house. He had his eyes closed, and I *knew* what he was doing. Didn't have to tell *me*.

I heard a noise in the street, a sound of people yelling and one man in perfect English saying "Watch out!" A white electric car rolled to a stop in the middle of the street, and there, slumped in the driver's seat, was bald, bleeding Gideon.

Mark

It was my job to see that his body lay in state for the two days required by his will, and I would fulfill that for him. Asher had been my dearest friend, and had become my savior and my lord.

We prepared his body in accordance with what he had instructed, ensuring that no preservative chemicals were used. We dressed his head as best we could, but the damage was extensive. The bullet had entered near the center of his forehead and exited out the back, taking with it a good chunk of his brain. We covered the wound with putty and makeup, and did our best to make him look presentable, but there is only so much one can do with limited resources. Although we had stockpiled and collected all the supplies in the region, certain things were still out of our reach, and the manufacturing plants planned for the future were still planned for the future.

I supposed there would be time for that after phase two.

I arranged for musicians to play around the clock at his funeral, and the pilgrims began arriving almost immediately to his building. We had to tell the mourning people to leave, but they loved Asher, and so did I. He had brought this city from a pile of rubble to a glowing city of gold with the sheer force of his own will, believing in the power of the human spirit to help us all rise from the ashes of war and ignorance.

I missed him, but phase two was already in place and operating smoothly. The people were mourning Asher, as they should, but soon there would be a new era of humanity, when we would push ourselves further along the evolutionary chain and create a world free of hunger, pain, or any hindrance that would stop us from reaching our full potential.

I thought back to that meeting we had last year, when we raised the tethered wind turbines, when Asher called me to his home and made drinks for us from liquor he had distilled himself. It was sweet and went down smooth like the greatest scotch.

"Mark, my friend," he said, his eyes like diamonds. "I want to talk about phase two with you. I want you to be my beneficiary."

"Asher," I said. "Lord, I just don't think I am worthy of that."

"Hah," he grunted. "Worthy does not enter into it. When I finish what I have started, you will be granted powers beyond your imaginings. Mark, the human race is on the cusp of something spectacular, the next step in our evolution. We homo sapiens have been ruling this planet and wrecking it for millennia, but what if I were to tell you that I have found a way to speed up the evolutionary process, to skip ahead on our genetic path?"

"Asher," I said, trying not to let him see my eyes roll. "What do you mean?"

"I am speaking of a new era in human kind. What I am able to do, the whole human race can do. In my search for a cure for Volos, I discovered something unseen in the human genome, something that I was able to enhance and magnify, something I was able to harness. It's amazing, Mark. I feel exhilarated by it, energized. I literally see things on a different level now, as if the very atoms are visible to me."

He continued to tell me about the plan, and then showed

me the evidence as we rode the elevator to his laboratory. He said that he would sacrifice himself in a coup for the fate of the human race, that he would use his newfound discovery to beat death, and then help us all to do the same. After much convincing, I saw the truth in the science, the evidence that he had indeed found a way to make us all immortal.

The evidence Asher revealed to me was at once marvelous and terrifying.

We lay Asher's body in state on the temple mount, right at the spot where the two preachers had been killed, and for two days he lay there as all the people of the city formed massive lines to see him, left gifts at his massive marble casket, and wept at his passing. It had all been planned months in advance. It had all been masterfully orchestrated by Asher, the great Asher, and soon he would make good on all that he had promised.

I had faith in that.

Howard

Clayton, Kashif and Amy pulled a severely injured Gideon out of an electric car and carried him carefully to the alleyway. The crowd parted, and some of them ran down the street, only pausing to look over their shoulder and mutter "traitor". It was only a matter of time before they revealed the whereabouts of my charges.

Four of my friends stood guard around the crowd, and others were arriving every moment as the new believers gathered, some of them won by the witnesses and then hidden from the enemy's view until now. Amy held Gideon in her arms, gently rubbing the soft, dark stubble on top of his head.

"Gideon," she said, her tears falling on his cheek. "Gideon come back to me. Please come back to me. Don't leave me."

Clayton and Kashif turned to face the crowd, and I stood with my friends, all of us at the ready for any trouble that should arise. We had to get these charges out of the city along with all the other saints who had just been born again. It would be a thick battle, but we were ready, ready to do anything to stop the enemy now that we had been given carte blanch.

Gideon slowly woke, his eyelids parting gently, his dark eyes slowly widening as he saw the soft and gentle face of Amy, her smile breaking through her sorrow, her heart on fire with love for him, a pure and honest love.

"What kept you?" he whispered, and then groaned with pain. His arm had begun to swell, and I could see that three of his ribs were broken.

The darkness that pervaded this city was beyond anything that had ever been witnessed by my eyes. My brethren stood in unison, weapons at the ready as a host of the enemy fell on us, swirling around us like a cloud of flies blowing on a carcass, but this cloud had gnashing sharp teeth and razor claws. Clayton looked at me again, his head bowed in prayer, the light of it scattering the darkness around us and causing a bubble of power to envelop us, energy straight from the throne of the Most High, feeding our strength, causing everything within us to explode in a nuclear reaction of warlike speed and agility.

I had not moved like that since a third of my brethren chose to leave us.

Clayton and Kashif lifted Gideon carefully as they made their way back toward the ruins. We followed them, knowing full well that the battle was long from over, that very quickly all of them would be tested, and we would be there to help.

Kelly

I stood just outside the square, not able to reach Mark who had was overseeing the crowd of mourners. I felt somehow sick.

Throngs of people crowded the casket, and suddenly there was a cold wind that blew past me, as if it were a sweltering summer day and someone opened a freezer next to me. It brushed my skin and I shivered, as if some invisible monster slipped past me just at the edge of my vision, and then Asher sat up in the casket.

He then stood, a smile stretching across his face, but somehow it was not him.

I ran, I'll have to confess, I ran. It was like one of those movies where the vampire sits up in the casket and looks around at the living before he jumps on them and sucks the life out of them.

Oh, at first it was like a zombie movie, but he was really calm for a zombie, just holding up his hands and smiling and then he started speaking to the fleeing crowd…and I could hear him as clearly as if he were standing right next to me.

"People of the world," he said, his voice somehow changed, the cadence somehow slightly different, with something growling beneath it. People stopped running and turned to face him, their knees bent as if wary of a threat from the sky.

Asher continued.

"I bring you peace. No longer will you be shackled by the confines of your mortal nature. I will show you the secret of immortality, the way to beat death and to live to create the greatest civilization known to this planet, to evolve to our highest potential, to reach out to the stars and beyond. Give me your allegiance and I will see to it that you will never go hungry, never thirst, never worry about where to live, never be lonely. All I ask is your loyalty."

I felt sick. I could see him at a distance as I stood at the edge of the square built around the temple mount, and he looked out at the crowd, holding his arms high over his head as if he were to fly away at any moment, his face still pale, his eyes still sunken and dark, and the people were bowing down in front of him.

They went to their knees like a wave from the casket outward, and I stepped around the corner into an alley and the tears welled up in my eyes. What was happening? This was all wrong. This was all sickly wrong. I couldn't place it, couldn't put my finger on the driving force behind my uneasiness, but it was probably that a man whose brains I had worn on my face only days ago was standing on the temple mount as if nothing had happened, somehow changed but still a living corpse.

I took a deep breath, my chest hitching, and stepped back out into the street to see the screens that were placed at every intersection announcing the resurrection of Asher, the image of this temple mount scene being broadcast all over the world to every device that had been miraculously re-activated by some kind of new technology invented in this city, by this man. The production value of the video announcement was also much too good to be on the spot.

They *knew* this would happen.

I turned to see Mark standing near Asher, a microphone

in his hand, and a curious mark on his forehead. Several security personnel approached the outside of the crowd, a few of them mounting the platform where Asher stood, his arms outstretched as if to welcome them all, that smile stretched across his ashen face.

"Come," Mark said. "Come and show your loyalty to the one who would give us immortality. If you want everlasting life, come and receive the mark of your loyalty on your bodies. It contains the genetic code to help you reach your full potential, to never die. Soon you will see the power that the mark gives you over death."

The security personnel each had some kind of device in their hand like a scanner, and the people were lining up and letting them put it against their forehead to leave some kind of implanted tattoo there. I started to feel sick again, and I turned to go, to walk away from this strange nightmare.

Mark had become something else. He stood smiling with Asher who was also smiling, and the people were standing from their kneeling position to get in line, and I looked as people were crowding down the street to see what was going on, to see the resurrection of Asher, and falling in line.

I tried to push past the people, tried to get through them, but they were all so bent on getting to the temple mount to express their allegiance, to see the miracle that was Asher, to become immortal.

I would have none of it.

I ducked into a storefront and met three women who came out into the street to get in line, and they looked at me like I was odd or out of place, and that was when I knew I had to get back to the apartment and grab Anya.

I had to get out of there.

I ran down the street, not looking behind me, and I felt a
hot wind begin to blow, to pick up the dust that lay in the
streets and fling it, stinging, into my eyes. I found one of
those golf carts that the security personnel drove but there
was a young man sitting behind the wheel wearing his black
fatigues and his sidearm. He saw me coming and looked at
me nervously.

"Um, ma'am," he said. "You will have to go to the
temple mount. We're being called there now."

I looked directly at him, my face set as hard as I could set
it. This had to work.

"I left my niece back at the apartment," I said, trying not
to stammer, trying not to let my voice shake. "Can you take
me there so that I can get her?"

"This is highly irregular—"

"I am Magistrate Knight's fiancee, and if you do not take
me there immediately I will have him deny you the mark."

"Hop on in," he said, and we were off to the tower. I sat
silently in the seat next to this young man, this agent of what
I now saw as a monster. I just had to get Anya out of the
city, out of this horrible nightmare and far away.

The young man dropped me off without incident, and I
ran through the eerily vacant lobby, took the elevator to my
apartment and knocked on the door. The door opened, and
there stood Darla, Anya's nanny, holding Anya, a set of keys
in her hand, a mark on her forehead that was a circle with
the three curved lines coming out of it, curved in a clockwise
fashion, the symbol on the flag that flew all over this city.

"I was just about to leave," she said. "We have to get
down to the temple mount to swear allegiance to him. Isn't
it all amazing? We'll live forever…I'll live forever."

"I'm not going," I said, clenching my fists. "And I'm taking Anya with me."

"What?" she said, her mouth open, eyes wide. "Why?"

"Don't make this hard," I said, as calm as I could in front of Anya. "Just give her to me and there won't be any trouble."

"No way," she growled, this girl barely out of her teens screamed as she tried to slam the door on me, but I had my knee in the way.

Man, that hurt.

I forced my way into the room, but she put Anya down who then ran screaming to the bedroom, slamming the door. I saw Darla reach behind her and pull out a gun and I grabbed her hand, but it went off, bouncing a bullet into the floor and then somewhere in the room.

There was a smell of gunpowder, and this girl was strong, but I gave her a knee to the stomach and she let go of it, and I pointed it at her face.

"Get out on the balcony, Darla." I said.

She screamed ugly insults and epithets at me, spittle flying from her mouth, then backed out onto the balcony, and I locked her out there.

"Watch your mouth in front of the baby," I said through the glass.

I knocked on the door to the bedroom, and heard a little voice on the other side.

"Who...Who is it?"

"It's me, baby," I said. "Everything is fine. You can come out now."

The door slowly unlatched and precious Anya stood on the other side, tears streaming down her plump cheeks. I grabbed her up, threw some canned food from the cabinets into a backpack, and darted out the door, down the elevator, and out into the street. Just as I was rounding a corner, I felt someone grab my arm.

It was a short, squatty middle eastern man, a panicked look on his face.

"Lady," he said. "You look like you're the only one not going to get the mark."

He looked terrified, and his face had some bruises like he had been in a fight.

"I know a holocaust when I see it," he said, his voice strained, as if he had been running. He was out of breath. "And you look like you are as uncomfortable about all this as I am. My great grandfather told me about this kind of thing. Are you fearing this too?"

"Y-yes," I managed, somehow feeling like our meeting was not chance.

"Then let's get you and your baby out of here," he said, his face and hands animated. "I'll have none of this. This Asher has got all the people acting crazy."

I followed the man who led us down the street where he had parked a delivery truck, a large electric vehicle with a big sealed box on the back of it. He helped Anya and I into the passenger side, and then went around the front and climbed in, then reached across Anya and stuck out his hand.

"I'm Josiah Malachi," he said. "Now...*Yalla!*"

He stepped on the gas pedal, and we rolled down the street, only to see a line of security personnel in their black fatigues waving us down.

"Leave this to me," he said.

Clayton

Yeah, I'd always read about that mark of the beast thing but I never thought I'd actually *see* it, right up there on the big screen right over the intersection. Man, all I knew is that we had to get on out of there before they started lookin' to mark us as well.

I sure as shootin' wasn't gonna take it. All them people was filin' out of their apartment buildings and headin' on up to the temple mount to get their mark, all except the folks who had just turned their lives over to Jesus who stood in the alley with us. They was lookin' to me to figure what to do, but I was straight outta options. I could see the evil swirlin' around us like some kind of dark smoke from a chimney fire.

"Which way we go?" asked Kashif, his face lookin' all bug eyed. He was pretty weirded out, as all of us were. "Must get Gideon to doctor or someone must look at arm. It is very bad."

"I know, I know," I muttered, tryin' to reassure him. "First we gotta get outta this city or I have a bad feelin' we's gonna end up on the wanted list with ol' Gideon here."

I handed Gideon's unbroken arm off to Amy, and went through the small crowd of folks standin' with us to look back the way we'd come. Security goons started linin' up down the street and marchin' toward us, goin' from door to door, wearin' them black fatigues but this time with helmets and them clear plastic riot shields. People was movin' down the street ahead of them, and pretty soon they'd reach this alley and we'd be found out. Far as I could tell, we was boxed in. We was in this narrow alleyway where the streets on either side of it ran crossways to make the letter "H". Security was startin' to get as thick as thieves, and Gideon for sure was on their wanted list. I guess we'd be on there as well by association.

Gideon was all groggy and his head was lollin' back and forth between Kashif and Amy. Once in a while his feet would drag and they'd have to pick him up or shake him a bit so's he'd stay awake.

I peeked down the other street (the way we wanted to go) to see a white vehicle headed our way flanked on each side by them black clad security guys, some of them carryin' riot shields but others carryin' guns.

We was in a pickle, for sure.

"We's gonna have to head back up to the temple mount and see if we can duck in a buildin' and wait it out," I said, shruggin' a little. "We can't face off against them guards or we're done for. Maybe we can get in with the crowd over on this side and when they pass a door we can duck in 'till they roll on by."

"Sounds like as good a plan as any," said Amy.

I took Gideon from Kashif and she and I held him up, and Kashif explained in Farsi to the other people what we was gonna do. They didn't like it, but we all got the sense that if we didn't do somethin' then we was gonna be horse meat.

We all waited for the crowd of civilians to come by, and we ducked in with them, kind of falling out into the street like lemmings and then once we got a ways down the street we started funnelin' people into open doorways that folks just left to the wind when they lit out to get their marks.

That's when we started noticin' the security guys in front of us.

They was watchin' what we was doin' and started gettin' closer. They would put both hands on their rifles instead of just slingin' 'em around their shoulders, and the air started to get real thick. I started to prayin', askin' God to come and save us once more, to help these people out of the city who had decided to follow Him.

"Dear Jesus, give these people a way out," I said aloud. "Part the red sea and roll back the Jordan. This is our last resort, and we are completely relyin' on you for help."

I could hear others prayin' as well, but I could also now see the faces of the guards through their plexiglass face shields.. They was lookin' mean as ever, and it was like they knew who we was talkin' to.

And they didn't like it one bit.

Gideon

I was floating in and out, and I could see Amy, but the guy on my left was a stranger. He was helping me to walk so I guess that was alright.

They dragged me uphill along a street and through my half closed eyes I could just see a line of goons headed toward us, guns at the ready.

"Gotta get in the doorway," I moaned, my right hand trying to indicate the direction, but pain shooting from my arm to my skull. "Over there…safe."

They ignored me, mumbling prayers to themselves and aloud, and then I could see Clayton to my left, walking along, his walking stick striking the ground with every other step. He was striding forward as if on the march. Man, something big was about to happen.

I totally didn't expect to see the truck racing around the corner up the street, followed by two of those electric security cars. Some of the men in the column turned to fire at it, but it barreled on through. It was almost playing out in slow motion.

The security noobs were so focused on staring us down that three of them didn't even notice, and the truck drove right over them like they weren't there, one of them being knocked across the street and into a lamp post like a little G.I. Joe doll.

The truck screeched to a stop right near us and I heard a woman screaming something but couldn't make it out, and then they were trying to get the back door of the truck open while the two security cars parked all catty corner. The guys with very high powered rifles set up and aimed across the canopies and hoods with muzzle flashes flaring…

I heard a scream, and then my left leg was on fire just above the knee.

I didn't really react, but people started pulling on me and I could hear Amy screaming.

Clayton stepped up, though, and I saw something I couldn't quite believe as they were dragging me along. Someone laid me in the back of the truck and from there I noticed something was stopping the bullets, or at least most of them. I couldn't really make it out because I was floating in and out, but something that looked like a large man appeared, caught a bullet, then disappeared, and there were a lot of them, like ten or so — flashing in and out of my vision, moving toward the guards like a storm, and Clayton standing in the middle of the street between us and the soldiers like some superhero. It was like a big wall of yellow fire in front of him, pushing out toward the soldiers, Clayton raising his hands up above his head, one fist firmly grasping that stick of his.

Clayton was the last one to get in the truck before they closed the freight doors and it got dark. All I heard before blacking out again was the sound of sobbing, of the weird whine of an electric engine, and the ping of bullets striking metal.

Hui

"Do you think it will be long, Father," I asked, my children playing at my feet.

"Not long, Hui," he said, writing the characters on the broken concrete with a wet sponge attached to the end of an old broom handle. The sponge was tapered to resemble a paint brush, and he used it to draw the character for *vessel*, consisting of three other characters: *mouth*, the number eight, and *boat*.

I could predict my father's thinking as he stooped over toward the ground, his shoes off, his linen pant legs rolled up to his knees, writing on the shattered concrete.

He was probably thinking about the man from America who came to his school so many years ago. The man asked about this very character and then used it to share with him something he had never heard: the Bible.

My father slowly wrote these characters on the concrete and they faded, evaporating in the sun as we waited atop that ancient fortress of Masada, the place where the Jewish people came to raise a defiant fist against the Romans.

I stood, stretching my arms out from my body, feeling the heat of the sun on my skin, and looked out across the desert, across the field of ruin devastated by the war to see a golden glint on the horizon, the glint of the towers that rose out of the dust called New Jerusalem.

Defiant, but foolish.

I had been allowed to see the helpers, the great soldiers that had joined us on our journey to this place. I and my group of followers, followers of Shang Di but not the Shang

Di of idol worship, had gathered here after leaving our
ravaged land where the feudal system had returned. We
were the result of one American who came to visit my
father's English school forever ago, long before the war.
This humble man had shared with my father the grace of the
true Shang Di, the one who sent his son Jesu to die and then
rise from the dead. In turn, our entire family had accepted
this graceful gift, and for the longest time trying to
understand the mystery that it did not need to be paid back.

We had seen the resurrection of the false one in the city of
the dead. Our old cell phones and walkie talkies worked for
some reason, and had been working for about a year, and we
followed the signal to this place after Jesu told my father to
bring us here.

We had faced many hardships along the way, suffering
for our Lord Jesu, for the name of the true Shang Di. We had
lost many friends, seen many horrors that the war had left
on our world, and many sacrifices had been made.

I walked to the edge of the plateau and climbed to the
top of the broken wall of the ancient fort to look out across
the desert and pulled my shirt up to just above my belly to
keep cool. I took my binoculars from my pocket because I
saw a small plume of dust rising in the distance, and
thinking it was yet another dust devil, I almost did not look.
Curiosity overcame me, and when I peered at it, I saw a
truck moving toward us across the wasteland.

I felt my father's hand on my back.

"They need our help, son," he said. "Go take some men
and retrieve them. We will feed them, treat their wounds,
and see that they have a place to sleep."

"Yes, father," I said, bowing to him slightly at the waist.

I walked through the crowd of people, this people who had been brought from so far away to stand on this mountain fortress, to camp around it by the thousands. I climbed onto my old horse and rode the road down to meet our new friends, passing the brothers and sisters we had met who had traveled from Ghana, Norway, Italy, India, Bangladesh, France, and all parts of the globe to be here for what purpose only Shang Di knew.

For now to wait.

When I finally rode up on them, their vehicle was dying, and had taken heavy damage from gunfire. A man, a stocky middle eastern man climbed out of the driver's seat.

"I have many people injured and needing help," he said, his accent from this region, but speaking English. I understood English.

"Come," I said to him, climbing from the saddle and planting my feet on the ground. "We will help you. There are food and medical supplies. What is ours is yours."

He was grateful, and we all helped the people climb out of the truck, and there was one man badly hurt, shot through the leg, arm broken. I called for help and many ran to our aide, many of them doctors and nurses from before the world became broken. Our people went to work treating wounds, offering water and food.

They were all very happy to see us, but the middle eastern man, the blocky man, stood aside, his arms folded, looking at everything with strange eyes. I approached him and offered him some of my ration of noodles.

"No," he said. "I...I don't eat pork. Thank you, though."

"It is not pork," I said, jabbing at the mutton noodles with chopsticks. "It is good. You try."

He did, and his face lit up as he slurped up the noodles. He said his name was Josiah, and he had lived in this area for a long time. I led him to a large rock where he sat down with a heavy sigh just as the sun was starting to dip below the horizon. Soon the campfires were the only thing glowing other than the stars and he sat silently for a long time after dark.

I was patient.

"What is all this?" he asked, handing me the empty bowl of noodles.

"We are waiting," I told him. "We have come here because we have all been told that we must meet here."

"Why?" he asked.

"I suppose the answer will present itself soon," I said. "Until then, we wait."

He had many more questions, and told me he was Jewish and I was so excited to meet a member of the chosen people of Shang Di, the people He chose to carry His holy message, to bear the Savior of the World. I was so sad that Josiah did not know about the prophesies of Jesu from the old testament, and I shared with him about it from my Chinese Bible, but he did not understand.

I told him about my father, about the American man who came to his city to share the story of Jesu with him, and share about the Chinese characters and how they express stories read about in the pages of the Bible. I told him about our experiences coming to this land, that Shang Di had parted two rivers so that we could cross on horseback, that he had healed many who had contracted Volos, that he had fed us when we had nothing to eat.

These stories amazed him, and soon he began asking

questions about Jesu and how to follow him. I told him the simple message of my faith, and he accepted, simply, like a child. He simply saw what we had, saw the miracles that Shang Di had performed, and suddenly something switched on in him as if it lay dormant for his entire life. In his excitement, he ran shouting through the camp, praising Shang Di, praising Jehovah, and this started a firestorm of praise among the brothers and sisters.

Our songs rose from the desert into the starry night, a fragrant incense for Shang-Di.

Mark

We had given the mark to nearly everyone, and the line had at last grown much shorter.

Where was Kelly?

"Don't worry about her," said Asher next to me as he touched the heads of people who had come to be blessed. He had somehow read my thoughts. To be immortal. It was more than I could imagine, but his skin was still the gray color of death, and his head was misshapen where the bullet had exited.

"This immortality…When will we feel the effects of it? When will we feel its power?" I asked.

"All in good time," he said, that reassuring smile on his face, his gums black. I am sure that with time he would be looking like his old self again. At least I hoped he would.

"First we must insure that all have been brought into the fold," he said. "Then we will hunt down and destroy all those who oppose us. Then we will indeed have peace. We must purify the blood line."

He laughed, and I felt strangely at peace, greater than I had felt when I first met Asher and greater even than when we broke ground on this magnificent city of ours. I wanted to know when I would feel the power surging through me. Surely I would be one of the first to experience it.

To be immortal. To truly be free of death.

The lines of people, the last of them, stretched down to the edge of the square. The rest of them, the ones who had already received the mark were celebrating, a sublime party of revelry and debauchery. We were no longer tied by the confines of our cultures and other nonsense. This was a new era, an era of the human animal.

Then I noticed something.

One of the people in the line, a woman, a young blonde woman, started to push out of order and walk to the side. She then turned to run.

"I don't want this!" she screamed. "It's wrong, all wrong!"

I was about to react when the people around her clawed at her arms and legs and would not let her go. They laughed as they began to pull at her limbs, balling up their fists to punch her and then kick her, and then they began to pull at her until they tore her apart, the mob spilling her blood in the square as Asher and I looked on.

Asher laughed.

"Look at what power will do to people," he said, his pupils cloudy. "The human being understands the truth when it is confronted by that truth. Little do they know that they are only selecting that which is purely to better our existence. We will reign for thousands of years and nothing will stop us."

"What of the unbelievers who have gathered at Masada outside of our city?" I asked. "What will we do about them?"

"Phase three, friend," he said. "Phase three. I have been in contact with the armies of what is left of Russia, Europe and China. They are coming here to join us and to destroy the interlopers. Their blood will run so deep that the horses will not be able to wade through it. All the rest will take the mark as I have been marked."

I thought about phase three. All of those weapons and

vehicles of war that we secretly spent so much time restoring and outfitting with all new devices invented by Asher. Soon we would drive out onto that old battlefield and destroy the gathered unbelievers.

Their screams would be exquisite.

Kashif

I rose for morning prayer, rolling up my cushion before laying out my prayer rug. This time, I knelt and bowed to the ground, saying prayers to Isa, thanking him for another day of life. I prayed quietly so as not to wake the others, and after prayer I walked the road to the top of the fortress of Masada to see beyond what I could see on the ground.

Having working eyes was a joyous thing, something I had not taken for granted in this new life.

It was a long walk to the top, and as I walked through the believers camping there, people from all over the world, the sun began rise above the horizon to the east revealing a cloud of dust that caused the sun to take on the most beautiful color. Clayton had said that it was something called orange, but it was such a gorgeous color that it needed another name. Orange was such a strange word for the sensation it provided.

My new friend Hui woke, moved to stand beside me and watch the large sun bring new light to the world. He put his arm around my shoulder, careful to not bump my broken arm. His wide, flat face decorated with a smile, his almond shaped eyes squinting in the new day sun.

"So pretty," he said with a little laugh that sounded almost like a cough. "Piàoliang."

We stood for a moment, looking out at the desert as it awoke, the orange light spreading across the landscape, and then my friend squinted his eyes and put his hand over his brow to shield them from the sun. He ran to his small satchel near his bed roll and brought back some binoculars, holding them up to his eyes and staring out across the wasteland.

His hands dropped to his sides and his shoulders slumped, then he handed the binoculars to me.

"You look," he said, and I took the binoculars from him and peered through them to see something that even in that hot arid desert chilled my bones.

Horses, thousands of horses, hundreds of thousands, all of them carrying a rider galloping across the desert toward us. I handed the binoculars back to Hui and he said three words: "We must warn."

I nodded my head and ran through the camp, down the trail that led to the camps at the bottom of the mountain, frantically warning the others. These men were headed toward us, and hostile or not, I had experienced what raiders could do to a group of defenseless people. I had to find Clayton to discuss what must be done.

In moments I had reached the camp near the truck where Clayton and our friends were sleeping, only to find them rolling up their beds, all but Gideon who lay on his small mattress with Amy sitting near him, holding his hand. I do not think she slept all night.

"Clayton! Clayton!" I shouted. "There is army coming this way. We must go to top of Masada, flee with what we can carry."

"We ain't never gonna outrun 'em," Clayton said, his face expressionless, his eyes set as he put his bedroll away in his bag. "We are all in this one spot for a reason, man. I don't think God brought us here so's we could be run down and slaughtered like a bunch o' sheep."

I could not believe his reply. I protested.

"But Clayton," I said, placing my hand on his arm. "We must find a way to defend ourselves. Go to the mountain. Some of us have guns."

Clayton smiled, and I was wondering if he had indeed gone mad.

"We'll pray," he said. "God will help us. He always does."

Others were not as calm as Clayton. As word spread through the camp, people began grabbing whatever they could carry, and for some it was only their children, and everyone went as fast as they could travel up the trail to the top of Masada. We helped Gideon along, carrying him on a stretcher we had made from two tent poles and a piece of canvas. He moaned as we went, and Amy walked beside him, holding his hand. The splint we had used to set his arm might not be enough if we could not get something to keep the infection from setting in. The bones had been ground together and the muscles and tendons stretched. He was in great pain.

As we climbed to the fort at the top of Masada, we could see the horsemen approaching and they filled the wasteland from edge to edge it seemed, the dust from their hooves nearly blotting out the morning sun.

I passed Hui on the way down. He followed his father who was walking slowly in the opposite direction that we were going, heading back down to our evacuated campsites. Hui was arguing with his father in Chinese, but the old man ignored him, and was even laughing a little, his long white beard wiggling when he did. The old man waved his hand, only saying "Dui, dui, dui", while Hui pleaded with him, following close behind his father.

We were halfway up the side of the mountain when the horsemen finally arrived at our campsites, and they wore torn and faded uniforms with holes and tattered edges. Many of them wore a red head scarf and all of them had long hair and long beards.

One of the men, out in front of the rest of them, riding a black horse that was slinging snot from its nose, shouted up at us in Chinese, something I could not possibly understand, but then the old man was shouting back at him, his raspy old voice echoing off of the walls of the mountain. Hui had stopped pleading with his father to come back, and the soldier on horseback rode over to the old man, drawing a long sword out of its scabbard, shaking it, screaming something in Chinese. Many of the other horsemen had swords as well, and guns, and there were men screaming in other languages, most likely Russian, and I realized that these men were the remnants of a mighty army.

I looked around me and all the people had stopped, had bowed their heads and were praying. Clayton looked at me and grinned.

"Pray, Kashif," he said. "Watch what God can do."

I did. I knelt down in the dust, bowed my body, ignored the pain in my arm, and put my forehead on the ground to plead with the Most High to bring peace. In an instant I heard the most awful sound of screaming I had ever heard in my life. I dared to look, opening my eyes slowly to see the men on horseback falling off of their horses, some of them with hands covering their faces, some of them stripping off their uniforms, and many of them rolling on the ground as if they were being stung by a swarm of bees.

Sores.

Horrible bleeding sores covered their skin, so bad that in a few minutes I could smell the stink of it. These thousands of soldiers with awful sores like that of people with leprosy no longer cared about taking our supplies, hurting us, or anything else for that matter.

In my pocket, I heard the sound of the iPhone we found at the broken battlefield, the sound of screaming. I pulled it out, and there on the cracked screen was the image of a correspondent, his hands out in front of him like claws, his surprised face covered with the runny, bloody sores.

"What is happening?" shouted the man on the screen. "What is happening?"

And then the camera switched to the square at the temple mount where thousands of people were lying on the ground in agony, moaning and clawing at their faces.

"We're close," said Clayton. "Won't be long now."

Amy

I totally didn't know that the sores had appeared on the riders until I heard their screams from the plain below. I guess it's pretty callous to say that I didn't care, because I had other things to worry about. I guess the world could have been opening up and swallowing people whole at that point and I wouldn't really care.

Gideon had become my world.

As best as I could tell, his arm was in such a bad way that if he hadn't already developed ostomyalitis it might happen really soon, and that was a slow death without antibiotics, and of course nobody had any. There was also the matter of his ugly gunshot wound that pierced his left leg just above the knee. It went clean through and I'd cleaned and dressed it, but again, without proper antibiotics he would get infected and that could be a very bad day. He'd also broken or cracked some ribs but without an x-ray I couldn't really tell, and could only see some awful bruising. From the looks of things, from the way his abdomen was swelling, he probably had some internal bleeding.

I just couldn't stop the tears from coming every few hours. Gideon would slip in and out of consciousness and I'd try to bring him back, but then it was also important that he get rest. It really stunk that we had to move him so much, and once we got up to the top of that ancient fort we lay him down on the ground and he groaned again.

The pain must have been really bad, but when he was awake you could barely tell. He was always smiling and trying to cheer me up. Kelly was with us again, and she filled us in on the horror show that was New Jerusalem, about the mark and the creepy zombie lord Asher. When Gideon came to and saw her, he smiled really big, and I couldn't believe how beautiful it was to see that smile of his.

"Hey, Kelly," he said, his voice weak. I gave him a sip of water. "How are you? Long time no see."

"Too long," she said, tears in her eyes, gently rubbing his bald head. "I missed you, I really did. I am so glad to be back with you."

"Don't ever leave me again," he said. "Or I'll move heaven and earth, understand?"

"Yeah," she said, smiling.

He smiled back and then looked at me.

"Water," he groaned. I gave him some, and he sipped a little. I felt his forehead and it was burning hot, the sweat dripping off of his skin and beading up. He was probably getting an infection, but there was nothing I could do. Nothing any of us could do. Just sit and watch him die.

"Gideon," I said, trying to be strong. "I think you've got an infection. I really don't have a way to treat you here 'cause there aren't any antibiotics. If you want, I can just keep getting you water, but..." and I broke down.

I heard him take a breath and there was a wheeze, a very faint wheeze.

"It's ok, Amy," he said, smiling, always smiling. "I'm fine. I've had a lot worse than this. I used to sneak in and out of militia camps and steal food and supplies all the time, sometimes getting caught, sometimes getting tortured, but I always figured out a way to live. Just don't worry about me."

I couldn't say anything. I just knelt there, asking God to

please help Gideon live, to give him life that wouldn't go away. I didn't want to lose him, too.

"Let me tell you something, Amy," he said, letting out a raspy cough. That was such a bad sign, but I didn't want to think about it. Couldn't say anything, just put my fingers over his lips. He kissed them and then took my hand in his left hand, and I found his skin to be so soft, so warm.

"I'm so tired of running, Amy," he rasped. "I've run all my life even before the war. My dad was such an abusive man, always telling me I wasn't good enough, always teaching me how to survive and then belittling me when I didn't follow through. I guess I showed him, huh? It's all the people I've killed Amy. I just don't think I can live with it anymore. I had to, you know…to survive…but it's just eating at me. Here I am at the end of the world and I'm still alive, but for what? To be with you? I don't deserve you. It's…it's time to rest Amy. It's time to sleep."

"No," I said, the tears flowing.

I looked at Kelly and she could not speak, covering her mouth, her eyes looking back and forth at me and at Gideon.

"No Gideon," I repeated. "I refuse to let you go. I refuse to let you die. Just hang on. We'll find a way to get some help, I know it. Just have some faith."

"Faith," he whispered. "I have seen some strange stuff on this trip with you. I can't explain it or square it away. I never thought I'd see you again, Amy. I never thought I'd see your beautiful face ever again, yet here you are. That in itself is a miracle. I can't deny that. Please tell me what you have. I need that. I want that. I want peace whether I'm dying here on this mountain or not. I'm so…tired of running. So tired of feeling the guilt about what I've done."

So I told him. I told him about grace, about Jesus, about what had happened to me, that He could forgive even murder, that all sin was the same, and he listened, his beautiful eyes focused on me like a child. Kelly and Gideon listened intently, locked in on my every word. After a few minutes, they started asking questions, mostly Kelly, and then they asked to receive the free gift, the gift of grace that is free to all people, the free gift that all on this mountain had received.

After Gideon said a small prayer, asking Jesus to become the lord of his life, to finally stop running, to forgive him of all the death he had caused, he fell asleep and breathed deeply, his breathing no longer shallow and weak. Kelly just sat there and cried, giving up all the horrors she had witnessed, all the wrongs she had done, giving them to the Father, accepting the free gift.

At last, I thought, we had hope.

Mark

Cain Asher was not bothered by the sores. He relished in them. He sat upon a golden throne that had been placed by our followers upon the temple mount. The people saw him more as a god than the highly evolved being that he had become, that we all would soon become. They were still so primitive even if they had been given immortality. They didn't deserve it. They didn't deserve *him*.

Asher stood.

"This is an attack," he said. "An attack on all that we are. This is an attack from God."

"What?" I asked, my eyes wide. "You do not believe in God, Asher. You are a god among men."

"I am not so naive to think so," he said, laughing. "Watch this."

He walked forward, climbing the few steps to stand on his now closed casket.

"People of New Jerusalem," he boomed. "Do not fret about the sores that cover your skin. Soon this sickness will pass like all others. I was wounded in the head, dead for two days, and yet here I am. We will eradicate the lesser humans from the face of the earth and build a new world! This...this plague is an act of defiance by the God of the Christians. It is *he* who has placed this plague upon you. Rise up! Take up arms! Your enemy lies only nine and a half kilometers outside this city at the ancient fortress of Masada. We will go there and kill every last one of the Christians and then we will send a message to all the rest that their god is dead!."

The people roared, a large mass of angry flesh that looked to the figure of Asher who stood on top of the casket, the symbol of his resurrection, and all of them raised their fists in support of our cause.

"In fact," he screamed, his voice shrill and yet full of deep resonance at the same time, a deep roaring beneath. "We shall rename this city! It shall no longer be known by the filthy religious name of Jerusalem…but a *new* name…a *proud* name…a defiant name…"

The crowd was chanting "Asher, Asher, Asher" and I could feel the blood boiling in my body, my breath getting faster, my heart beating with every syllable of his name, his holy name. Was this the beginning of the evolutionary change in my body, the change that would make me immortal?

"We shall call this city…*Babylon!* A city that shakes its fist in the face of all that is religious, all that has brought the human race to its knees. Long live Babylon! Babylon the *Great!*"

The people changed their chant, thousands of them, crowding the streets to get a glimpse of Asher, a glimpse of me, climbing over one another like rats, for I was his prophet, his Magistrate. They chanted the name of our city: "BABYLON! BABYLON! BABYLON!"

Yes! I thought. *We could wipe out the Christians, the last vestiges of religion on this planet, and finally be free of them.*

At my verbal command over a handheld radio, my lieutenant led the bulk of our new arsenal out of the parking garages that we had built into every basement of every building in this city. It was a sight to behold: Modified Abrams tanks refitted with rail guns, RG-31 Nayala's mounted with sound cannons and mini guns, Bradleys with M-60's that fired bullets that homed in on heat signatures. We were ready for one final battle, a battle to further the human race beyond its current state, to emerge like a butterfly from a chrysalis and spread its colorful wings across this planet and eventually beyond our own.

Then one of my aides ran into the square and over to me, out of breath.

"Sir," he said, his eyes wide, bandages covering his oozing sores. "It's the water supply."

"What is it?" I asked, a smile on my face, trying to stay calm in the face of what I knew was more bad news.

"It's the water, sir," he stammered. "It has turned to… turned to blood."

I shoved him to the ground, walking away from him, trying to ignore this obvious prank and focus on my lord, the one who had made us all immortal, the one who had truly beaten death.

Asher hopped down off of his casket and strode across the small black stage proudly, sticking out his arms as if to wrap the entire mob in a personal embrace.

"Behold your army," he shouted. "The army that will ensure our inevitable retaking and rebuilding of our planet."

The vehicles rolled into the square, and Asher bounded to the top of one of the new Abrams, straddling the rail gun like a horse. The new white paint on the vehicles shone in the sun like freshly found pearls.

"Onward!" he shouted, his pale face beaming a toothy smile. "We will crush them utterly! We will spit in the face of their god!"

As the vehicles rolled by and people climbed aboard each

one, taking up weapons that were being passed out to each citizen, man, woman, and child, I pulled out my canteen to take a drink of cool water...

...and spat out blood.

Hui

My father was so stubborn. I was not able to make him stay with the group, but he insisted on talking to the soldiers, these soldiers who had followed us from our broken country and had joined up with the forgotten armies of the world. He would only say "yeah, yeah, yeah" as he wandered away from me laughing. His faith was so powerful.

These men, these soldiers, were what was left of the armies that fought in the last war, bent on not losing face and saving their honor. It did not matter that the nuclear attacks had nearly destroyed our lands, that the virus had ravaged our families. Their greatest concern was conquest, and when the country split into provinces, each ruled by its own feudal militia, we knew it was time to abandon it and come to our final destination: the fort at Masada.

Father only wanted to warn the soldiers of their fate if they chose to harm us. He did not want them to face the wrath of Shang Di. He pleaded with them to follow Jesu and give their lives to Him. The men would not listen, screaming obscenities at us and demanding that we turn over all of our food, supplies and medicines.

The strangest thing happened.

Many of the boil covered soldiers began to mount their horses and ride away. It was as if they did not see us or had lost interest in threatening us. My father waved at them as they rode away toward the city, but perhaps they reasoned that the city would be more of a prize than a mass of near starving refugees from all over the globe.

Some of the soldiers stayed to threaten us, but for some reason they seemed like small children to us, and that these threats were empty. The world around us suddenly felt as if it were melting away.

My father had seen enough. I offered to help father to the top of the mountain again, but he insisted on walking unaided. He used to climb the Great Wall every year, claiming to others that a real man would be able to reach the top regardless of age. He would go to the wall each year to secretly write gospel messages on the parapets when no one was looking.

Father was a rebel.

When we reached the top, we looked out on the wasteland to see the horsemen riding toward the city, the clouds of dust rising up from the horse's hooves, and out of the city came the vehicles we had seen on the smart phones. I could see them through the binoculars, the strange weapons on the vehicles firing on the horsemen as the horsemen tried with utter futility to attack tanks with machine guns and swords. The tanks rode them down like grass, and the sonic weapons caused man and horse to fall to the ground and writhe around like worms on a hot plate.

It was a battle of desperation.

The sun was particularly bright that day, and not a cloud could be seen, only the gray sky and the haze of faint moisture in the air. The noise of the guns was faint, but growing louder, and we knew that it was only a matter of time before they reached us.

I watched in horror through my binoculars as thousands of men and horses were mowed down by the guns, their blood spilling on the ground in bucketfulls. I prayed for their souls and wished that they had come under the protection of Shang Di.

And then another strange thing happened. The sun, the beautiful sun that had risen this morning and sent that wonderful glow of orange across the ground suddenly stopped shining, and the entire world was plunged into utter darkness.

Not completely, however, for we could see a faint light emanating from our skin as if we ourselves were emitting light…and we were. I looked at my father who was smiling, the few teeth he had left purely visible, and the saints all around us were glowing like lights in the sky at night, like stars.

"What is this?" said Father, his eyes wide, looking at his glowing skin. "Praise be to Shang Di!"

I heard laughter from others as we stood on top of Masada, and some children giggled and pointed at one another as we marveled at the miraculous light emanating from the saints.

Gideon

"Freaky," I said to myself, looking at my left arm glowing as I lay on my little bedroll and tried not to wince from the pain.

Amy and Kelly had left me for a bit to look down at the wasteland below, watching the battle as the armies of Babylon moved to our position to wipe us off the face of the earth as that Asher guy said.

I couldn't believe he was still alive. I totally didn't miss.

I had to get up, to see what was going on, and then I just…well…I just did. I stood up, suddenly feeling no pain, and flexed the fingers of my right hand, my splint no longer needed. I removed the splint and walked without effort, but as if I had just been on a long run, and man was I hungry. I put my arms around Amy and Kelly, and it wasn't hard to find them at all even though the entire world had gone completely dark. You couldn't even see any stars, and the guns were firing down on the plain, but you couldn't see any muzzle flashes at all.

It was freaky weird, but somehow right, somehow cool.

"What are you?…*Gideon!?*" screamed Amy, and Kelly kissed my cheek as Amy nearly squeezed the life out of me.

"The reports of my death were greatly exaggerated," I said, the laughter falling out of me. I didn't think Amy was going to stop holding on to me, and then she kissed me and I let her, putting my arms around her and holding her warmly, our love more than physical, more than just two lovers, but real and powerful and holy. There was a sudden electric quality to the air, as if we were waiting for something to happen, something epic.

Usually when there was danger bearing down on me, like the militia in the U.S., or the threat of the security personnel or the crazy zombie king, I'd be ready to run or ready to fight, but not now. Now I felt like staying, 'cause it didn't matter anymore. Something told me to stay, to not worry, to just be calm.

That something was about to show up.

Big time.

Mark

The insolent fools on horseback were no match for us.
How dare they fire on us after making plans to join us in the
fight. Hunger was a great motivator, I suppose.

We plowed them down and moved on through, but it
was the sudden darkness that baffled us, as if we were not
only without light but blind as well. None of our
illuminating lamps worked at all, and when the technicians
pulled out flashlights to make repairs, those didn't work
either.

"Look!" said Asher in the darkness, speaking into the
walkie. "On the mountain! Masada! Our enemy is glowing!
Drive this army toward them and kill them! Only then will
this darkness end!"

I sat next to him in the back seat of the Hummer as we
looked out the window at the glowing mountain top.
Masada looked like it was on fire, but as I felt for the trap
door in the roof, opened it and stood up to look through my
binoculars, I could see people walking around on top of the
ancient fort, glowing like some kind of strange incandescent
bulbs.

I sat back down as we started toward the mountain, and
Asher leaned over to me and touched my leg. That was
when I noticed that Asher smelled like a corpse.

"This will be all over soon," he said, his voice taking on a
gravelly, serpentine quality, his breath like an open grave.
"And then you will have your reward."

"Reward?" I said, my heart racing.

"Oh yes," he said. "You will be richly rewarded in my

kingdom, Mark. We both will."

I felt a jarring as we banged into something metal in front of us in the darkness, but Asher only laughed and grabbed my leg again, his grip like ice. It was not long before I heard chatter on the walkie.

"We are in range, my Lord," came a deep voice.

"Then fire, you idiot!" screamed Asher with a rasp in his voice that sounded strangely desperate.

I could hear the electric hiss of the rail guns and the mini guns ripping out forty seven hundred rounds per second, but as I looked, all I saw was a bubble of light forming around the mountain, and the bullets were being directed back at us. I climbed out of the Hummer and hid behind the door on the side facing away from the glowing mountain, hearing the superheated steel bolts bouncing back and slicing through the heavy armor of the Abrams in front of us.

How could this be!?

In the faint glow of Masada, I could see the black silhouette of Asher standing on top of the Hummer having climbed out of the trap door in the roof, and he was shaking his fist at the sky, screaming until he was hoarse, and his vocal chords failed.

"NOT NOW!" he hissed.

Something exploded above us, and I crouched to look into the sky and a light appeared, brighter than the sun, and out of it poured a billion people, flying at us with swords and shields, riding horses that flew on the winds, and riding at the front was something I could not fathom.

It was Him.

HIM!

He had a large crown that looked like it was made of

light but filled with many golden crowns, and he carried a sword of glowing flame like a solar flare, and then he spoke a word, a word that is unintelligible to my insignificant human ears, but it meant "JUDGEMENT", and there was a blast of something unknown, something of utter and absolute power, greater than the power of a billion supernovas that blew me completely off of the ground, upended every vehicle in our army, and then there was a fire, and…and…darkness…

…darkness except for a faint light far away, far away in front of me.

In an instant I was standing in a sea of people. I couldn't tell the size of the crowd but it was massive, and I brushed elbows with someone and he turned, and he had short cropped black hair with a small mustache in the middle of his lip. He looked at me wide eyed, and then someone else bumped me, and I turned and it was a man I had seen before, one of our security personnel. In front of me was Cain Asher, and he was furious, cursing at the top of his lungs, but there didn't seem to be any air and it was hard to breathe, and his voice sounded very small…weak.

But then there was light. Hard, oppressive light from the front of the crowd and then I could see the size of the crowd and it was more than anyone could count, a sea of people from all ages of time standing all together in a massive throng of bodies, and the light was blinding, and the sounds of the wailing began.

We knew Who it was. We all knew. The sobs and wailing reached a crescendo as we all saw Who was sitting before us on a gargantuan white throne, His face obscured by the power that emanated from Him. But we did not look…NO! We did not look for we could *not*. We began to bow down not out of worship, but out of understanding of how small we are, how insignificant, how weak in the sight of a HOLY GOD. I saw in an instant every sin I had committed that separated me from His love, His forgiveness, His favor, pouring over me like a black ooze of death.

I, like everyone else understood in an instant who we were before Him, and it frightened us, terrified us, and if we had been on earth and experienced this we would have expired from fear, but we were spared that for now.

And then we heard the Voice. He spoke to us and I imagined that this must be what ants hear when we speak to them. It was not the voice of a tyrant, the voice of a dictator, but the voice of a Judge, the supreme Judge, and justice was being served to us…

OH GOD! PLEASE FORGIVE…but it was too late.

"Depart from me into everlasting torment, for I never knew you."

It burned so badly, and still does.

Clayton

Babylon was on fire, but that weren't really important anymore. Not to us.

Jesus, King of Kings, Lord of Lords, Creater of the Universe, hovered in mid air on his powerful white horse, and then he looked our way, his eyes like two suns, and I could hear His voice in my head, echoin' through every atom in my body as I was now bein' made new.

"Well done, good and faithful servant. Enter into your rest."

And then we were floatin' up, all of us, Amy and Gideon and all the rest, flyin' toward that openin' in the sky, and I could see someone comin' to meet me as the broken earth fell away and I lost control of all emotions, but they was replaced by joy, joy, joy! My tears started rollin' down my face, 'cause it was my Momma and my Sister and my...my Daddy, comin' to meet me and they was all smiles, all full of peace, glowing' like fire in the heavens, and there was Ralph and Jacob and Amy and Gideon and Kelly and little Anya and all the rest with us, and then...well...

...I'd describe the rest of it for you...you know, what heaven's like...but then there just ain't words for that.

Roger Colby is an English teacher by trade, making the lives of teens in his class difficult yet rewarding even if they cannot see the use for the important skills he is teaching them (for the most part). He is a father of four rambunctious children and is husband to a wonderful, beautiful, understanding wife who gives him space to write about weird places and even weirder happenstances. He has many dogs, cats, chickens, and birds.

It is a noisy house.

Other novels by Roger Colby

The Transgression Box, 2009
Come Apart, 2014